THE TIES THAT BIND US

MEGAN JAMIESON

Black Rose Writing | Texas

©2026 by Megan Jamieson
All rights reserved. No part of this book may be reproduced, stored in a retrieval system or transmitted in any form or by any means without the prior written permission of the publishers, except by a reviewer who may quote brief passages in a review to be printed in a newspaper, magazine or journal.

The author grants the final approval for this literary material.

First printing

This is a work of fiction. Names, characters, businesses, places, events, and incidents are either the products of the author's imagination or used in a fictitious manner. Any resemblance to actual persons, living or dead, or actual events is purely coincidental.

ISBN: 978-1-68513-713-7
LIBRARY OF CONGRESS CONTROL NUMBER: 2025945576
PUBLISHED BY BLACK ROSE WRITING
www.blackrosewriting.com

Printed in the United States of America
Suggested Retail Price (SRP) $19.95

The Ties That Bind Us is printed in Garamond Premier Pro

*As a planet-friendly publisher, Black Rose Writing does its best to eliminate unnecessary waste to reduce paper usage and energy costs, while never compromising the reading experience. As a result, the final word count vs. page count may not meet common expectations.

This book contains subject matter that might be difficult for some readers, including elements of violence, torture (off page), sexual abuse (off page), domestic abuse (off page), suicide (off page), PTSD (off page), and death. There is coarse language and sexual situations depicted throughout the novel. The material is not suitable for younger readers.

PRAISE FOR
THE TIES THAT BIND US

"Twisted officials, perversions, and a trail of impossibly connected and unsolvable crimes"
–Scott Eveloff, author of *Do Not Resuscitate*

"*The Ties that Bind Us* is a well-crafted slow-burn police procedural that kept me guessing. A complex cast of characters, each with their own flaws and peculiarities, builds an undercurrent of tension that makes every interaction feel charged. At times, the story evokes the chilling atmosphere of The Silence of the Lambs, with the author unraveling the mystery and revealing the villain in a way that made me audibly gasp. Dark, atmospheric and haunting, *The Ties That Bind Us* is as moody and relentless as a rainy Oregon night"
–James Foley, author of *Treasure Coast*

"Megan Jamieson's debut novel is a true page turner that keeps you guessing until the very end. Maeve, an eager, newly-trained forensics homicide detective, moves to a small town in Oregon to begin her career. Initially, she is disappointed to be assigned to a cold case instead of an active investigation, but the case turns out to be much more than she or her handsome partner, Ben, bargained for. Ben is a seasoned detective from the small Oregon town, and though he is intimately connected to many of the people involved in the case, he is happy to have a new set of eyes, especially a beautiful and smart pair of eyes, digging through the case once again. Maeve's cunning and relentless determination lead to shocking discoveries that just keep unraveling one mystery inside of another. The twists and turns are cleverly disguised and the red herrings are so believable, it is impossible to put down."
–Kim McCallum, author of *What Happens in Montana*

*Dedicated to those who feel trapped in the life they once dreamed of.
Pride hurts, but nothing is as devastating as inaction.
Do it all, do it now.*

THE TIES
THAT BIND US

CHAPTER ONE

April 2019
Grants Pass, OR

Maeve walked to the doors of the precinct, anxious and uncoordinated. It was miserable outside, the sort of gray that lingered over Oregon in the spring, a continuous damp fog. Fortunately for her, she was in the minority of people who preferred a rainy day to a sunny one. It was something about the crisp, clean, earthy smell that had her feeling rejuvenated and alive. She allowed a slight smile as she thanked herself for choosing to move to one of the wettest places in the United States.

The 59th precinct was made entirely of brick and looked like it hadn't been updated since the 1980s. She attempted to open the glass doors using her free hand as she balanced a coffee and her oversized bag with the other, a surge of unease rippling through her. She tended to live on the klutzy side of the spectrum, and these situations never ended well. She was cursing under her breath when a large and impeccably toned man with a buzz cut ran to open the door for her, his masculine cologne overwhelming. She muttered a quick, "Thanks," as she ducked under his arm, and he followed her inside.

"You are very welcome, ma'am. I'm Ben Striton, by the way. It's a pleasure to meet you." He shook her hand with a bone crushing grip.

Maeve raked her eyes over him quickly. She felt his self-assuredness as she took in his dark jeans and black collared Lacoste T-shirt that looked like it had been ironed one too many times.

"Hi, I'm Maeve...same here." She was never one for awkward first encounters that often transitioned to forced small talk.

"You don't have to be shy, Maeve, I won't bite," he said, giving her a show-stopping grin.

Maeve knew he was the kind of man who was aware of his effect on women and used it to his advantage. She gave a polite, closed mouth smile back as scanned the space. Her discomfort was alleviated as a glass door opened across the room and a round man in a faded brown suit waddled out with his arms raised. He was average height, but his robust center seemed to throw him off balance as he moved toward them.

"Maeve, darlin'! How are ya?!"

She recognized him immediately as Chief Joe Briggs. They'd met briefly over Zoom the previous month, he had a commanding presence. What she wasn't prepared for, was the smell. He approached with such velocity she braced her core in response, anticipating a hug of back breaking intensity.

"It's so good to finally have you here! We've been looking forward to having a new member on our team. We're up to our knees in cases," he said, his body and accompanying body odor barreling into her all at once. Her coffee sloshed, burning her hand.

She winced at the burns as he pulled away and apologized for the spill. "This here is Ben Striton," Briggs started, motioning to the handsome, and significantly better smelling, stranger who had been watching their interaction with mild curiosity.

"He's one of our senior detectives here at the precinct," he said, placing a hand on Ben's shoulder. "Leave her alone now, Ben, and let her get in the damn door."

Time felt tight as Ben held her gaze for too long before acknowledging the chief and quietly walking in the opposite direction, turning back ever so slightly to give Maeve a heavy nod. Maeve swallowed and took in her surroundings. Despite the cold exterior of the building, the inside looked like it might have been renovated in recent years. The light oak vinyl flooring and stark white walls brightened up the space, giving it an air of cleanliness and professionalism.

Briggs pulled her back into reality as he put a hand on her back and guided her to the reception desk.

"This here is Beatta, our receptionist. She's an absolute saint. Anything you need help with, she's your gal."

A middle-aged woman with tight brown curls and tired eyes gave Maeve a kind smile and wave before she went back to typing, her long neon pink gel nails making an irritating clicking sound that echoed throughout the foyer. Maeve opened her mouth to introduce herself but was abruptly cut off.

"Follow me to the conference room, and we'll get you all sorted, darlin'." She gave a half smile in apology to Beatta before trailing after the chief, doing her best to keep what remained of her coffee inside the cup. For a man who undoubtedly sat on the cusp of the morbidly obese category, he moved at an alarmingly fast pace. Standing at a generous five foot three, she had to jog to catch up.

Briggs spoke over his shoulder and in between large breaths. "As you can probably guess, your partner, Ben, takes some getting used to, a little hot headed at times, but he's the best detective we've got here in 59."

The fluorescent lights above them were oppressive as Maeve took in the disorderly cubicles filled with various officers chatting with colleagues or eating at their desks. There were no perps in sight and no need to be anywhere anytime fast. She frowned as she noted no other female officers. They were usually the minority at any police department, but it was still unusual not to see at least a few.

"My partner?" she stumbled, eyes bulging as she righted herself again. Briggs slowed his pace. "Oh yes, darlin', we need you to hit the ground running. Ben will get you up to speed and guide you through a 'learn as you go' process. I wish I could ease you into things, but we have a lot of unsolved cases. Minor ones to be sure, but still not closed. I've got the commissioner hounding my ass. I've put in a request for more enforcement personnel, but Grants Pass being the small city we are, we tend to get overlooked," he said, a small bead of sweat rolling down his forehead. "Also, I know you're trained as a forensic homicide detective, but GP is a small place, and we don't get all that many homicides. So, in addition to your work here, you may be called on neighboring municipalities' cases. My detectives here in 59 deal with whatever comes up. That also means from time to time you'll be doing enforcement work in uniform on an as-needed basis."

She swallowed her frustration. Briggs hadn't mentioned her scope including grunt work during her interview. She'd done her time doing traffic stops and welfare checks during basic training. Her specialty was in forensic work.

He picked up on her silence. "Listen, I know you don't need taking care of, darlin', but Ben can be a real asset when it comes to practical work. You're going to want him on your side."

"Yes sir, I understand."

They arrived in a small windowless room with wood paneling on the walls and a dull fluorescent glow emanating from the drop ceiling. A musty, damp smell washed over her. Clearly the room had been overlooked in the renovations.

Briggs motioned for her to sit on one of the metal chairs before squeezing himself into the one next to her.

"Maeve, I've been through your file, and I just wanted to start out by saying I don't make staffing decisions based on years of experience or time in the field. Hell, I wouldn't be in this position if that were the case. Someone took a chance on me, and I like to extend that same courtesy to my staff until I'm proven otherwise."

He looked at her with dull brown eyes and an unshaven beard only months of persistent fatigue could have caused. "I understand this will be your first experience as a detective, and I'll try to make it an easy transition for you." She nodded and he flipped through a brown folder of documents. " You used to be a nurse?"

"Yes sir, for a few years. As we talked about in the interview, I've changed career paths a few times recently, but I'm committed to this position, and I'm eager to gain some experience."

Maeve was constantly justifying herself to others. She could never understand people who wanted to work in one position their entire life, and she often got bored when she was in the same position for too long. She thrived on change and internal progress, always wanting to learn more and be more. Sometimes that scared her more than anything else ever did. "Darlin'," he leaned over, "you don't have to explain yourself to me, I've read your resume. I was only asking because I think it could give you a leg up on your first assignment. As part of a training initiative, we like to introduce you to cold cases before we get you in on active ones. It's high profile, but the trail went cold almost right after the investigation began. Ben was lead detective on it at the time and can fill in the gaps for you as you familiarize yourself with the case. If anything, it will give you some insight into what goes into a crime scene and how to proceed with an investigation."

After nearly an hour of going over various HR and orientation documents with Briggs, Maeve looked around her new office space. It seemed more like a maintenance closet than an office, only large enough to fit a desk and two chairs, but it would do. The walls were painted the off white tone that was themed throughout the entire building, but she noticed a small window with a view of the back parking lot as rain tapped gently against the glass.

She jumped as a strange man entered her office pushing a dolly with three large brown boxes. The frail man with gray hair and thin metal glasses did not acknowledge her presence as he promptly unloaded the boxes on the ground and left just as quickly. Exhaling, she got up and took the lid off the first box, finding the inside filled with various colored folders shoved in at all angles. Her dark chestnut fell in strands out of her bun, and she did her best to tuck them back before pulling out a folder at random. It contained photographs, witness statements, interviews, and detective notes. She felt a tight knot of excitement in her stomach and smiled. She knew she probably shouldn't be excited looking at crime scene notes, but she couldn't help it, it was what she'd been looking forward to. Two years of forensic investigation specialization after her nursing degree had been rough and had tested her sanity more than once, but she'd finally made it.

She placed the reports in ascending order based on dates and picked up the first. A glossy 4x6 print took up the top half of the first page. The woman in the photo was devastatingly beautiful in a harsh way with shiny flaming-red hair, large blue eyes, and an infectious smile. She was in a black cap and gown, yellow tassel hanging off the left side with an out of focus courtroom in the background. Maeve flipped through the first pages of contact information and next of kin before finding the first statement.

Liam McAllister (L.M.) reported on Tuesday, May 2, 2019, at 12:30pm that his sister, Lara McAllister (Lara M.), had been missing since yesterday (May 1) after work. L.M. stated Lara M. usually texts in the morning, and when he didn't receive a text, he called her several times with no answer. L.M proceeded to drive to Lara M.'s house. L.M. stated he has a key to his sister's house in case of emergency and to look after the place when she goes away, so he let himself in. He stated nothing seemed out of place, and the house was locked up. He then called her office (Bert & Callahan Law), reception answered the call (Rebecca Raley) and said Lara M. left after work yesterday (May 1) but never came into work that morning. She stated Lara M. told Rebecca that she had a couple more people to meet up with before the end of the day and not to wait up. L.M. then came into 59 to file a report at the time and dated stated above.

Maeve rifled through to the last report and at no point saw any mention of a body. Was it a missing person's case?

"Hey, gorgeous."

Maeve jumped, holding a hand to her racing heart as she looked up at her new partner hovering in her doorway, arms crossed, eyes scanning the mess she'd already made.

"I see you found the Lara McAllister files," he said as he moved into the office, gently moving into the chair opposite hers.

Maeve cleared her throat, ignoring his inappropriate greeting. First the chief with darlin' and now her new partner. There really was never any shortage of objectification in the workplace. Or in the world, really.

"Yeah, I was reading the initial reports filed," she replied, looking down. He leaned forward. "Her brother was the first. Liam McAllister. They were very close. They did everything together. He was an absolute wreck when she went missing," he said, running a hand over his buzzed head.

"I noticed the brother and missing victim have the same initials. That's going to make this confusing."

Ben let out a deep laugh that raked over her. "You're telling me. Even better, there's an older half-sister too, and her name is Lydia."

"Honestly, I'm not one to judge. My mother did the same thing. My brother's name is Matteo and my sister's is Maya," she told him, shaking her head.

"Nice." He chuckled, extending the word into one long syllable. "Do they live here too?"

"No, we're kind of spread out. I'm the only one here," she said, looking down as she tried to bring the personal exchange to an end. Luckily, her partner got the not-so-subtle hint.

"Hey, what do you say we take our coffee break and head out for a bite? Shelley's Diner has an unreal mushroom omelet you're gonna want to try. Plus, then you can start to get involved in our small community. Everyone goes to Shelley's."

"No thanks, I think I'll work through. I've got loads to catch up on, and I need to get familiar with this case. I didn't even know there was another sister," she said, offering a half smile.

"Suit yourself." He got up to leave, the disappointment showing on his face.

"Wait! There's one thing I was going to ask. Was her body found? I can't seem to find a coroner's report here or any mention of the discovery."

"There's no body, Maeve. Lara McAllister was never found," he replied before making a hasty exit.

Never found? That would make it a missing person's case, not a homicide. Why on earth was she being assigned to a missing person's case from…she glanced at the date on the bottom of the report, just under a year ago. Most missing person's cases dropped off within a week. If they couldn't be found within the first forty-eight hours, chances are they wouldn't be. From that point, it was almost always a body recovery.

Maeve walked apprehensively to Chief Briggs' office and knocked on the door frame. The man in question was standing, putting on his blue suit jacket as he grabbed his keys. He looked up and gave her a tired smile.

"Maeve darlin', what can I do for you? I apologize, but it'll have to be quick, I'm on my way out."

"Sorry, sir, just a quick question. The Lara McAllister case you assigned to me…am I supposed to be looking into this as a missing person's case?" she asked tentatively.

He looked at her, pausing his rushed movements.

"Ben has been relentless. He thinks he has reason to believe there was foul play, but we don't have a body. There is some circumstantial evidence, but nothing concrete. We're also surrounded by acres and acres of densely forested land, which also happens to be a great place to dispose of bodies." He sighed, moving toward her.

"At one point, we had officers, residents, and volunteers from neighboring communities sweeping the county, but it just wasn't sustainable. Financially or otherwise. We just don't have the resources. Personally, I think it's time to let it go. I was going to start you out with a different case, but Ben insisted you use your objectivity to offer a fresh set of eyes into it. He's bound and determined to close it. I've told him a few times to put it to the side of his desk and focus on the present, but it haunts him."

He gave her a defeated look before glancing down at his watch. "Look, Maeve, I'm sorry, but I have to run to a meeting. If anything urgent pops up, call me on my cell," he said, handing her his card on his way past.

She meandered back to her office, hitting the card back and forth on her palm as she went. She thought back to her initial impression of Oregon when she had first driven through it on a road trip with her sister. The state was almost entirely dense forest with soft, damp, easy-to-shovel earth because of the relentless precipitation. She was sure there were still stretches of land that still remain untouched. It was the ideal setting to dispose of any evidence relating to a crime.

Three hours and a persistent throbbing headache later, Maeve still hadn't finished going through the files. Her stomach grumbled, and she decided she'd grab some lunch. She walked through the line of cubicles to the exit of the building and noticed the place was empty, a heavy silence filling the room.

She shivered, zipping up her windbreaker as she walked outside, the rain hitting the ground in a faint drizzle, creating a blanket of mist around her as she made it to her car. She cranked the Mazda's heat and settled into the leather, warming her hands over the vents. Even though she loved the rain, she couldn't deny that she hated the bone chilling cold that often came with it.

The nostalgia of being back home in Hawaii hit her, potent and unyielding as she thought of the islands' warm humidity. Maeve was trapped in a whirlpool of intrusive thoughts as she drove around town. She knew Google Maps could probably direct her to the nearest fast-food chain, but she preferred to discover things the old fashioned way. Especially being new in town, she felt she owed it to her circumstance to explore a little bit.

After driving around in circles, she finally passed a large yellow sign for Shelley's Diner. Out of sheer desperation, she gave in, parking along the street and reluctantly making her way inside.

With her sudden appearance in the restaurant, several tables filled with patrons paused their discussions to glance her way. She cursed to herself as she glanced down at the badge on her hip, reluctantly offering a small smile and wave to the room. As much as she would have preferred to become one with the wall, she was going to be working in Grants Pass for the foreseeable future in a job that required forming trust with members of the public. Being aloof wasn't an option. Especially in a small town.

Maeve was not used to the level of interaction her new position required. She enjoyed the occasional small gathering with close friends, but she was an introvert through and through. She preferred to be at home with a large glass of red wine and a Shonda Rhimes re-run, and that was partially to blame for her lack of meaningful relationships. When you are your favourite company, spending time alone is a gift.

She averted her eyes away from the customers that had returned to eating their meals and walked up to the hostess stand, asking to place an order to-go. After a quick glance at the menu, she gave her order to the bubbly hostess and sat down on a bench under a giant hand-painted portrait of Elvis.

She scanned the diner. It was a modest size, booths on one side, tables in the middle, and the kitchen on the other. It had the kind of open kitchen where patrons could see what was happening behind the grill. The aesthetic was pulled together with vivid portraits of famous characters painted across the walls. Marilyn Monroe, Minnie Mouse, and Elvis on one side, James Dean and Audrey Hepburn on the other. The smell of coffee and bacon filled the space. Shelley's was maximum level tacky, but some of the best restaurants were.

After Maeve grabbed her bag of food and cup of coffee, she turned to leave, slamming full force into a hard body in front of her. Her hot coffee smashed to the ground, and with it a harsh, crude curse. Bending down, she quickly started cleaning the mess to avoid drawing any more attention to herself.

"Oh my god, I'm so sorry," the stranger said, crouching down to help her clean.

She lifted her dark eyes to the offender. Even though they were both kneeling, he was towering over her, a goofy grin plastered on his face. He held her gaze as he stood, reaching down to offer her a hand. Once fully upright, she muttered a thanks, bracing herself for the awkward encounter. The man towered at least a foot above her, his fit body on full display as Maeve took in his toned arms and legs. He looked to be in his mid 30s, his dark red hair falling over his forehead as he reciprocated the exploration of her body with his deep blues.

Just as she started to feel uneasy, their interaction was abruptly cut off as the blonde hostess broke in between them, handing her some napkins and mumbling about getting her another coffee.

Maeve looked down at her white top and noticed a coffee stain all the way down the front. She closed her eyes, frustration seeping out of her as she re-opened them again to find the handsome stranger still standing in front of her with an amused look. Something about him was familiar. It threw her off balance.

"It's no problem," she finally replied. "I'm the one who's sorry. It was my fault. I'm a huge klutz. This happens on a daily basis, to be honest," she said, disoriented.

He extended his hand to her. "No need to apologize, the only casualty was your top it seems," he said, eyes flickering over her chest quickly before returning to her face. He smiled, his perfect teeth on display. "I'm Liam McAllister."

CHAPTER TWO

She had literally run full force into a person of interest in her new case. Maeve, unable to find words, awkwardly shook his hand.

"You're the new detective, I see," he said as he pointed to her badge. Shifting on her feet, she nodded and offered up an awkward smile. Thankfully, the hostess re-appeared, handing her a new coffee and giving her an opportunity to excuse herself and duck out the door. "It was nice to meet you!" Liam called after her, lifting a hand. Maeve drove back to the office at a speed too careless for the slick condition of the road as she tried to get her heart rate back down.

Once back at her desk she flipped through the background notes collected by the original detective working the case at the time, and her new partner, Ben Striton. The last thing she needed was more caffeine, her body still slightly jittery, but she dismissed the toxic thought as she took a sip of her coffee and started reading.

Name: Lara McAllister (MISSING PERSON)
Age: 30
Gender/Appearance: female, 5'10", red hair, pale complexion, blue eyes, freckles, dimples, fit build.

Occupation: Stanford Law graduate, worked as a junior partner at Bert & Callahan Law.
Contacts: Close friendship/roommates with Rebecca Raley, Dating Marc Hallman, friends with Jason Boukesh, Shirin Khorram.

Name: Lydia Droughton (formerly McAllister)
Age: 42
Gender/Appearance: female, 5'5", half Latina, brown hair, brown complexion, brown eyes, curvy build
Occupation: Part owner of Droughton Farms
Contacts: Married to Raymond Droughton, no kids, half-sister to Liam and Lara McAllister (same father).
Statement: "I haven't seen Lara since March. Her and Liam came over for dinner. We haven't been in contact since, but that's not abnormal for us. We only see each other every few months or so, we all have our own things going on. Life is busy, you know?
Name: Liam McAllister
Age: 32
Gender/Appearance: male, 6'3, dark red hair, pale complexion, blue/grey eyes, fit build.
Occupation: Owner and physiotherapist at Kother Holistic Health Contacts: No current romantic relationship, friends with Carl and Nikko Jackson, Robert and William Cartosen, Emma Holmberg, Amelia and Marco Silva, Luna Chang, and Noah Blackburn.
Statement: *refer to initial report
Name: Rebecca Raley
Age: 29
Appearance: female, 5'6, blonde hair, pale complexion, green eyes, slim build.
Occupation: Receptionist at Bert & Callahan Law

  The notes were cut off and Maeve flipped to the next page of the folder as a glossy photo fell out onto her desk. In the picture were two people, both with red hair, arms around each other, and giant youthful smiles plastered across their faces. Although taken several years ago, she recognized the subjects immediately as the younger versions of Liam and Lara. They both looked happy and carefree posing on a hiking trail, like nothing in the world could ruin their day. They could easily be mistaken for twins, both with that same thick red hair and striking blue eyes, Liam's hair and eyes only slightly darker than his sisters'. Both had large teeth that showed through their genuine smiles, Lara with dimples.

It brought the realism of the case into focus. Maeve flipped the photo over and saw that it was dated August 9, 2015. Liam looked just as charming back then as he did when she ran into him at the diner, a bit more youthful and unkempt, but still easy on the eyes. He was lanky in the photo, he must have grown into his build in the past few years. The world was grateful for it. Maeve exhaled as she shook off the problematic direction her mind wandered.

Maeve spent the rest of the afternoon compiling a list of people she wanted to interview along with potential questions she wanted to ask. Even though Ben had done it all the previous year, she wanted to start fresh with her own investigation. Her stomach jolted as she thought about meeting with Liam. She'd made a fool of herself and she desperately needed to re-establish her professionalism. She'd need to meet with him again.

A few hours later she drove home in a daze. She was tired but eager to relax with a glass of Merlot. She had rented a small house in town, a two-story with navy siding and white trim around the multitude of windows. It looked as though there had once been the beginnings of an herb garden under the large living room window, but all that was left were some tulips and the rest all overgrown. Maeve had never had a green thumb and couldn't be bothered to take over the endeavor that had been left to her by the previous owners.

Even though it was in an older neighborhood, the house itself had been renovated and had modern touches with high end appliances and light hardwood throughout.

After she'd caught up on previous episodes of The Bachelor, Maeve headed up the stairs to bed, her feet brushing the soft cream-colored carpet that covered the entirety of the second floor. It was only nine, but she'd never been a night owl. The routine of having her morning coffee while watching the news brought her contentment and clarity. She climbed into her silk sheets, and her last thought before drifting into oblivion had been of Lara McAllister.

The next day brought with it an epic sunrise filled with oranges and pinks that eventually fell away into a clear sunny morning. As much as Maeve loved rain, she also couldn't deny the energy the sun provided as she dressed, throwing her long hair into her low bun and dialing Chief Briggs.

"Morning sir, sorry to call you early, but I wanted to let you know I won't be in until later. I want to go by and talk to some residents about the case. I brought some of the files home last night, I hope that's okay."

A short chuckle in response. "Morning darlin', you don't have to let me know every step you take, you're an independent investigator, you have free reign in this position. Just bring me the bad guys."

Maeve smiled to herself. Briggs was growing on her. There was nothing worse than a boss who was always breathing down your neck. "Just make sure you call Ben and let him know what you're up to. He needs to be involved as well," he told her before ending the call. Fuck. She'd completely forgotten about Ben. He texted her his number yesterday "in case she needed anything" and she hadn't responded. Unfortunately, she couldn't put it off any longer as she sent him a text to meet her at Bert & Callahan Law, Lara's place of work at the time she went missing.

The sunlight bounced off the pavement on the drive, the trees lifting up toward the sky in hopeful desperation as the residual damp undertones lingered on the ground below. The drive was a short one and her google maps led her into a lot directly across the street from Shelley's Diner. One of the few perks of living in a small town, everything was close by.

The firm was an impressive building in comparison to the majority of the architecture in Grants Pass. It looked out of place in the small, outdated town with its tall glass walls and futuristic features. The kind of place Elon Musk would work. Maeve waited for her partner, but after fifteen long minutes she got tired of playing Wordle and grabbed her bag to head in. The firm had an open floor plan, and whatever wasn't made of glass was painted in stark white. The layout was loft style, a large spiral staircase in the middle and offices around the perimeter. The reception area was directly in front, surrounded by hard leather armchairs, overexaggerated space between each one to give the illusion of more space.

The young woman at reception was already smiling at Maeve as she approached.

"Good morning! I'm Sarah. What can I do for you?"

Maeve returned the polite smile, disappointment raking through her. "Hi...Maeve Kalani. I'm a detective over at the 59th and I'm actually looking to speak to Rebecca Raley, does she still work here?" Rebecca Raley had been Lara's best friend and roommate at the time of her disappearance, as well as a receptionist at the same firm. Maeve was eager to speak with her.

"Yes, she does! She's in the office right back there, you can just walk right in." She pointed past the grand spiral staircase.

Maeve walked to the back of the building as she pulled her navy-blue blazer tighter around herself. She ended up at the last office, the sign on the door reading "Rebecca Raley - Paralegal." Behind the large glass desk sat a delicate woman who looked to be in her early-thirties, blonde hair curled to perfection with a bright red lip. Her eyes sparkled as she looked up, a reflection off her computer monitor no doubt. The effect was mesmerizing.

Maeve introduced herself and Rebecca motioned to the seat across from her desk. The small office showcased floor to ceiling windows, two pink velvet armchairs, and a sheepskin rug. She wondered if the Legally Blonde vibes were purposeful or just a happy coincidence.

"So, detective, what can I do for you?" Rebecca asked confidently, leaning back.

Maeve decided to dive in headfirst. She was running with the idea that most people also hated small talk and those who said they didn't were lying. Just like those who say they don't pee in the shower.

"I've been assigned to Lara McAllister's case. I know my partner, Ben Striton, has already interviewed you about this, and I apologize if it's hard to talk about, but I was wondering if you wouldn't mind if I asked a few questions of my own."

Rebecca gave a tight nod. "Detective…"

"Maeve. Please, call me Maeve."

"Maeve, I don't want to sound rude, but I've been over this so many times already. Have you not read my statement?"

Maeve wasn't sure what she'd been expecting, but it wasn't that. "I have yes but seeing as I'm not overly familiar with the case, nor was I around when it occurred, I like to carry out my own investigation. If you're agreeable. You certainly don't have to speak to me today if you don't feel comfortable."

Rebecca rolled her eyes before standing up to close her office door. Maeve took in her tight, baby pink dress and five-inch heels. Heels with red soles.

"What did you want to ask me?" Rebecca asked, seated back in her chair. Maeve got out her notepad. "Miss. Raley, please tell me about your relationship with Lara McAllister."

Rebecca cleared her throat and ran a finger under her false lashes. "You can call me Rebecca. We were close. She was my best friend. When she moved here and joined the firm, we became close fairly quickly. Most people in this city already had their pre-judgements about me from high school... but with her, I could have a clean slate. She didn't care about my reputation or who I used to be, she just cared for who I was."

"What was she like?"

A tense silence lingered for a moment before Rebecca spoke again. "She was incredibly successful, hardworking and driven. She had everything going for her and every guy in this place was interested in her. She was perfect without even trying," she finished, offering a closed mouth smile.

"I also read that you and Lara lived together?" Maeve asked.

"Yes. Lara was fresh out of law school and didn't have two pennies to rub together when she started here. I offered to let her stay with me so she could get out of Liam's place, and I had more than enough room. We lived together for two years."

"You saw her the day before she was reported missing, correct?" Rebecca fiddled with her nails as her eyes roamed around the room. "Yeah, she worked that day then left at 4:30. She said she was headed out to see some clients before heading home and she told me not to wait up."

"Isn't that a bit out of character for her? From your statement in the initial report, you mentioned she was often in bed pretty early."

"Yeah, but it was a Friday. She tended to push those boundaries on the weekend. She also slept over at Marc's place from time to time. It wasn't unusual for her to say she'd be home and then change her mind and stay with him instead. Or if she had a few drinks, she obviously wouldn't drive home. It wasn't out of character."

Maeve nodded, making notes. "How was her demeanor before she left that day?"

"Well, she seemed the same way she always did, anxious…determined. She worked her ass off her first year here. She felt like she had something to prove, being the youngest associate."

"Did she often do business with clients outside the firm?" Rebecca lifted her magnetic green eyes. "Yes. She prided herself on being approachable and flexible for her clients. She would meet them for lunch or stop by their place to have them sign paperwork. She hated being confined to her desk all day. She used to say her spirit couldn't handle being stuck in an office," she finished, rolling her eyes and letting out a small laugh, her gaze moving to the large corner window. Despite her attitude, Maeve thought she seemed genuinely affected by her friend's disappearance.

"Did she let someone know where she would be when she met up with clients outside the office? Seems like it may have been risky meeting people by herself."

Rebecca laughed mockingly. "You're new here, hey? I can tell."

She cocked her head to the side, hair falling off her shoulder. "Grants Pass is a small-town, detective. Things like that don't happen here. You can walk around alone in the dark and feel perfectly safe. There's always someone watching. And not in a creepy way, in a nosy way. Nothing like that ever happens here because no one would risk being seen by someone else."

"Except for when something like that did happen."

Maeve looked into Rebecca's eyes. She had struck a chord. Maeve could see it as Rebecca's face contracted in a way that would show crow's feet on most middle-aged women if they hadn't had an obscene amount of Botox. "Yeah. I guess you're right on that one," she scoffed.

Maeve, realizing she'd been a bit harsh, moved on. "Did you notice if her car was there that night? Did you see it when you got up the next morning?"

Rebecca took a breath. "No, I didn't see her car there when I got home that night around midnight. It wasn't there the next morning either." Maeve quietly made notes. She'd read that Lara drove a black Honda Civic. It was never found.

"But that wasn't unusual. She sometimes got a ride home from Marc or, like I said, she would stay at his place. She's an adult, I wasn't going to text her to ask where she was every moment of the day."

Maeve left the silence for a minute before shifting gears. "How well did you know her boyfriend Marc?"

"Pretty well. He's been a friend for a few years now. I introduced them since I was dating his best friend at the time. It just made sense. He's...well, you'll see when you meet him. Let's just say she did well for herself. Not that she acted like it," she snorted.

"What do you mean? She wasn't very interested in the relationship?" "No, it's not that. She really liked him. I just think he liked her more, you know? There's always one person in the relationship who's more into it than the other...that's all. She was having fun, but he was completely smitten. She just didn't know what a good thing she had. She didn't appreciate him and she worked way too much. Marc needed someone who was ready for a committed relationship with a common goal, and Lara just wasn't in the same place. They were kind of destined to fail I think."

Maeve inhaled quietly, steeling herself. "Were you ever interested in him that way? Did you two ever...?"

"What? Are you kidding me? Of course not! That was my best friend's boyfriend. That's like Girl Code 101. I would never do that to her." She paused, fixing her hair. "Plus, Marc was never interested in me, and I was with someone else at the time."

Maeve lifted her hands. "I apologize, I didn't mean to insinuate anything, I meant in the distant past."

Rebecca relaxed, looking away. "No, Marc hasn't been here that long, he only moved here a few years ago." She leaned back. "Look, are we done here? I have work to do and I've had more than enough of reliving the past. I live with this pain every day. I miss my best friend, and I've had enough of rehashing this shit over and over again with no progress."

Maeve packed up her stuff and got up to leave. "Of course. I'm sorry Rebecca. Thank you for your time today. I'll give you my card. Don't hesitate to call, day or night, if you feel like you may have missed anything."

Maeve left the firm at a quickened pace, desperate to get out of the uncomfortable situation. She was walking to her car when a sleek black Chrysler 300 ripped into the lot. It stopped in front of her before backing into the spot next to her SUV. The chrome on the rims was polished to perfection and tinted windows blocked out her view of the driver.

She was still frowning as Ben Striton got out of the driver's seat, coffee in hand and jubilant grin smacked across his face.

"Hey babe, sorry I'm late, shall we head in?"

Maeve had to stop herself from letting her jaw fall open. "Ben, I was in there for thirty minutes. I texted you like an hour ago."

His grin faded away and was quickly replaced with genuine disappointment.

"Shit. I figured you meant you were headed there at a reasonable hour Maeve, not eight o'clock in the fucking morning. I mean come on; we don't typically start our day until we've at least had one cup of coffee at Shelley's."

"Okay, well I wasn't aware of those work guidelines," she shot back.

He walked up closer to her. "Look I'm sorry, but I wish I had stopped you before you wasted your time with Rebs. I questioned her thoroughly right after Lara's missing person's report was filed."

Almost as if he was reading her mind, he held up his hand. "Listen, before you think I'm undermining you or mansplaining or something, you should probably know…" he hesitated, looking down. "We were sleeping together at the time of Lara's disappearance. So yeah, I do think I got all the answers from her that we're ever going to get." Maeve couldn't help herself as she let out a short laugh. "Figures."

His eyebrows lifted. "Keep your judgments to yourself. You don't know me."

He moved forward, stepping past her to toss the coffee into the garbage. Maeve watched with quiet regret as he slipped back into his car and raced back out of the lot.

A few short hours later, Ben and Maeve were elbow deep in police reports in her office. After Maeve had swallowed her pride and apologized, Ben had uttered a don't worry about it before hastily redirecting the conversation. He'd filled her in on the details of the case she hadn't yet discovered on her own, and despite the initial impression, her new partner seemed like a decent guy. He'd explained to Maeve the McAllister family history in detail, with a timeline and poorly sketched family tree.

"Lydia McAllister had a different mother to Liam and Lara. She told me that when she was nine, their shared father, Gerald McAllister, had met Liam and Lara's mother, Cora Young. They'd had a quick one-month courtship before they eloped, and Liam was born eleven months after the wedding. Lara followed two years after that. Cora was then found dead in the bathtub when Liam was seven and Lara was five. It was ruled a suicide, as both her wrists cut vertically five inches. Liam had been the one to find her."

Maeve's stomach twisted as she thought about the effects that kind of trauma would have on a child that age. She looked up from her work to meet Ben's honey-colored eyes.

"Their father, Gerald, worked as a security guard at the local country club in a city in northern California, Chico. This family has some sort of dark omen that follows them. He then died in California a few months after his wife."

Ben answered Maeve's confused expression. "Yeah, I know. Apparently, a fire broke out at the country club one night, in the maintenance shed, and Gerald was inside at the time. The coroner's report states he died from a collapsed airway. The fire investigation was deemed inconclusive. No one has any idea how it started."

Liam and Lara lost both parents within a year.

"What about Lydia's mother? What was her name again?" she asked, shuffling her papers.

"Grace Brawley. The three of them were not one big happy family. Apparently, Grace was more of a promiscuous drug addict than a mother, and her and Gerald never really had much of a relationship past a few drunken nights. Lydia doesn't remember knowing her mother at all, and it makes sense because Grace died when Lydia was four."

"Jesus. How the hell did this one happen?" she asked, frowning.

"Heroin overdose."

Maeve jumped. The answer had not come from Ben, but from Chief Briggs who was standing in her doorway.

CHAPTER THREE

"Christ! Sorry sir, you scared the shit out of me," she said, moving a hand over her chest as she took a breath to calm her racing heart. He forced a polite smile, his presence bringing in a foul mixture of sweat and sour apples.

"Quite the mouth you have on you. Sorry darlin', I was just coming over here to see how things were going with the case."

Maeve mumbled an apology, silently cursing herself. Luckily Ben answered the chief, filling him in on their progress. After Briggs left them to it, Ben reached and opened her small window, his bicep bulging with the movement. She looked at him and mouthed a silent thank you. He simply winked in response, tossing her the file she reached for.

"What happened to the kids after their parents died? Foster care?" "No, Cora has a sister, Charlotte Young. She lives in Chico. The three of them went to live with her there until they were old enough to go off to college and move out. I only met her briefly when she came to help with the search last year, but she's a super nice lady. Those kids got lucky with her," he said.

Maeve nodded, making notes. "I think I want to talk to Liam next."

Sitting on the heated leather seat of her Mazda, Maeve pulled her hair into a bun and called her partner. He sounded half asleep, forgoing any words and instead moaning a slight huff.

"Good morning to you too. It's 7:45 Ben, we're supposed to meet Liam in fifteen minutes at the diner."

"Yeah, yeah, I know, I'm up. Leaving the house now," he responded, sounding sluggish and angry.

"Bullshit. I'll see you soon," Maeve replied, ending the call. Shelley's was significantly quieter than the last time she'd been there. The small sounds of cutlery being sorted and the sizzle and pop of fatty bacon reached her as she scanned the room. A blonde woman who looked to be in her sixties, dressed in tight fitting jeans and a red apron, was pouring coffee grounds into a machine near the kitchen. She turned to look at Maeve, giving her a warm smile.

"Hi honey! Just have a seat anywhere, I'll be by with some coffee in half a moment."

Maeve nodded and moved to find a table. She did a double take as she noticed Chief Briggs sitting in a booth across the room. Briggs was already looking at her and lifted his mug in acknowledgement. The man across from him, turned to look at her, his head catching the sunlight coming through the window. He was a large man, even from his seated position he towered over the table. Unlike Briggs, his presence felt cold, discomforting.

The men went back to their conversation and Maeve took the not-so subtle hint to keep moving. Moving toward the back of the diner she felt a slight tingle up the back of her neck. Someone was looking at her. She paused, her eyes roving. Her gaze finally clashed with Liam McAllister's amused smirk.

A black ball cap covered his unmistakable copper hair, and he had on a simple gray T-shirt. It was the kind of outfit someone wore when they didn't desire any attention. She took note of his toned upper body in the short sleeves, skin pale but smooth.

Maeve wasn't one to deny that he was a good-looking man, but, unlike Ben, it was in a simple and understated kind of way. Maeve thought back to the photo of him and Lara. Lara's beauty was obvious and intense. Her charisma was discernible even through the faded 4x6 snapshots. Liam's beauty was subtle.

Liam raked his eyes over her as she approached the table. "Good to see you again, detective. I ordered you a coffee. Figured it's the least I could do after last time."

She slid into the booth, offering a polite smile.

"Please, call me Maeve. I appreciate it. Our last run-in wasn't my finest moment. Especially in front of the entire town."

He laughed, leaning back in his seat and adjusting his hat. "Honestly it wasn't that bad. Moments like that always feel worse than they actually are. Most people who witness things like that instantly forget it once the moment has passed. We always assume people care so much about us and judge us, when in reality, people are inherently selfish and focused on themselves. I guarantee you most of the people haven't thought twice about it."

She raised her eyebrows, dragging her coffee toward her, quietly avoiding eye contact as she grabbed a sugar packet.

"Fair enough. Thank you for saying that. I hope that's true, because I was mortified thinking about how I handled that. I just kind of panicked and rushed out. I'm sorry."

The side of his mouth titled up. "It's no problem, Maeve, really." She took a sip of her coffee and cleared her throat. "Listen, thanks for agreeing to meet. I want to first start out by saying I'm sorry for everything you and your family has gone through this past year. I can't imagine how difficult it must have been for you."

Liam looked away, the playfulness between them gone in an instant. Her obtuse partner chose that moment to slide into the seat next to her, his body flush with hers. She bit back her frustration as Ben smiled at her, giving her a heated perusal and completely ignoring Liam. His smoky scent surrounded her, making her temporarily lose focus.

"Hi. Sorry I'm late. What did I miss?" he asked, finally directing his gaze across the table.

He was dressed in dark pants and a navy-blue button down, his badge hanging around his neck and a hint of stubble on his face. He had made it quicker than she expected. That was one thing she envied about men; they could look presentable in half the time women could. Ben stretched out his right hand and shook Liam's across the table.

"Good to see you man, how have you been?"

Liam looked slightly put off, taking his hand. "Hey, I'm doing alright. Just keeping busy with work and helping Lydia with the farm now that Ray is injured. You know, same old." His eyes drifted over to Maeve as he finished talking.

"Do you have a good relationship with Lydia?" she asked, using the opportunity to jump in.

His deep blue eyes moved to her. "I do now, but that wasn't always the case. We didn't get along much growing up. My father always created this divide between us, and we were very different. It got a bit better when we went to live with Aunt Lottie, but it just wasn't the same as what Lara and I had."

"Your aunt was the one who raised you after your parents died?" she asked, opening her notebook.

"Yeah, that's right. She's the best. She had to work really hard to provide for all three of us. She was never married, so it was just us four for a long time. She was a lot like my mom; gentle, kind, nurturing. It was a nice change after living with my father."

"What was he like?"

Liam turned to look out the window, avoiding eye contact. "He was strict. Regimented. He was super doting towards Lara but was a dick to Lydia and me. More so Lydia, really. With me he was just constantly disappointed. I was a momma's boy, and I was really shy. He could also be..." he quieted, looking back at her, "I don't know, he was just kind of a shitty guy. As bad as it was, he was all we had after mom died. After we lost him later that year, we all kind of spiraled, and my poor aunt had to pick up the pieces. After that I had to be the man of the house. I resented it."

"I'm sorry Liam, that must have been difficult, I can't even imagine. When did you guys move to Grants Pass?"

"We moved here about three years ago. Lara and I were fresh out of university and needed a fresh start."

Beside her, Ben remained silent, sipping his coffee, seemingly content to let her take the lead.

"A fresh start away from Chico? Did Lydia come with you?" she asked.

Liam took a deep breath. "Yeah, Chico. Lara had gone to Stanford, and I was working at the hospital there. We both decided we needed a change of scenery. And no, Lydia didn't come with us at first. She came to Grants Pass a year after we did. She was content running her B&B there with her boyfriend at the time."

"What made her change her mind and come to Oregon?"

He leaned back against the booth, wrapping both hands around his mug as he dropped his eyes to focus on the black liquid inside.

"Her boyfriend Trevor hit her. He'd always had a temper, but I didn't know the extent of it until Lydia called me one night. I told her to pack up and leave everything, and I would help her deal with it all. Even if we weren't close, she was still my sister, you know? I had to do something for her. I paid for her to get here and have her stuff sent the following week. She met Ray six months later and moved into his farmhouse."

Maeve had read up on Ray Droughton and found a photo of him on one of the farm auction websites. He was a hefty brute of a man, not hugely overweight, but thick. He came into his family's farmland when his parents passed, and he was fifteen years older than Lydia. Ben told her Ray had a good reputation around town and people generally seemed to like him.

Maeve ripped the band-aid. "Liam, do you have any opinion on what you think happened to your sister?" she asked, noticing Ben's hand tighten around his mug.

Liam looked out the window, absently shaking his head side to side before letting out a soft laugh. "You know, in all the months this has been going on, no one has ever asked me that," he said, pausing. "I only wish I had a better answer. I genuinely have no idea what could've happened to her. That's what pisses me off the most. I was her brother and her best friend, and I don't have the slightest inclination as to what could have happened."

He met her eyes. "It kills me."

"Liam, tell me about the night she went missing. What were you doing?"

"My alibi you mean?" he asked, lifting his eyebrows. "I was out with friends. We went for dinner and then they all came over to my place for a nightcap. A few of them stayed overnight."

"Sorry…I know you've probably shared it a million times. I'm just trying to get a handle on this case."

He lifted his hat, running a hand through his hair before replacing it again.

"I get it…but you don't have to beat around the bush. You can be direct with your questions, Maeve. I'd actually prefer it if you were."

She smiled apologetically. Ben shifted beside her. "Noted. When was the last time you saw her?" she asked.

Liam's brows pulled together. "I think it was the weekend before she went missing. We'd gone climbing at Northwest, a climbing gym on the other side of town. And since you're going to ask, she seemed fine. Nothing out of the ordinary. She was her usual loud and energetic self."

"Forgive me, but in your statement you mentioned that you knew something was wrong the morning that Saturday. How did you know?"

"We texted pretty much every day. I hadn't heard from her since that Friday morning when I texted her to ask if she wanted to get brunch on the weekend and got worried. It wasn't like her to not respond for that long. After I tried calling a few times and Rebs and Marc both told me that they hadn't seen her either, that's when I went to the precinct. I knew…I just knew something was wrong. I felt it," he said, pressing his lips together. She nodded, looking at Ben as they exchanged silent communication. "We'll let you get to work Liam. Thanks for meeting with us, we really appreciate it."

She felt increasingly small as they walked out to the parking lot, the men flanking her. Ben was at least six one, and Liam at least a couple inches taller than him. The feeling was a dichotomy of intimidation and safety.

The morning haze had cleared as the sun made its appearance, hesitant but warm. Maeve thanked Liam and they said their goodbyes before he meandered over to his red Subaru.

She turned slowly to Ben, who was awkwardly hovering behind her. She crossed her arms. "I still can't see why this could be anything other than a missing persons case. I mean, maybe I'm missing something, but I don't see the evidence for any foul play. It also doesn't make sense that she'd just skip town without telling anyone."

Ben leaned back against her car.

"Okay, so there's the fact that she excelled at her job at the firm, happy and successful," he started. "She was last seen telling her best friend she was going to see some clients and then would be home. Her car was never found, and all her things are at her house, photographs, personal items...all untouched."

She stepped closer, the sun warming her face.

He went on. "There's been no contact to her conjoined-at-the-hip brother in a year. She vanished right in the prime of her life never to be heard from again. She didn't run away. I just know it."

"Okay, I get it. Still, if there was foul play involved, there's usually at least some shred of actual evidence. I hate to say it, but there's also a chance she's still alive and being kept somewhere."

He nodded, touching his scruff. "Yeah, I've thought about that too. We staged a massive search party with the Medford Police Department and volunteer residents from GP. We did a clean sweep of this place. We walked arm and arm through acres of this shit," he said, gesturing to the rolling, lush-green mountains surrounding them.

"Yeah, Briggs told me. It's so weird that there wasn't a single ounce of trace evidence. Not even a shoe?" she asked.

He pushed off her car, stepping closer. "Nothing. Fucking...nothing." She took a breath, his proximity distracting her. "Okay, so did you look into her client list? Who was she scheduled to see last?"

"I'm not a complete idiot, of course I did. The firm gave me a roster of her ongoing clients, and I visited each of them. All of them said they hadn't done any work with her that week. Apparently, she'd rescheduled all their appointments to make room for a new client. Only problem is, the firm has no record of who the new client was. Seeing as she would work from home, coffee shops, client's houses, the chances were that she had all her work on her person or in her car. Then, Rebs confirmed it when I asked. She said she had a briefcase she took everywhere with her. Brown leather with a large gold lock on the front. Liam gave it to her when she passed the bar."

He searched her eyes. "And no…before you ask, I didn't find it. It was never found."

CHAPTER FOUR

Maeve made it to Bert & Callahan Law just after nine, pulling on her hood as she made her way inside. The rain had returned with fervor, but despite the hateful climate outside, Maeve felt focused and motivated. She'd made arrangements to speak with Jason Boukesh, a junior partner, and Lara's former colleague. He'd worked side-by-side with her at the time of her disappearance and had since been promoted. It was odd how Rebecca and Jason had both been promoted in the year since Lara's death, but when she'd queried it to Ben, he'd told her that promotions moved quickly in places the size of GP. Limited pool of competitors and all. It hadn't sated her suspicions.

Ben had texted he wouldn't be joining her for the interview as he didn't really get along with Jason and hadn't wanted to derail her interview. Small town problems.

The firm was clinically spotless. Maeve felt guilty as her shoes tracked in mud across the white tile floors. She approached the front desk and greeted Sarah, thankful for remembering her name from her last visit. Becoming a detective had forced her to come up with learned habits that were important, if not essential, to the job. Remembering people's names was one of them. It built trust.

Sarah returned Maeve's polite greeting and asked her to have a seat on the white leather sofa behind her, the desk phone ringing just as Maeve backed away.

After a solid ten minutes of waiting, a short blonde man strode confidently toward her. His light brown dress shoes made a clicking sound against the polished tile, and she immediately felt underdressed. He had a concerned look on his face, gaze down at his phone. She noted a haircut she'd once been told was called a fade, his white-blonde hair short on the sides and long on top, and he was wearing what looked to be a very expensive navy-blue suit. She could see the outlines of his defined shoulders and arms through his suit jacket and could easily picture him flexing in a tank top at the gym as he took endless pictures of himself. He finally dragged his eyes away from his phone and moved toward her, extending his hand.

"You must be Detective Kalani. I'm Jason Boukesh. It's a pleasure to meet you."

He shook her hand with uncomfortable pressure, his gaze moving over her too slowly before moving to the coffee on the glass table in front of her, grin spreading across his shiny face. She'd grabbed herself a high-calorie vanilla latte with extra whip and a black coffee for her interviewee.

"Please tell me that's for me...I'm exhausted."

She returned the smile. "Yes, it is. I wasn't sure what you took in it, but I figured you'd have cream and sugar here. Please, help yourself." He eagerly grabbed the coffee, thanking her and gesturing for her to follow. They walked up the large spiral staircase in the center of the building, the large gaps between each wooden step spiking her cortisol. It was illogical to assume someone could step at such an odd angle that they would slide right through the tiny gaps, but tell that to your mind.

After they made it to the loft-style second level, Maeve had to actively hide the fact that she was breathing much heavier than he was. She took some quiet, deep breaths as she tried to lower her heart rate after the embarrassingly small climb to the top.

Jason's office was one of only two offices on the second level and was triple the size of Rebecca's. It housed floor to ceiling windows on three sides, several large bookshelves, and a large leather sofa in the corner. The office could have been right off the set of suits.

Jason dropped into the leather chair behind his oversized desk and leaned back, looking her up and down in an unnerving way.

"So, I'm guessing this is about Lara?"

"Yes, it is. I just wanted to ask you some questions and take some notes, if that's okay with you? I know you've probably already answered them many times before, but I'm new to the case and wanted to speak to you personally."

He nodded but didn't respond, instead gesturing with his hand for her to get on with it. She hadn't been invited to sit, but she did her best to remember she held the power in the room and dropped into the fine leather seat across from him.

"How about we start with when you first met and your relationship with her in the years you knew her," she said, crossing her legs. He sighed, placing his coffee on the desk and interlocking his fingers over his stomach as he pulled his gaze from her chest.

"Well, she and I started here at the firm pretty much at the same time. I'd been working in Medford and moved out here in the hopes of getting the promotion to junior partner. That was the deal I made with Dave, our Managing Partner. Lara was a new Associate, and I was in a similar position. We ended up spending a lot of time with each other since we were assigned to the same cases," he offered, pausing. "And we also had a relationship."

He delivered the news with a smirk, the information meant to throw her off. Maeve's brows lifted but she didn't need to ask a follow up question, Jason rambled on without any prompting.

"It was going really well...in my opinion...but she ended after a few months. Lara decided all on her own that she wanted to go back to being friends because she didn't want to ruin our friendship. She said she wanted to focus on work," he finished with a huff.

"You didn't want to break up?" she asked, writing notes.

He squinted at her. "I don't see how that relates to the investigation."

"Humor me."

He rolled his eyes. "No, I guess I didn't. We were having a great time. She was magnetic." He cleared his throat and awkwardly shifted forward. "She was also very intelligent and driven. I'm not gonna lie, she was a catch. But I guess it didn't mean as much to her as it did to me. She could be...stubborn," he said, struggling to find the right word.

"I mean in hindsight I see it now. Lara didn't tell many people about us. She didn't want to start gossip, or have it impact our work until she knew if it would become something more. Or maybe she knew we wouldn't last," he said, looking down.

"Did Liam know?"

He seems surprised by the question, eyebrows lifting. "No, he didn't. Lara didn't like to bother him with things like that, and she asked me to keep it quiet. She said she didn't want him to worry or get involved in any way. He could get..."

She lifted her eyebrows in return.

"It's not like it still bothers me or anything. I'm not hung up on it anymore. I'm over it. There will always be others. I tend to prefer brunettes now anyway," he said, smirking at her.

She cleared her throat and redirected him.

"I can understand why she wouldn't want her older brother to know, but what did you mean when you said Liam could get...?"

Jason shifted. "Oh, I didn't mean anything by it. He was just protective of her, as an older brother should be. He could be a bit controlling at times, and they were really close. Lara was used to his overbearing nature, but they had some co-dependency issues if you ask me. It was kind of like we were constantly fighting for her time and attention. If she wasn't with me or at work, she was with him. We used to argue a bit about it because she felt bad leaving him alone even though he's a grown adult. It was weird."

Maeve nodded, writing notes. "You remained close friends then up until the night she went missing? Can you tell me about that night?" "Yes, detective, we remained friends. Contrary to popular belief, you can still be friends with someone after you break up," he replied. "What do you want to know? She left early. I went to ask Rebs where she went, and she told me Lara had gone to meet up with some clients. I didn't think anything of it at the time. I left work shortly after and went home to pack. I went on a trip that weekend with some friends."

She held his gaze, allowing some time to pass before continuing on.

"A trip? Where to?" she pressed, even though she'd already read his alibi in Ben's notes.

"My alibi you mean? You can just come right out and say it hun, I'm an attorney after all. I understand this line of work. I went hunting." "Who did you go with? Where did you go?"

"Ganesh Varma and Alex Marintha. My family has a cabin in the southern part of Rogue River National Forest. That should already be on file at your precinct," he quipped.

"My apologies, I'm new to this case and there's a lot to remember," she lied, "How far is that?"

"About three hours. You can't get there direct from GP, so you have to go down through California and back up and around. It takes longer than it should but that's why we like it. Isolated and off the grid."

"And you left that same Friday evening?" she asked pointedly.

"Yeah, we did."

Maeve let the silence and the direction of questioning linger before she spoke again.

"So, you weren't concerned that Lara was going to see clients outside of the office on her own? Did she do that often?"

Maeve noticed the clench in his jaw.

"No, I wasn't. She did it often. She was meeting up with these new clients quite a bit. We just assumed she was going to see them again. She spent a lot of time on that case."

"Did you know who Lara's new client was?"

He leaned forward, adjusting his cuff link. "When this investigation was active a year ago, your office got a subpoena for that information already. As you're also probably aware, there wasn't anything to find. She hadn't logged them in the B and C system as clients, and the firm hadn't taken any deposit from them at the time. She was either still in the vetting stage or she kept all her documents. There was nothing on file here. It took us a few weeks to gather her historical client list, but apparently Striton had no luck anyway. They all said they hadn't seen her for a few weeks. Looks like she pushed everything aside for these new clients."

"What kind of cases do you guys typically take on here? What kind of lawyer was she?"

"Well, we don't have the luxury of specializing much in a place this size, but we all have our preferences. I usually take on business, estate, and corporate law. A few associates here do family and divorce, and Lara typically took on criminal defense and civil rights."

That backed up Ben's notes. The McAllister's had endured a traumatic childhood. It was a perfect roadmap to a life dedicated to advocating for justice and protecting the innocent.

"Listen, thanks for seeing me, Jason. I know you're busy."

She slid her card across the desk toward him as she stood up. "Please call if you remember anything else you think may be important."

He stood and buttoned his jacket before extending his hand. The act was gentlemanly on first impression before it was subsequently exposed as his eyes dipped to her chest again.

She was walking back down the extravagant staircase when she made a split-second decision. She arrived at the office, did a slight knock and appeared in the doorway. Rebecca Raley looked like she was texting, looking up as before she let out a small but noticeable jump.

"Jesus, you scared the shit out of me!" she exclaimed, red flooding her cheeks. She put her phone down, a guilty look on her face before looking at the calendar on her desk. "I didn't realize we had a meeting today."

"We don't. I'm sorry. I was meeting with Jason upstairs, and I was on my way out, but I decided I needed to ask you something else, if that's okay?" Surprisingly, Rebecca was agreeable, nodding her head. "Sure." "Did Liam know about Marc? Jason just mentioned to me that he didn't know about their brief fling, so I was curious."

Rebecca shifted uncomfortably, her blonde curls moving off her shoulder.

"We were trying to keep it quiet from Liam. She didn't want him knowing about every aspect of her life. Especially since he wouldn't have approved."

Rebecca opened her top drawer to grab her pocket mirror and started re-applying her lip stain. Her gold bracelets caught Maeve's eye. "I know it sounds like Liam is a crazy person, but he's not. He just really loved her and didn't want her to get hurt. He's a good guy. He'd never do anything to jeopardize their bond."

Maeve wondered how a paralegal's salary could support Rebecca's extravagant taste, the Louboutin's, the jewelry.

"Look, you should ask Ben. He'd know more about the Marc situation. He knows him best for sure."

Maeve frowned, stepping forward. "What do you mean?" Rebecca lifted her eyebrows, smacking her lips together as she finished her touch up.

"Ben and Marc are best friends. We all used to hang out, the four of us."

CHAPTER FIVE

Maeve exhaled loudly, tossing her book on the couch next to her and dropping her head back. Distraction and sublimation never helped her racing mind. She really wished she could successfully read any one of the books her sister Maya sent her, but it was a lost cause. She couldn't sit around any longer.

She waltzed through the precinct twenty minutes later to find it completely abandoned. The main lights were shut off and the office was dimly lit by the natural light from outside, the effect post-apocalyptic. She moved to the only light source coming from an office down the hallway. Ben looked up at her, his expression tired and apologetic.

"Hey. What are you doing here on a Saturday?"

She took a breath, flouncing into the extra chair in the space.

"Pot, meet kettle," she said, gesturing to him. "I can't relax to save my life, and I don't really have a social life here so what the hell else am I going to do," she paused. "Also, I know it's the weekend, but it's also kind of odd we're the only ones here."

"Yeah, it's always like this. Briggs doesn't run a tight ship and most officers that work the weekends are out on patrol anyway. Though I agree this is unusually quiet. Even for 59."

Maeve exhaled. "Hey so…I spoke to Rebecca again. She told me about your bestie Marc."

Ben frowned, spinning his hat backwards as he looked at her.

She leaned forward. "How am I supposed to be successful in this if you pick and choose what to share and when to share it? Don't you think that's extremely important information I should've been told?"

He had the decency to look genuinely apologetic as he reached for his mug. "I know I know, I'm sorry. I was going to tell you, I just didn't know how. I'll have to thank Rebs for that," he said, rolling his eyes. She remained quiet, expectant. He leaned back in his chair and took a sip of his dark roast before meeting her eyes again.

"Marc is my best friend. I was trying to save him another painful drag through the suspect ringer. He was cleared when it happened, and he doesn't deserve to be put through that again."

She pulled her hair out from behind her and crossed her arms over her chest.

"Cleared or not, Ben, I still deserve the respect of my partner telling me every aspect of this case. What exactly cleared him?"

"Airtight alibi."

She raised her eyebrows.

"I'm not an idiot. I realize it's a conflict of interest, me investigating him," he said, "but I did my job properly. He didn't see her that night. He knew she had another meeting with a client and couldn't stop by, so he went out with me instead. I'm his alibi, Maeve."

Her shock must have been apparent because he lifted his hands to stop her before she spoke. "We went out that night, to The Shipyard, like we always did. He told me his plans had fallen through and asked if I wanted to meet up for a beer. Marc ended up having one too many and passed out on my couch at my place that night. I was with him the entire night."

As if reading her mind, he continued. "Now before you go and start getting suspicious of me, you'll want to check with Briggs. He checked with Carl, the manager at The Shipyard, and five other patrons that were there that night to confirm."

Maeve nodded but inside she was still thinking it left a good chunk of time at night where Ben and Marc were at his place, unseen. They were best friends, what better alibi was there? What was the saying? A good friend will help you move, but a true friend will help you move a body.

There was also the possibility that Marc could have left after he had passed out on the couch under the assumption that Ben was asleep. The small town and interconnectivity of the residents as it related to Lara's disappearance was making her paranoid. She felt like she had no one left to trust. And now to add on another layer, it was a major conflict of interest that her partner was connected. It meant she might just be the only truly objective person investigating the case.

After a few minutes of painful silence Maeve spoke again.

"Were you friends with Lara?"

He looked sincere as he nodded slowly.

"We hung out, the four of us, pretty often. She was good for Marc, and it was just convenient that I dated Rebs. Rebs was always wanting to hang out as a group. She told me I was boring on my own," he said, letting out a short laugh. "She was super insecure around Lara. Apparently in high school Rebs was..." he winced, shifting his gaze away, "...popular with the boys, and after Lara came to town she was like the shiny new toy. She got drunk one night and told me she used to have a thing for Marc, and that's when I ended it. She was also getting more and more clingy and neurotic, and it was too much for a surface level fling."

Maeve met his honey eyes. "I can't believe you knew Lara that well. You're close to this."

"I'm not that close to it, Maeve. I'm close to Marc. Lara was a bit intense, but Marc was in deep. I only knew her from the brief interactions we had on double dates," he explained, fidgeting with his pen. He was quiet for a moment.

"Meave, I was a Marine. I've seen...done...some really fucked up things. He's the closest thing I have to a brother. He was the one to convince me not to drop out of college. That's where we met, at Uni in Portland. Honestly Maeve, he's the reason I'm a detective" he said, voice tight. He swallowed audibly. "No...he's the reason I'm still alive."

The room was quiet, and she didn't know how to fill it. She didn't know if she should.

"I'm sorry, Ben. You're right. It's not your fault you're intertwined in this, and it's not like we can have someone else look into it. From what Briggs tells me, you're all GP has," she offered, laughing quietly. "I can't begin to understand what you've been through. Thank you for telling me." He offered a small nod in response.

That sat together as Maeve went through the rest of the investigation notes and Ben filled in the blanks as she went. By the time the afternoon came around, her mind was foggy. Ben had been asleep in the chair across from her for nearly an hour, but she'd successfully made it through the rest of the files. She kicked the bottom of Ben's shoe to wake him, and he jolted up with a snort, subtly trying to wipe the drool from the corner of his mouth as he ran a hand over his head.

"Did I fall asleep?" he asked, voice thick and deep.

"Yes. You were snoring."

"Jesus. Sorry Maeve, you could have woken me."

"It's okay. Seemed like you needed the rest, and I enjoyed the silence anyway."

He nodded, straightening up and gathering his things as he looked at his watch.

"Wanna head to The Shipyard? They have great pub food, and you can have a look at where our girl spent a lot of her time. Plus, it's Saturday. Sangria Saturday."

She laughed, despite herself. "Big sangria fan eh?" she teased.

Ben smiled, his eyes intense. "Absolutely. Drinks aren't masculine or feminine. They're just drinks."

She nodded. "Fair enough. I'm in. I need some fries."

The pub was a direct imitation of its British counterparts, complete with dim lighting and the faint smell of stale beer. Tacky license plates from all over the country plastered the wooden interior, sailing memorabilia, and fishing nets strewn about. She smiled as she took it in. She would choose a pub over a fancy restaurant any day. The booming laughter, the greasy food, and the general calm, it was magnetic.

The tattooed bartender sauntered over to them and took their orders as they slid onto the navy-blue bar stools. He had a perfectly groomed mustache that twirled up at the ends and sported a tweed flat cap. Ben made quick introductions.

"Carl? You must be the same guy that Ben always gushes about. He loves your sangria," she mocked.

"Excuse me, I do not...nor would I ever, gush," Ben huffed. Carl laughed, clapping him on the shoulder in greeting. The three of them fell into easy conversation for the duration of their meal, Carl occasionally stepping away to fill orders.

"How long have you worked here?" Maeve asked, polishing off her fries.

"I've been managing for just over five years now, but I've been saving up to buy it. Gotta make some responsible moves now that we have a baby on the way."

"Oh amazing! Congratulations. Does your partner work here too?" she asked.

Carl opened his mouth to reply but stopped himself as his attention was drawn to a petite Japanese woman in a light blue linen jumpsuit gliding through the front door. She quickly closed her clear umbrella and patted her black hair into perfection. Carl grinned, moving out from behind the bar as the woman habitually moved into his arms. After a small embrace and peck on the lips, Carl gestured to the detectives.

"Perfect timing, babe. Nik, this is Detective Maeve Kalani and, of course, you know Ben. Maeve moved here a couple weeks ago."

Nik surprised her by turning to her with a bright warm smile, extending her delicate hand. "Maeve! It's so nice to meet you. Ben, nice to see you as well," she greeted them, encompassing Maeve's hand into both of hers as Carl slung an arm around her small shoulders.

"I'm sure you can figure out that this beautiful woman here is my wife, Nikko," he paused, touching her round stomach, "and this is our little one on the way." He beamed at his wife in admiration.

Maeve smiled. "Congratulations. You look great by the way." "Oh, you're too kind. I feel like an unstable troll," she laughed.

"Look Maeve, there isn't much to do around here, but Nik and I usually have people over on Saturdays for drinks and cards after I'm done work. If you want to join, you and Ben are welcome."

"Yes, both of you must come! I know it doesn't sound like it, but it's actually fun, and we could always use new people to join, spice things up a bit!" Nikko chimed in.

Despite Maeve's initial urge to decline, the alcohol she'd ingested had other ideas as she felt her mouth move against her will.

"Yes, let's do it. What time?"

Ben looked at her in astonishment.

"What?"

"I didn't know you liked fun. I'm shocked. Honestly, I didn't even know you could laugh until today when I forced it out of you with my witty, elite level humor."

"Oh, fuck off," she shot back.

Maeve accepted the ride with Nikko and Carl back to their place. Ben had been right about the Sangiras, a pitcher was a non-negotiable and her head was swimming. Her partner had claimed he was too tired to join at Carl and Nikko's and had taken a cab home instead. Buzz kill. It was just after nine by the time they pulled into the driveway. Maeve's stomach surged as the effects of the booze wore off and her social anxiety crept in. Had she really just gotten in a stranger's car to go to another location to join for games night with people she'd never met before? What had gotten into her? She could have bailed when Ben did but something in her had pulled her to go. To make friends as her mother would say.

She pulled self-consciously at her top, noticing two other cars pull in and couples sift through the front door without pausing to knock. She was immediately jealous of the level of familiarity that would take.

Candles of varying shapes and sizes were placed delicately around their home and pictures framed in metallics cluttered the walls. Where there wasn't art, there were plants. They filled all the remaining spaces, large or small. It wasn't what Maeve expected, and she loved it. The modern minimalistic greys and whites that had become popular for homes in recent years was usually as tasteless as the people that lived in them.

After she greeted Nikko, Maeve made her rounds introducing herself to the guests. On the green velvet couch were Will and Rob, a handsome couple who both worked in finance. Nikko's friend from college, Emma, who was a teacher and had curves to die for. Maeve was inherently jealous of women who didn't have the shapely outline of a rectangle.

On the stools across the kitchen island chatting with Carl, were Amelia and Marco, and the woman who sat on the floor leaning against the fireplace was Luna. She had bright yellow nails and red rimmed plastic glasses. Her raven black hair was sleek as she tossed her head back in a deep laugh at something Will had said.

Maeve had just dropped down onto the sofa next to Will and Rob as a tall figure emerged from the hallway, moving into the open kitchen. Maeve's heart did a somersault when she recognized the red tinge of his hair. Just as luck would have it, Liam fucking McAllister.

He entered the living room, taking a drink from a bottle of Corona. He tensed, noticing her on the couch but recovered quickly, hiding his shock before placing his beer on the counter and sauntering over. Carl raised his voice. "Maeve, this is Liam. The last of our group and the one with the best hair."

He tossed Liam a wink as Liam ran a hand through the silky auburn strands and rolled his eyes. Everyone laughed as Liam moved to sit next to her on the couch. She knew there was literally nowhere else for him to sit, but it still felt deliberate. She was lightheaded as she took in the faint smell of mint as he moved closer.

The tension dissipated as the evening shifted into board games, wine, and hearty laughter. She relaxed as the night progressed, despite the walking conflict of interest in dark jeans.

Liam had been easy to talk to. Less intense than she remembered, and a worthy charades partner. He hadn't made anything uncomfortable, and although he spent time with Maeve, he also made sure to catch up with his other friends as well. He was genuinely interested in the well-being of the group, and it showed. Overall, it had been a fun and easy evening. Maeve was grateful for the social interaction and inclusion, but she still felt unsettled.

Her mistrust laced every interaction, and she wondered if she would ever be able to form meaningful relationships in a town where everyone was a potential suspect. The line between paranoia and sanctioned vigilance was growing increasingly blurry.

• • •

The oppressive trees lining the dirt path swayed as Maeve pulled up outside of Marc Hallman's house, their diverse foliage dancing in rhythm with the turbulent weather. Marc lived on a large plot of land, the area marked by linear rows of soil, planters and gardens. His small brown farmhouse appeared well maintained but was grossly overshadowed by the greenhouse adjacent to it. The oversized dome was double in size and helped round out the garden nicely.

Maeve stepped out of her car, tucking her hair back as the wind whipped fallen pieces against her cheeks. A high-pitched whine caught her attention as she turned toward the greenhouse, the door open as a man stepped out. She waved awkwardly and he returned the gesture before locking the door behind him and began walking toward her, wiping his hands on his dirt crusted jeans. She swallowed thickly as a surge of uncertainty clawed its way through her.

"Detective Kalani?" he yelled, stomping over to her in heavy rubber boots.

She pulled her jacket tight around her, a light rain starting.

"Yes, hi. It's nice to meet you, Marc. Thank you for meeting with me on a Sunday, I really appreciate it."

He smiled, waving her off. Even through his loose clothing Maeve could see the ripple of refined muscles beneath, his skin a warm brown and his eyes almost as dark as her own. He was deeply handsome, but the farmer look didn't seem to suit him, his beard too well manicured, teeth too white, and plaid shirt too crisp.

"It worked out for me too, I didn't need another investigator coming into my work, they might start to get suspicious," he said, ending in a laugh and waving her toward the house.

Once they were both warm and dry inside, Marc spoke first.

"Your last name…Hawaiian?"

She nodded. Shaking off the oppressive chill that had settled within her as she scanned the space. It was light and airy, the whites and woods providing a simple backdrop for the minimalist decor and foliage placed artistically throughout the home.

"Excellent deduction skills. Most assume I just have a nice tan year round," she replied, smiling and meeting his eyes, her apprehension from before melting away.

He laughed, leading her into the tight living room. "I get it. My mother moved to the US from Haiti when she was eighteen. Left most of her family there and met my father in Portland. My last name tends to confuse people, and I always feel like I have to explain why I'm not white."

"I get it," she said, offering a smile. "Good for her, that's an impressive move at eighteen. Do you speak Creole?"

"Yeah, I do. Not as good as I used to, but I still get by. Not much use of it here though," he replied, leaning forward. They were sitting in the cozy living room on green velvet armchairs.

"Do you get a chance to go back and visit often?"

"I used to go a lot more when I was younger, but now I can't really get life to slow down enough, you know?"

"That's fair. I don't get to see my father and brother much either. They're still over there. I have good intentions, but like you said, I never actually end up going. Something always gets in the way. As my mother used to say, 'how can you focus on the important things when all the unimportant things keep getting in the way?'" she said, laughing at herself for quoting her mother. It wasn't something she did often, but when she did, she always cringed. Her narration ran through her brain when she least expected it. Luckily, Marc echoed her reaction, letting out a supportive laugh in response.

Maeve grabbed her notebook.

"Marc, do you mind if I jump into things? I just have a few questions, if you don't mind."

"Of course, ask away, Maeve."

"You and Lara had been dating when she went missing, correct?" He stood, moving to the adjoining kitchen and putting a kettle on the stove. The sudden shift through her off. He replied to her, back still turned. "Correct."

"How long were you together before that night?" she pressed, lifting her voice.

He turned, crossing his arms and leaning back against the counter. "About six months."

"How was your relationship?" she pressed, struggling to get more information from him.

"I mean we were fine I'd say. Every couple has their petty fights, but we were good at communicating. We were also independent enough to pursue our own goals as individuals before putting pressure on us as a couple. We were trying to keep things light. We wanted to just see where things would go without the pressure of a long-term commitment. We both had goals we wanted to achieve before we wanted to settle down."

"Makes sense," she said, making notes. Marc returned with the tea, pouring a cup for them both before settling back down.

"What do you do for work?" she asked.

"I work for the Bureau of Land Management. I work in the Environmental Science Department."

"Here in GP?"

"My office is out of Portland actually, but I work remotely from home. I only need to go in once a month or so for important meetings," he said, taking a sip from his mug. She nodded, looking around the small space for an office.

Picking up on her line of thinking he replied, "I have a desk upstairs in the loft area if you want to see."

"No, that's okay, thank you. Can you tell me about the night of May 1st, 2018? What were you doing?"

He clenched his angular jaw. "I was with Ben," he said, giving her a knowing look. "Lara canceled our plans to get drinks while I was at work that day. She said she needed to see her new clients, so I asked Ben to meet up for a beer instead. We were at The Shipyard until late, probably around midnight I'd say, then we took a cab back to his place to crash. Since I live so far out of town I usually stay at his place when it's convenient. I was there all night."

"Ben mentioned there was a period of time where you were presumably both asleep, you on the couch and him in his room...did you leave at any point in the night?"

"No, I didn't. I was passed out all night. Woke to a sore head and dry throat the next morning around nine. I got up and made us both eggs and then left to go home and shower. I hadn't heard from Lara at all. Not since she first texted me to cancel. I sent the proof of our texts to the precinct, directly to Chief Briggs instead of Ben. I understand having the lead detective as my alibi is a problem, but there's not much I can do to prove I was actually at Ben's the whole night."

She made a note. "You weren't worried about her?"

He frowned. "No, honestly I wasn't. She just canceled a date; it wasn't a big deal to me at the time. I respected that she had a busy life, and her career was important to her. She blew me off quite a lot in those last few weeks. I was kind of frustrated by then anyway, I assumed she was trying to quietly remove herself from our relationship." He paused, taking a drink and exhaling. "At the time, I had no reason to be worried that I hadn't heard from her all night. That was normal for us, unfortunately."

Maeve nodded, assessing his reaction. "Did she seem different in the days before she went missing? Anything out of the ordinary or peculiar about the way she acted or the things she said?"

"I honestly hadn't seen her since the weekend prior. We'd gone for a hike out at Watertail and then brunch after. She seemed her usual self that day, lively, stubborn...busy."

"Watertail? Sorry I'm not familiar with this area."

"No problem, yeah, it's about ten minutes south of here. I'm really lucky, there's some good walking trails near here and not many people know about them so they don't get too busy."

She made a note. "Did you know about the case she was working on at the time? Did she ever mention anything to you?"

"Not specifically no. She was good at keeping work at work. She never shared anything about her clients or what she was working on, but would often just share her frustrations in general. The only thing that stuck with me about this case in particular, was that she used to say the case was a dead end, but she felt she owed it to the family to keep digging. She was going above and beyond though, working more than usual. Like I said, she kept canceling or rescheduling our plans."

Maeve made a note and pivoted the conversation. "Did you know her siblings well?"

He let out a deep chuckle before crouching down in front of the fireplace, adjusting the logs.

"Well, to be frank, not really. Liam and I had only met briefly once through mutual friends, but even then he didn't know I was with his sister. It's not like I didn't try to meet him; I suggested dinner multiple times, but Lara was adamant that she didn't want him to know about us. Whenever I picked her up from his place she'd always make me park a couple houses down. She said she wanted to keep us private for a while before involving Liam, but it felt like she was paranoid, I don't know."

"What was Lara's relationship with them like?"

He stood, turning back toward her. "She saw Liam every few days at least, they were really close. She told me that he had been overprotective since their parents died but that was about it. She definitely looked up to him. He was absolutely destroyed after she went missing," he paused, moving back to the armchair and meeting her gaze. "I mean, we all were, I guess."

"I'm very sorry this happened, Marc."

He looked away, nodding his thanks. The silence held for a moment before he spoke again, clearing his throat.

"I never met Lydia. Lara just said they weren't close and that was the end of it. Who was I to pry into or judge their family dynamic, you know? She always said she wanted things to settle down before we brought our families into it. Whatever that means."

Maeve closed her notebook. "Is it easy to grow things out here? Do you get lots of fresh vegetables and herbs?" she asked, nodding to the basket he'd brought in from the greenhouse.

He followed her gaze, lingering a moment before offering a close mouthed smile as he leaned forward, arms braced on his thighs.

"Yes, actually. The moisture is good in this region, but it's too cold to grow anything outside in the winter. I'm just starting some seedlings in the greenhouse before summer comes. I keep it heated in there year-round."

"Nice, well good for you. I could never. I don't have the patience."

He laughed. "That's fair. I tend to be very meticulous when it comes to things I care about, but it's a meditative outlet for me more than anything."

Her shoes made a squelching sound as she trudged through the damp gravel back to her car. The rain fell down in fat drops, soaking through her layers. She quickened her pace past the greenhouse and her gaze landed on a thick padlock. The spotless shiny silver a vivid contrast to the rusted rings on which it hung. Maeve lingered, moving closer. A sudden loud bang jolted her and she turned, her heart racing. Marc was standing on the covered front porch, watching. Once Maeve realized the source of the loud noise was his wood framed screen door, she took a breath in an attempt to lower her heart rate. He lifted his hand, offering a soft wave in dismissal. Even though he was too far away to see, she still gave an apologetic smile. This is what she got for snooping.

Driving through the tree lined path, Maeve glanced in the rearview mirror. Unease crawled up her legs and into her core as she saw him standing there, hand still raised.

CHAPTER SIX

The Monday-est Monday rolled around unapologetic and unrelenting. The rainy haze outside persisted and the vibes in the office responded in like. There was minimal motivation and a lazy pace. Over the past week, the detectives moved into an easy flow, a camaraderie that was no longer forced or uncomfortable. At least her partner seemed to have the same work ethic as her or she'd be losing her mind. The detectives were sitting in Maeve's office, three cups of coffee deep.

"He's got a nice place out there, kind of gave me the whole organic granola vibe," she said, referencing Ben's best friend.

He huffed, kicking up his feet on the desk. "Yeah, he is. He's all about whole foods and growing your own. He's a diehard climate activist and I think he'd love to live completely off the grid if he could. Too bad he had to go and get a real job," he said, ending in a laugh.

"Yeah, I could see that. Huge greenhouse he has out there, hey? Does he sell any of his produce? I'm sure he could make a profit at a farmer's market or something."

"Yeah, and it's actually double the size if you include the cellar. He has a full system, irrigation, heating...the whole shebang. It's crazy. But no, he's never sold anything at a market."

She nodded and Ben jumped as his cell phone buzzed loudly through his pants. He lurched, swinging his feet off the desk. He answered and his hazel eyes met hers, his face draining of color.

"We'll be over as quickly as we can. Don't touch anything," he barked, ending the call.

"What is it?"

"They've found a body."

Time stood still. The distant rumblings of the road nearby and the phone lines ringing were the only sounds passing through her mind as she held her breath, the weight of the situation paralyzing her. There was only a slim chance the victim was Lara, but it was still a chance. Even if it wasn't her, then they'd have another homicide case on their hands.

She took a breath. One step at a time. It was the mantra that had saved her more times that she could count. She had a bad habit of taking on too much at once, and it had more than once resulted in a mistake. She'd learned the hard way that getting things done on time was not nearly as important as doing things right. Especially when those things saved peoples' lives.

Ben grabbed his jacket off the back of the chair and moved in a controlled but quickened pace. Maeve, contrarily, moved in slow motion as she collected her things.

Ben leaned out of her office, yelling across the space. "Joe, you're going to want to come with us!"

Only as all three of them entered Ben's Chrysler, did Chief Briggs ask what was going on. Ben peeled out of the parking lot and onto the street that connected directly to the 15 northbound. The faint smell of BO coming from the backseat started to permeate the air.

"I got a call that a body was found behind Umbele Correctional in the woods. We have no other information other than that right now," Ben explained, glancing at Maeve.

When there was no immediate response, she turned to the backseat. Briggs was completely still, the utter shock on his face forcing her instincts to watch his chest for breathing.

"Sir?"

She watched as her boss re-entered the present moment and focused back on her.

"Fuck. Is it her?" Briggs asked, leaning forward.

"We don't know. Gary said it was a young female but that he didn't want to get any closer to make out details. I told him that was the right call."

Briggs cleared his throat. "Gary?"

Ben met his eyes in the rear-view mirror. "Yeah."

An unspoken communication passed briefly between them. "Who's Gary?" she asked tentatively.

"The warden," Ben replied, offering no other explanation. Maeve took the hint and slipped into silence. She relaxed into her seat, glancing out at the vast all-encompassing firs, junipers and pines filling her view. The sheer density of it was overwhelming. Confining and liberating at the same time.

So easy to hide a body.

The chief spent the rest of the drive making calls to organize the tactical response. Ben had his eyes on the road, hands at ten and two, white-knuckle grip on the steering wheel.

After twenty minutes he finally slowed down, and they coasted through the ghost town that was Azalea. They passed an old Foodmart from circa 1922, and Maeve could almost taste the stale muffins and weak coffee it most certainly provided. It looked completely abandoned, other than the zombies that undoubtedly dragged themselves through the aisles. She shuddered, trying to pull back her intrusive thoughts.

After various left and right turns onto unpaved roadway, they arrived at a stop sign a few minutes outside the town limits. Maeve noticed a large blue road sign with Umbele Correctional Women's Penitentiary. She zipped up her black windbreaker as best she could and glanced up toward the end of the dirt path that appeared to lead into nothingness.

Three large buildings appeared like shadows through the haze resting on top of the landscape. It reminded Maeve of a scene from The Walking Dead. The misting rain surrounding the gothic, gray buildings loomed before them. The area was surrounded by tall brick walls and looming gates, two guards posted in the small shelter between the entrance and exit gates. A quiet eeriness spread through the car.

Ben provided his name and badge, and the officer radioed for approval before the gate was buzzed open. As they rolled toward the buildings, Maeve spotted a figure standing near the top of the small hill directly in front of the prison.

The distance was too far to see his features, but close enough to notice he was holding a shovel.

CHAPTER SEVEN

The man before them gave off an aura of comfortable superiority. His looming presence and impeccable tailored suit made Maeve feel small. He was surrounded by three correctional officers who resembled the Queen's Guard at Buckingham Palace. Not in appearance, but in demeanor. They didn't shift their weight, blink, or even breathe. Their arms were behind their backs like soldiers in formation, waiting for their next command.

Briggs and Ben greeted him with familiarity and Maeve awkwardly introduced herself.

"It's a pleasure to meet you, Miss Kalani. I'm Warden Gary Managan. It's about time Joe brought new blood to the team," he said. He shifted his stance, passing his shovel to a filthy elderly man next to him dressed in overalls and knee-high rubber boots. The man scratched the white scruff on his face before dipping to take the shovel and backing up a few steps, avoiding eye contact. Gary tracked his gaze over to Maeve, eyeing her for a moment before looking at the chief.

Briggs walked forward, grabbing him by the shoulder gently and turning him away. Maeve and the others followed the pair around the prison perimeter, the COs falling behind the group to take their positions. The warden started to tell Briggs what had happened, and Maeve had to move into a slight jog to be able to keep close enough to hear the exchange. Ben walked next to her and snorted at the effort she had to put in to keep up. Tom, the older man carrying the shovel, was one of two groundskeepers at Umbele. Tom had contracted an arborist to bring down some of the large trees behind the cemetery to allow for expansion. After clearing away some of the dense brush, Tom had immediately called it off and radioed for the warden.

"...I walked out with Tom and Henry to where the backhoe was sitting and saw a woman's arm sticking out of the ground. I was in shock, but luckily Tom took it upon himself to call 911. Sorry I wasn't able to warn you ahead of time, Joe. It just went through dispatch."

Ben leaned toward her, lowering his voice. "Gary and Joe are good friends. They go way back. They have breakfast every morning together at the diner."

He'd read her mind again.

The group finally made their way through the cemetery, and Maeve was shocked at the state it was in. The overgrowth was so dense it covered most of the gravestones, and there were piles of dirt and fallen trees scattered around the space. It was disrespectful, but unfortunately due to the nature of the inhabitants, not all that surprising.

Maeve had a strong opinion about the justice system, and her decision to work in enforcement was not made easy due to her unyielding beliefs. It was a shame that even in death people saw criminals before they saw human beings. Death should demand respect and dignity above all else.

Before she'd become a detective, Maeve had always had issues with what was considered acceptable punishment in the justice system. It was as corrupt as the people who enacted it in the first place, and she'd struggled with the fact that her work oiled the wheels for the system as a whole. Voltaire said it best: "It is forbidden to kill; therefore all murderers are punished, unless they kill in large numbers and to the sound of trumpets."

Maeve dragged her focus back to the present as they left the perimeter of the cemetery and toward the back of the lot. The trees were thick, the edge of the forest clearly defined. Large gaps in the earth where large trunks with deep rooted systems had been forcibly removed were everywhere. The imagery was crude and immoral. A few graves had been placed within the treed area farther back from the flatland and amongst the saplings and firs.

It began to rain with more fervor, the steady downpour surrounding them as the warden pulled out a black umbrella and moved toward a large mound of upturned dirt in the woodland. Apart from the sound of shoes crunching in the damp underbrush and rain falling on various umbrellas, a deafening quiet settled in the woods. The timid silence followed behind them like a shadow until they reached their destination.

Maeve turned back to look at the prison behind them. They were far enough away from the buildings to only make out the ant-like outlines of the inmates walking into the building from the yard. It must have been deliberate, to bury the dead not within the walls that both confined and condemned them but instead to allow their final resting place to be within the natural elements. The irony of allowing some semblance of humanity only once it was made redundant.

Henry Rolal approached each of them and shook their hands politely. His hands, as her grandfather's had been, were covered in dried dirt and blisters formed from a lifetime of hard labor. Henry had a receding salt and pepper hairline and looked to be in his early sixties. He was slightly taller than the average male and had the burly handyman look going on, but his eyes were soft and kind as he gave Maeve a gentle smile.

"You guys help yourself to whatever you need, just let us know if we can be of any assistance. We'll be on the north side of the admin building fixing the exteriors," he explained, pointing to the lights that surrounded the outer walls of the prison. "If you need my statement, I'll be in the office in about an hour to gather my things and head out for the evening. I wish I could do it now, but I've gotta get those done today," he said reluctantly, glancing quickly at the warden. "Again sir, we're very sorry. Didn't mean to cause such a mess."

Gary gave him a slight nod in return, waving his hand in his general direction to dismiss him as he turned back to Briggs. Tom and Henry made their way back toward the prison at a leisurely pace, Tom with a slight limp favoring his left side. The detectives approached the scene slowly.

Maeve's gaze landed on the contorted, ashy human arm sticking out of the earth at an unnatural angle. The arm was undeniably that of a female.

Long, lean, and delicate with minimal hair. The skin had noted pallor and signs of mottling around the elbow, but the nails were well manicured despite being covered in dirt. Ben dropped down into a crouch and removed his hat. Maeve made a mental note of the scene as she mimicked her partner, crouching down. They worked quietly and independently as they took their own notes. The differences in perception of the same reality were incredibly valuable in a situation where the smallest of details could help solve a case. Maeve adjusted her ponytail as she stood back up, her knees cracking. "So, what's next then? What do you want to do first?" Ben shook his head back and forth before replacing his hat.

"Can't be sure until god damned forensics arrives and does their shit first. Not sure what the holdup is, chief called them ages ago," he said, looking behind him.

"Are they coming from GP?"

He looked at her and huffed a laugh. "No. We aren't big enough to warrant our own crew. They usually put a call out to see who has the capacity to send their team to us. My guess is Medford," he paused, turning around to get Briggs' attention. He was lingering farther back, assessing the scene and talking to some officers.

The last bits of light slowly faded away and Maeve wandered to the outskirts of the cemetery and deeper into the forest. Her shoes squished as she trudged through the damp moss in her black runners. Maeve had always been an observant person; she could take in a scene she'd seen a million times and pick out any minute differences. Her best work was not with witness statements and interviews, but with the setting. With the body.

The context of the crime.

She took her time, letting her mind wander. A short while later she grabbed her upper arms, the damp cold seeping in through her thin jacket. She looked up and noticed Ben, Briggs and Gary looking up at her from where they stood near the body. Maeve's pulse leaped as she noticed the intensity in their stares before Ben lifted an arm and aggressively waved her back. Four sets of headlights in a straight line headed their way.

Muttering, "it's about damn time" Ben came up to stand beside her, playfully nudging her shoulder with his own.

They both unconsciously raised their hands to shield their eyes as the vehicles closed the distance between them, the harsh light piercing through the night. Three large black Ford cargo vans and one black town car pulled in. Briggs and Gary walked up to greet the arrivals as the detectives hung back.

Men and women wearing navy blue jackets with MCSU plastered across the back hustled out of the vans and started unloading a variety of equipment. Briggs approached the man who exited the town car and shook his hand.

Ben nudged her to join him, and they made their way over. Chief Regan Maxwell from the precinct in Medford introduced himself to Maeve and greeted Ben. Regan Maxwell's presence took up the space around them as he barked commands at the team and grabbed Briggs shoulder, asking for a recap. Maeve's perception of Briggs was immediately minimized by Chief Maxwell.

Over the next few hours, Maeve filled her green notebook with intrusive questions and details that had been forcing their way into her mind since they'd found the body. She had spent a great deal of time hovering as she watched the MCSU team unpack and get set up, and Ben had kept himself busy interviewing potential witnesses, the warden, and the prison employees. They'd watched the back and forth between Chief Maxwell and Chief Briggs as they both tried to gain the upper hand and pull rank. It was a tense pissing match but eventually Maxwell had relented, stepping away to release some of the idle officers and tighten up the scene.

The forensic team had taken hundreds of photographs and samples before they gave the go-ahead to have the body removed. As the team carefully uncovered the dirt surrounding her, the group fell into complete silence.

Ben moved to stand next to her, tension rolling off both of them. Maeve held her breath as the partially decomposed body was revealed. The dirt was swept away to reveal a head of platinum blonde hair. The detectives exchanged glances as the rest of her sickly body was uncovered. Although decomposition had already progressed quickly, one thing was clear. It wasn't Lara McAllister.

Dr. Mason Gertree, Grants Pass Medical Examiner, was the first to move in. He was a frail man with large eyebrows and thin metal framed glasses, his technique demonstrated comfortable competence as his hands moved with expert skill and precision. Maeve watched as he prodded the victim's trachea and the discernable dark ring surrounding it, splatters of tiny burst vessels peppering the skin of her neck. Her head sat at an unnatural angle to her neck, the near perfect right angle unsettling. Her large natural breasts hung heavy against her emaciated body, the angles of her limbs abnormal and inhuman. Some of her skin, fat and muscle had since melted into the earth below, her cheeks open and skeletal, the connective tissues visible between jaw and skull. The broken neck and tracheal trauma were enough to suspect a suicide, but if that's what happened, someone would have had to move her to this place. And if it truly was a suicide, why hide her at all?

CHAPTER EIGHT

Incessant pounding echoed throughout the house as Maeve padded to the front door. She swung it open to find her partner leaning against the door frame, grinning fiendishly. A sharp cold breeze hit her bare toes, and she curled them, crossing her arms expectantly.

He dragged his gaze over her. "Sorry to…wake you?" he said, his mouth tipping at the edges. "Dr. G called. He has the prelim ready. He wants us down there ASAP."

She frowned. "Did you drive over here just to tell me that? You couldn't have relayed that message with a simple phone call?" she asked, grumpy and exhausted.

"No, 'cause then I wouldn't have been able to witness…this," he whispered, gesturing to her green Harry Potter pajama set, giving her a suggestive wink. She scowled, stepping back to let him in before trudging up the stairs to go change.

"You didn't tell me you were a Slytherin! This changes things!" he yelled after her, the sound traveling up the stairs as she shook her head, craving her first hit of caffeine.

"Ben, can you at least try to drive at a reasonable speed? I mean, my god, you're a cop."

They were driving out of Maeve's subdivision as she attempted to put on mascara in the mirror. They'd gotten to know each other better in the past few weeks, and the unfamiliarity had eased, and they had both shifted into the mocking stage of their partnership.

Adjusting his grip on the steering wheel Ben looked at her.

"Not a chance, babe. I've been waiting for two days for this report." He was dressed in his usual dark jeans and black jacket but had on a basic white T-shirt underneath. His usual light stubble around his jawline was thick and disheveled, but it worked for him.

Thanks to a brief gap in cloud cover, the sharp cold from the morning had begun to give way to warmth. The sun climbed higher into the sky, the dew still lingering on the ground from the humidity of dawn.

They entered the medical examiner's office through the glass doors, bell chiming above them as they were engulfed by the offensive smell of medicinal chemicals. It was a smell that Maeve had become accustomed to from her years working in a hospital, but her partner did not have the same luxury. Maeve snorted as Ben's expression gave him away. He was scowling at her as Dr. Mason Gertree breezed through the swinging door in front of them in full surgical attire.

"Detectives! Good to see you. Give me half a minute and I'll be right with you."

They moved toward the front office and Dr Mason Gertree – Chief Medical Examiner – Forensic Pathology was noted on a small name plate on the door. They let themselves in and sat in the perfectly placed lounge chairs as Mason swiftly entered the room. His disposable surgical equipment had been removed, and he was dressed in a wrinkled brown suit. Mason looked to weigh about as much as a large racoon, his pronounced height making him appear off balance.

"So sorry to keep you guys waiting," he apologized, sitting down and extending his hand first to Maeve and then Ben.

"Dr. G, nice to see you. Wish it were under better circumstances. How's the missus?" Ben asked, dropping his arms casually over the arms of his chair.

"Good, good, Deb is doing well. Having trouble with the empty nest since Bohman left for university this past fall, but we're hanging in there."

He paused, removing his glasses and leaning back in his chair. "Mind if I get right into it?"

"Please do."

"Listen...the deceased matches the profile of one Amanda Brinks. Dental records confirm it."

Maeve opened her notebook.

"She's a previous inmate at Umbele Penitentiary, but I think you're going to want to look into the reports filed with this one. Cause of death, time of death, and context surrounding it. In short, she'd already been listed as deceased."

The detective exchanged glances.

"I know this, because I was the one to examine her fourteen months ago. Notable petechiae was present all over her body, subconjunctival hemorrhages in both eyes, cyanosis in her lips and nails, and significant deep tissue injury to the anterior trachea and cervical vertebrae, including a hyoid fracture."

Ben exhaled. "Dr. G, we've been over this. English, please man." Mason exhaled. "The cause of death for Amanda Brinks was a broken neck and asphyxiation. She was found hanging in her cell by her own bed sheets. I ruled it a suicide at the time."

Moments passed in tense silence. Maeve could hear the ticking of the clock filling the room, monotonous and deafening.

"The family had a closed casket funeral and buried her at Umbele. I'm not completely done with the examination this time round, and I haven't yet written a final report, but I just wanted to be able to give you the facts so you could get started on this. I have a feeling things are about to get complicated."

Ben returned a grateful nod. Maeve's throat was dry as she attempted to clear it.

"Dr. Gertree, can you provide some preliminary photos taken at the autopsy? Ben and I are going to need copies."

"Mason. Please, call me Mason. I prepared a file for you both, of course. Just a prelim," he replied, giving her a gentle smile that emphasized his crow's feet. "Listen guys, I'm sorry to just drop this on you and run, but I've got a lot of work to do. Can you see yourselves out?"

Maeve's mind finally cleared as they moved outside. Ben put on his aviators, leaning back against his car.

"So, um, elephant in the room here, but is there a slight chance we just accidentally exhumed a woman who was peacefully buried in her final resting place?" he said.

She shook her head and let out a short laugh, her hair falling in her face. "I wish it were that simple. How the hell did she wind up relocated from her coffin without anyone noticing?"

"I think the more important question is why. I mean, it should be pretty easy to walk this back and find her headstone, dig up what's under it and see what's inside." He opened his palms. "If it's gone then we figure that out, but if it's there...I'd be very interested to see what's inside."

Maeve called the chief and updated him on the situation as Ben tried to balance eating and driving at the same time, occasionally yelling his own thoughts at the phone like they were on speaker. In an effort to protect her hearing, she finally switched it so they could both hear Briggs.

Maeve felt the chief's anxiety from the other end of the line as he told them to call the warden.

"We didn't think that was a good call, sir. We have no idea what happened to Amanda, and the last thing we want to do is tip him off before we get there. We need the element of surprise on this one," Maeve replied, looking at her partner for support. Mayo dripped down the side of Ben's mouth as he forced out unintelligible words of support. She scrunched her nose at him.

Briggs chuffed a laugh. "Ben, I didn't understand a damn word you just spat at me. Either way, I trust you both. Just keep me in the loop. I need to fill you in on what happened after she died. Her parents had their panties in a bunch about it. They're going to rip us a new asshole on this, and frankly, I don't blame them," Briggs said, breathing into the phone. "We need to have the team excavate under her marked gravestone. If she isn't there, we need to know why. There's no way someone can dig six feet under with a shovel and some perseverance. Not a chance. Not without anyone noticing. I'll get the search warrant..." he paused, "oh and darlin', tell Ben to stop eating while driving, he's a fucking cop for god's sake."

They pulled into the prison grounds just before mid-day, dust kicking up behind them as Ben drove quickly up the gravel path. The first signs of summer in Oregon were starting to show as the sun decided to linger for most of the morning. Maeve closed her eyes and let it warm her as she thought of her hometown. Honolulu had a reputation to be equally wet in the winters, but the summers made up for it. She thought of her father back home with a pinch of homesickness, and she made a mental note to call him when she got home that evening.

They exited the car and made their way in, Ben frantically wiping at his jaw as he tried to dislodge the stubborn crumbs in his facial hair.

The detectives exchanged glances as the sounds of diverse voices echoed throughout the halls as they made their way through the locked gates. Even though it was just the administration building, the compound was still connected on both sides to the east and west wings where the inmates were housed. Their voices carried, bouncing off the concrete.

They were brought to a small waiting room with several metal chairs along the outer walls and a petite brunette sitting at a small oak desk directly in front. The young girl looked up, surprise flashing across her face before she recovered and forced out a smile.

"Hi there!" she exclaimed, eyes darting from her computer screen to the closed door on the opposite side of the room. "I didn't realize anyone would be coming in today. What can I help you with?"

The girl looked much too young to be working in a prison, her innocence salient. Ben spoke up, lifting his badge from under his jacket and flashing it to her.

"Detective Ben Striton with my partner, Detective Maeve Kalani. We're here to speak with the warden."

Maeve took a slow wander around the room, perusing the brochures.

"Oh! Okay, well I didn't realize he had an appointment today. He has a very busy schedule and I'm not sure when we could squeeze you in," she replied, typing frantically on the keyboard.

Ben's frustration was all over his face as he leaned on her desk, hands gripping the edge. His badge swung forward.

"With all due respect..." glancing down at her name plate, "Spencer...we don't need an appointment. So, if you could just let Gary know we're here, that would be great."

Spencer looked at him and squirmed. She picked up the phone and pressed a key. "Sorry to bother you sir, but there are two detectives here to speak with you..." a short pause, "yes...in the waiting room...yes right now. I tried sir...yes...okay."

As abruptly as Spencer hung up, the door next to Maeve swung open, startling her. Warden Gary Managan filled the doorway, his presence all consuming. His green snakeskin shoes were a stark contrast to the musty carpet below, and the scent of luxury cologne overwhelmed Maeve as she gave him an awkward smile. The fluorescent lighting above them reflected off the warden's bald head as he stood to the side, opening his door further in invitation, eyes flashing to Ben. He was quiet as he adjusted his tie, his tight poker face showing nothing about how he was feeling about their surprise visit.

Silently, the three of them moved into his office. Ben reached out and gently placed his hand on the back of her arm, lifting an eyebrow in question. The touch felt welcome, supportive. She gave him a reassuring smile and he reluctantly moved away.

The warden's office was decorated in crimsons and purples, an ode of decadence and royalty. She noticed a large window on the wall behind his desk framed by heavy maroon curtains with a view of the cemetery to the south. His grandiose mahogany desk took up most of the space, and perpendicular to it were several floor to ceiling oak bookshelves lining the entire wall. The room was otherworldly and inappropriate in comparison to the building that housed it.

The detectives dropped into the armchairs across from his desk.

"Gary, we're sorry to just stop by like this, but we needed to speak to you about the body found on your property," Ben started, briefly glancing over at Maeve.

Gary intertwined his fingers on his desk. His eyes moved slowly between the pair.

"I'd assumed as much, detectives. What exactly can I help you with?" he said, his deep voice too loud.

"Well, the body discovered was that of Amanda Brinks. She was an inmate here for some time. We need some information about why she was here and what happened to her," Maeve said as she leaned forward in the brown leather armchair, fidgeting with her pen and notepad.

Gary was quiet for a moment as he registered what they were saying. He frowned and then quickly rose and walked over to the bar cart, pouring himself a glass of amber colored liquid from a crystal decanter. He extended the offer to Ben with a gesture who responded with a subtle head shake.

"Maeve, did you want a glass of scotch in the middle of the day with the warden?" Ben asked, his eyes dancing with mischief. Her mouth lifted as she swallowed down her laugh.

After an audible swig, the warden looked at Maeve and tilted his head. He moved his glass in a slow circle as it hung from his fingertips. "She died last year from what I recall."

He turned, pulling out a file before sauntering back to the desk.

Maeve instinctively leaned in, trying to read the fine print on the report.

"That's right. Suicide. She hung herself in her cell using her bed sheets," he said, lifting his gaze and sliding the folder across the desk. Ben grabbed it, handing the photos inside to Maeve as he looked through some of the papers. She analyzed a close-up glossy photo of Amanda Brinks postmortem. The anterior portion of her neck was covered in blue and purple markings, green eyes left open with deep red filling her corneas. Although her current state came with a lot less flesh, the resemblance to the corpse in the woods was unquestionable.

She knew how to look for the difference between markings made from hands and markings made from objects, but despite Maeve's intense scrutiny, it wasn't clear. If there hadn't been proof of the hanging, it could have been inconclusive. Maeve froze as the next photo stole her breath. She held a photo of Amanda in what must have been the first few minutes after she was found. Her limp body being held by her neck, arched at an unnatural angle. The room was dark, and her stringy blonde hair fell over her ashy, unseeing eyes.

"Can I ask why you have this?" she asked, frowning.

"Certainly, detective. I took the photo. I knew it would be important to capture the moment when she was found, but we also wanted to move quickly to get her down in case she was still alive. We didn't want to waste any time if we still had a chance of saving her. I gave them to Joe. Your department has copies of these," he replied evenly.

She nodded, making notes. "I assume you keep this office and this cabinet locked when you aren't here?"

"Your assumption is correct."

"Mr. Managan, can you recall what kind of inmate Amanda was? Was she quiet? Strong willed? Violent?"

She felt Ben shift beside her. The warden's brows came together in the middle, furrowing his entire face into apprehension.

"Well, from what I remember, Mandy was definitely on the quiet side. I didn't see or hear a lot about her during her time here, which is usually a good thing," he said, leaning back in his leather chair, forcing the metal springs to let out a prolonged high-pitched squeak.

"What was she incarcerated for?" Ben asked.

The warden rummaged through the file folder on his desk, pulling a single sheet out. "She was doing time for manslaughter. She was driving under the influence a few years ago and she ended up killing a seven-year-old boy on his bike."

Ben gestured to the file and the warden slid it over to him.

"It looks like she was serving five years. She'd been at Umbele for three and was up for parole," he paused, squinting at the print in front of him, "in the summer of last year," Ben said, looking at Maeve. She obligingly made a note.

Gary removed his red reading glasses and threw them on the desk, as he settled back into his chair. "It was such a shame that she was so close to the end of her sentence. I guess when you're mentally ill, the lows can strike at any time. Let me tell you...for some, the idea of walking free after something like that can cause a lot of anxiety. They just bottle it all up and hope for the best once they're released instead of working through the healing journey. Many of them don't ask for penance or absolution and their sins fester and multiply. After that, it's in God's hands," he said, letting his gaze fall somewhere behind them.

People typically didn't kill themselves a few months before they were to be released, but the idea that Amanda couldn't live with herself after what she'd done had some credibility to it.

"Are you religious, sir?" Maeve asked.

He looked at her intently. "I am a man of God, yes detective. I try to heed His teachings as best I can. And for some women here, it has worked. Their souls have been made lighter by their confession and quest for clemency. I'm not a priest, but I do what I can. I've asked Father Derick from Good Shepherd to stop by on Sundays for Mass, and we've had quite the turnout in recent months."

She nodded, eyes dropping to the oversized brass cross on the wall behind him.

Silence fell as they worked through the contents of the file, the warden excusing himself. He returned some minutes later with a coffee pot in hand, giving them each a styrofoam cup and pouring them some of the black sludge. "Figured you guys have probably been up since the crack of dawn...thought you could use some of this."

Maeve was warmed by the sentiment and Ben smiled politely before downing his in one gulp and proceeding to grab the pot to fill it a second time. The man liked his coffee even more than she did, and that was saying something. The warden moved back behind his desk and as he reached to open his laptop.

"Sir, just a few more questions for you if you don't mind?"

Gary nodded his head and gestured for her to go on.

"I was wondering about the cemetery..."

"Yes?"

"Well, I'm wondering why it's there. It's a little odd, people typically don't bury their family members inside the perimeter of a prison. Why is Umbele different?"

He smiled through closed lips. "It's a good question, detective. Unfortunately, the answer is substantially less intriguing. The cemetery was here first. A church used to sit on the property, it was torn down about fifty years ago. The prison was built to accommodate the rapidly increasing female inmate population on the west coast, but they couldn't exactly exhume all the bodies that were in that cemetery, so they left it. At first we didn't add to it, but then as the population increased, we had to use the space."

"People had trouble finding places to bury their loved ones, and in the end, the convenience of it tipped the scales. Some families started agreeing to bury the women who passed away here in the cemetery. Some of these women don't have families close or aren't in touch anymore, so it makes it an easy decision after they pass."

He'd shifted to the window behind the desk, gazing out as he let silence fill the room for a moment.

"Unfortunately, a lot of the time, it comes down to money. Transporting a body isn't cheap and the state isn't going to extend a helping hand for a dead convict. To be clear, it's not like we bury an astronomical amount back there, only a few a year at most. The area was large enough for the first few years since I became warden, but recently we've started to run out of room. That's why Tom and Henry have been clearing out some of the forest."

Maeve nodded and followed his gaze to the view outside his window.

"In the past six months, have you noticed anything out of the ordinary back there? Any indication as to how she came to be found outside of her coffin and left in the dirt?" Ben asked, knee bouncing.

The warden frowned. "No, not that I can recall. My groundskeepers are always doing work out there, but I would have noticed if someone was digging six feet under. Tom and Henry can't even handle the burials on their own, we have an excavator and we use it to make a hole ahead of time. I definitely would have noticed someone using it when they shouldn't have been."

"Is it locked up when not in use?"

He tipped his head. "Yes, always. Tom, Henry and I are the only ones with a key."

A flash of light from outside caught Maeve's eye as she stood, moving to the window, her partner closing in behind.

"They're here. Perfect," Ben whispered, his breath grazing across her neck in his proximity.

"Thank you for your time, sir. We appreciate you talking to us. The team just arrived and is setting up outside. We've got a warrant to dig under her gravestone to see what's going on down there."

Gary lifted his eyebrows. "That was quick. Joe must have put a rush on it," he said, pausing, "Let me know if you need my assistance at all. I'm here all day," he finished, stepping closer as he peered out the window, boxing them in.

"One last thing..." Ben chimed in, looking up at the warden as he stepped around, creating some distance. "Her cellmate, can we pay her a visit? Would be good to hear a first-hand account of the incident."

The warden nodded, his gaze landing on Maeve as he told them the inmate's name and cell number.

They'd decided to split up, Ben to speak to Kristina Remino in the east wing and Maeve to the west wing to ask some questions to the other prisoners.

"How'd it go? Looks like you were fitting right in there, jailbird," Ben teased, giving her a wink.

She rolled her eyes and gave him a playful shove. "Listen, we can't leave yet. I want to take a look in solitary."

He frowned at her but nodded in support.

They were taken through a series of locked doors requiring varying amounts of keys and buzzers before they ended up in the basement below the administration building. The tall female correctional officer that had been escorting them silently gestured for them to take a look around.

Umbele, the small minimum-security penitentiary that it was, only had two solitary confinement rooms. The rooms were on opposite sides to each other and were located behind thick reinforced iron doors. There was a tiny slide-across window to peek into and a lower slot big enough to fit food trays through.

The low hanging fluorescent light had an irregular flicker, and there was water dripping from some unknown location that caused a musty damp smell. The basement was at least five degrees cooler than the upper floor, and Maeve crossed her arms over herself. Ben noticed, shifting closer to her as he spoke.

"Good god could this be any more stereotypical...this is fucking creepy. Hello Clarice" he said, grinning at her.

She indulged him and let out a slight smile as she turned to ask the guard if they could look inside one of the cells. The guard silently obliged, using most of her body weight to swing the door open, the metal letting out an extended creak.

Inside was a concrete bed, void of a mattress or linens, and a small metal sink and toilet duo in the back corner. Maeve quietly walked around the room, a chill settling in behind her rib cage. She noticed something shiny on the floor in one of the corners. Frowning, she crouched down. A small circular hook was coming out of the concrete. She spun on the ball of her foot and noticed that there was one in each corner. Strange.

Ben was tracing his fingers along the floor as he halted abruptly, gesturing her over with a flick of his head.

"See this?" he whispered, turning to look over his shoulder as Maeve squinted to where he was touching the ground.

A tiny smudge of crimson red.

Maeve's heart pounded in her ears as she turned to find the guard. The cell was empty.

When had she left?

They exchanged weighted glances. Ben fished his phone out of his pocket to take a quick photo.

"Is that blood?" Maeve whispered.

CHAPTER NINE

The afternoon sun warmed the air as Ben and Maeve took off their jackets, lingering in the parking lot. Maeve closed her eyes and looked up toward the sun as she tried to rid herself of the deep chill that had settled within her, courtesy of the visit to solitary at Umbele.

After dropping off their jackets, they wandered out to the cemetery.

"So that was weird" Maeve started, fixing her hair.

"Yeah, it was, but also not a major red flag."

Maeve looked at him.

"I mean, I assume some inmates who go into solitary could be bleeding at the time…a fight, a stiff hit from one of the guards, self-harm…but still, it's concerning. It might be something to look into, especially if there is mistreatment happening. I mean, I wouldn't be surprised, sadly, but I have no idea how we would even have a leg to stand on. It could be a very simple explanation, and we have no way to confirm or deny it. We'd have to take the warden's word as gospel," a grin, "pun very much intended."

Maeve rolled her eyes and started to fill him in on her visit to the west wing. She told him that an elderly woman, who they all called Nanna T, had seen an inmate named Dakota attack Amanda Brinks. Or Mandy, as they called her.

"Nanna T had been on work duty in the library at the time and had witnessed a fight from behind one of the shelves. She told me she'd been sorting books when she noticed Dakota approach Amanda and start taunting her about Robbie, the little boy on the bike who Amanda killed. The accident that landed her in prison. Apparently, Dakota had gone on

and on about how he wouldn't get to grow old or see his family again all because Amanda had decided to drive home drunk that night. She said Amanda had done her best to ignore Dakota, and had mostly succeeded, right up until said something about her dad."

Maeve paused, turning to him.

"Everything came to a head when Dakota pushed her a bit too far when she mentioned that Amanda took after her father, getting boozed up and taking it out on a kid. Nanna T said it was like something snapped and Amanda jumped up and started beating the shit out of Dakota."

They slowed their pace as they reached the crime scene.

"She grabbed a large book that was on one of the desks and hit Dakota on the side of her face. Dakota collapsed to the ground instantly. Amanda was in a frenzied state and kept kicking her while she was down. She told me it was a very different version of the Amanda they had all gotten to know, and it had been strangely uncharacteristic behavior. Apparently, the CO posted in the library had attempted to pull her off on her own, but Amanda was in a rage, and she'd been forced to radio for backup. By the time Amanda was dragged off of her, Dakota had sustained…" she paused, flipping her notepad as she turned to him, "a severe concussion, fractured cheekbone, ruptured eardrum, three cracked ribs, a lacerated spleen, and countless contusions deep tissue injuries. I spoke to the nurse onsite. Dakota had been rushed into emergency surgery at the hospital in Medford. She'd been there for weeks for post-op observation and Amanda Brinks had been thrown into solitary for three months."

Ben turned his hat backwards, looking at her.

"That's a long fucking time to be in solitary. Especially for a fight. As brutal as it was."

Maeve nodded, kicking up some gravel. "Yeah, that's what I said, but Nanna T told me it wasn't all that uncommon here. She said the warden got off on the power and control and often pushed his catholic teachings on all the women there in the interest of cleansing their souls. She said there's almost always someone in solitary on a rotational basis, and it's directly correlated to how the warden was feeling week to week. That being said...there's no one down there right now. There could be something to gain from bending the truth to make it seem worse here than it actually is. There's no love lost between the inmates and the staff."

They turned and finished the walk to Amanda's headstone. Henry was in the backhoe, excavating the area, a large mound of dirt piling up beside them. Ben raised his voice slightly, crossing his arms.

"Yeah, that's not unusual, anything for a little reprieve. Especially when it's directed at the man running the show. What concerns me is that the warden failed to mention any of it. Get this, when I spoke to Kristina, she said a lawyer with red hair had been coming by to ask her questions about Amanda's death. She also validated what you just told me about Amanda being in solitary in the months before she killed herself. So that's either corroborated or they're all in on the same lie," he exhaled. "What about Dakota? Did you talk to her?"

Maeve shook her head. "Dakota sat in her cell quietly drumming her tattooed fingers as she'd watched her fellow inmates rat her out. It was weird. When I tried to talk to her, she gave me the finger and turned around."

Realization clicked in. Maeve did a frantic hand motion. "Whoa, back up. You're saying Amanda Brinks just gave us our first new lead in the Lara McAllister case? They're linked?"

Ben nodded, hope shining in his eyes. "Briggs is going to have to agree to formally re-open it now."

"What do you mean agree to re-open it? Isn't that what we're already doing?"

He looked back at the dig happening in front of them.

"Nah, it's still technically a cold case, but I never really stopped investigating it. It's been like a shadow, hovering behind me for the past year. Every time I run into Liam or Lydia...it's just there. I told Briggs that I let it go just to get him off my back. He didn't want to waste any more time or resources on it...but I couldn't stop. Then he told me you were coming, and I asked if I could bring you in, help ease you into things and get an objective opinion on it. I was just planning to brief you on it and then I'd let you decide where to take it, but here we are. I couldn't help myself."

She looked down as the machine reached the hard exterior of the coffin. Ben followed her gaze.

"Amanda's case, at the time, would have been a very straightforward suicide. Especially with the added piece that she was in solitary for months right before it happened. The cause of death was consistent with suicide by hanging, and thanks our warden, there's photo evidence in the moments after she was found. It would have been odd for Lara to be investigating it. Seems pretty open and shut to me."

She watched as the coffin was hoisted out of the ground and lifted onto the metal support stand. Members of the forensic team moved about in front of them, setting up equipment and donning protective gear. The wind kicked up, tossing her hair in front of her face.

"I'm concerned about this connection. I'd really like to know why the warden didn't mention that she'd been there that week, or that Amanda had been in solitary."

Ben's eyes tracked the team in front of him. He clenched his jaw.

"Unless he didn't know. Unless she was just visiting the inmates before making her way up to the top. I doubt he knows every single lawyer that makes a visit to his various inmates. It's not like he would check the visitor log randomly, and he can't exactly be there 24/7," he turned to look at her. "Either way, we're going to have to meet with him again. Morbid as it sounds, I'm glad the groundskeepers accidentally dug up Amanda Brinks's body. It takes us one step closer to finding Lara," he paused, looking toward the coffin. "This connection and these new circumstances...what the hell happened here? What happened to both of these women?"

"Answer that detective, and we're rendered unnecessary," she replied, tossing him a wink.

"Did you just make a stupid joke and wink at me?" Ben asked, taking off his aviators as he looked at her, amusement plastered across his face.

She rolled her eyes. "I guess I did. I must be spending too much time with you. I'm starting to pick up your annoying mannerisms."

Ben smiled at her, large and uninhibited. The effect warmed her core and swept away the last bit of uneasiness left inside her. A throat clearing from behind them had Maeve flinching. She recovered just as Briggs sauntered up between them.

"I called Mandy's parents to let them know what was going on. They were absolutely irate, understandably, but once I explained the situation, they were agreeable. Seems they're just as motivated to try and figure out what's going on," he paused, taking a breath. "They were volatile and reactive when she died, and they blamed me...blamed the force. They refused to believe she killed herself, and they called me constantly to try and get the department to investigate it. I tried to tell them there was nothing to investigate, but they wouldn't let it go. Eventually they stopped calling, I figured they finally got some closure. Anyway, they're on their way from Portland."

He took a step toward the coffin, nodding to the team to start prying it open. "Did you get some answers in there?"

The detectives took turns filling him in on what they'd learned, and Maeve described their trip down to solitary. She was careful to leave out the bit of blood on the floor. It was inconclusive and therefore irrelevant to the current status of the case.

Briggs was attentive. "You went down there on your own? Did Gary know?"

Ben stepped in to cover for her. "No, we went on impulse after we finished our interviews with some of the inmates. It was my idea."

Briggs nodded, the lines between his eyebrows more pronounced.

"We have to be careful here. We need Gary on our side. Did you find anything down there?"

"No sir. Nothing of note."

Briggs took a breath and scanned the area. It was sectioned off well. Police tape closed in the entire cemetery and neighboring woods where Amanda had been found. A tent had been placed over Amanda's gravestone, and there were various members of the unit taking photos and collecting samples. The sharp wind had increased in intensity, howling through the trees. Ben somehow sensed Maeve's anxiety and gave her shoulder a gentle squeeze. With the coffin open, the team acknowledged the detectives with respectful nods before they backed away from the scene to give them space. Maeve approached the open casket with slow deliberate movements, careful not to disturb the environment around her. A lull settled over them, and she sensed her surroundings at a supersonic level. The leaves blowing in the wind, the raspy sound of her boss's inhales, a bird singing its morning song yards away. The coffin wasn't empty.

The corpse's red hair had darkened with decay and her face had sunken in, emphasizing protruding cheekbones and a sharp jaw. Her skin was so pale it was nearing gray. Purple and blue veins were visible just below the surface. She had changed, but not so much as one would expect in a year's time. The embalming was exceptionally done, the woman instantly recognizable.

The wind picked up limp strands of the woman's hair and tossed them over her unseeing ice blue eyes.

CHAPTER TEN

Lara McAllister. Maeve was surprised it wasn't shock that encompassed her, but anger. She knew most missing person cases had the same result, but it somehow felt personal. She'd spent the past weeks researching Lara's entire life. She knew her friends, her family, her past, her interests, her aspirations, her shoe size. To find her like this felt like cheating.

Ben turned around and dropped his head, hands going to his hips. Maeve knew exactly what he was thinking, what he was taking responsibility for. A year's worth of his investigative work had done nothing to save her.

Briggs was still, looking down at the body. The songbird's melody faded away, the wind halting its onslaught. They were left in disturbing silence, the air a preternatural quiet.

The crunch of footsteps on fallen leaves from behind had her spinning quickly as she came face to face with the warden.

"So, what have you found on my property?" he asked, looking at Maeve a moment longer before turning to the chief.

Briggs looked at Maeve in apology before leading the warden away from the scene and back toward the admin building. A soft murmur of conversation started between them as they walked away.

Maeve focused back on Lara and frowned. Lara was in a floral dress with pink, white, and green peonies pasted throughout. It bore short sleeves with a light lace outline and looked uncomfortably tight and much too short for the body it was covering. It was inconsistent with

the picture she had of Lara. All the photos she'd seen of Lara had been in athletic wear or business casual work attire. There were women who liked pink and there were women who didn't. Lara had most definitely been the latter.

A deep purple blanket, stiff and worn, had been laid over her legs. Maeve put on disposable nitrile gloves before carefully picking it up and pulling it back. Lara's long pale legs stretched out before her, riddled with blue and purple markings. Bruises. Deep tissue injuries that must have occurred close to the time of death, delaying the healing process. She glanced over Lara's ankles and nausea rolled through her. Thick, angry, abrasive red lines surrounded each of them.

Her death was one thing, but this...this was so much worse. She'd known it was a possibility, but it was still distressing to see it first-hand.

Lara had been restrained and abused.

Shock poured through her, her legs feeling as though metal had replaced bone. She immediately thought of Liam. How was she going to tell her overprotective brother?

Ben moved to Maeve's side, hands in his pockets. His perfect resolve back in place.

"Un-fucking-believable. I've been looking for her for over a year and she was right under my nose this whole time."

Maeve said nothing as she lifted the blanket for him, showing him what she'd just uncovered. He stilled, his respirations increasing as his gaze traveled over Lara's body. He clenched his jaw and looked up at the sky, letting out a forceful curse. His frustration was primal, alive.

She took a breath and got to work, cataloging the findings while the forensic team took photos and collected samples. After some time, Briggs returned and took control of the scene.

The detectives made their way back to Ben's car and sat in silence, neither of them ready to confront the path forward. Lara's image was on loop in her mind. She'd seen hundreds of dead bodies when she'd been a nurse, but most had died from natural causes. Patients that were at the end of their life and ready to drift into oblivion. This was different. This was a life taken far before her time. A crime against nature. Every woman's worst nightmare.

A shift of warmth settled into her and landed deep in her stomach. The clarity eased its way into her mind like a warm cup of tea; she was going to find the person who did this to Lara. Some sick fuck had been keeping her somewhere, chained up, used, abused, and possibly tortured, before preserving her for their own satisfaction.

Ben, as usual, read her mind.

"Did you see that coffin? I've never seen anything like that in my life," he said, rolling down his window and lighting a cigarette, much to Maeve's surprise.

"Yeah, the gold trim surrounding the dark red and brown swirls. It was beautiful," she said, rolling her window down even further as she held in a cough. He took a long drag, his gaze finally landing back on her.

"I bet that thing is worth at least ten grand. The gold, the mahogany...."
"You know about coffins, do you?" she teased, raising her eyebrows.

He looked away, his gaze lingering out the window. She sensed a shift in the air, the question hanging between them for too long.

"Yeah...my Ma...she died a couple months after I got back from the Middle East. She didn't have two pennies to rub together and neither did I. I had to do some searching to find something worthy of her and something I could afford."

Maeve hadn't heard Ben's southern drawl come out before, but she didn't hate it. He'd told her when they first met he was from Kansas City, but it was easy to forget. She shifted toward him, guilt washing over her.

"I'm sorry Ben. I didn't mean..."

He tossed the cigarette butt out, rolling the window back up and turning on the heat.

"It's alright, Maeve. You didn't know," he paused, looking at her. "You're allowed to tease me," his honey-colored eyes locking on hers.

"In fact, I kind of like it when you do," he said, shifting into gear. "Buckle up."

On the drive back to Grants Pass, Maeve looked at the dense rolling hills surrounding the highway.

"Why go through all that effort just to relocate a body? To make her easier to find? The fact that someone went through the trouble of preserving evidence of their crime first with the embalming and then the coffin, it's contradictory. It's stupid. It goes against everything we know."

"Unless that is the point. Someone wanted us to find her. A breadcrumb," Ben replied, holding her gaze. "The killer is so meticulous that it's all purposeful. Skilled. Elevated. One step ahead. This isn't just some messy accidental murder. This is something entirely different. This is practiced."

They exchanged glances. They both knew what he was alluding to. The implications.

Finally back home, Maeve walked in a daze to her bedroom. Her mind was racing as she undressed, turning on the shower in her ensuite and cranking the handle to the highest temperature setting. Mid-way through her deep conditioning treatment, a gentle thud sounded from the level below. Her eyes flew open and she turned off the water. Paralyzed, she listened intently as the conditioner dripped slowly into her eye. When she heard no follow up noise, she quietly stepped out. She wrapped her wet hair in a towel and put on her robe as she tip-toed out of the bathroom. She moved for the gun she'd left on her bedside table and tucked it inside her pocket. She knew she was acting paranoid but being a young single woman living alone in the midst of investigating a murder, one could never be too careful.

Her pulse racing, she cleared every room on the second floor and silently descended the stairs, stepping on the only loose floorboard. A loud creak emerged and she paused, cringing. When no return movements sounded, she continued on.

Only after she had finished checking the entire first floor did she relax. Thinking a large rodent had potentially knocked something about in her backyard, she pulled back the curtains covering the glass patio doors.

Her gaze dropped to an envelope neatly placed on the back deck just on the other side of the doors. Goosebumps peppered her arms and the familiar tingle in the back of her neck re-appeared.

A flicker of movement caught in her peripherals. A quick glimpse of something in the dense bush behind her fence.

Maeve tensed, hand moving to her pistol as she felt the adrenaline begin to surge through her once again. She carefully slid open the door and jogged to the back fence, scanning the woods. She didn't intend on going any farther, but she needed to see if someone was still on her property.

There was nothing there in either direction. She paced back and forth, trying to get a view of anything out of the ordinary. The wind whistled through the trees as dusk approached, the leaves dancing in disorder. A loud call sounded through the trees and she jolted, her eyes falling on a brown-striped owl staring down at her.

Delayed realization swept in as she looked down at herself. She was standing outside in her robe with a hidden firearm in the fleece pocket. The product left in her wet hair starting to form into clumps.

Toes numb, she jogged back to the house and picked up the note. She stepped inside and locked the door behind her, scanning the backyard again. Her soiled feet left a trail as she paced around her living room. She looked down at her name written in delicate cursive on the front of the envelope. A regular civilian wouldn't hesitate to open it. A note was harmless. A friendly neighbor welcoming you to the neighborhood. As a cop, things were different. It was expected that she should use logic to sift through the potential outcomes and weigh the risks. Maybe she should call Briggs. Text Ben. Something. Anything.

She took a breath and ripped open the envelope.

STOP DIGGING, OR YOU'LL BE NEXT.

CHAPTER ELEVEN

Dialing Ben she dropped onto the couch. He answered on the first ring. "Maeve? What's wrong?"

Her hands shook but she managed to keep her voice level as she told him what happened.

"What the fuck? I'm on my way. Stay on the phone with me until I get there, I won't be long."

"Where are you coming from? I'm fine, Ben. Whoever dropped it off is long gone, I just wanted to tell you."

"No, I'm coming, not an option. Oh uh…across town, I'm not at home, but I'll be there in twenty minutes, max."

True to his word he barged in exactly twenty minutes later.

"I'm sorry, did I just waltz into your unlocked home moments after you were threatened by someone who was trespassing on your property?"

He was disheveled, his jacket hanging like it had been thrown on carelessly and his face flushed. She rolled her eyes, inviting him in and walking to the kitchen.

"I unlocked it right before you came, Ben. The profoundly unnecessary force you use to knock on my door would have scared me more to be honest."

Peeling off his jacket he followed after her. "Are you okay?"

She turned, offering a nod. "Fine yeah, just a little shaken up. Nothing like a death threat on your first case," she said, forcing out a laugh. Maeve sensed his anger as he reached out to take the note from her, his eyes traveling over it.

"It's handwritten. That's something to go on at least. Talk me through it again."

And she did. Several times. When she'd finished, he'd walked around her property. Then, even though it was nearing midnight, Ben called the chief and put it on speakerphone.

"Jesus fucking christ. Just what we need, two dead bodies and now a death threat on one of my detectives. Maeve, darlin', you need to be careful. Keep your wits about you. Ben's right, this is a big deal," he said, catching his breath.

"I'm going to station a patrol vehicle outside your house for the next while. At least until we solve this or there are no further threats. I have a feeling this case is going to get even bigger and messier than it already is, and I need you both safe. Don't do anything stupid. And that goes for both of you. If you find a lead, if you do any exploring...call me first. I mean it."

Ben paced quietly with his hands on his waist before looking through the back door again. The chief wasn't finished.

"I want you to have backup when you need it, and someone should know where you both are at all times. You know as well as I do that there's a strong possibility that whoever moved Mandy may have also had a connection to Lara. I want you both to be careful not to dismiss any potential avenues. Even though it looks like Lara may have been taken and killed near the prison, we can't discount that that's exactly what the killer wants us to believe. There's still a chance she was taken away from the property, killed, and returned there in order to lead us astray. It's not out of the question, and it would be incredibly convenient to pin it on someone else."

Ben and Maeve made charged eye contact.

"Either way, keep me in the loop and look out for each other. Try not to contaminate the note any further and drop it in a plastic bag or something. I want that logged into evidence first thing. Oh, and Maeve?"

"Yes, sir?"

"I'm glad you're okay, but if you ever feel you aren't, please tell someone. I know that was probably a lot for you, even if you'd never admit it. We support you and we've got your back. We'll find the fucker."

She smiled and Ben ended the call.

• • •

They pulled up in front of Mason's office to find Liam's red SUV parked out front. He was sitting with his back against his car, knees up and his hands knotted behind his dropped head. The sun-kissed day had taken a turn on the drive over, and a drizzle of light rain was coming down. A hyperbole for the moment.

Maeve stood awkwardly under the awning covering the front door, giving Liam another minute alone before nodding to Ben and lifting her hood. Her shoes made a scraping noise along the damp pavement as she made her way over, her partner trailing behind. Liam was dressed in black joggers and a sand-colored hoodie. His red hair was damp and smelling of mint and pine, the scent strong enough to drift in the distance between them. He looked up as they approached.

His eyes met hers, swollen and pink. He answered her unspoken question.

"Yes, I'm fine. I just needed a moment," he offered, looking to the side to avoid her gaze. The light sound of rain bouncing off the cars magnified as he hesitated.

"It's hard knowing I held on for so long hoping she was still alive somewhere. And now finding out she was thirty fucking minutes away." He shifted, his hands balling into fists.

"I should've been there to help her. I'm her big brother, that's my job," he said, voice cracking.

"I'm sorry this happened to her, Liam. To you."

Maeve had always been terrible at receiving support and was equally terrible at comforting others. It had previously been flagged as an area for improvement all throughout her training. She was closed off and guarded. It was a coping mechanism, an essential adaptation from working in healthcare. If you took that work home with you, you'd never get out of bed. The residual effect left her desensitized, her compassion almost always forced and sometimes even fake.

The three of them made their way inside. Mason greeted them in the reception area and brought them straight through the back and into the exam room.

Liam looked down at the outline of his sister's body under the white sheet. He had a slight tremor in his hands. Mason spoke up in his small raspy voice.

"Liam, I am so sorry for your loss."

Liam didn't make any motion to acknowledge the sentiment and Mason looked like he hadn't expected one. He lifted the sheet off her face and rolled it down to chest level.

The instant tension in the room was suffocating. Maeve felt like the walls were closing in on them. Ben put a hand on her shoulder.

The detectives hovered near the back of the room. They watched as Liam tilted his head back towards the ceiling before taking a deep breath and dropping it down again. He stood unmoving, looking at the body for what seemed like an eternity. Finally, he placed a hand on her forehead and pushed her hair back gently. Affectionately. Lara was still dressed in the tight summer dress she'd been found in, her angular face unnaturally alive. The embalming process required training and materials. Typically, the only people who had the right materials were funeral directors. There was a slight chance that whoever had done it had been self-trained and purchased all the tools themselves, but it was still a lead worth pursuing.

Mason walked slowly up next to him, asking in a gentle tone if there was anything out of the ordinary or remarkable about her.

Liam took a moment to process before whispering.

"Everything about her was remarkable."

The detectives exchanged glances. Maeve noticed that Mason had deliberately kept the rest of her body covered with the sheet so as to hide the distinguishable markings on her ankles and wrists. They planned to tell Liam what they found, in time, but it was one thing to hear it, and something else entirely for him to witness it. Especially on his little sister.

Liam's voice drowned out her thoughts.

"This dress... it's... so...not like her, but somehow it seems familiar. It's so odd...she hated dresses. She hated girly things. She wore more workout clothes than I did. And it's way too small..."

Mason cocked his head, making brief notes on his clipboard. Then, before anyone had time to react, Liam moved in a calculated, confident manner as he reached for the sheet and pulled it back in one swift movement. The doctor nor the detectives had time to step in.

Liam had just uncovered his own worst nightmare. Everyone intrinsically stepped closer in case they needed to de-escalate the situation. Liam turned around to look at Maeve, his eyes darker than she'd ever seen them before, the deep blue gone and replaced by a sinister shade of gray.

"What the fuck happened to my sister?"

Maeve recoiled. Liam always seemed so muted and meticulous. It was a side of him she was not prepared for, as justified as it was.

Ben stepped forward.

"Whoa whoa whoa, let's just take a minute Liam. We can discuss this outside if you need to take a breather, but I won't allow you to speak to my partner like that."

To her own surprise, she stepped around Ben, placing a hand on his arm. "I'm so sorry Liam. We were going to set up a family conference. We really didn't want you to see it first-hand. It's something you shouldn't have to witness."

"So, she was kidnapped? Taken? Fucking abused? All this time? How long ago was she killed? She could have been saved! She was so close!"

"Honestly Liam, we aren't sure about everything that happened yet, but it's our top priority. We'll look at every angle, every lead," she paused, glancing at Ben. "As bad this sounds…we now have something we can work off of. A lead. I promise we'll do our very best to solve this and bring her justice," she said. Ben stepped forward.

"All that said…in the interest of full transparency, yes, it does look like she was kept and restrained by her wrists and ankles. Unfortunately, we don't know for how long. Dr. G is going to do his best to try to figure out how long ago she passed away so we can work off of that, but there was nothing you or anyone else could have done to save her. We had nothing until the ground at Umbele was dug up. It's highly unlikely that this could have been prevented, Liam."

"Highly unlikely isn't going to work for me, detective. There was still a chance. There was still a chance I could have saved her," Liam replied, voice breaking before turning away.

After a few tense moments, Liam moved to exit through the doors before hesitating and turning back around toward his sister's body. He tilted his head to the left in confusion, squinting slightly. He reached down to touch her right wrist, delicately trailing his index finger along the inside.

"Where's her watch?" he asked, first looking at Maeve, then at Mason. "Watch? What watch, Liam?" Ben asked, stepping closer.

Liam looked back down at Lara. "It was gold with little diamonds in the face. It was our mother's. She never took it off."

CHAPTER TWELVE

Maeve set her notes down before she grabbed the remote and turned on the news. She yawned, sipping from her third coffee of the morning in an attempt to compensate for her restless night. It'd helped knowing there was an officer stationed outside, but she still woke up hourly, reaching for her gun to ensure it was still close.

A BREAKING NEWS banner across the bottom of the screen caught her attention and she turned up the volume. The elderly reporter, infamous to Grants Pass as Goudreau the Grey, was front and center, his deep, earthy voice coming through.

"Good morning Grants Pass,

More to the ongoing story coming out from Umbele Penitentiary... sources report that several bodies have been discovered on the grounds of the prison. Although both bodies were found within the cemetery located on the property, the details surrounding the discoveries are indicative of foul play. One of the bodies is noted to be that of a young female with red hair, approximate age late 20s to early 30s. This is consistent with the local resident Lara McAllister who went missing in early May of last year. The search that occurred at the time lasted several months but yielded no evidence or leads surrounding her disappearance. At the time, no foul play was noted, but as the situation stands now, the case will be re-opened for further investigation. Sources say the body of the other young woman, still unconfirmed on the identity at this time,

was removed from the prison several days prior. Sources confirm the two victims may somehow be linked as circumstances surrounding their death are slowly being uncovered. Crime scene investigation units were seen mobilizing the area as of around 6pm on Saturday, April 22nd, and the area is still reportedly closed off for the ongoing investigation. The Grants Pass Police Department, the Medford Police Department, and the Umbele Penitentiary personnel have all declined to make a statement at this time. The question remains…what happened to Lara McAllister last year and how did she end up in a prison cemetery thirty miles away? Who is the other woman that was found, and could they be connected? Do people of Grants Pass need to be worried? Stay tuned for further updates as they come. You heard it here first on ODR11, right people, right time, right news."

She made it to the precinct by 10:30 and beelined it directly to the conference room. It was filled to maximum occupancy. Surely the entire department was crammed in along with a few additional faces Maeve didn't recognize. She scanned for her partner and found him positioned at the front behind a wooden podium, fidgeting with some papers. Sensing her gaze, he lifted his eyes, offering a gentle tired smile and waving her over. He tapped roughly on the microphone, startling everyone in the room as the chatter dropped off immediately. Maeve moved closer.

"Thank you all for being here today. Due to the nature of what was recently uncovered, we need all the help we can get. I'm sure you're all anxious to hear what's going on with our Jane Doe." He paused, clearing his throat. "We've received confirmation from Dr. Gertree that the victim is in fact Lara McAllister."

She looked around the room and noted an obvious differentiation between those who had known Lara and those who had just come to help out. A mix of surprise, despair and excitement rumbled through the space.

Law enforcement may be the only demographic to show excitement at the discovery of a dead body.

Briggs, moving forward from beside Ben, quieted the crowd, clearing his throat and causing a slight cough to emerge as he adjusted his tie.

"Now although we have confirmation of her identity, the report and cause of death are not confirmed as of yet, so we're taking this one step at a time. What we do know is that her time of death was reported to be approximately two months ago. Lara was likely kidnapped and held captive before her death. I just received confirmation from Warden Gary Managan at Umbele Penitentiary that Lara had attended an appointment with him on May 1st at just after five in the evening. He said she came in to ask questions about Amanda Brinks' case and then left about an hour later to speak to some of the inmates. The visitor log shows she signed out just after seven that same evening and video footage confirms it. The brother, Liam McAllister, already came in to confirm her identity. The victim's half-sister Lydia and her ex-boyfriend Marc Hallman have also been made aware of the situation. Detectives Striton and Kalani will be taking the lead on this due to the historical nature of this case, and you'll all report to them. It is expected that you support them with whatever they need to solve this."

Ben and Briggs broke up the workload on the whiteboard. After the uniforms left, Maeve approached her partner and the chief. She let her hair out of its bun, attempting to massage away the headache that was beginning to form.

"What the hell was that?" Ben blurted to the chief.

"What the hell was what? Don't speak to me that way, Ben. I let you get away with a lot of shit here, but don't be insubordinate in front of your colleagues," Briggs shot back, his face the color of red sherbert.

"Gary met with her that night? Why didn't he fucking say anything a year ago?! He was likely the last person to see her alive!"

Briggs crossed his arms over his chest.

"It wasn't purposeful, Ben. He didn't mean to hold back information. He thought we knew already, and he thought it wasn't all that relevant to bring up again, since she left the property. I watched the footage myself. She gets in her car and drives away. It doesn't make sense that her body ends up back there. That's where you two come in. Figure it out," he ordered, looking between them. The detectives made eye contact.

"You got it, sir" Ben replied, attitude lacing his tone.

Briggs stared at him a moment before giving in, shaking his head back and forth. He waddled briskly out of the room, mumbling about the joys of being chief.

Ben spun his hat around and crossed his arms. Maeve tried and failed not to notice the way his biceps bulged.

"Maeve, you're not going to like this, but I don't think you should do anything alone anymore. Even interviews. If it relates to this case, I want to be there."

Her first instinct was to argue, but she thought about the threatening note and reluctantly agreed. Ben's surprise showed on his face.

"Thank you. One less thing for me to worry about. We'll talk to Amanda's parents first then head out to the Droughton Farm to talk to Lydia. Deal?"

They made their way out to Maeve's SUV, the rain soaking into her nylon coat.

"They live in Portland. So once Briggs called to let them know about Amanda, they agreed to come and stay in a hotel here to help out with the investigation. They're up at Morrisons River Lodge. Nicest place in town."

They arrived just after one in the afternoon. The downpour happening outside escalated as they approached Cottage 13, their shoes sinking into the wet soil as the earthy smell of nature enveloped them. Twenty-five log cabins of various shapes and sizes were placed deep in the damp woodland. Stamping off her shoes and suppressing a cold shudder, Maeve knocked.

A refined blonde woman in her fifties swung open the door and quietly ushered them inside. Her pearl earrings and high cheekbones gave her a dignified, elegant appearance. Once inside, she introduced herself as Judy before gesturing to her husband.

"This is my husband, Jack. Please, come in."

They settled around the oak dining room table with fresh coffee. The luxury of the space distracted Maeve. The interior was framed with the classic log cabin aesthetic, but everything else was elevated. High end, starchy white furniture and minimalistic decor filled the spacious A frame. It looked like the classic ski and spa getaway in the mountains. It was out of place for Grants Pass.

"Well, it's nice your precinct could actually meet with us this time," Jack Brinks started, leaning back and draping an arm over the back of his wife's chair. He was in a knit crewneck sweater, his salt and pepper hair short and meticulously groomed.

"This time?" Ben replied, frowning.

"Yes. We'd tried for weeks to get your precinct to listen to our theories about Mandy's passing, but everyone just kept saying it was a suicide. But, you see, there's no way she did that. Our girl just wouldn't do that. She was raised well, and she had a good head on her shoulders, despite her...circumstances," he said, rubbing a large hand along his sharp jawline.

Maeve wrote notes as Ben replied.

"Can you tell us why you think it wasn't a suicide?"

Judy sat back from the table slightly behind her husband. She avoided eye contact as she tucked pieces back into her immaculate chignon. Jack pulled Maeve's attention back to him as he leaned forward across the table, talking louder.

"She didn't mean to kill that little boy. It was a terrible accident is all. No one should be locked up for an accident. It's inhumane. She was a good girl. She respected authority and she'd never step out of line like they say she did. My Judy visited her right before the so-called fight, and she was perfectly happy, right honey?" He flashed his wife a brief glance.

The detectives shifted to hear from Judy, but before she could open her mouth, Jack barreled on.

"Warden Managan was trying to keep everything quiet. He didn't want anyone else to know what was going on in his prison. You know, that someone had died under his watch. He'd have to admit to locking her up like a dog in a cage."

He huffed. "I pushed as much as I could, but he pushed back. I wasn't getting answers from him, and your department refused to investigate it as anything other than a suicide. So, I took matters into my own hands and hired someone." He shrugged. "Lara had been skeptical at first, but a few weeks after she started digging, she found something. It's amazing what you can accomplish with a little financial incentive."

He paused, waiting for their surprise or admiration. The detectives offered neither.

"Anyway, after a few weeks Lara called me and told me she found something and asked if I could meet her here in town. I asked why she couldn't just tell me over the phone and save me a trip from Portland, but she insisted we meet in person. She sounded...I don't know...paranoid. A few days later I went and waited for two hours, but she never showed. I called and texted, but it went straight to voicemail. I called her law firm to see if she was there, and that's when they told me she was missing."

"Did you call the precinct?" Ben asked, leaning forward against the table. "Yes of course I did, but apparently they didn't really care. They already knew she was missing."

"What do you mean they didn't care? Did you tell them that you were supposed to meet with her and that she was working on your daughter's case?" Ben asked, frustration seeping into his tone.

"Of course I did! I'm not misspeaking. The lady who answered the phone told me she would transfer me to someone who would take my statement. I talked to an officer for a few minutes, gave my report and he said he'd follow up with me. But no one ever did. I tried calling a couple times after that, but they said they were aware of my statement and were looking into it, and there was nothing more I needed to do." Jack crossed his arms.

Ben and Maeve exchanged glances. "Who did you speak to?" Maeve asked.

"I have no idea. A guy...sounded white I guess."

"A white male? That's it? You didn't get a name?" Ben pushed, irritated. "No, I didn't think I needed to take the officer's name, I thought it was his job to take mine" Jack shot back defensively.

Silence descended for a few moments before a loud thunk filled the room. Maeve jolted, turning to see a large tree branch through the rain-streaked window, swaying in the wind. Jack looked at her, amusement in his features.

"Just the wind detective, nothing to be afraid of," he said, giving her a wink.

Ben leaned forward, drawing Jack's attention away. "I assume you've been to identify Amanda?"

For the first time since they arrived Jack remained silent and subdued. He wrapped his hands around his mug.

"Yes. It's her. She looks much the same as the last time we identified her," he said quietly and with malice.

"I'm so sorry for your loss. For both of you. It can't have been easy going through that the first time, let alone a second time. I apologize for the circumstances that brought this about," Maeve offered.

Jack nodded his thanks and Judy kept her gaze down. Ben asked Jack about Amanda's coffin as Maeve studied Judy. Maeve cleared her throat and spoke quietly.

"Judy, would you be able to show me where the bathroom is? If you don't mind?"

Her green eyes lifted for a moment before darting to her husband, a brief glimpse of panic in them.

"The bathroom is down the hall, second door on the right. Help yourself," Jack responded, effortlessly pivoting from his conversation with Ben as his dark eyes bore into hers.

Maeve swallowed. She thanked him and excused herself. After she was done pretending to use the washroom, she opened the door and jumped, her hand landing over her chest. Jack Brinks was standing on the other side, waiting.

"Sorry Mr. Brinks, you scared me," she said, looking over his shoulder at her escape route.

"My apologies, detective, I didn't mean to frighten you. I just wanted to be sure you found it okay," he replied, eyeing her a moment longer before walking back to the dining room.

"Well, that was enlightening" Ben murmured, shaking his head as they weaved through traffic. Maeve turned to look at him.

"Tell me you saw what I saw, Ben. I feel sick just leaving her there with him."

"You mean the clear signs of domestic abuse happening? Yeah, I did. She also had yellow bruising and swelling on the side of her face. It was well covered with makeup and her pieces of hair, but it was there. I wonder if she wanted us to know."

Maeve leaned her head back against the headrest. "I don't know. I wish I could've spoken to her alone."

"Yeah, like hell Jack was going to let that happen. What an alpha male dick wad. You gave her your card though, right?"

"Yeah, I slid it against my coffee mug as I handed it back to her. She has it. Either way, I'm going to pass this along to domestic. They need to follow up on that situation."

"Did she say anything when he followed me to the bathroom?" she asked, fixing her hair.

"No. I tried, but nothing. She wouldn't even look at me. That was the only reason I didn't follow him when he went after you though. I hope you know that. It killed me to not be in both places at once. I had to prioritize, and I knew you could handle yourself if he tried anything."

"Of course, Ben, I get it. I was fine. He was just trying to intimidate me. I'm glad you tried to speak with her alone."

"Honestly, I wouldn't be surprised if Dakota Patrieko had been right and that's why it sent Amanda off the deep end. If he used to abuse Amanda like he abuses Judy, it would add credibility to the story," he paused looking out the window "the question is though ..."

"How did Dakota know that?" Maeve interjected.

He smiled at her interruption, running a hand along his stubble. He'd taken off his jacket and was wearing a white button-down dress shirt with the sleeves rolled up. Maeve eyed his vascular forearms.

"We need to figure out what happened to Jack's missing statement. I was still working homicide at the time and covering her case; it should have been passed to me. That's protocol, no matter who answered the phone. Even if I was off duty that day, it still should have come back to me eventually."

Maeve let out a small sound, looking down. "What is it?"

"Well, I mean, I hate to be the devil's advocate being the newbie and all, but do you think this might have something to do with the culture at the precinct? It's not exactly the NYPD in there."

"The culture? What like the fact that we have a bunch of lazy idiots working at 59?" he laughed, sparing her a glance. "I think you could be right. We have a couple of good guys, but if any one of them were working at the time, I wouldn't be surprised if it got caught up in someone's Subway wrapper and tossed in the garbage."

She remained quiet, turning to look out the window.

"What is it, Maeve? I can practically hear you thinking."

She took a breath. "I mean, it's either that, or it's possible someone at the precinct knows something."

"I honestly don't know what to think. For now, let's keep this information tight. A need-to-know basis. The officers at 59 have been like that since I got to GP, but at least they aren't in charge of solving murders. Their incompetence gets overlooked when it's just parking tickets and barking complaints," He looked out the window. "The other problem I have is that I don't trust Jack Brinks. As far as we know, he didn't even make a phone call. He could be hiding something and covering his ass. What's worse than lying to the police about passing on relevant information to a case?" he said, tightening his grip on the wheel.

"Not passing along anything at all."

CHAPTER THIRTEEN

"It's so strange. Lara is obviously abused and chained up, then embalmed and put in someone else's coffin. But Amanda? Amanda is taken out and thrown away like trash, yet no mistreatment is noted on her. Apart from the mark on her neck of course. That aligns with it actually being a suicide." Maeve paused, sighing. "I know we think these two are linked somehow, but if they were both killed by the same person, the MO would be the same."

They were sitting in the McDonald's parking lot inhaling a late lunch in Ben's car.

"You're assuming this is one person?" he challenged, a piece of lettuce falling out the side of his mouth.

She turned to him. "You think there could be more than one?"

"It's not out of the question. I mean, as soon as we figure out what Lara discovered prior to her disappearance, we may have our motive. That kind of effort, the digging up of a coffin, the embalming, the swapping out and re-burying...it's a hell of a lot for one person. Especially without being seen."

"True. Either way, we need to talk to Lydia."

"Yes ma'am." He smiled, his accent coming through.

Droughton farm was straight out of Little House on the Prairie. Diverse shades of greens and browns covered the rustic landscape, and livestock roamed the endless expanse of land that framed the gravel road. Just as Maeve swept her gaze across the cow filled pasture in the distance, she was also hit with the scent of their excrement, foul and sharp, causing a roll deep within her stomach.

Farm life was definitely not for her.

She enjoyed the level of outdoor activity that came with lying on a beach or wine night on a patio. There was nothing more contradictory to her personality than being on a farm.

The farmhouse was a moderate size. Although the house was a harsh rectangle, the deep green siding and brown brick accents softened the perspective. It was a simple one-story build, but it was elevated by a beautiful movie-worthy wrap-around porch. White hydrangeas reached up from the ground below and covered the front of the deck.

They were greeted at the door by a small woman with dark chestnut hair that hung in a thick bob. Her skin was a bronze color, shiny and smooth. She gave the detectives a kind smile and introduced herself. The gentle upward curve at the corners of her mouth didn't reach her puffy, reddened eyes. Lydia Droughton looked exhausted, and nothing like her half siblings.

She ushered them inside toward the living room and introduced her husband Ray, who moved toward them and extended a calloused hand.

Raymond Droughton looked to be in his early sixties, strands of gray and white apparent under his red cap, and a lifetime's worth of sunspots on his arms. He sported a small beer belly and walked with a slight limp. All Ray could muster up in greeting was a quick pleasure before he slowly situated himself onto a gray leather recliner. Lydia moved to her seat by the large bay window that overlooked their land.

"Liam called me after he found out. That was the second worst phone call I've ever received in my life. I mean, I'm glad the uncertainty is gone. The worrying. It's painful you know, to lose all hope that quickly," she said as she sniffed, turning away.

"We are so sorry for your loss Mrs. Droughton, we can't imagine what you must be going through. Please, take a moment if you need it," Maeve said. With some effort, Ray stood, walking over and placing a hand on his wife's shoulder. She looked up at him and smiled, placing a hand over his.

"No, no, it's okay. I'm okay, really. I mean we'd been preparing for this. The odds were not in her favor. Now I just want to do what I can to help your investigation."

"Okay, let us know if you need a break at all," Maeve started, opening her notebook. Ben shifted beside her, leaning back. His presence was soothing as she took control of the interview.

"How was your relationship with Lara?"

"It was good, I'd say. We weren't close like Liam and her were, but we got along fine. It was different when we were young, but as we both grew up and matured, things evened out."

"What do you mean by that?"

"Well, looking back on it, I probably resented them for having the life I never did. They had their mom and dad alive and well, all living under one roof. I was just the bastard child that was always trying to fit into a family that didn't want me. They were both kind to me, but there was just no fixing the space created between us," she explained, putting down her mug as she shifted to one side.

"I used to resent them for everything. The way they looked, their education, their privilege. I tried to shrink myself, change myself to be more like them. My father didn't care much for me, and I was starved for attention and a sense of belonging. I was ignored and left to my own devices, and instead of being thankful that I had all the freedom in the world, I was jealous. I was jealous of Lara, his golden child. He was extremely protective and possessive of her. He set a curfew for her and felt she needed to be escorted everywhere she went. He used to say that it was his duty to protect her from the sins of this world. He didn't want her to end up like my mother I guess," she said, rolling her eyes.

"She got everything she ever wanted and Liam and I were left in the dust. I hated her for it, even though it wasn't her fault." She took a deep breath, running her fingers through her curls.

"As I got older, I moved past those insecurities and we were civil. Lara had gone off to Stanford and my father was gone. I think it helped patch things up for us. It's amazing how much more siblings can get along when they have some separation," she laughed, pausing. "Liam, however, kind of took over the overprotective role after my father died. He wasn't nearly as intense, but he did his best to protect her. Shelter her. Naturally, that backfired when she was in college..." she broke off, laughing again. "Liam helped me through a time in my life when I had no one, and for that I will always be grateful." She lifted her gaze to meet Ray's, who had moved back to his recliner across the room. He gave her a tight smile, his crow's feet deepening.

"I guess I never really thanked him properly for bringing me out here. It's the reason I met this old sack of bones over here."

A deep, coarse chuckle came from Ray and Maeve smiled in response.

Ben waited a respectable amount of time before jumping in.

"Did Lara rebel in college?"

"I guess you could say that. It wasn't anything more extreme than most people in college. Just a big change for her. Going from living such a sheltered, innocent life to having full freedom as a young adult. It was just partying, staying out late, hanging around guys she shouldn't have been. It was normal college stuff, but Liam had never seen her like that. It scared him. He would drop in and make unexpected visits to check on her. Eventually it was too much, and she told him to stay away for a while. I think they didn't talk for quite some time, but they patched it up in her last year of law school. She'd settled down a lot by then."

Ben nodded, writing notes. "Did you have much contact with them in the past couple years?"

She tilted her head back and forth. "Not all that much, detective. They used to come for dinner every other month or so, but that fizzled out a couple months before Lara went missing." Lydia bit her lip, a tick that Maeve guessed was used to keep herself from becoming too emotional. She'd done the same thing herself once or twice.

"I guess it's just going to be one of those things that I'll never forgive myself for. If I'd known...." she broke off, turning her head to look out the window. "Hindsight as they say."

"I'm so sorry Lydia," Ben replied, handing her the box of tissues from beside him.

"Liam had been making an attempt in recent months to come by once in a while to work on the farm when we needed it. He was such a huge help after Ray's knee injury."

"That's good of him. Also gives you both a chance to reconnect," Maeve replied. Lydia smiled at her and nodded.

"Did you get along with your stepmother Cora?" Ben asked, rubbing a hand over his jaw. Lydia's demeanor shifted instantly. She looked apprehensive, reserved.

She cleared her throat.

"Well, things were normal, I guess. Cora was kind. She did her best to include me, but it was still obvious I wasn't her child. Every time I did something wrong I could see the judgment in her eyes. I was the product of sex work and I never forgot it," she said quietly, dropping her head.

"Anyway, after Cora died, Liam wasn't the same. He became more reserved and careful. I guess finding your mom dead in a bathtub would do that to a person. I can't believe Liam has lost both his parents and his baby sister in his short lifespan. He's just left with me. He deserves better" she said, her voice cracking. She took another sip from her coffee.

Maeve returned a polite smile.

"My apologies Mrs. Droughton, if this is too much we can come back a bit later. We just want to get as much information as we can so we don't have to keep bothering you. We need to know this kind of stuff so we can try to figure out what may have happened to your sister."

"I get it. To be honest, I'd rather just get this over with anyway. Please, carry on."

Maeve nodded. "From what I read, it wasn't long after the loss of Cora that your father died, correct?"

"That's right. He used to work nights over at The Links Country Club. He was night shift security. One night there was a fire in the maintenance shed. I don't remember any other details really, I just remember an officer and a lady from social services came and took us to Aunt Lottie's. After his death, Liam and Lara were inseparable, and I was the third wheel," she finished, shrugging her shoulders, looking between the detectives. "I'm not complaining, I did fine on my own. It was still nice to know they were there if I needed them. They didn't leave me out on purpose, it just happened naturally. They were never cruel to me, and they can't be faulted for loving each other too much, now can they?"

Ben nodded and spoke up then, asking the question in Maeve's mind.

"One last question. Was there anything different about Liam or Lara in the days or months before her disappearance? Did either of you notice anything peculiar about Lara?"

Lydia went quiet, avoiding her gaze.

"No, not at all. Although I hadn't seen her for a couple months before that. Everything seemed fine with both of them last time they came for supper...Ray?"

He jolted forward. He must have started to doze off. "No, nope. Nothing. That said, I didn't know either too well to begin with."

Admittedly, Maeve had forgotten about Ray's presence throughout the interview and used the opportunity to ask him if there was anything else he wanted to add to Lydia's statement.

He looked to Lydia, Ben, then finally back at Maeve as his brows pulled in. "Nope, nothing to add. I don't do or hear much other than what goes on at my farm. Lydia knows best about her own family."

The detectives thanked the Droughton's and headed outside. Maeve immediately grieved the loss of the warm smell of apples and cinnamon that had filled the Droughton home.

Ben put his hands on his hips and leaned back, forcing a gentle crack from his spine. "Fuck, we're just chasing our tails on this. Not a single one of these interviews have told us anything about what could've happened to her those last few days. They are literally making the exact same statements they made to me last year." He turned to her, extending his arm out in a larger gesture. "I mean, GP is a fucking tiny ass place where Mary Burch from down the street knows when my god damn doctor's appointments are. How the hell does something like this just go unseen? How the hell does no one know anything?" He turned, kicking at a patch of gravel. Maeve felt the sun on her face and lifted her hand to shield her eyes.

"Ben, I feel like we're missing something. Something we may already know but can't quite piece together. I can't think straight out here with the smell of cow shit. Let's call it a day and come back to this tomorrow. We're tapped out."

Tuesday morning rolled around and they found themselves in Maeve's office, files thrown on her desk and floor. She was sitting cross-legged on the stale carpet, aimlessly flicking her pen against her leg. Her partner sat in her chair, legs propped up on the desk as he read through reports.

"I think this case may just kill me. I mean, it was difficult when it first happened, but now...now I can't even fucking get a moment of peace. It's all I think about," he said, ending his sentiment with an audible exhale and tossing the folder onto the desk.

Maeve didn't respond, she was too deep into a report and he'd been making his internal monologue external for over an hour. He huffed and started to pace above her, stepping on photos and nearly crushing her fingers.

"Alright, Ben, you either need to sit down or get out of my office, because this pacing isn't gonna work for me."

He looked down at her, blinking rapidly. "Oh sorry...sorry Maeve, I'll relocate," he replied, stepping over her. "I need to get out of this office and away from these files anyways."

"Wait! Something you said earlier had me thinking. The fact that you've already interviewed these people before...I don't think it's a problem. I actually think it could help. I mean, are there any statements or alibis that are exactly word for word the same? Anything too rehearsed? And then on the other end, is anything different? I mean, after a certain amount of time has passed, most innocent people would forget minute details. Unless of course, they've been practicing them to re-create their truth. In that case, they'd remember everything. Their freedom would depend on it."

"Brilliant Maeve. You're bloody brilliant. Let me grab my old interview notes, I'll take them home with me and take a look."

She smiled back, warmed by the compliment as she watched him move toward the door before stopping abruptly and turning back.

"I almost forgot, please call or text once you get home. Just to confirm patrol is still there."

She agreed, rolling her eyes before her partner made a successful exit.

She sifted through old photos of the family and something caught her eye. She reached under a stack to find an old polaroid shot, curled at the edges and riddled with brown spots.

The photo looked like it had been taken in a 1970s-style living room, brown and yellow shag carpet on the ground and oak furniture in the background. A young red-headed woman sitting cross legged on the floor with her back against a gray couch took the focus. She had a scrawny little ginger boy on her lap. The woman had her head tilted back mid-laugh, pure joy radiated off her. Her hair was a deep shade of copper, tied back in a high pony with a bright yellow scrunchie. Deep dimples on both sides of her cheeks identical to the ones her daughter had. The woman must have been Cora, their mother.

The little boy had to be Liam. He looked no older than four. Their hair was almost the exact same shade, and he was looking up at her as she laughed, love and admiration on his face. The photo would've been taken only a few years before he'd found her dead in the bathtub. Cora's eyes were slightly closed but Maeve could see they were dark, the only apparent difference between her and her kids. They must have gotten their blue eyes from their father. Her thoughts traveled to Gerald McAllister, and she rifled through the remaining photos on the floor trying to find one of him.

Suddenly, the loud pitch of her phone ringing echoed through the room. Jumping, she placed a hand over her heart and fumbled to answer it.

"Hey, sorry to bail on you with vague ideas and musings. I was getting a little claustrophobic in there. Anyway, I'm headed to The Shipyard for a cold beer if you want to join. I know we're in the middle of a homicide investigation, and it's the middle of the day on a Tuesday, but I need a break" Ben finished, sounding out of breath.

She agreed to meet him, her empty stomach the primary motivator.

As she walked out of the precinct, she glanced over to Briggs's office and noticed the door was locked and the lights were off. He hadn't yet come in for work. Maeve assumed that he was most likely at the crime scene dealing with the press or talking to families.

She made her way over to Ben sitting at the bar, pulling off her jacket and fixing her hair. Her partner smiled as she approached and stood up, gesturing to the empty booth on the opposite wall.

Carl wasn't on shift to give them a special deal, so they ordered the half-price pale ale on draught and fell into easy conversation. The nature of the dialogue revolved around the case, but this time was framed with ease rather than frustration. Maeve was half-way through her second beer and starting to feel swirly when she realized she was genuinely enjoying herself. Ben took a sip from his drink and re-directed the conversation.

"So, are you liking it in GP so far?"

"Yeah, I think I'm settling in well enough. I'm not one to connect with people easily so I tend to live life on the introverted side of the spectrum anyway. I've been hanging out with Nikko, Carl and some of that group lately though. They're super nice."

"You didn't have friends or...boyfriends that you had to leave back home?"

"I mean, yeah, I had some girls from university that I was close with, but nothing serious in terms of relationships," she replied, averting her eyes and taking a long sip of her beer.

"Shame" he deadpanned, bringing her attention back to him before letting out a small lopsided smile, emphasizing the lack of sincerity in his comment. She was just about to ask him the reciprocal question when her attention was drawn to the pub entrance. A tall figure in a rain jacket came busting in, bringing the storm in with him.

When had a storm rolled in? It had been sunny and dry when Maeve had arrived. Ben turned to follow her gaze and they both stiffened as the man strolled casually toward the bar, pulling off his hood and revealing the shiny auburn hair below.

CHAPTER FOURTEEN

Liam McAllister stopped dead in his tracks and looked over at their table, giving Maeve a tentative nod before making it to the bar. She slowly brought her eyes to Ben. He was already looking at her.

"Why are you looking at me like that?" she asked, playing with the condensation on her glass.

"Like what?" he said, cocking an eyebrow.

She opened her mouth to answer but was cut off by the figure that hovered at the end of their booth.

"Detectives. Mind if I join you?" Liam asked, his tone light.

Stunned into silence, Maeve moved over on the bench. Liam slid in next to her effortlessly, his scent cool as the smell of mint enveloped her. His thigh grazed hers ever so slightly under the table, sending an electrical jolt up through her lower back.

"Thanks. The only thing more depressing than drinking yourself into oblivion, is doing it alone," he said, glancing across the bar. "Although, alone would still be more tolerable than making small talk with Jason Boukesh," he finished, tossing a thumb toward the spot near the exit.

Ben cleared his throat, clearly uncomfortable as his eyes shifted to where Liam pointed. He squinted in disdain.

"How've you been, Liam?" he asked, pouring himself the last bit of beer left in the pitcher.

"Oh, pretty fucking peachy thanks, you?"

"Sorry, stupid question. I'm truly sorry for what happened to her, man. No one should have to go through what you have."

Liam shifted slightly, placing his elbows on the table and running a thumb along the outside of his jaw.

"Thanks, Ben."

Maeve crossed her legs, leaning away as best she could to give herself some space and counteract the effect two beers had on her resolve. Sensing her shift, Liam turned to her. His gaze resting on her lips before moving to her eyes.

"Maeve, please change the subject. How did you wind up moving to this hell hole?" he asked, moving closer.

Ben's hand tightened around his glass.

"Honestly it's not all that interesting. I was born in Honolulu and was raised there until I was thirteen. I moved with my mom and sister to Vancouver when my parents split, but my brother stayed with my dad. My mom is from Canada, originally, and only moved to Hawaii to be with my dad when they first met," she paused and took a sip of her drink.

"I loved living on the west coast, but it wasn't the same as the islands. I went to UBC for my nursing degree and then UVic for my masters in forensic investigation and behavioral analysis."

Ben gestured to the server for another pitcher.

"Why did you choose GP? Seems like a very random choice when you have the entirety of the United States at your disposal," Liam asked, dragging a hand through his messy hair. He dropped his arm along the top of the booth behind her. She looked at the outline of his bicep beside her.

"I chose Oregon. Grants Pass kind of chose me when this position opened up. Not many people want to hire a rookie with minimal frontline work as a detective. I didn't have enough experience for most places, and I really didn't want to do grunt work. I love it here though; the intense rain and the overwhelming amount of nature just makes me feel at home."

Liam nodded but didn't respond, his gaze finally moving to Ben. Maeve thought about how inappropriate it looked for the lead detectives on a case to be sitting with the victim's brother. She was about to excuse herself when Ben spoke up, once again reading her mind.

"It's okay Maeve, you don't have to worry about how this looks. It's a small place and a close-knit community. People can assume what they want, but it's not against the rules."

She nodded her head, giving him a tight smile and cursing herself for missing her only excuse to get out of the situation unscathed.

"Is your family still in Canada then?" Liam asked, taking a sip of his Guinness.

"Yeah, my mom and sister are. They love it there and I don't think they'll ever leave. My dad and brother still live in Honolulu. I don't go back to see them nearly as much as I'd like though. That being said, I'm not close with my sister, and my brother is living his own life with his wife and kids. I've grown accustomed to being on my own for a while."

"Guess you and I have that in common now," Liam responded tightly, turning away from her to hide the emotion behind his words.

"So, you're saying this may be a temporary thing before you find something better?" Ben asked her, holding eye contact.

"No, not exactly. I do get bored with jobs pretty easily, but that was mostly because I wasn't happy with what I was doing. Things are different now. This...this is something I've always wanted," she replied, giving him a reassuring smile. His shoulders dropped as he relaxed back into the seat. It was something she'd never witnessed before from her partner. He was always so controlled, tense.

The conversation moved to Ben's childhood in Missouri and his time overseas. Maeve learned that he was born and raised in Kansas City up until he enlisted in the army, which led him to two tours in Afghanistan. Once he returned, he completed his police training and found a job in Grants Pass with Marc.Despite the wealth of personal information they'd both shared, Liam was a brick wall. He was active in the conversation, probing them both with questions, but stonewalled every attempt they made to change the subject. The idea that they'd both shared way too much about their personal lives with a person of interest in the case didn't sit well with Maeve, but the damage was done. Throughout the afternoon, Ben and Liam must have had around ten beers and several shooters between the two of them. Subsequently, they both ended up on an entirely different level than Maeve. She'd stopped after three pints and took it upon herself to be the responsible one, but she was enjoying herself just as much as they were. They were incredibly entertaining, and she was surprised at how comfortable and at ease she felt with them.

As the evening wore on, they were loud and inappropriate. She hadn't belly laughed that hard in months. She didn't want to leave, but she knew she needed to get the both of them home. Reluctantly, she led the way toward the exit with her sloppy, unsteady company trailing behind.

Upon nearing the exit, she accidentally dropped her car keys on the ground. Bending to pick them up, she heard a loud whistle from the table next to her.

"No wonder the chief hired you, that really is something to look at. Are those tight jeans part of the dress code over there, detective? Cause' if so, I think I need to change my career path."

Maeve halted, anger surging through her as she looked over at her catcaller.

Jason Boukesh was eye fucking her, his shiny forehead gleaming off the antique chandelier above them. His friends laughed in support and nodded their heads as they looked their fill. Maeve went to take a step, but a blur of motion came from behind her. Ben launched himself at Jason so quickly she didn't have time to react.

Her partner dragged the lawyer up by the neck before shoving him through the exit door. A crowd of people swarmed instantly, and Maeve elbowed her way outside to help her idiotic partner. Liam trailed behind, helping her push her through the crowd.

Ben had Jason up against the building, his forearm pressed just below his neck as Jason squirmed. He moved again, and in less than a few seconds, Jason was on the ground with a knee pressed into his back and his arms pinned behind him. Jason was red-faced and panting while her partner didn't even look winded. He leaned over Jason.

"Speak to my partner like that again and you'll never practice law for the rest of your miserable life, you piece of shit. Actually, you know what? If you even look at her again, I'll make sure every person in this place knows just how small your dick really is, Jason."

Jason's so-called-friends, no longer bursting with testosterone and pride, hovered awkwardly. They were smart enough at least to not get involved with an ex-marine turned cop. Maeve knew better than to get between two full-grown men in a pissing contest and let her partner collect himself.

"Nothing to say now hey tough guy? You're pathetic. I look forward to the day you end up in one of my jail cells, " Ben spat, kicking Jason on the inside of the thigh forcing a squeal out of him.

Shifting his tone, he turned to her. "Ready to go?"

Maeve had to actively close her mouth before jogging after him. His seamless shift in demeanor unsettled her.

Ben apologized to the staff and patrons left in the pub and cleaned up the mess he made. By the time they made it back outside the crowd had dispersed. Liam awkwardly shuffled beside her giving her a concerned look as they followed their reactive friend out into the street. They'd just blown off half a day of work to get torched, and her partner had gotten into a bar fight in an effort to defend her honor.

What a fucking day.

She typically hated when overprotective men solved their problems with violence, but for some reason she felt herself smile as she made her way to the taxi idling at the end of the street.

• • •

"So, how did it go yesterday?" Briggs asked, moving his papers aside as he finished up his call. He met Maeve's eyes as he dabbed his forehead with a tissue.

"I'm sorry I didn't update you sooner on my progress, sir. It went well I think."

He shifted, pulling at his tie in an effort to get more air past his constricted lungs. "No problem darlin', it happens. Did you have a long day?"

She decided it was best to bend the truth a little. She cleared her throat. "Yeah, I just got caught up in an interview with Ben and it ran late. Liam was curious about the dress, as we all are, but he kept his composure until he left the exam room and let himself fall apart a bit. He did, however, mention a missing watch. Apparently, it belonged to their mother and Lara never took it off."

"Huh, weird. I guess we can add that to the case notes. Good work, Maeve. What about Ray and Lydia?" He leaned back, taking a deep breath as he crossed his fingers over his large abdomen.

"Ben and I visited them the other day, nothing new there unfortunately."

"Alright, well I'm glad you guys met with them anyway. Unfortunately, there's no shortage of dead ends with this," he paused, catching his breath. "Listen, I apologize I wasn't available yesterday. I was out at Umbele with Gary and Chief Maxwell."

"It's no problem, sir. We have your number if we need it."

He smiled. "What are your next steps?"

She felt a dull throb begin in her temple. Her reliance on caffeine was becoming a problem. She took a deep breath, anxious to get out of the cramped room.

"We're thinking we need to dig deeper into Amanda's case. Ben and I think there's something we're missing. When we spoke with Jack and Judy Brinks, they said when Lara had first gone missing they'd called to make a statement. Apparently, someone here took their call and said that they'd get back to them, but no one ever did. Jack said he called again to follow up and was told it was being handled."

Briggs lifted his eyebrows, letting her finish.

"That being said, we aren't discrediting the idea that he's lying to cover his ass. Do you happen to know anything about that? Ben said he never got a statement."

Briggs frowned. "I definitely didn't get a call from either of them after Lara went missing. If I had, that would've changed things."

He leaned forward, the smell of his BO drifting over to her. "I'd met with Jack several times when she first died. He would come in all hotheaded and full of theories. He used to get so wound up he actually had to be escorted out of my office at one point. He would call me incessantly at work and on my cell, leaving me all kinds of threatening messages. I told them again and again that the evidence suggested it was an open and shut case…a suicide, but they didn't want to hear it. I wish I could've spared the time and resources to spend more time on it, but it had no basis for further investigation. She was found hanging in her cell and the cause of death was asphyxiation." He coughed, a dribble of spit hanging off the side of his mouth."Leadership told me to close it and my hands were tied. I mean, eventually he got the message and backed off, but he was relentless for a while there. I hadn't heard from him since then and he definitely did not call about Lara." He frowned, concerned. "Leave it with me. I'll look into it with Beatta and see if we can find a call log or statement of any kind. I don't trust that guy as far as I can throw him, but we'll do our due diligence just in case."

She nodded her head, leaning back in the chair.

"What, no invite?" Ben said, looming in the doorway.

"Sorry Ben, I was just getting an update from your capable partner," Briggs explained, giving Maeve a reassuring smile. Ben leaned casually against the door frame with his arms crossed. Her partner was textbook handsome. His signature buzz cut was starting to grow out and he sported his usual backwards hat and all black outfit, his silver badge and dog tags tangled on his defined chest. His eyes were a shade lighter than usual as they drifted over to hers. His presence had brought with it a sense of calm, warming her like a weighted blanket. She felt safe when he was around.

She didn't trust it.

Reading her mind, he gave her a mischievous grin."Well Joe, if you don't mind, I need to steal my partner from you."

The possessive tone of his voice had her swallowing the excess saliva that had gathered at the back of her throat. Briggs nodded his head, muttering a thanks darlin' before turning back to his computer.

Maeve followed Ben into his office, his smoky scent distracting her. She tried to regain control of her thoughts as they divided up their workload. Ben's office space was only marginally larger than her own but felt claustrophobic from the lack of windows. The space was in pristine condition, not a single pen out of place. She wasn't at all surprised to learn that Ben was a neat freak. Her mess must cause him heart palpitations.

• • •

Back home, Maeve tucked Lara's call logs back into the file and ran upstairs to change into her pj shorts. Just as she dropped onto her couch and covered herself in a soft throw blanket, she received a text from her mother. Groaning, she decided to rip off the Band-Aid and FaceTime her. She'd been dodging her calls long enough.

Helena Kalani was a regal woman. Her hair was coiffed perfectly, not a rogue strand to be found as the blunt length fell just above her shoulders in a dull ashy shade of blonde. Her mother had an uncanny resemblance to Janet McTeer. The thin lines spider webbing out from her high cheekbones were the only hint of softness in her features, and they multiplied as she smiled at Maeve.

She was so unlike her mother. Her sister, Maya, was an exact duplicate of the woman on the screen, but the only semblance of their father's genes in her sister was the shade of her hair. Maya was as thin and angular as Helena, and as equally poised. The divide between her and her sister had grown deeper with each passing year as their differing beliefs and values grew too large to overcome. She cared for her mother and sister, but she felt out of place in their world. They needed the sleek, fast-paced city lifestyle, while she was more similar to her father and Matteo. They liked to stop and smell the roses.

After Helena commented on how tired Maeve looked, she asked how things were at work and Maeve updated her on the comings and goings. She made sure to leave out the gory details of the case or the mention of her new friends. She also managed to evade any questions about her love life, and her mother had been happy to hear that she was finally settling in and "becoming less of a hermit."

Once Maeve was done with her updates, Helena spent the following forty minutes telling her about her new-found love of gardening and the man she met at the bakery. As predicted, Helena still couldn't help herself as she had to drop the slight that Maya missed her terribly and that she was family. Like that was some sort of excuse. Being related by blood to someone did not mean that person had any assumed right to be in her life. Maeve did her duty and apologized for not calling both of them more often and was finally able to end the call a few minutes later, rounding the total time to just over an hour. A new record. Helena Kalani loved nothing more than talking about herself.

Despite herself, the small bit of familiarity from the call had brought some warmth back into her soul. Painful as FaceTime was, it was nice to see a familiar face. Maeve had been a little short on human connection in recent months. Her friends from college were all married with children, and she was unable to find anything in common with them anymore. She'd almost completely severed any connection with them in the past few years, other than the occasional text or strained coffee chat. She had a sudden realization she hadn't heard from them since her move. She was no better. She hadn't reached out either.

She'd been lost in an ocean of her own thoughts, having downed a glass of Mission Hill Pinot Noir, when her phone buzzed beside her. She lifted it and saw Liam McAllister on the screen. Perching gently on the edge of the sofa, she answered.

"Maeve! I've been having lots of thoughts about who could've done this. I think I have some leads! I think we need to look more closely at Jason. I don't trust him. Especially after what went down at The Shipyard. He's always been skeevy. Also, have you thought about maybe someone who may've been stalking her? She always got lots of attention. Especially right after we moved here." He rambled on, finally pausing after realizing she'd yet to reply. "Maeve? Are you writing this down? Are you even listening to me?"

She stood up, pacing. "Yes…yes of course I'm listening, Liam. Why don't we talk about this tomorrow? I can drop by your clinic."

"No, that won't work. I've taken some time away. I already told you that. Plus, I don't think I'll be thinking as clearly tomorrow. I have so many thoughts about this right now and I think maybe Ben didn't cover all his bases…." A beat later, he added, "I have a better idea, I'll just drop by. That'll be easier than trying to do this on the phone."

"Wait! I'm not…" she started, but it was already too late. He'd hung up.

She texted him telling him it wasn't a good idea to drop by, and when he didn't answer the texts, she tried calling.

Her mind raced as she worried about her next move. Should she text Ben? It was late. She didn't want to disturb him for no reason, and they'd just spent time with Liam. She moved to the front window, glancing out toward the patrol car still parked out front.

At least she had backup if she needed it.

Liam knocked at her door less than ten minutes later. She opened it to find him on her front steps soaking wet and wild-eyed. His hair was sloppy, some of it pinned against his forehead and his eyes were cerulean blue, large and frantic. He was in a thin white athletic shirt that was plastered to his frame. It did nothing to hide the shape of his muscles that lay beneath. Her breath hitched as she took in his rigid abdomen, heaving under the effort of his increased respiratory rate.

"Liam, you're soaking wet. Tell me you didn't walk here."

"Okay, I didn't walk here," he replied, grinning fiendishly. "I ran."

CHAPTER FIFTEEN

Her brows pinched as she ushered him inside, peering behind him to wave at the patrol car parked across the street.

"How did you know I wasn't at the precinct? How do you know where I live?" she asked, heart racing.

"It's a small town, Maeve. Don't have to be a detective to figure it out. Do you have a bathroom?" he asked, gesturing to his soaked outfit.

"I'll go get you a towel," she said, moving to the stairs. He muttered his thanks as he dried his hair aggressively, causing the strands to stick out in different directions. The mess made it look longer than usual, some of it hanging past his ears and some standing up at the back. He looked significantly younger than he was. Without so much as a glance her way, he proceeded to peel off his shirt and towel dry his upper body. She had every intention of turning around to give him privacy, but instead she was unable to drag her eyes away from his body. His biceps. His chest. His abs.

She dared to look lower, Liam completely oblivious to her captivated gaze. Her toes curled as she saw both lines that began at his hips and descended into his pelvis, just below his waistband. Lord have mercy. Those lines made even the strongest women weak.

With extreme effort, she cleared her throat and turned away, heading into the kitchen. "You couldn't have done that in the bathroom?"

"Nah, too far," he replied from behind her. Maeve grabbed herself a glass of water in a hurried attempt to counteract the effects of both the wine in her system and the abs in her front entrance. She politely asked him if he wanted anything, and he padded to the entrance of the kitchen in his bare feet, turning to point to the bottle of wine on her coffee table in the attached room.

"I'll have some of that," he said, winking at her before waltzing confidently into her living room and dropping into her couch. He still hadn't put his shirt back on and had the towel draped over his neck.

Still standing at the sink, she downed another glass of water and grabbed another bottle of wine before following the scent of mint into the living room.

"Liam, I don't think you should be here. And I really don't think you should have any wine."

He ignored her concern, glancing at the bottle in front of him. "Why is there a police car out front?"

She swallowed at the abrupt change in topic. "No reason. Just the chief being overly cautious."

He eyed her intently.

"I'm sorry, Maeve, I didn't mean to interrupt. I know it's completely unprofessional that I'm here, but I just need to run some things by you. I can't sleep."

"Okay, well go ahead then. Tell me what you need to tell me."

He leaned back, running a hand through his hair as he eyed the bottle of wine. "Not until I have some of that."

She poured the Crown and Thieves into the glass she'd set on the coffee table. She knew it was a terrible idea, but she also knew she wouldn't get anything out of him unless she played along.

"What? I'm drinking alone?" he whined, the side of his mouth tilting up. She rolled her eyes and poured herself some too. After she'd taken a tiny sip, she made an exaggerated gesture for him to continue.

"Okay, so. Jason Boukesh. I don't like him. He's a perv, as you know. Lara was a pretty girl, and I think there's a chance that maybe someone liked her a little too much. Jason was way more into her than she was him."

"Liam, I looked into Jason. He's clear. He has an alibi."

"What is it?"

"You know I can't tell you that."

He took a long drink from his wine, almost emptying the glass completely. "He was a fucking prick to her when they were dating. I always hated that guy."

She looked at him intently. She was careful not to reply as she realized Liam knew more than everyone thought he did.

"What about Marc Hallman? You know she dated him too, right?" he pushed, ignoring her silence.

Maeve was dumbstruck. Everyone she'd spoken to had told her point blank that Liam hadn't known about Lara's relationships. He eyed her, waiting for a response as he topped himself up.

"Liam, I looked into both of them. They both have alibis. That being said, we never write anyone off entirely. We'll always keep an eye on whoever may be involved, and since they were both close to Lara at the time of her disappearance, we've been keeping tabs on them."

He clenched his perfectly angular jaw.

"I don't know why she didn't think she could trust me enough to tell me about them. All I ever wanted was to protect her from the same shit we went through as kids. She didn't see dad like I did back then. She was young and she didn't understand what was happening with our fucked up family. She was also so sure of who she was, confident and strong. I knew she could handle herself, but it was the rest of the world I didn't trust. She was too kind and forgiving. She would take people at their word. She had a big heart, and people took advantage of that." His voice cracked, his grief filling the room and surrounding them both.

"I just...I just wanted to protect her from something bad happening. Someone taking advantage of her kind-hearted nature. That's what dad did to my mom and look how well that turned out," he huffed, "Ironic, isn't it? Things turned out exactly as I always feared they would," he said, tears finally falling from his bloodshot eyes. He tried to compose himself as he took a breath.

"Our family has some sort of bad omen surrounding it. Everyone we love is taken away. It was just Lydia, Lara and I left, and we almost lost Lydia to that fuckhead she was dating in Chico a few years ago too. Lara was the most important person in the world to me and I couldn't let anything happen to her. Who was going to have her back if I didn't? We didn't have anyone left. Mom always told me to look out for her...and I...I failed them both."

Maeve felt his anguish, hot and suffocating.

He dropped his head into his hands as his shoulders shook, his pale skin peppered with goosebumps. Her own eyes fogged up, but she blinked it back as best she could. She got up and turned the electric fireplace on before moving to sit next to him on the couch. She put a friendly hand on his back as they sat in quiet resolve.

After a few long minutes he stopped shaking. He leaned back to look at her, taking a breath. Then, as if in a trance, he started absently playing with her split ends. Much to her own surprise, she allowed the friendly gesture.

"Your hair is beautiful down. I've never seen it like this," he whispered, scanning her face.

She shrugged him off and removed her clammy hand from his bare back. Maeve noticed the goosebumps all over his skin and she wondered if it was from his damp clothing, the conversation, or her touch.

Her heart rate increased, her face hot. She dropped her gaze behind him as they sat next to each other, both unsure how to proceed. Liam moved to touch her face with his right hand, thumb tracing back and forth across her cheek. His other hand had shifted to her thigh as he turned to face her. She froze, dragging her gaze up toward his crippling baby blues.

She was about to tell him off when he gently lifted her chin, his eyes dropping to her lips. Before she had time to comprehend his intentions, his lips found hers, just a light graze at first as he tested her. Her mind, previously spinning, became a void as she found warmth and comfort in the kiss.

After a few uncertain moments, something came over her and she began to move with him, gripping onto his forearm as he cupped her face. Her panic fell away as his lips grew more demanding. His other hand tightened on her leg, dragging her closer as his tongue explored her mouth. Playfully biting his lower lip, she could feel him smile. She chuckled before she shifted, moving over him to straddle his hips.

He made a sound of appreciation and took the opportunity to move his experienced mouth to her neck. She weaved her fingers through his damp hair as his lips made their way down toward her chest and back up again. After some diligence on her neck, his mouth returned to hers. They stayed that way for a few long minutes and Maeve felt him begin to harden beneath her. He pulled back momentarily, cheeks flushed and lips red.

"Are you aware how many layers of clothing you have on?" he said, eyes shining. She laughed, pulling off her top layers before standing to allow him to do the bottom. His eyes were hungry as he expertly pulled off her sweatpants, his brow furrowing in concentration.

He paused, looking up at her. "Sweatpants and shorts?" He kept pulling and Maeve silently stepped out of each layer as he went. "And granny panties. Maeve, I dare say, you make loungewear very sexy."

She felt entirely exposed standing in front of him while he lounged, arms stretched out on the back of the couch, legs wide, soaking in the view. He stood then and she watched his eyes shift as he moved quickly, grabbing her wrists and wrapping her arms around his neck, his hands on her lower back. "I need to take you upstairs now before you let your morals get the best of you, but first, I need you to tell me that you want this," he said, eyes searching hers. She felt a responsive pulse run through from her stomach to her pelvis and she tightened her hold on his neck.

"I want this. But don't quote me on that tomorrow," she said, her voice raspy and laced in desire as she pulled his towering six-foot-three frame down to meet her mouth. She felt the rumble of his laughter on her lips as his hands fell below her ass, allowing himself a handful before lifting her off the ground. Her legs wrapped around his waist as she held the kiss.

He laid her back gently on the bed, his core flexing. Dragging her hand down his chest, she gripped onto the waistband of his pants and impatiently pulled them down, sliding her hand over his boxer briefs and along his firm length. He moaned into her mouth, and she swallowed it, frantic with need.

She continued her pursuit, sitting up on the end of the bed and pulling his briefs down, exposing his manhood as it burst free, bobbing slightly. As he stood before her, she took a moment to drag her gaze from the glazed tip up his muscular chest and into his eyes. They burned into her own.

His breathing hitched as he looked down at her.

"You're...mouth-watering." He reached down to drag a thumb over her bottom lip, his cock twitching with need and causing the pulsing between her legs to increase. He quickly found her mouth again and she wrapped her legs around his waist, his slick erection pressing into her stomach. Pulling back, he took one of her breasts into his mouth, sucking greedily as he squeezed the other one and teased her nipple.

"Liam, get on with it. I can't wait any longer," she ordered. She reached down to pull off her own underwear.

"Beg me again," he growled, intensity outlining his features as he helped her wiggle out of her last bit of clothing.

"I swear to god Liam..." she started, her threat immediately lost to a loud moan as he thrust himself inside in one quick movement.

"What was that?" he teased, fully seated within her as he nipped at her ear.

"Fuck...start moving," she demanded, wrapping her legs around him tightly and arching until her breasts grazed his chest. Shuddering, he complied, pumping in and out with force.

"Fuck, you're so wet and ready for me already."

His movements were frantic as he thrusted at a frenzied pace, pulling all the way out to the tip before slamming back into her, shifting her closer and closer toward the headboard. He kissed her, long and deep before placing both hands against the headboard and increasing the intensity, hips rolling into her in waves. She was writhing beneath him, breathless and moaning at each forceful movement, still eager for more as she clenched around him forcing an animalistic groan from him.

He slowed slightly, finding a deeper rhythm as she dug her nails into his back, and he clenched his jaw in an effort to hold off his release. Adjusting his position, he grabbed her legs, putting both over his shoulders as he reached down to rub her swollen, sensitive bundle of nerves with his thumb.

Maeve, responding instantly, felt the beginning of her release as the tingling sensation began up her legs and toward her core. Closing her eyes she tilted her pelvis, squeezing her thighs around him as he moved at a more deliberate, intentional pace.

"Oh my god," she breathed. He leaned down to touch his forehead to her own as he continued his movements. She shuddered, eager to chase her own orgasm, and he instantly swelled within her, thrusting frantically as he trembled through his release, tightening his grip on the back of her knee.

After they caught their breath, Liam lifted up on a shaky arm, sliding out of her before walking to the bathroom. She rolled onto her side, sliding under the covers.

"I've been wanting to do that since I first laid eyes on you at the diner, but that was better than I ever could have imagined," he said, walking back to her and trailing a sweaty hand down her exposed back before sliding in next to her. Maeve could only smile in response as the numbing effects of her orgasm and the wine wore off and the implications of her decisions crept in.

CHAPTER SIXTEEN

The next morning, Maeve woke with a dull headache and an accompanying surge of dread. She opened her eyes one at a time, slowly sitting up and hoping to hell what she remembered of last night hadn't actually happened.

After getting up the nerve to look at the spot next to her in bed, she was relieved to find it without a naked murder suspect. She let go of a breath she didn't know she'd been holding and grabbed her phone. There were no texts, but she paused on the date.

Tuesday, May 2, 2019.

Yesterday marked a year to the day since Lara was reported missing. Which explained Liam's heightened emotional distress. He'd had an excuse for their mistake.

What was hers?

Groaning, she did what she did best and shoved her feelings down. Avoidance, the unhealthy, but incredibly convenient solution to everything. She quickly jumped in the shower, turning the dial to a scalding level heat in an attempt to cleanse herself of the booze and the boy.

She arrived at the prison just after ten. Maeve walked toward her partner and instantly regretted not dressing in layers. The sun was relentlessly bright. The heat pouring through the fabric of her sweater made her feel like she was draped in plastic wrap. She tossed her sunglasses on and sent a silent plea to the universe to help her through the day. She looked up to see Ben holding a coffee in each hand, a ridiculously exaggerated close-lipped smile smacked across his face. She moaned, moving to throw her arms around him as she mumbled that he was literally saving her life. His familiar fresh but smoky scent comforted her instantly. He stiffened, clearing his throat before returning the gesture as best he could without spilling the cups. He let out a small laugh at her dramatic welcome.

"What was that for?"

"It was a long night," she replied, avoiding his gaze as she stepped back. Much to her relief he narrowed his eyes at her but didn't push the subject. She trusted Ben, but not enough to tell him that she'd crossed that line. The sex was out of character for her. It wasn't in her nature to bend the rules, and she hated doing the wrong thing. It was like she had lost control of her own actions, her own body. She must be in week two of her cycle. She took a sip of her hot coffee, burying her inner turmoil. There wasn't time for a personal crisis.

"Hey, did you end up following up about the embalming?" she asked, lifting her hand to shield her eyes.

"Yeah. I talked to the four funeral directors here in GP and made a call to Chief Maxwell in Medford. He's going to poke around a bit there too. I also looked into some of the hardware stores that sell that kind of equipment, but none of them could remember anything helpful. Doesn't help it's been a year. I mean, I get it, I barely remember what I had for lunch yesterday," he said, dragging a hand over his unshaven face.

"And then there's the whole online shopping idea," Maeve added.

"Yup. We can't exactly investigate all the possible suppliers that may have delivered to this area," he concluded, once again finishing her own train of thought.

As they made their way into the building, Maeve quickly glanced at the area surrounding the cemetery. It was all still taped off, but there were no uniforms or lab techs in sight. All the vans and equipment were gone, and what was left of the scene was a disaster. Forgotten dirt piles were everywhere, grass and shrubbery were tossed about and leftover trash scattered the scene. Maeve was ashamed of what she saw, voicing her concern out loud as Ben simply shrugged her off and told her it wasn't their problem.

The atmosphere in the prison was overstimulating. The hallways were too warm and the lights too bright. It smelled like dirt and rotten fruit, and she instantly felt her gag reflex kick in. After some tedious lefts and rights, they found themselves face to face with Spencer Caldwell again. Spencer avoided eye contact with Maeve, her eyes darting behind to look at Ben as the side of her mouth curved up. She undressed him with her eyes and Maeve felt her agitation doubling.

"Hi, Spencer. We need to see Warden Managan as soon as possible. It's important," Maeve said, leaning on the desk.

"He's not here. We didn't know you were coming in," she said quietly, eyes darting to his office. Maeve rolled her eyes as Ben walked over and knocked harshly. No sound came from behind the closed door. He knocked again, adding more force. After another silence he tried the doorknob. It was locked.

"Spencer, while we have you here, can we ask you something?" Ben said, sauntering closer to her.

She lifted her large eyes. "Sure."

"The night that Lara McAllister came to conduct her investigation here, May 1st of last year, did you see her? Did she sign the visitor log?"

Spencer flushed, looking up at Ben. "Yeah. She was here just before I was supposed to leave for the day. I remember her well, she was so pretty. So confident."

"What time did you leave?"

She shrugged her shoulders. "Once I escorted her in to meet with the warden, I packed up my stuff and left for the day. Not sure the exact time, but I typically head out just after five. Sometimes I stay a bit later if I have a lot of work to catch up on."

"Then you came in the next morning and checked the visitor log?" he pushed, grabbing his badge that was swinging forward.

"Yeah. I do it every morning. The COs follow up on visitors when I'm not here. It's their job to keep track of who's still in the building after hours. One of them probably made sure she signed out."

"Any chance we can get a copy of that?"

She hesitated. "I wouldn't be comfortable turning over any records we have without the warden aware of it. I think it would be best if you waited for him," she said, swallowing.

Ben took a deep breath and nodded, not wanting to push the young girl who was clearly in a difficult position. They thanked her and turned to leave. Once they rounded out of sight, Ben gently grabbed Maeve's elbow, bringing her in the opposite direction of the exit and lowering his voice.

"I think this could work in our favor. Assuming the warden isn't here at all, we can see if we can get a few more people to chat," he said, giving her a wink.

He led them to the west wing and made his way toward cell 412. Kristina Remino was sitting at her desk in the corner of the room, using a pen to fill in her tattoo of a phoenix on her left forearm. She looked up and leaned back in the chair, moving to flick the pen back and forth on her thigh. Her hair looked freshly washed, a shade so dark it looked violet under the fluorescents. Maeve noticed her heavy liner and similarly colored nails bitten down to stubs. Ben introduced them before diving in.

"Kristina, I'm sorry to drop by again. I know how much you love talking to me..." he deadpanned, giving her a sarcastic smile and sitting on the lower bunk across from her. She began picking at her cuticles.

"What do you want this time, pig?"

"There's just a couple more loose ends I need help figuring out about Amanda."

She stopped picking, her gaze darting between the two of them. She dropped her head back against the concrete wall and gave a small wave of acceptance.

"The night she was found hanging in this cell, I know you weren't there, but did you hear anything?"

"No. Like I told you, one of those fuckin' guards hit me in the head for talking back and I was in the infirmary getting stitches. It's way on the other side of the other wing. I was nowhere near here," she paused. "They wanted me to stay there overnight for observation. Something about a head injury," she said, pointing to a faint white scar above her left eyebrow. Her eyes shifted to the female CO pacing slowly in the common area.

"The CO hit you?"

She nodded, shrugging her shoulders. "Don't act so surprised, detective. Happens all the time in here. Warden runs a tight ship."

Ben looked over at Maeve with concern before he turned his attention back to Kristina. "So how was she first found? I would assume the others would notice this happening."

"The other bitches in here saw it as soon as they turned the lights on that morning. I heard them all screaming all the way from the other end. I tried to get up to go see what was going on, but I was handcuffed to the cot. Nanna T told me later what happened. I hadn't seen Mandy for three months, and then just like that, she killed herself," she said, running her hands up and down her thighs. "Honestly pig, it's not that big a deal. Mandy isn't the first to off herself and she won't be the last. You fuck up in here, you go to the shoe. That's just how it is."

Ben scowled in response, looking at Maeve as they both watched Kristina's demeanor shift. She stiffened, her eyes moving to something behind Maeve in the doorway. Kristina immediately looked down, turning herself back toward her desk and picking her pen back up.

Maeve felt the hair on her arms rise and a familiar tingle on the back of her neck as she turned to see what Ben was already looking at. The female guard that Kristina had gestured to was standing directly in the entrance to the cell, not two feet from her. She was unnervingly tall, at least six feet. An obvious brute of a woman. Her brown hair was pulled back in a tight pony that barely touched her upper back, and her dark eyes were fixed on Kristina.

"What's going on here, Tina?" she asked, hand moving to her nightstick. Kristina stopped scribbling but shrugged her shoulders in response, refusing to turn around. Bobbie, as Maeve saw on her name tag, panned slowly from Ben to Maeve, raising an eyebrow into her peaked cap. Ben stood, holding up his badge as Maeve followed suit with her own pinned on her hip. Bobbie simply nodded, walking out toward the common area. She turned back around, waiting for them to follow.

"Did you make an appointment to talk to our inmates today? Was this approved by the warden? Cause' if so, I wasn't told," she said, dropping her hands onto her black leather belt.

"No. We tried to get in to see him, but it seems he's not here. We've been trying to come back here for quite some time to conduct our investigation, but we can't track him down. Any ideas?"

Turning the tables on her. Brilliant man.

Bobbie stood only an inch or two below Ben and her bust was almost touching his chest as she stepped forward. "Maybe you should wait until you get clearance then next time before sneaking around the halls without permission."

"With all due respect ma'am, we're homicide detectives, and a homicide victim was found on this property. We have every right to be here. With or without the warden," he fired back, stepping even closer to her.

Bobbie stared at him for some time before realizing she didn't have a leg to stand on and finally stepped back. Ben gestured for Maeve to go first as he fell into step close behind, keeping his mouth shut on their way out.

Once back at his car, Maeve spoke up. "So that was actually somewhat helpful. I don't, however, like that no one saw Amanda in the hours before her death, and I don't like what Kristina said about the treatment here. That's messed up. Even for a prison."

Ben had lit a cigarette and was taking a long drag, blowing it out away from her direction. "Yeah, there's a lot I'm concerned about after that. I wonder if the staff are aware when the warden isn't on site. I wonder if that's why Kristina was more forthcoming this time. Either way, we need to get into the prison files and access a copy of that visitor log. We need to see dates and if there's some sort of pattern here. There's no way the warden is going to let us have access on our own, and I don't trust anyone not to alter things. I don't trust that someone hasn't already. Lara found something, I know it."

He took another long drag, shifting his weight and letting his frustration flow back onto Maeve. The sun was hostile, its unrelenting heat dulling her senses.

"God, I hope not. I think this has to be one of those airtight data systems that tracks those kinds of changes. They couldn't very well just have people adjusting dates and crimes. They'd know about it. It's like electronic medical records and systems. There are flags when people access files they shouldn't. There's foolproof tracking and monitoring going on all the time. This is our justice system for god's sake. I'd hope it would be similar. I'd hope there would be some accountability."

Ben looked at her for a long moment, contemplating the accuracy of her statement before finishing his cigarette and dropping it on the pavement, squishing it with his shoe and sliding into his car.

"You could be right, kid. Let's go with it."

. . .

They sat in Ben's car in the parking lot as he passed Maeve Lara's autopsy report to read out loud. The sun was still gracing them with a warmer than usual spring day and Maeve's mood had shifted for the better. Turns out she just needed to eat.

"1.1 Ligature marks on wrists and ankles – deduction: consistent with use of restraints for an extended period of time.
1.2 Trauma to the vaginal and anal cavities – deduction: repeated sexual assault for an extended period of time.
1.3 Contusions to the temporal area of the brain – deduction: potential cause of death, blunt force trauma.
1.4 Severe trauma noted to the anterior tracheal region in the form of petechiae and deep tissue injury consistent with strangulation and asphyxiation. Noted consistencies within the trachea itself. Trauma markings are noted to be linear in nature, 1 inch in width and encompassing the entire circumference of the neck – deduction: potential

cause of death, likely made with some sort of rope or linen as no markings were left on the skin from the instrument used.

1.5 Lacerations present: posterior upper right arm, lateral aspect of right mandible, and inner portion of right thigh – deduction: repeated physical assault, unknown cause.

1.6 Bite marks on the outer aspect of breast tissue bilaterally and gluteal area bilaterally, approximately 8–10 separate marks – deduction: consistent with a bite from human origin, all incisors and molars present.

1.7 Bilateral conjunctival hemorrhage – deduction: hypoxia or strangulation, potential cause of death.

1.8 Third phalanx missing from right foot, severe trauma noted to the area – deduction: consistent with forced removal."

CHAPTER SEVENTEEN

Maeve's insides once again became unsettled as she read to her partner, pausing to glance up at him. He had removed his aviators and all the color had drained from his face.

"Ben, there are still two full pages left," she said quietly. His eyes searched hers. "Are they important?"

Maeve scanned them quickly, deciphering the likely conclusions from the report. They were helpful in making a case at trial, but the additional details didn't directly impact their ability to solve the case.

It was gruesome.

The report encompassed every detail of the treatment Lara endured in her time held captive. It was thorough and detailed. An unnecessary torture to share.

"No, it's just more details about her injuries. It's not necessary to go over in detail, in my opinion. I'll take a closer look later just to be sure. The gist is that Lara was tortured and raped for an extended period of time," she said, as she tossed the report on the dash and took her hair out of the bun. She had the beginnings of a headache. Ben shook his head back and forth. "Fuck. I hope all that didn't happen to her the entire time she was missing," he sighed and ran a hand over his head, muscles flexing in his arm. "The only upside to having something like this come out is that the people that live here may be more vigilant. They may be more likely to come forward with a lead. The press won't release all the details, but it'll be enough to scare everyone."

She nodded and changed the subject.

"Hey, whatever happened with Jason's hunting friends. Everything checked out again?" she asked in an attempt to distract the rage-fueled detective before her.

"Yeah. Alex and Ganesh. They said the same thing he did. They all left after work for the hunting cabin, Jason was there the whole weekend. No suspicious day trips back to GP, then they all left on the Sunday. Despite how much I hate that dickwad, his alibi actually seems legit. It's not airtight by any means, but Ganesh is a nice dude, and I trust him. He's a realtor and he's worked with some people I know. He's a good guy. Honestly I'm not sure why he's friends with someone like Jason."

She leaned back, crossing her arms. "Speaking of...what happened after that night?"

He let out an exhale, the side of his mouth tipping up.

"Chief got a couple calls from a few of the customers complaining about my professionalism, but Ty, the bartender there that night, had my back. He told Briggs that Jason instigated it, and I didn't actually do anything to him really. I dragged him outside and then scared him a little," he said, shrugging his shoulders.

"Before nearly choking him out against a wall and kicking him on the pavement?" she deadpanned.

He let out a burst of a laugh and Maeve was powerless to stop herself from joining in.

"So, you didn't get in shit?"

"Nah, not really. Liam also put in a good word, believe it or not. He had my back when he said Jason started it. Chief yelled and threatened some code of conduct bullshit, but he was just as furious when he found out what Jason had said to you. You should've seen him. I thought he was going to have a coronary. I do have to apologize to Jason though...horseshit," he said, muttering the last word under his breath.

"I wish I could've been there. I would've loved to see you get yelled at," Maeve said, grinning. "But Ben, don't ever do that again. I can handle myself. I mean, I appreciate it, you standing up for me, but it makes me look incompetent. If I was a random damsel in distress maybe, but I'm your equal. And I'm also a cop."

He looked at her quietly for a long moment. "Fair enough. I respect that. I'm sorry I made you feel that way…I just…I get a bit protective over the people I care about. I can't help it. It's not just who I am, it's also what I was trained for. But that's no excuse, I know you can handle yourself Maeve. I just think you shouldn't have to."

Her eyes glazed over at his words, threatening to sabotage her self-restraint.

"That's fair. Thanks for saying that Ben, I appreciate it. It's nice to know I have someone in my corner. Especially when I don't really have anyone else."

. . .

The dull light of the morning made its way into her room and Maeve grabbed her phone to see a Hey, can we talk? text from Liam.

She immediately laid back down, her head hitting the pillow with force. She tossed her phone onto the bed and looked at the clock. It was only seven in the morning, and she was still exhausted from the previous nights' events. She'd taken home Amanda's autopsy report and turned to where it was now resting on her bedside table.

1. Overall observation: Patient is noted to be a female approximately late 20s to early 30s, blonde hair, blue eyes, 5'8" tall, 130 pounds, skin intact, extreme trauma noted to the anterior portion of the trachea.
1.1 Bilateral conjunctival hemorrhage – deduction: extreme hypoxia due to strangulation.
1.2 Significant petechial hemorrhage and deep tissue injury to the anterior portion of the neck.

1.3 Exterior lining of the trachea shows signs of complete collapse – deduction: extreme hypoxia as a result of trauma to the tracheal region, likely cause of death.
1.3.1 Note: Patient found hanging from the roof by bed linens. Above Nottage is consistent with same.

Maeve couldn't shake the feeling they were focusing on the wrong details and diverting attention away from facts that may be more indicative of what happened.

People see what they want to see. Especially when they're desperate. It had been part of the reason Ben had brought Maeve onto the case. Fresh eyes, fresh perspective. She forced herself to think objectively about the facts.

There was no way it was a crime of opportunity. It was too personal, too meticulous. She was targeted. If she was taken by a random stranger, why would the stranger have chosen her? How would they have found her? Why would they have buried her near the prison? And if she was going with the stranger line of thinking, then it was likely the killer had done this to women before.

Had a system. A pattern.

There hadn't, however, been any other homicides in the area consistent with her manner of death, and it was too well executed for it to be someone's first try. There would've been signs of a struggle. It would've been sloppy.

If the killer wasn't a stranger, and they'd just been trying to keep her quiet about the Amanda Brinks case, then why keep her captive for an extended period of time? Why hold her and abuse her? Why not dispose of her and be done with it? Why embalm her at all? Why preserve the evidence of their crime? Why toss Amanda out to be found if they were trying to bury evidence in the first place?

There were too many contradictions. Too many whys.

Lara was put in a ten-thousand-dollar coffin, dressed in a child's dress, and embalmed enough to resemble Annabelle. Taking into consideration that Lara had been sexually abused by a male at some point, didn't necessarily mean women could be ruled out either. There was also a chance the killer didn't work alone. There were plenty of cases where the crime was orchestrated by a female lead for ulterior motives.

Maeve tried to focus on simple statistics. In cases such as Lara's, the victim was usually taken and killed by someone they knew. Or hired by someone they knew. Someone they trusted. If she took what she learned in school and applied it, if she trusted her gut and made an informed decision based on the facts, it was the most logical deduction.

She thought about Lara's friends and family and felt her pulse rise in response. There was a slight chance Lara had had a secret relationship with someone no one knew about behind Marc's back, but there was a higher chance that Maeve had already interacted with Lara's killer without knowing it.

The discovery of her remains found on prison land meant that there was a high probability she didn't leave the prison at all that night. It didn't make logical sense for her to drive away, then be kidnapped and killed, only to be placed back at the prison. Unless it was purposeful. Clues meant to divert attention toward a logical scenario instead of the truth. It could go either way.

Her mind raced and she sent a reluctant text to Liam telling him that things were busy and she would be in touch when she had some time. She was blowing him off, but she didn't care. She needed to get a handle on her job, and fooling around with the victim's brother was out of the question.

Well, technically, fooling around again was out of the question.

A press conference was scheduled for later that afternoon and although Briggs agreed to take the lead, she was still nervous. Being the center of attention wasn't her thing.

Her phone made an incoming text sound and she groaned. She prepared herself for a snide response from Liam but was relieved to find Ben's name on the screen. Sliding the message open she read that the warrant for the prison had come through. Finally. They'd been waiting an unusually long amount of time to get the clearance.

Taking a steadying breath, she crawled out of bed and grabbed the only formal wear she owned, a burnt orange colored pant suit. She tossed on a simple black v neck underneath and emptied half a bottle of dry shampoo into her hair. After she'd curled it and put on some light makeup, she finished the look with her go-to gold hoop earrings.

She looked at her work in the mirror as she tilted her head to the left and fidgeted with her blazer before muttering a good enough. She bounded down the stairs, clipping her badge onto its usual place near her hip.

She heard the sound of Ben's car outside and made her way out the front door, tripping on her lone flowerpot and letting out a swift curse. She slid into Ben's passenger seat and the heated leather instantly warmed her. Ben handed her a to-go cup from Shelley's, grinning.

"What?" she half yelled at him, flustered.

"I noticed your flowerpot got in the way of your foot. I could read the foul language coming out of your mouth from here," he finished, laughing and shifting into reverse. She looked at him, scowling.

"I bought it in the hopes of making the place more welcoming but all it does is get in the way," she said leaning back against the seat. "I didn't have time to make any coffee this morning," she said, lifting her cup. "Thank you."

He gave her a wink in return and floored it out of her neighborhood. "Listen, I've been thinking about it, and it seems unrealistic that she was taken somewhere else, abused, killed, embalmed, and buried at Umbele."

Ben nodded. "Yeah, I've been thinking the same thing. I mean, if someone had her and did all this to her, killed her, embalmed her, why would they randomly choose Umbele Cemetery to dig up Amanda's coffin and put her there. But we also have video evidence that she left. It also wouldn't make sense that she was there the whole time. If she came back, it would have been captured. There's just no pattern, no matter what way you look at it."

"Unless she came back through different means."

"Different means? As in, hogtied in someone's trunk?"

Maeve nodded. "Yeah, it would immediately take suspicion off the prison. We know there was a connection between Lara and Amanda. She was investigating her death and then went missing, so someone doesn't want her to find out the real story behind her death and gets rid of her. The problem is, it's incredibly intentional to dig someone up and use their coffin for someone else. Way too much effort for it not to be. Lara was important, cherished. She deserved the coffin. She deserved to be preserved. It's the significance of it. The symbolism. That doesn't fit the motive of trying to cover up Amanda's death. That's personal. This entire thing is contradictory. I can't get a handle on it."

"You and me both, kid. Still, if she was in the prison the whole time, where and how? How do you just casually embalm someone? Can't exactly just use a maintenance closet." He paused, glancing over at her. "Maybe there are some underground tunnels," he said, raising his eyebrows.

She rolled her eyes.

Twenty minutes later they beelined it directly to Spencer's desk. As usual, the young girl jumped in surprise as they exited the hallway and came through her doorway.

"Detectives! I didn't know you were coming this morning..." she quipped, frantically re-arranging the papers on her desk. Ben lifted a paper up in front of her.

"Spencer, we have a warrant to search the premises, including the electronic files. We need to see the warden right away."

Spencer stared at him before she hastily got up and waltzed over to the warden's office. She knocked abruptly.

"Sir, the police are here again. They have a warrant," she said, eyeing Maeve intently as they all stood waiting. Spencer, visibly eager to be out of the tense situation, lifted her hand to knock with significantly more force.

The door finally swung open.

Warden Gary Managan stood inside, his arm half raised in welcome but his face remained neutral. Spencer avoided eye contact and silently returned to her desk.

Everything in the warden's office was, as usual, impeccably tidy and in its rightful place. Gary, by contrast, looked unkempt. He was wearing his usual three-piece gray suit and leather dress shoes, but his dress shirt was slightly untucked and there was a few days' worth of stubble on his face. He looked exhausted.

The detectives politely declined to take the seats that the warden had gestured to and instead handed him the warrant. Ben informed him they were going to be conducting a search and seizure, and there were no signs of surprise or distress. He simply nodded in compliance.

"I understand, detective. Let me know what my officers or I can do to help. I'll need to let the inmates know as soon as possible, as I'm assuming you'll be looking in their cells as well?"

Ben nodded and returned his thanks. Maeve seized the moment and asked the warden if he could login to the system hard drive. He nodded and strode behind his desk, leaning forward to type in his password before gesturing for her to proceed.

"Electronic files in the Umbele database are on the desktop, and there are duplicated paper copies in this filing cabinet behind me. They should be directly identical. If not, it would likely be an inputting error. Feel free to look through both. The search function works best when you input last name and then first, and the records go back about twenty years or so. Anything prior to that would be in storage in the basement," he explained, moving toward his open door. "I'm going to speak to the inmates, give them a heads up. When will your officers be arriving?"

Ben inched closer to him. "Gary, I hope you understand that I'll need to come with you. I can't exactly have you wandering about, potentially removing evidence as you go. Briggs has organized it so that the rest of our team will be here within the hour, but, as you said, we should warn the women first. Detective Kalani will stay here."

Maeve wasn't sure what she was looking for, she'd know it once she saw it. She clicked on the search bar and typed Brinks, Amanda. The blue circle of death appeared for a few minutes before it finally loaded. Maeve hit the control print keys and while she waited for all fifteen pages to print, she searched in the filing cabinet for the hard copies. She located the same file the warden had shown them previously and tossed it on the desk before rummaging through the rest.

The day dragged on and Maeve, Ben and various officers from Grants Pass and Medford Police Departments made headway with their search and seizure. Maeve had remained focused on the electronic files with the tech crew, and Ben and the warden were lurking in the gen pop common area of the west wing trying to keep the peace. Briggs had joined them and become command central, barking orders and giving direction.

The search was throwing the inmates off their routine, something that never went over well in prison. It was a delicately placed card tower, one shift in position and the whole thing would crumble. As expected, the women were pissed off that members of law enforcement were snooping in amongst their possessions. Possessions that may or may not be all that legal or easily obtained.

All in all, the warden had been surprisingly calm, understanding, and helpful. It had unnerved her partner all day.

Just after lunch Maeve checked her phone. Cursing, she headed out of the warden's office. Spencer reached out to grab her arm on her way by.

"Detective, I got the visitor log you wanted," she said quietly, handing Maeve a white binder as she looked around. Maeve eyed her trying to read something in Spencer's eyes before accepting it with thanks. She didn't have much time but briefly opened it, flipping to the date in question. Sure enough, there was a log in and log out signed by Lara in the same color ink. Maeve glanced through some of the previous pages of scribbled ink and noticed an odd sense of familiarity but couldn't quite place it. Her mind was in too many places at once.

Glancing at her watch she cursed, moving into a jog as she made her way down the hall to the east wing. They had twenty minutes until the press conference started in Grants Pass and it was a thirty-minute drive. She found her partner chatting with the warden and a few other inmates. She lingered quietly, not wanting to drag him away from an important conversation. Ben, sensing her there, glanced up and cocked an eyebrow. She tapped her finger to her wrist and tossed a thumb over her shoulder.

Luckily, her partner excelled at pushing speed limits and lived up to the challenge as they pulled into the parking lot at the station with two minutes to spare. She slid out of the car as Ben walked around to hold her door open.

"What are you doing? This isn't prom," she said, scrunching up her face as she looked around.

"Why am I not surprised you take a kind, gentlemanly gesture as an insult," he said as he leaned in closer, moving a strong hand to her lower back. "Before the day got away from me, I just wanted to tell you that you look really nice today. I figured you wouldn't want me saying it in front of our whole department," he reasoned, stepping away all too soon and taking his comforting presence with him. She cleared her throat, adjusting her sunglasses as she followed behind him.

God, she was such a bitch sometimes.

Members of the press were hovering like eager vultures as they formed a semicircle at the front of the building. Briggs was at the center of it, standing awkwardly behind a wooden podium. The detectives slid casually in behind the chief and moved off to his left. He turned to them, tossing them a disappointed look and adjusting his navy-blue tie. He looked dapper in his official blue uniform but, as usual, he was sweating profusely and the buttons over his stomach were holding on for dear life.

Only after she'd settled slightly and Briggs had begun speaking, did she allow her gaze to travel over the crowd. She jolted as familiar intense blue eyes caught her attention.

CHAPTER EIGHTEEN

Liam was standing casually with his hands in his structured wool jacket, his red hair tidy and styled back. Without warning, the image of her weaving her fingers through the soft, messy strands forced its way into her mind and her cheeks warmed. She turned away quickly but not before she saw his all consuming eyes sweep over her with hunger.

After Briggs had successfully communicated the details of the case without giving out too much information, he gestured for Liam and Lydia to join him on his right side. Maeve stepped as far away as she could, but she was still off balance by the scent of him so near her. Ben kept looking over at her, sensing her discomfort but she successfully avoided his gaze.

Next, Briggs ushered Jack and Judy Brinks up and allowed them to say their peace about Amanda. Although the connection was still unclear, it was known that there was a link in their deaths. It was only fair that both families were involved.

Once they finished up and Briggs had answered enough questions to be able to end the conference, Ben opened the door to the precinct and escorted friends and family of the victims inside.

Over the course of the afternoon, both of the detectives had tried to escape to make it back to the prison. They desperately wanted to get away from small talk and pastries, but Briggs had forced them to stay. They were the faces of the investigation.

Jack Brinks had been, to put it bluntly, an arrogant asshole most of the afternoon. He rambled on and on about the negative image that had been portrayed about Amanda and the positive one that had been laid out for Lara. Judy just sat like a china doll on the edge of her seat looking uncomfortable and out of place as he spoke, casually adjusting the white tassel on her Louis Vuitton and sipping her tea.

Lydia hadn't stayed long, her and Ray citing work that needed to be done at the farm. Liam had intermittently cast Maeve some glances, but she'd been successful in avoiding him most of the afternoon.

She was leaning against the white board holding a large mug of coffee in comfort as she made small talk with Brian and Wyatt and a few other officers from the 59th precinct.

"Detective Kalani, have you been avoiding me?" Liam asked from beside her, mischief in his voice.

She lifted her eyes reluctantly to the man that had appeared out of thin air. His hair was a bit messier than it had been earlier and he was sporting a black collared shirt with the sleeves rolled up. He was intense, holding her eyes and his coffee in a tight grip as the corner of his mouth lifted. She gave him a polite smile and responded in what she hoped was a casual tone.

"Liam, hey. Good to see you. No, I'm not avoiding you, I just wanted to give you space during this difficult time," she said, rocking back and forth on her feet, glancing at her colleagues. Ben looked at her from across the room.

Brian and Wyatt muttered their condolences, but Liam didn't take his eyes off hers as he thanked them. She was about to excuse herself, but Briggs stepped in and interrupted the small group, requesting she join him in making rounds. She looked to the spot Ben had been standing to find it empty. Little weasel.

After the precinct emptied out, she wandered around to find her partner holed up in his office casually scrolling on his phone. She gave him a what the hell gesture and he chuckled, murmuring a piss poor apology for ditching her. He put his phone on speaker and called the team at Umbele.

"Listen, can you just bring a copy of that hard drive back to the station and ask Beatta to help sort it? We'll be in this weekend at some point to go through it all. Go ahead and send everyone home for the day, it's been a long one."

He ended the call, standing and putting his jacket back on before tossing an arm around her shoulders.

"Why would I schmooze when you're obviously so much better at it and significantly better looking" he teased, jostling her playfully. She shoved him off and they grabbed their things, making a hasty exit.

• • •

"Hey, it's me. Listen, I have something I want to talk to you about, can I stop by?" Ben asked over the phone, his voice eager and energetic.

She leaned back on the couch, absentmindedly playing with a kernel of popcorn.

"Ugh, can't it wait? It's Friday night and I need some alone time. We spent all day together."

He held silence on the line as she tilted her head up to the ceiling. She was lying to herself if she thought she wasn't going to keep working on her own anyway. "Fine. Bring wine or I won't let you in."

"You got it."

She had a sneaking suspicion he'd already been on his way, and sure enough, not five minutes later, the man himself was letting himself in through the front door. Which apparently, she'd forgotten to lock. After he finished pestering her about the importance of safety, he poured two glasses of wine and joined her in the living room. Over the past few weeks, he'd been over a number of times, but she didn't realize how comfortable he'd gotten in her place until she watched him move about her house with familiarity and ease.

She still hadn't been to his. Hadn't even received an invite. She wasn't sure of his reluctance, but it unsettled her. He had seen into her private life, why couldn't he extend the same courtesy? He was a closed book.

After they ordered Chinese food from Al's, Ben pulled out a giant stack of files he'd taken from the prison. She took a long sip of the merlot as he set the files in front of them on the coffee table at chest level and they made themselves comfortable on the floor. Maeve put on a trashy reality TV show for background noise and divided up the work.

About two episodes later, Maeve abruptly stood, papers in hand, hair falling around her face. "SHIT! Shit, shit, shit, shit, shit. Ben, look at this!"

He stood to his full height, towering behind her as he leaned down to read what was in her hand. Maeve was momentarily caught off guard as she found herself noticing how good he smelled. The usual perfect mix of smoky and citrus. Like a walking old-fashioned.

"I was just looking through the files of each of the women associated with the case and I found this," she said, pointing to a line on the page. "Dakota Patrieko, sentenced to ten years for assault with a deadly weapon and multiple parole violations. She was sentenced in 2014, which was five years ago, and the date here says she is due to be released next year. On good behavior."

"How the fuck would she get out five years early for good behavior?! Especially seeing as she just provoked a fight severe enough to land someone in solitary. That makes no fucking sense."

"Something is wrong. Even if the warden had something to do with this, it'd still be impossible for a warden to convince a judge of something that profound," he said, grabbing his glass and draining it in one motion. "Unless there was some shady shit going on. Blackmail...extortion... bribery."

"You're right. Something with this prison just doesn't add up. The cases intertwined like this, both bodies found there, and now this," she replied, holding up the papers.

He looked at her, sly grin appearing across his masculine face.

"What? Why are you looking at me like that?" she asked, scowling at him.

"You said I was right. I've never heard those words come out of your mouth before," he said, his eyes swirling with satisfaction.

"Don't get used to it," she said, swatting him over the head with the papers before sliding back into the spot next to him on the floor. He feigned injury, rubbing his buzzed head dramatically.

They spent another thirty minutes sifting through the prison records, collecting data. Ben sat forward.

"Maeve, there's a pattern. There's a history of women either being let out early for good behavior or dying prematurely. I'd have to do a data comparison just to be sure, but that seems highly unusual for a minimum-security prison with such a small inmate population. I'd like to take this back to the station and cross reference it with any police files around the same time. If we can find one of these women who was let out early, maybe we can talk to them. I know for damn sure Dakota isn't going to have a nice friendly chat about why she's getting out. She wouldn't want to risk messing it up."

"Ho-ly shit. That's why Lara kept going. I bet she figured it out. Maybe she wasn't just investigating Amanda's death, maybe she was investigating all of them. This is motive, Ben. The warden is looking more and more guilty by the second. Even if he isn't involved, there's no way he doesn't know about what's going on."

"To get away with altering records, signing off on early releases, covering up deaths…it would need to be someone extremely well connected or high up. What I don't get is the reason behind it. I mean, why bend the rules to let these women out early, what does this person get out of it? It doesn't make sense. I think you're right. This has Lara written all over it. Of course she took this on." He pulled out the visitor log binder, scanning it.

"There's a line each for sign-in, sign-out, and then one for validated, which I assume is where Spencer or the COs sign as witness. Lara signed in at 16:41 that night and signed out at 19:48, just like Spencer told us. There are different validation signatures, Spencer's for the sign-in and Bobbie's for the sign out that night. Lara's signature is identical in both, definitely not forged. Or if it was, it was an expert. The video footage showed there were no differences between the woman who entered and the woman who left other than the fact that her hair was up when she went in and down when she left."

"Okay, let's go over this again. We have Lara hired to investigate the death of Amanda Brinks. While looking into the case, she disappears. Then, we find her body a year later. She had a normal day at work, then told everyone she was leaving early to see clients around four. She makes it to Umbele just after five and stays there for a couple hours before she leaves in her car. She's never seen or heard from again. All CCTV footage in GP was analyzed, and her vehicle was not spotted again after that day. She's kidnapped, held captive and killed.

"Then during some landscaping work at the prison, they find Amanda's body in the woods. When we excavate her coffin, we find Lara inside. No one has seen or heard anything fishy at the prison other than the fight between Dakota and Amanda, which of course led to Amanda being in solitary confinement for a few months. However, when she returned to her cell, there were no eyewitnesses that actually saw her come back or hang herself. The first ME report states nothing out of the ordinary with Amanda's death, straight forward suicide. The second time round, the report aligns with the same thing but isn't as conclusive as her body suffered more decomposition over the past year or so."

Maeve paused, running her hands through her hair. Ben watched her quietly.

"Lara's report, on the other hand, shows evidence of extreme mistreatment before her death. The way she was laid to rest indicates the killer or killers likely saw her as a trophy. She was something to be preserved and cared for, which can be indicative of a connection between the killer and the victim. And if her watch truly is missing like Liam mentioned, the theory holds more weight."

Ben murmured quietly. "A possible trophy."

"Now, we see that there is a pattern of missing and dying women at Umbele. Likely conclusion, something fucky is happening there."

Ben nodded along with her summary as she went, and as she finished, he slammed his fist down sideways on the coffee table. "HEAR HEAR!"

She gave him an eye roll and dropped dramatically into the armchair.

"I'm exhausted and you're drunk. You should go. We can go over our next steps tomorrow. God knows we won't get the weekend off."

He gave her a deep chuckle in response before getting up and grabbing his coat. "How much longer is that patrol going to be outside?"

"Not sure. I kind of think it's time they moved on but it's not my call," she replied, cleaning up the glasses. "You're not driving, are you?"

"Hell no. I'm a cop, Maeve. Give me some credit. I'm not that much of an idiot. I texted Marc, he's on his way," he replied, walking toward her front door. He paused, turning to look back at her. His mouth opened briefly before he closed it again, tossing her a cordial wave as he slipped out without another word.

. . .

Way too early on her weekend morning, Maeve received a call from Briggs. "Maeve! Morning darlin', how'd you sleep?"

"Fine, thanks sir. Sorry, did I miss something? Am I late for something?" she asked in a panic.

"No, no, nothing like that. It's not even expected that you work on the weekend, but I'm sure I couldn't stop you if I tried," he said, coughing.

"You're right about that, sir. There's too much going on, no way I can sit still all weekend."

"Right, well I thought you could meet me for lunch. I need an update on the case and Ben said he isn't feeling up to it. He sounded legitimately unwell, so I didn't want to push it."

She cleared her throat. "Okay. Tell me when and where and I'll be there," she replied, getting out of bed.

Half an hour later, Maeve pulled into the lot of a winery just outside of Wilderville, southwest of town. She noticed the chief in a cozy spot near the back corner of the tasting room, and he gestured to her aggressively.

The winery was not busy by any means, but there were a few couples and groups scattered throughout the aesthetic room. It was a tasteful establishment for a tiny little place in rural Oregon. Healthy ferns and vines were hanging from the exposed roof, white lights strung about, and velvet couches placed eclectically around the room.

She sat down across from Briggs. He was dressed in jeans and a worn-down cotton shirt, the image unnerving. It was like running into a teacher at the grocery store as a kid when you forgot they were real people too.

"Maeve, darlin', thanks for meeting me here. Sorry it was a bit of a drive, hope it wasn't too bad?"

"No, not at all," she replied, shrugging off her jacket.

They made meaningless small talk, Briggs asking about her family and how she was settling in before she eventually steered the direction of the conversation back to the case. She'd ordered herself the mimosa special after Briggs insisted it was the weekend and she could have whatever she wanted, and he'd ordered himself a beer.

At first, she was put off by the fact that the chief had invited her to a winery out of town only to order a beer, but then he'd ordered the oysters and the mystery was solved. He spent the subsequent ten minutes detailing why they were the best in the state in vivid, unwanted detail. She'd updated him on the case as he'd noisily slurped the moist, garlic-covered mollusks, and somehow, she'd miraculously managed to keep her gag reflex from kicking in. She hated oysters as it was, and watching him use his hands to devour the unsavory dish had been the ultimate test of self-control. He'd remained quiet as she spoke, only nodding his head occasionally between bites. After she finished, she asked if he had any questions.

"Just one. What do you think is going on?" he asked, dabbing his chins and leaning back in the strained chair.

She hesitated, sipping on her drink and looking out past him to the tangled vineyard. A hummingbird drinking from a red feeder attached to the window caught her attention for a moment before she re-focused back on the chief. He was watching her, waiting for an answer.

"I have some thoughts, but I can't be sure. There are too many coincidences, and I think that's the solution rather than the problem. It definitely has something to do with Umbele, but we need to go back into police records to see what happened with some of these women. If there's a pattern, we could be looking at a serial. That being said, I don't want to jump to conclusions just yet. Ben and I need to rule some things out first."

Briggs shifted in his chair, causing a sharp noise to emerge from the frame. "A serial hey? Here in Grants Pass? Could you imagine. Good god I hope not. The last thing we need is the FBI coming in and taking over."

Her eyebrows lifted as she realized he was right. If it was confirmed to be a pattern, the investigation would be taken from them without a second thought. She became antsy as she thought about the work that lay ahead and told the chief that she needed to get back.

"Thanks for meeting me here darlin', I had a craving and I knew you'd like it out here. It's one of my favorite places but I don't get to make it out here too often. Anyway, good luck today and let me know what else you find. I'll see you on Monday," he said, walking over to his blue truck.

Maeve returned to her Mazda, sifting through her purse trying to find her cell phone. Ben had texted her while she'd been with Briggs, and she sent him a quick reply.

As her eyes lifted her pulse followed. A white envelope sat under her wiper. She got out of the car and grabbed it, hovering as she ripped it open.

DON'T TRUST ANYONE

CHAPTER NINETEEN

Maeve quickly scanned the parking lot, her hand resting on the empty space where her holster usually rested. A few cars were scattered about and even fewer people were around. The only person she could see was a short man leaning against his car casually, talking on the phone. She stepped closer to try and get a view of him and he looked at her and frowned. Whoever left her the note was long gone.

The wind picked up as she dropped into her car and locked the doors. The paranoia was crawling under her skin and up her arms, a sentient being coming to rest inside of her. No one else knew she was here. Someone had been following her, and she hadn't had the patrol car with her. She'd been going to meet with the chief, it wasn't necessary. The writing and the ink were the same as her first threatening letter.

She held the steering wheel and tipped her head back against the seat, closing her eyes. It took the entire drive back to town for her nerves to settle.

She made it to the precinct by mid-afternoon and the warmth of the day had settled comfortably in Grants Pass, bleaching out the fear that had latched itself around her neck. She could still smell the dampness from the previous weeks, but the heat of the day had brought about an obvious shift in energy. Spring had always been her favorite; the promise of warmer weather and extended daylight. The anticipation of long walks and day drinking. It was like an awakening.

The halls of the precinct were dark and it felt odd to not be greeted by Beatta as Maeve walked in. Although it was a Saturday, she still expected at least one person to be there. They were working on a high-level murder investigation; the entire department should be working extended hours. At the very least, officers working the weekend shift should be in and out. It was unsettling.

After dropping her stuff in her office, she booted up her computer and opened her blinds before setting off to find her partner. She rounded the corner into his office and found him seated in his old brown leather chair, hunched over his desk with a pen between his fingers. He had a deep-set frown across his unshaven face and looked up when he sensed her there, stiffening and giving her a quick once over. He offered her a timid smile and gestured to the chair across from the desk. His response was contradictory to his usual self-assured demeanor, and it put her off slightly. He looked uncertain, off kilter.

"Hey, how was your relaxing morning at home?" he asked, intertwining his fingers on his desk.

She was unsure about the intent behind the question but answered anyway.

"It was only relaxing for a few hours until I had to go give Briggs an update on the case. That's where I just came from, I thought you knew that? Otherwise, I'd have come straight here so we could get started."

He looked genuinely confused.

"What? You didn't think that inviting me along would be the decent thing to do. Seeing as we're partners?"

She was dumbfounded. "Ben, Briggs said he texted you and that you were sick. I assumed you were hungover."

His eyebrows pulled together. He grabbed his phone from the desk and scanned it. "I didn't get a call or text from him at all today. What the fuck is he playing at? Is he pissed at me or something?"

She leaned back in the chair, crossing her legs.

"Maybe he just wanted my unbiased perspective. He was also a bit chatty, so maybe it was just him trying to get to know me. I mean, we haven't really interacted much since I started, so maybe he just felt bad...I don't know. Anyway, it doesn't matter, I have to tell you something."

She showed him the note she found on her car.

"This is what happens when you go somewhere without me," he said, looking at her for a long moment before taking an audible breath. Maeve spent the next few minutes calming him down and re-directing him back into the headspace of an investigator.

"I'll tell the chief about it. I have to call him anyway," he said, standing abruptly and leaving the room.

Maeve dropped the note into an evidence bag and met him back in his office. Tension took hold of the room. She couldn't help but feel like it was somehow her fault. He lifted his eyes to hers and she cleared her throat, dropping hers in a poor attempt to make it look like she hadn't been looking at him.

"I've been going through some of our old cases to see if there are any reports that align with the dates we found last night, and I found something. I've been waiting to show you," he said, leaning forward and turning the monitor toward her.

She stood, leaning over the desk.

"Two women are listed in the prison records that were released early for good behavior. I went to look them up to see if I could find their contact info and maybe give them a call, but then I found this," he said, pointing.

She squinted, on the line across from the name Jordyn Cunningham was a missing person notice.

"Wait, so she was released and then reported missing...three days later?"

Ben nodded his head. "Not just that. I found two others. Anne Barder and Mikaela Rokanier. Same exact thing. Released from Umbele and then reported missing several days to weeks later."

"What the fuck."

"My thoughts exactly."

"Which case dates back the longest?" she asked rounding the desk to hover behind him, strands of her hair briefly falling onto his arm.

He cleared his throat. "Jordyn Cunningham. She has a weird file. I was trying to find out what she was charged with, but it's all very vague and a lot of details are missing. I mean, it was almost ten years ago, but still. She worked at the Super 8 in town and had no priors. I read through the very limited investigation notes, and it looks like her friends and family said she was always quiet and withdrawn. It was highly unusual for her to end up in that kind of situation. She'd been a straight A student, and she'd been taking fine arts classes at the community college when she'd been arrested." He paused, leaning back to look at her. "The officer's notes say that it was disorderly conduct, assault of an officer, and resisting arrest. Problem is, the evidence tab is lacking and there's no other statements. All it says is that an officer was called to respond to an incident at the hotel she worked at," he quieted, leaning up to look at her. "Maybe she was drunk and went off the handle. Maybe she got into a fight or something and then when an officer got involved, she got violent. Who knows. She was sentenced to five years and transferred to Umbele."

He pointed at the monitor again. "After that, I looked into her records from the prison. Jordyn Cunningham, age 24, stayed at Umbele for two and a half years before she died. Suicide. She sliced both her wrists using shards from her glasses."

"So that's our second suspicious suicide."

Ben leaned back in his chair, crossing his arms and forcing a rusty squeak from the springs. "And as the final damning piece of circumstantial evidence I'd like to share; nothing like this is recorded prior to Gary Managan becoming warden. The dates line up with his arrival. Nothing suspicious happened prior to 2009."

"So, we just found our first lead?"

He looked at her and grinned. "You bet your ass we did."

The prison was still swarming with uniforms. At least one team was doing their job today. Maeve met up with Wyatt, the team lead, and he gave her a quick update. Wyatt was a strange character, smart but quirky. The type of kid who walked on his tiptoes in school, mumbling to himself. He didn't fit the cop persona, but Maeve knew better than to stereotype. She noted his crippling OCD the moment they met, his frequent counting and need for cleanliness. He had always been kind to her, but Maeve had the sense that there was more to him than what he let people see. She couldn't quite decide if it was innocent neurodivergence or calculated manipulation that made him hard to read. The differences between the two concepts were endless, but on the surface, there were too many similarities.

The team had completed their thorough search and found nothing out of the ordinary at the prison, but she wasn't disappointed. She knew the answer would be in the records.

She gave the all clear for them to start packing up before making her way to the warden's office to meet up with her partner. She knocked on the door gently before stepping in.

The warden was sitting in one of his two leather lounge chairs, casually sipping on a glass of scotch. He wasn't wearing a full suit, but instead a simple white dress shirt, gray slacks, and a coordinated gray tie. She wondered if he also showered with his tie on.

"Detectives," he said, his voice deep and laced in venom.

"Afternoon Warden, Maeve and I need to talk to you. Can we sit?"

He didn't respond. He gestured openly to the room. Maeve moved to sit in his office chair while Ben pulled up the armchair next to him.

"After looking through the prison database, we noticed some dates that lined up with some police records pertaining to missing women."

The warden cocked his head slightly to the side, taking a long sip from his glass before meeting Ben's gaze. "Oh?"

Maeve's blood heated.

"Do you know anything about that? Jordyn Cunningham was one of them. Also, Anne Barder and Mikaela Rokanier. They were incarcerated here and let out on good behavior. Then they were reported missing right after they were released."

The warden nodded. "Jordyn…I think I remember her. The other two I'm not sure about. I'd have to double check."

"Do you know why they were released early? I mean, I know it was good behavior, but how is that realistic when Anne and Mikaela were in for incredibly violent crimes?" Ben asked, leaning forward. His badge swung loose around his neck. The warden shrugged, polishing off his drink and getting up from the armchair to wander back to the bar cart.

"Sometimes, when an inmate has had no priors and doesn't get herself into trouble here, they're released early. That's all there is to it. It's not my decision, Ben. It's the decision of the criminal justice system."

The last part of the sentence was spoken quieter than the rest, no doubt meant to lead the detectives elsewhere and take the blame off of himself. Luckily, Ben was good at his job.

"Okay, so if that's the case, why is Dakota Patrieko being released early? She definitely didn't demonstrate good behavior, as you call it."

The warden stilled, turning slowly to lean on the wall. He looked at Ben. "I can assume you're referring to the fight?" he said, his demeanor threatening as he walked slowly back to the chair. "Seeing as she was on the receiving end of it, I don't see your point."

"You know exactly my point, Gary. We have a statement saying she instigated the fight, saying things that would surely put any one of us into a frenzy like the one Amanda Brinks experienced. Especially after her history."

"Saying a couple mean things to someone doesn't justify getting beaten to a pulp, detective" the warden replied evenly.

"True. However, it seems out of the ordinary for these two. No prior history of arguments, disagreements or fighting before the incident. No one even saw them speak to each other before what happened in the library. Seems odd that Dakota would know something so intimate about Amanda's life and use it against her in that way...and for what benefit?"

"Seems like you have a lot of questions you need answers to, detective. Not my place to assume what went on between them that day. I don't advocate for adding years of lockup to women who say mean things. Otherwise, this whole place would be empty. Surely you should know that."

Ben stood, putting his hands on his hips as he began to walk slowly around the room. "What about the suicides? Can you speak to those?"

"As you know, I don't agree with such acts. No one should play God. We belong to Him, and it is He who should decide our fate," he said quietly, lifting his sharp eyes to Maeve. "That being said, there has always been a history of suicides in prisons. People are locked up for most of their adult life, and when there's no light at the end of the tunnel, no hope for a future outside the walls, no hope of penance, they'll take any chance they get to take matters into their own hands. To end their suffering."

"Fair enough, but there are at least two separate cases of women who have taken their own lives inside the walls of your prison."

"Two women taking their lives over the course of several years is not abnormal. In fact, I bet those stats are pretty low compared to other institutions."

"It's low for maximum security penitentiaries, not for prisons of this size."

The warden stood tall, squaring up to Ben.

"I've been here for over ten years. I'd say two deaths in ten years isn't all that unreasonable. We do our best here to prevent things like that from happening, but when they're that desperate, they'll always find a way. It's a tragedy. It really is. But until you've spent considerable time locked up for a crime you may or may not have committed, you can't begin to understand what these women have gone through," he said, moving to stand in front of the window that overlooked the cemetery beyond.

"Okay, what about when it happens right before they're due to be released?" Ben pushed, moving to stand between the warden and Maeve.

"What are you talking about?" the warden asked, turning to him. "Jordyn Cunningham, due to be released the year after she killed herself. Amanda Brinks...killed herself mere months before her release."

Maeve still hadn't moved a muscle, not wanting to derail her partner as she quietly took notes. Every one of the questions that had popped into her head had also seemingly popped into Ben's. He knew what he was doing.

"Again, detective, I cannot speak for what Jordyn went through while she was here, but I can guess it would be daunting figuring out how to start your life over in a small town like this after being in lockup. Everyone knew her around here and she assaulted a police officer. People don't react well to that. As for Mandy, my guess is, the idea of living with what she did to that little boy weighed on her. I mean, she damn near killed Dakota over it. Maybe, on a subconscious level, it was her way of keeping herself locked up so she wouldn't have to face what she'd done," he offered, pausing as he adjusted his tie. "Have you ever seen Shawshank Redemption? Not an unreasonable train of thought. I can't speak to what these women went through, Ben."

Ben rounded on him. "Ah, but you did. Multiple times."

・・・

The interview had gone in circles for over an hour, the warden reserved and calculated with his responses. The detectives were determined to find a judge with a link to Gary Managan, but they had yet to find anything. They'd gone through the remaining list of judges presiding on the women's cases before concluding that no two judges had been the same. The judges were from all over the state, and none could be officially connected to anyone in Grants Pass, let alone the warden.

Ben had then taken a gamble and gone back even further in the police records, extending his search past Umbele and Grants Pass. Numerous accounts of missing women were present all throughout the state. Most were young women with little or no family and weren't reported missing until months after it occurred, with no pattern. No link. It didn't dismiss the theory, but it did make it highly unlikely.

The unfortunate truth was that women went missing all the time.

When they compared the numbers with those across the country, they weren't unreasonable. In order for these cases to remain as missing persons, no bodies had been found. Which meant that people assumed the women simply ran off.

When Maeve had done some digging of her own, there'd been no connection to Gary Managan on a personal level either. She'd tried to track down any friends or family he may have had, but was stonewalled every time. The warden was a solitary man with few friends and no family. At least none that could be tracked down. Either their theory went right out the window, or he was really good at covering his tracks. They'd hit a dead end.

The case had been all over the news and the detectives had been avoiding the public all week. Liam and Lydia decided to wait to host Lara's funeral until their aunt, Charlotte Young, could make it from Chico. It had been hovering over Maeve like a shadow. Liam had invited both detectives, and although they'd been desperate to get out of it, Briggs had made it clear they were both expected to attend.

The day finally arrived, and Maeve had swung home at lunch to change into her black dress. Her mind was spinning from the idea of seeing Liam again. She walked to her full-length mirror, tilting her head as she looked at the dress, the silhouette flattering but conservative. It was embellished with sleeves that covered her shoulders a black lace overlay and a hem length that stopped just above her knee. She hadn't worn a dress in years, and it was uncomfortably stiff, reinforcing her negative feelings toward them. She paired it with simple black wedges, knowing she'd be walking in grass, and then pinned her hair up in an artistic twist. She kept her makeup light and applied a nude-pink shade of lip color. Once she was satisfied enough with her appearance, she texted Ben.

Although it was beautiful outside, there was still a slight breeze. Maeve grabbed her long black jacket on her way out and waved over to the ever-present patrol car. Its presence had been extended after the second note.

Ben hadn't gotten out of the car to meet her as he usually did, and instead had his phone pressed up against his ear when she slid into the passenger seat. He stopped speaking to whoever was on the line, dragging his eyes over her before giving her a nod in welcome. He focused back on his conversation and shot back short, one-word answers.

Maeve was flushed, her dress starting to feel constricting. It wasn't just the scrutiny of his gaze; it was also the way he looked in his suit. He'd gone without a tie, but the black dress shirt under his suit made up for the informality. He'd undone the top button, the chain from his dog tags slightly visible, and it had flawlessly wrapped up his look. Luckily, neither of them addressed the unmistakable shift in the car as Ben ended his call.

The service was just beginning as they pulled up. Ben offered his elbow to her as they hurried into the funeral home and squeezed into the back row next to Briggs. Maeve spotted Liam in the front, wedged between Lydia and a small woman she didn't recognize. The woman had a short gray-blonde bob, her arm looped through Liam's as she leaned on his shoulder. Maeve turned to see Ben focused on the same thing before looking back at her, and they exchanged a silent agreement. The woman had to be Charlotte Young; the aunt who helped raise them after they were orphaned. They'd need to speak with her before she left town again.

They sat quietly through the service, both attempting to sink into the benches and pretend they didn't exist. Unfortunately for her, because of her close proximity to the chief, his leg had been plastered up against her own. The feel of the dampness that had settled there made her feel queasy. He'd been fidgeting non-stop, likely due to the fact that he barely fit between benches. She did her best as she tried not to focus on the way he smelled. Mercifully, the service wrapped up quickly after Liam brought it to a close with a heart-wrenching eulogy that elicited a mist to form over her eyes.

The three of them slipped out before a crowd could form and made their way back to their vehicles. Ben handed her the service pamphlet pointing to the back page.

With the cremation, no burial will be held. The wake is set to be held at 1991 54 Ave at 4:00pm. Food, drink, and merriment to be had.

Maeve turned to him. "Are they Irish?"

He was carelessly playing with a lighter as he turned to her.

"You mean the pale, flaming red-headed children with the last name McAllister?"

She scowled.

"Come on Maeve, I thought you were a detective," he mocked, dropping an arm over her shoulders.

Loud music echoed throughout the large Victorian Lara had once called home. The house was sizable, as expected, but in direct contrast to the modern open floor plan that was on trend. A grand staircase filled the entryway and light distressed hardwood was present throughout. To the left she could see the formal sitting room with a grand piano in the corner, a brick fireplace that took up the entire back wall, and poised gray couches that were without a doubt, stiff and uncomfortable. To the right of the entryway was an identical-sized room with a large oak dining table, and an attached kitchen that took up the back portion of the home.

It had the familiar scent of an older home, a wooden, dusty smell but with a lighter, citrus scent lingering behind it. The character had been maintained and perfectly woven into the decor with antique accents and brass sconces in every room.

The detectives placed their coats on the rack in the entryway, exchanged apprehensive glances, and went their separate ways. Ben, she assumed, to join the liquored-up guests at the bar, and Maeve, to find Charlotte Young. As luck would have it, she moved through the dining area, past the table filled with an assortment of pastries and finger foods, and plowed shoulder first into her worst nightmare.

She righted herself and turned to look at her victim. Her toes curled at the familiar cold, alpine scent as it surrounded her. She looked up to see his piercing blue eyes looking down at her, faint amusement dancing in them. Liam touched her upper arm, stabilizing her, and she stepped back. He took an exaggerated breath and leaned against the archway, crossing his arms, smiling. "We have to stop meeting like this."

She pulled on the hem of her dress as she failed to form a response. When it was clear she wasn't going to speak, he went on.

"I mean, I don't mind. Your lack of coordination is partially responsible for our few interactions."

She forced herself to look into his eyes as she offered her condolences and praised his eulogy. He simply nodded his head in thanks as his grin quickly faded.

"Come with me," he ordered, grabbing her elbow as he led her out of the room and toward the stairs.

Liam brought her into the brightly lit primary bedroom near the top of the stairs, closing the door gently as she made her way inside. She stepped away from him, already uncomfortable standing in Rebecca's room. Liam picked up on her hesitation.

"Look, I'm not trying to have sex with you at my sister's wake. I just want to talk."

She let out a breath as he stepped back.

"Maeve, I'm sorry for what happened that night. I was drunk and I was emotionally fucked up and I know it's not an excuse, but I still want you to know that I didn't mean for it to happen. It wasn't my intent when I came over. I just got caught up in the moment," he finished, taking a step toward her as she leaned against the back of the door.

"I'm not sure how you feel about it, but I do know you've been dodging my calls, and I can only assume you also agree it was a mistake. I've been trying to let you work through it on your own, but I just couldn't let it go without apologizing. I realize how messed up it is, especially with Lara's case, and I'm not stupid enough to not know that if it got out it would jeopardize your career. I won't let that happen."

He watched her, waiting for a reply. After a few moments of silence, she uncrossed her arms and pushed off the door, stepping closer to him. Despite her shame, she owed him something.

"Thank you for saying that Liam, but you don't need to apologize for anything. It was a drunken night and a decision that both of us made together. I was as equally to blame as you were. I think it's best we write it off and make a deal that no one can find out," she responded, reluctantly meeting his icy eyes.

At some point during her apology, he'd moved closer, his frame towering over her as he looked down. He made sure to hold her eye contact as he nodded at her response.

"All that being said, I would do it again in a heartbeat if you weren't one of the lead detectives on Lara's case. I don't regret you, Maeve. I regret the circumstances. You should know that" he replied quietly.

"I...I agree."

Surprise flickered in his eyes, the blue darkening to their gray counterpart as a slow lopsided grin followed. It was eerie watching the shift in color. It made him look like another person entirely.

After some tense silence, Liam mumbled something about getting back to the wake. He opened the door, giving her a parting smile before leaving her alone in Rebecca's room. She exhaled, letting her gaze scan the room properly as something caught her eye. It was on Rebecca's dresser in her jewelry, the subtle band of a gold watch. She looked to the open door that Liam had exited through before she made her way over to the dresser. She got closer, tucking back a piece of her hair as she grabbed her pen. She lifted under the edge of the watch, cocking her head to the side. If it really was Lara's, then it may be the only piece of solid evidence they had. She couldn't risk ruining the chance there were prints or DNA on it. Maeve's stomach dropped as she saw small diamonds around the face. Exactly like Liam had described.

A throat cleared behind her.

CHAPTER TWENTY

Maeve spun, her vision blurring. Ben was standing in the doorway, arms crossed and eyebrows raised.

"Whatcha up to, ya creep?"

Placing a hand over her racing heart she shushed him, ushering him inside and closing the door behind him.

"Maeve, as much as I'm willing, this isn't the time or place. Everyone will surely hear when I rock your world," he whispered.

She rolled her eyes and pointed to the watch. He froze, his entire body tensing beside her. "Is that…"

She nodded at him, reaching to take out her phone.

"Fuck!" he let out, his gaze meeting hers. "I mean it makes sense Lara's watch would be left at Lara's house, but why is it in Rebecca's room?"

He started pacing. "Maybe there's a chance she just saw it in Lara's room and wanted to have it as a keepsake?"

"I don't know, Ben, but we need to get out of here before we get caught snooping."

He hesitated but relented. They made their back down the stairs, exchanging a silent communication between them before Ben walked into the living room.

She watched as he made his way over to the bar, greeting a group of people with familiarity. She'd forgotten for a moment that some of the people in the house were his friends. That Lara had been his friend. It threw her off guard to see him so comfortable, so familiar.

Intrusive thoughts of his potential involvement in the case forced their way in and she shook her head. The threatening notes she'd received weren't helping the situation. She'd been warned not to trust anyone, but was the motive altruistic or manipulative? If it was the latter, it was working. She was increasingly paranoid about everyone she knew.

Rebecca and Marc were mid-laugh at something Ben had said, joy and admiration on their faces, but the mood shifted instantly as Maeve joined the group. Her stomach sunk as she nodded a greeting. Rebecca awkwardly sipped her drink in response, offering a small smile.

She leaned into her partner. "You do know we aren't supposed to drink on the job, right?"

"I'm not on the job, babe, I'm off duty at a wake that I was required, but not paid, to attend. So therefore, I will drink. With my friends. In honor of our friend."

He gestured across the next room to where Briggs was sitting with an older group, also sipping on a beer and laughing boisterously at whatever was exchanged.

"See? Even Joe is having a time. If he can do it, so can we. Perks of a small town Maeve, people treat you like family."

"That also has its drawbacks, Ben," she said, looking at the chief. "Fine, you keep drinking and I'll work for the both of us," she said, moving away.

She made her way around the room slowly, doing her best to avoid curious glances her way. With no success in finding Charlotte Young in the sitting room, she circled back to the north side of the home toward the kitchen. Sometimes, simple acts like hosting or cleaning helped people get through difficult situations. The feeling of usefulness helped to counteract the loss of control in stressful situations. Maeve was moving on a hunch. A hunch that turned out to be dead on.

She spotted Charlotte putting a bottle of white wine in the oversized refrigerator. The French doors connecting the kitchen to the patio were ajar, allowing a light spring breeze inside.

Maeve politely introduced herself and Charlotte gave a tired smile and limp hand in return. She knew better than to interview a family member at a funeral, instead offering her a business card and asking her to be in touch before she left town. Luckily, Charlotte agreed quietly before pocketing the card in her black slacks and moving to wipe the counters. She hummed along to the music playing from the other room.

At some point, the sounds of laughter and liveliness had greatly increased. The volume and intensity of the music had intensified, filling the space with gritty blues ballads. Assuming she'd stayed long enough to be socially acceptable, Maeve made a classic Irish exit and texted Ben on her way out the door.

• • •

Ben drove at his usual death race speed to Bert & Callahan Law. They were on their way to speak to Rebecca about the watch. Ben had also been not-so-gently reminded that he needed to apologize to Jason for the incident at the bar. Maeve was way too excited to witness the exchange.

They greeted Sarah at reception before walking back to Rebecca's office.

The door was closed, but as it was made of glass, they both peeked in to find it empty. Maeve jogged back to reception and Sarah told her Rebecca was in a deposition meeting with Jason and they wouldn't be out for another half hour or so. Maeve thanked her and emphasized that it wasn't urgent, moving to go get Ben from where she left him.

When she made it back to Rebecca's office, she found her partner sitting in Rebecca's white chair behind the desk, casually scrolling through his phone. He looked entirely too comfortable.

Like he'd done it a thousand times.

Maeve was about to scold him but was abruptly cut off by a voice behind her.

"Um...can I help you?"

They both jumped, awkwardly turning around to look at the door. Rebecca stood there, arms crossed as she looked between them in disbelief. Maeve's heart rate skyrocketed, and she exchanged panicked looks with Ben. She quickly stood up, smoothing out her top and taking a necessary step away from her partner. He looked at her in panic and she did her best to communicate without words that he should be the one to explain.

"Rebs! Sorry, we didn't mean to barge in here. We were just waiting for you."

Rebecca glided over to the decorative armchair in the corner, carefully sitting down. She crossed her dainty legs, her bright red heels matching perfectly with her bold lip color.

"So, you came to see me, even though you knew I was in a meeting, and then proceeded to intrude on my space? You couldn't have left a message with Sarah?"

Rebecca had an intimidating presence. An air of superiority surrounded her. It threw them both off their game as they did their best to avoid looking guilty. Ben nodded.

"Yeah, sorry Rebs, it was inappropriate for us to be in here," he said, before sheepishly looking at Maeve in silent apology. "Also, Maeve was wondering if she could ask you something."

What a coward. Maeve shot him her best death glare before turning back to Rebecca.

"Liam mentioned to us that Lara had a watch that she used to wear all the time, and we were wondering if you'd seen it? I know it's a bit of a stretch, but seeing as you're also her best friend, we had to ask."

She took a step closer.

Rebecca was quiet for a long moment before she stood, adjusting her top. She crossed the office and closed her glass door before gesturing to the seats across from her desk. The detectives moved to the chairs as Rebecca dropped into her own. She moved an elegant curl over her shoulder.

"I know it. She never took it off. It was her mother's. But no, I haven't seen it. She was wearing it the last time I saw her."

The detectives exchanged glances.

Maeve decided to risk it. "Rebecca, when I was at the wake, I got lost trying to find a bathroom and wandered into your room by accident. I saw...a similar watch to what Liam described."

Rebecca's eyebrows lifted through the Botox. She studied Maeve.

"By accident? Well, that's convenient, isn't it?" she replied, smiling. Ben looked at Maeve with wide eyes but stayed quiet.

After a tense silence Rebecca exhaled.

"It's Lara's. I've had it since October. I didn't know what to do with it. I know I should have turned it in, but I also knew how it looked. I knew no one would believe me if I explained how I got it," she said, leaning back in her chair.

"Especially since it had my fingerprints all over it," she explained, pausing. Without any prompting, she went on. "I found it. I was sitting on my porch one morning, having my coffee, soaking up one of the last warm days of summer when I saw it. It reflected off something and caught my eye. I went onto the grass and saw it sitting there...almost like it was just dropped carelessly. It was right on the edge, close to the sidewalk. Obviously, I didn't know it was hers until I picked it up."

She played with her gel nail.

"I went back and forth about turning it in, but the longer I waited, the more suspicious I knew it would look."

Ben cleared his throat but stayed silent. He interlaced his fingers on his lap. "Fair enough. If we're being honest though, this is the first lead we've had in a long time. Whatever went on with this watch, it's important that we look into it. Thank you for trusting us enough to tell us the truth," Maeve said, ending a well-placed note of intention.

"Do you know the exact date when you found it?" Ben finally chimed in, opening his notepad.

Rebecca shifted to look at him, her green eyes searching.

"I don't know the exact date, but I'd guess the first week or so in October, maybe mid-October at the latest. And it would've had to have been a weekend since I don't typically lounge outside in the mornings before work. It was most likely around ten I'd say."

She paused, crossing her thin arms. "And before you ask, no, there's no way it had been there all summer. I had Spencer mowing the grass once a week and she would've seen it. Or it would have been destroyed in the mower."

Maeve perked up. "Spencer? As in, Spencer Caldwell?"

"Yeah. She was looking for odd jobs around town to add to her work at the prison. She's saving for school. She has a shitty home life and gets no help at all, so she was going door to door posting flyers for anyone who may need some odd jobs done. She took care of the gardening and the lawn all summer. Helped with some cleaning inside the house too. She also does a lot of house sitting. I think she'll take any excuse to get away from that trailer park. She must have made some decent money, because she was doing quite a few houses on my street."

"What time of year does she stop lawn services?" Ben asked.

Rebecca shrugged. "Usually by the end of September, maybe the first week in October. Depends on the weather."

Meaning the watch was left there sometime in a one to two week window from the first of October. Which, if Maeve let her mind wander, meant there was a high probability that the watch was taken from Lara while she was held captive. If the killer had removed it randomly in the months after she was taken, it was likely important to them.

A trophy.

Assumingly important enough to not drop it on some random lawn in suburbia. Either way, it was likely the killer walked near or on Rebecca Raley's lawn at some point after Lara had been taken.

That was if Rebecca is telling the truth.

Maeve's heartbeat pounded in her temples as adrenaline spread throughout her system. The chances that the killer worked or lived in Grants Pass were high. She stood up and placed her hands on the back of her chair for support as she tried to expel the excess energy her body was making.

"Rebecca, that means the person who took Lara went back to your house after the abduction. Stood on your lawn. Or at least walked by it," Maeve started, her voice shaking despite her best efforts to control it.

"I'm worried about your safety. They know you live alone. And now that Lara is gone, they may target you next."

Rebecca looked over to Maeve. "Yeah, I know. I realized that may be a possibility a couple days later. I was on edge for a bit, but I have an alarm system, and I was sleeping with a cop next to me most nights. So that made me feel a bit better," she said, gesturing her head toward Ben. "Honestly it's been months now. As bad as it sounds, I think if they wanted me, it would've already happened. I'm not as strong or athletic as Lara was, either. I'd be a sitting duck."

"I can't believe you didn't tell me this. I could have kept a better eye out at the time," Ben said, leaning forward. Rebecca shot him a cold look.

Ben lifted his hands in surrender, the muscle in his jaw twitching. "Just let us know if you see anything suspicious."

"Yes, obviously," she said, rolling her eyes.

Maeve paced slowly, arms crossed. He looked at her in silent question, probing to see if she had anything else to say. She subtly shook her head. The overwhelming scent of Rebecca's Chanel perfume made her feel even more lightheaded.

"I'm going to stop by and grab the watch. And I need you to go down to the station to get fingerprinted. We're going to have to see who else's prints are on there and rule yours out. We'll also need a formal statement of everything you just told us."

Surprisingly, Rebecca agreed without pause and not-so-subtly gestured to the door. The meeting was over.

Maeve was following behind her partner as he made his way back toward the exit. "Hey, Speedy Gonzales, aren't you forgetting something?" she asked in a mocking tone. He stopped, turning back toward her slowly. His eyes narrowed. She held her ground, crossing her arms and nodding her head in the direction of the spiral staircase.

"Fuck. Fine. But you're not coming. I can't do this with you standing there."

"Oh yes I am. Are you kidding? I've been looking forward to this since we got here. I'm not missing it."

He rolled his eyes in an over dramatic, childlike way before gesturing for her to go first.

Jason Boukesh was in his office pacing back and forth quickly as he spoke to someone on the phone "...don't you dare threaten me. If you say anything..." he stopped, noticing the detectives hovering near his door. He immediately hung up, not even bothering to say goodbye to whoever he was speaking to.

"What the fuck are you doing here?" he asked Ben, closing the distance between them. Ben crossed his arms and lifted his chin in an alpha male show of dominance and Maeve snorted. Jason's eyes shifted to her and roved over her slowly. Ben responded immediately, stepping in to block his view.

"Look, fuck head, I don't want to have a dick measuring contest in your office for the next hour, so take your eyes off her and look at me."

Jason obliged, dragging his eyes from Maeve. "You've got a lot of nerve coming here. One call to the station and I could have your badge."

"Oh, fuck off Jason, I'm not here to beat your ass...again. I'm here to apologize."

Jason's eyes widened.

"I'm sorry I kicked your ass in front of all your friends. Apparently, I took it too far. Even though I strongly disagree. Honestly, that was me holding back. I used to kill men twice your size with my bare hands and not even break a sweat," he said.

A vein in Jason's forehead bulged.

"That being said, I'm not sorry that I defended my partner. You had no right to speak to her, or any woman, that way. And I think you know that. I know you didn't report me yourself, so I guess I owe you thanks for that. But, if it happens again, I'll happily lose my badge to put you back in your place. Know that, Jason."

Jason was obviously angry but had yet to respond. It was his first smart move.

Her partner wasn't done.

"Oh, and if I don't, Maeve will" he said looking over his shoulder to toss her a wink. "And she'd have no problem doing it to a short king such as yourself."

He gave Jason a hard look until he relented, nodding silently. Ben returned the nod and turned around, shit-eating grin plastered across his face. He grabbed Maeve's shoulder on the way out, steering her to walk in front of him.

Once they were back outside, Ben turned to her, sliding on his aviators. "How was I?"

"I think that's exactly what the chief had in mind when he asked you to apologize. Very kind, polite and sincere. Honestly, I think you nailed it, Ben" she deadpanned. He let out a loud laugh, dropping a heavy arm over her shoulders.

CHAPTER TWENTY-ONE

Later on in the week Ben and Maeve were dragged into Briggs's office. His voice had been demanding and authoritative over the phone and it had them on edge.

"Gary just called. Let me just start off by saying; what the fuck are you guys doing? He's so pissed off I had to pull out everything I had so he wouldn't press charges. And he's not usually an angry man. He's the most level-headed person I know."

Embarrassing as it was to be yelled at, she'd be lying if she said she hadn't expected it. Ben had all but accused Gary of serial disappearances, and by extension, murder. He had a right to be pissed. It was, however, a necessary step to get the information they'd needed.

She moved to answer the chief, but Ben inconspicuously lowered a hand next to her chair in an I got this gesture.

"Joe, we had to do it. I'm telling you, the link is there. It may not be evident on paper and we may not be able to prove it yet, but something is going on and it involves that prison. I know he's a friend of yours, but with all due respect, this is the whole reason Maeve and I are taking this case and not you. I mean no offense, sir, but you have to put your personal feelings aside for a moment and see it for what it is."

Briggs looked about ready to implode for a moment before he took an audible breath and intertwined his fingers over his large stomach.

"That's fair Ben, but be that as it may, you need to tread carefully. This is GP and we don't want to go around making enemies of our neighbors. Especially those in high places and especially those on the same side. Did you get any answers that justified your accusations?"

"No sir, unfortunately not. We got some insight into his emotional reaction to our questioning, but nothing concrete. It's obvious he knows the system and how to skirt his way around things."

Briggs held eye contact, nodding slowly. "No shit."

Maeve felt like she'd been slapped. She'd only known Briggs a short time, but his reaction hurt like paternal disappointment. She'd never seen him so riled up, his dull brown eyes boring first into Ben, then her. The warning was clear, and the conversation was over.

In an effort to escape the increasing suffocation in the room, she got up and left. Ben followed close behind. The sound of Briggs slamming his door shut came seconds later.

"Listen, don't take it personally. Gary and Joe are close. He's virtually the closest thing he has to a best friend. He has every right to be protective."

"I get that, Ben, but he's also the chief. It's like conflict of interest 101. You can't let anything get in the way of doing your job, especially this job. You should know, best friends with a suspect, previously emotionally involved with a suspect, double dating with the victim. Should I go on?"

"I mean, I wouldn't say emotionally involved, I'd go with physically, but I catch your drift," he said, bumping her shoulder with his. She rolled her eyes, creating some space between them.

"But in all seriousness, I get why you're thrown off. I've never seen him like that either and I've been here a hell of a lot longer than you. He's usually so un-phased, to a fault actually," he replied.

Ben's phone rang as they rounded into Maeve's office. He answered, putting it on speakerphone as he closed the door behind her.

Dr. Mason Gertree's voice filled the line.

"Listen, I tested the watch that you dropped off at the lab. There are multiple sets of prints, mostly partials and some not large enough to decipher, but it's what we expected. There's no doubt it had been passed around a bit before making its way to that lawn. So far, the complete sets I've pulled are from Rebecca Raley, Lara McAllister, Marc Hallman, yourself, Detective Striton, no doubt from when you picked it up from Ms. Raley's place, not wearing gloves I might add, and Chief Briggs, again likely from chain of evidence transportation. I swear you guys don't wear your PPE just to add in another level of difficulty."

Ben wrote the names down as he spoke. "Sorry doc, it was a precarious situation, and I had to grab and go. I did drop it in a bag at least. I also know that you're the best and you'd be able to easily separate out my prints. You're that good." He winked at Maeve, and she rolled her eyes.

Mason wasn't flattered. "Mhmm. Well, either way, those are the confirmed ones. I can't be sure about the partials yet. However, I don't think I'll be able to test them as comprehensively as I'd like. The samples are too small. Either way, I'll keep the watch here until we have exercised all testing avenues."

Ben thanked him and ended the call.

"I mean, all of those would be justified, but I guess we still have some more questions to ask," she said, crossing her arms over her chest as her partner's eyes tracked the movement.

"That's our entire job description," he drawled, grinning.

Maeve pulled up behind Ben's Chrysler as they arrived at his house. He lived on the other end of town in a moderately sized, quaint brick bungalow. His lawn was perfectly manicured and the pillars that flanked his front steps were oversized but charming. From the outside, the home showed its 1980s architecture, but the interior had a modern open floor plan with high end finishes. It was subtle but masculine, with caramel-colored wood and navy-blue accents. She warmed to it instantly.

She took off her shoes and crossed her legs on the couch, flipping on the TV for background noise and tossing her papers onto the trunk-turned-coffee table in the center of the room. Ben came out from where he was in the kitchen holding two cold beer bottles and paused, looking at her. Her eyebrows pulled together as she looked down at her position.

"Oh god! Sorry! I'm so stupid, I just made myself real comfortable here in your house that you've never let me come to before. Fuck. I'm sorry, I'm so bad at boundaries sometimes...I didn't mean to mess anything up," she squeaked, moving to shift forward and tidy up her papers. He placed the beers on the table, lifting his hands. "No, no no...that's not...you can...it just..."

She waited as he tried to form a real sentence. Finally, he placed his hands over hers, halting her movements. "Please stop cleaning. Make yourself at home, Maeve. I don't care if you mess things up, that's what a home is for. I just haven't had a woman here in a while, colleague or not. I don't...I don't typically like people in my space."

She nodded and relaxed some, leaning back and taking a long sip of the Corona. Ben followed suit and sat on the ground beside her, leaning against the armchair with his knees bent and arms hung casually over the top.

"I'm so exhausted I don't even want to do this anymore," he confessed, rubbing a hand over his head, his anxious tick.

"I know. I feel the same. Then I can't relax 'cause it's all I think about, and I want to solve it so badly. Does that make sense?" she said, laughing.

"Yes. Yes, it does. I am one of few people that would completely understand that feeling."

They fell into easy silence, both of them not moving to touch the files. "Why haven't you had a woman here for a while? What about Rebecca?" she asked tentatively, taking another sip of her beer.

"That was a long time ago and it was brief. I know I was making light of it, but it truly was only physical. For me anyway. We mostly went to her place. If she did come here, she was only here at night. And not for very long..." he said, taking a sip of his beer and avoiding her gaze.

"Okay, so none since then?"

After a moment his eyes moved to where she was threading her fingers through her hair. "No."

Feeling brave, she pushed. "Why not?"

He took a breath, dragging his eyes away from her as he looked straight ahead.

"Well for starters, GP has a female population of about twelve, and I've already vetted most of them," he paused, pulling on the chain that hung around his neck. "I've also...struggled in that area since I came home. Women aren't interested like they used to be. I know that's probably because of how I come off, but I can't really seem to soften enough for them," he said, the side of his mouth lifting up at his choice of words. "You know what I mean."

She cleared her throat, tearing her mind away from the dangerous place it had wandered.

"I seriously doubt it's all you, Ben. You may be different than you were before, but it doesn't mean that there aren't women out there who'd be accepting of what you have to offer."

He lifted his eyes to hers. "And what do you think I'm putting out there?"

"You've got the whole don't talk to me vibe going on, but I feel like a lot of people do," she explained, ending on a small laugh.

He nodded. "I don't mean to. I think I've just been hardened by my past and I don't think I can come back to who I was before. I don't have space for it."

"Ben, I don't think you need to go back to being who you were. What's wrong with who you are now? Who told you that wasn't enough?"

She paused, crossing her legs. "People change. They grow...evolve. We're shaped by our experiences and sometimes that changes us. I don't think it's a negative thing, I think that's a normal, expected part of life. I don't know what you've been through, but I do see how it's made you kind, selfless, and driven. Ben, you're a detective. A detective who hasn't slept well in weeks, because like me, you want justice. You want to do right by people. If you tell me this person you've become is someone who isn't worthy, then I will fight you tooth and nail on that. I didn't know you before you were deployed, but I know you now. And you are not hard," she finished, letting out a deep belly laugh as she noticed his eyebrows shooting up at her choice of words.

"You know what I mean, asshole. You are soft, in your own way. Fuck what anyone else says."

She paused, watching him struggle to accept her words and realizing that it was likely that no one had ever told him he was worthy.

"Thanks, Maeve. I have a hard time believing all that, but I trust you.

Rose, my ex-fiancé...her and I were two peas in a pod. She was my high school sweetheart, and we thought we'd be together forever. Like a goddamn fairy tale," he said, huffing a laugh before taking a long pull of his beer.

"She was small, delicate, soft-spoken. My mother adored her," he paused, tipping his head back. "After Ma died and I turned 18, I asked her to marry me. I enlisted soon after and was scheduled to deploy the following week. Our time apart was hard. She was all I had ever known. My safe space. My security blanket. When I came home, we were fine for a while, but we never really spoke about the wedding. We'd already been engaged for seven years, and I'd been back to visit a few times, but things just weren't the same. We didn't talk, we didn't communicate well at all, and I think that was mostly my fault. I just didn't know how to go from the harsh environment I'd been used to for so many years to one where people complained about their iPhones or the weather. It just seemed so God damn trivial, you know? I resented her for being exactly who she was before I left and that wasn't fair. I didn't have the energy or capacity to baby her or to take care of her like she wanted. I was barely even taking care of myself," he paused, taking another long drink.

"Eventually the divide grew so much it couldn't be stitched back together, and I left. And I guess I've compared everyone since to Rose, which was completely unfair and ironic since I didn't want another Rose. How fucked up is that?" He laughed, locking eyes with her.

"I guess I just figured my time over there changed me so much that I became unlovable. I couldn't wrap my mind around the intimacy side of things and give myself in that way. It was too much. So, I slept around a lot to fill the void. And now here I am, thirty-six years old, emotionally damaged and entirely alone," he said, looking at her with a forced smile in an attempt to cover the vulnerability.

Her heart nearly broke in two. Not just for him, but also for how painfully similar it was to how she felt about herself.

"Stand up."

"What?"

"Stand up!" she yelled, ushering him up with her arms.

He looked perplexed but followed orders, awkwardly adjusting his shirt where it had lifted up, his abs on full display. Her eyes tracked the movement, and she cleared her throat.

Then, she surprised them both by wrapping her arms around his stomach and resting her cheek against his chest in a tight embrace. He tensed, arms awkwardly hanging by his sides for a moment before he took a breath and relaxed. He moved his arms to surround her shoulders, their height difference making her feel like she was completely enveloped inside his huge frame. After some time, she felt him give in further, his head dropping into her neck. His breath whispered across her neck causing a slight tingle with each of his exhales.

They stayed that way for a small eternity before she forced herself to pull back, looking up as she did. His eyes changed from the softness they bore for the past several minutes to a dilated intensity she hadn't seen before. Captivating and needy. Unsettled, she pulled away and moved back to her place on the couch. The awkwardness and tension was palpable, so she bit the bullet and decided to reciprocate his vulnerability. If only to avoid acting on the fluttering in her stomach.

"Thanks for sharing all that with me Ben. It's not just you, though. Honestly, I've been the same way with relationships, but I don't really have a valid reason like you do. Somewhere along the way I distanced myself from my family and I ended up breaking off most of my connections with my friends, too. In a way, I think I was afraid to be stuck there. With the same friends in the same places with the same job. I think I was resistant to meet anyone because I didn't want to feel trapped in that kind of life. I've always craved more. I want to take as much in and do as much as I possibly can at all times. It's a blessing and a curse," she said, pulling her legs up.

"I went into every relationship with that mindset, and it scared me to know that I'd one day be trapped in a commitment, feeling like I was no longer living life for myself but for another," she admitted, pausing before getting up quietly, padding to the kitchen to grab two fresh bottles of beer and returning back to the emotionally charged living room. Ben just watched her from his spot on the couch, listening intently.

"I always hated the term other half. Like what the fuck is that? I'm not a half, I'm whole all on my own and someone can come in and also be a whole if they want, but I'm not going to give up who I am for someone. I mean, I get the idea of compromise, but I wasn't even close to feeling like I had finished working on myself, let alone being able to create space for someone else. I never wanted to lose my identity in another. To be so far intertwined you don't even know yourself anymore. I had to prove to myself for so long that I was independent and capable, and now I think I've just taken it too far," she paused, dropping back into the couch and handing him another beer.

"They say it's a trauma response. To be so overly independent so that you don't rely on anyone else so they can't let you down. All I know is that I'm not quite sure how to let someone in after all these years. I feel like I don't know how. And that I would somehow be bad at it."

He rubbed his unshaven face as he brought his warm eyes to meet hers. "Yeah, that's fair. I mean I can't pretend to know what you mean, since I'm not a woman and I haven't walked in your shoes, but I understand what you're saying. For whatever it's worth, I don't think you'd be bad at it, Maeve. You're too good of a person. It's not possible. Anyone would be damn lucky to have you."

She smiled at him. "Thanks Ben. I don't believe you, but I'm working on it."

He huffed a laugh. "I guess we're both equally fucked up, hey?"

She laughed as the heaviness lifted from the room. "Fuck work, let's watch something scary."

He looked at her, easy contentment on his face. "Anything you want, Maeve."

• • •

"Okay, alibis. Go."

"God, you're bossy. Hang on," he replied roughly, gathering his notes and flipping through some pages. They were sitting in his car after a breakfast at Shelley's, avoiding the confining walls of the precinct for as long as they could.

"Okay, Liam, out with friends the night of her disappearance, went for dinner and had drinks back at his place. The friends are Noah Blackburn, Emma Holmberg, Robert and William Cartosen. Liam brought Emma home with him and she stayed the night. Emma provided written testimony he was accounted for all night. I asked the others and they all corroborate that story, nothing seemed fishy."

She tried and failed not to picture Emma with Liam as she focused on Emma's tall lean figure, high cheekbones and perfectly groomed natural blonde hair. It was odd thinking about the new friends she'd made being intertwined in the case she was working on. Especially the fact that they were each other's alibis. She was annoyed as she realized she may have gotten a little too entangled in the community she was supposed to be investigating. Ben's situation was bad enough. She needed to be more careful.

"Okay, except there's a risk that Emma could be covering for her lover Liam on that one. I mean, just because he was there when she woke up, doesn't mean he was there all night."

He quirked an eyebrow. "Did you just say lover?"

"Yes, I did."

He smiled, the movement not reaching his eyes.

"Are you okay hearing about this? I mean, we just talked about Liam taking another girl home, a girl I think also happens to be one of your new friends. And his other alibis are also your new friends."

"I mean, yeah, this is my job and solving this case means more to me than causing a conflict of interest with my new pals. I only just met them a few weeks ago. If they were involved in any way, I'd still take them down," she replied, looking at him.

"Take them down," he echoed, laughing boisterously at her choice of words. She scowled at him and he cleared his throat, moving on.

"Next, we have Marc. He went to The Shipyard with me that night, then crashed on my couch. I got up to use the washroom and get water in the middle of the night and it sounded like a freight train was coming out of his mouth. Again, there's a chance he came and went while I was in bed, but it's very slight."

"Agreed," she offered, making notes.

"Okay, Rebs. She came home after work and Lara's car wasn't there, so she assumed Lara got a ride home from Marc and was in bed already, or that she was still out with him. Rebs goes to bed and gets up and goes to work the next day. She was alone that whole time, therefore, no alibi."

Maeve nodded as he paused to take a sip of his coffee.

"Lydia and Ray both state they made dinner, watched TV, and went to bed at eight-thirty. Their usual routine. They slept all night and woke up to start work on the farm around four-thirty the next morning. Nothing unusual there, but again no way to corroborate that. Next, Jason Boukesh, Grade A Asshole." Maeve rolled her eyes. Her partner barreled on.

"He claims he was out hunting that whole weekend with Ganesh Varma and Alex Marintha. Checked that out and there's proof of their weekend, and photos of them in the cabin that are time stamped from Friday night around six to Sunday afternoon around two. There is, however, the period of time from after work around four-thirty to when the first photo was taken at six, but the risk of something happening in that time is slight. Even though I'd love for it to be him."

She snorted at his admission. "Your bias is showing. Anyone else?"

"Yeah, the friends she shared with Liam. Emma Holmberg, of which we know her status that night, Rob and Will…same, Noah…same, Luna Chang was at her mom's place in Portland, checked and corroborated, Carl and Nikko Jackson were each other's alibis, both of them at The Shipyard most of the weekend. Finally, Amelia and Marco Silva. Both of them were on a weekend hiking trip a few hundred miles south, photos to corroborate. Then we have her friend Shirin Khorram. They used to go hiking and running and climbing and all that outdoorsy bullshit together."

She looked at him, tilting her head. "This is the first I am hearing about Shirin, Ben."

"Yeah well, she's in the files somewhere but there isn't much cause there isn't much to tell. She has a rock-solid alibi. She wasn't even in the country. She was in London at a marketing conference. She's like one of those artistic types with her own business making clothing, paintings, all natural beauty products and all that shit. I checked it out and the conference was about social media marketing for small businesses. She arrived the week before and returned two days after Lara's disappearance. I have hotel CCTV, ID, conference sign in, the lot. She's been single for ages, never married. Has a few cats, go figure. She's good," he paused, running a hand over his head. Maeve nodded, making notes.

"The problem is, that none of them have a motive. Or apparent motive, I guess. They were all her friends or family, and we would've picked up on any bad blood when we did our interviews. I mean, Rebs was always a bit jealous of her, Jason was resentful that she dropped him like trash, Liam was overprotective, Lydia and Marc had some resentment too, but all of that is not enough to want to kidnap, torture and kill someone. That's personal. That's as personal as it gets."

She leaned her head back, looking out the passenger window.

"I don't think anything is enough to justify raping and killing someone, Ben."

Before he had a chance to backpedal, his phone buzzed. Maeve couldn't hear the other end of the line, but from the look on his face she could tell it was something juicy. He said few words, only offering a few noises of acknowledgement and holy shits every so often. At some point he gestured at Maeve with some hurried hand movement, and she grabbed her notebook, passing it over to him and leaning in to see what he was writing down.

It looked like a license plate number, followed by HC-bl.

Finally, Ben hung up and looked at her, shit eating grin spread over his face. "That was the local PD in South Lake Tahoe. They towed a black Honda Civic from the forest a few miles off the shores and ran the plates after it got to the DMV. The plates don't match the registration and there was no paperwork in the glove box, but when they ran the VIN, guess who it belonged to?"

"No" she stared at him, disbelieving.

"Yes. Lara god damn McAllister. This is her car, Maeve! The plates are wrong, which means someone moved it, and had the time and means to change out the plates and dump it there, but this is it."

"If we hadn't just found her body Ben, I'd say it's likely that she was actually just there the whole time and case closed."

"The guy said it hadn't been found because it was so far off the touristy area in the deep brush. The area isn't heavily traveled, and the car was barely noticeable, covered in dead tree branches and leaves. They told me they did a thorough search inside and there's nothing in it. It was completely cleaned out."

"Except maybe if we're really, really lucky...DNA."

"My thoughts exactly. And we can trace the CCTV now that we know where the car actually ended up. Maybe get a glimpse at who was driving."

"Holy fucking shit, this is huge Ben!" she shouted at him excitedly.

"I hear that quite a bit actually," he replied, winking.

"Oh, for the love of god, just drive."

. . .

Maeve knocked on Ben's Motel door. Moments later her stomach entered her throat as he swung the door open in nothing but a towel around his waist. He leaned against the frame, brushing his teeth, his eyes dancing with mischief. She allowed herself a moment to ogle his damp muscular frame before tearing her eyes away and clearing her throat. He pulled out his toothbrush, giving her a cocky grin.

"Morning" he said, drawing out the word.

"Morning, sorry to...uh barge in on you, but I called the South Lake PD and told them we'd be there soon. I'll wait in the car," she finished, handing him a coffee and turning to leave.

"Are you sure? I don't mind if you want to wait in here," he said, his tone playful. She fought temptation and kept walking, tossing an arm in the air. "Nope I'm good! Hurry up please, I've been awake for hours."

They pulled into the South Lake Tahoe PD DMV. Her partner, thankfully, now fully dressed. She got out of the car and took off her sunglasses, admiring the perfect deep greens and sharp blues coming together over the horizon. It really was a beautiful landscape.

They were introduced to two officers from the local police department, a tall dark-haired duo that could pass as brothers if not for the stark contrast between their ability to grow body hair. Robbie, as Maeve came to know, looked like he was wearing a sweater under his short-sleeved uniform, tufts of hair coming out at his neck, covering his arms, and across his face. His partner, Jensen, was plucked like a spring chicken. They walked to the back end of the lot and the ground shifted from asphalt to gravel. Ben abruptly stopped walking as the black civic came into view. The rest of the group mimicked the motion as they fell in behind, eager subordinate wolves waiting their turn.

"I assume that forensics has come and gone?" Ben asked Jensen who lingered next to him.

"Yes sir, after you called yesterday we had them come down and check it for DNA and prints. You're good to go," he explained, handing him a pair of gloves.

"Did they find anything?"

"Not sure, sir, I watched them bag a couple strands of hair and dust for prints, but they didn't find any personal items from what I could tell."

Ben nodded his thanks and approached Lara's car, inspecting the frame before moving to examine the interior. Maeve watched him rummage through the compartments of the car, as she popped the trunk and searched the felt coating inside. She lifted the compartment housing the spare tire, freezing. The officer next to her took an audible inhale.

"Do you have any bags for evidence out here?"

Robbie shook his head, staring at the leather briefcase in a daze.

She sighed. "Look it's okay things get missed, but this needs to get bagged and sent for testing right away.

The officer nodded, Ben came to stand next to her.

"Is that...?"

"I think so. Brown leather, gold buckle. Just like Jason described."

CHAPTER TWENTY-TWO

In the hours that followed, the car was extensively documented and photographed, transportation was arranged for the vehicle to be moved to Oregon, and CCTV footage of the vehicle's journey had been requested.

In an attempt to rectify their misstep, Robbie and Jensen helped obtain the video footage from the South Lake Tahoe municipality, and had actually ended up being somewhat helpful as they sorted through all the logistics.

After what had felt like the longest day of her life, Maeve finally made her way into an empty conference room at the station in Tahoe. Ben followed quietly behind, closing the blinds and tossing the contents of Lara's briefcase onto the table. They'd received it back after it had been checked by the lab and were eager to analyze the documents.

At first glance it seemed like a random assortment of pages and notes with no real organization or logic to them. Chicken scratch cursive lined the sides of printed pages, poor quality photocopies of images taken from the internet, and police reports lay before them. Ben leaned in closer to try and read something.

"Holy mother of fuck," he said, leaning over the table, his arm bulging. "Look at this." He picked up pages from the desk and moved right up against her. "These are all the reports that you and I pulled weeks ago. This one is

JordynCunningham, Anne Barder, Mikaela Rokanier, Amanda Brinks...and a couple more I don't recognize."

She grabbed a few pages from his hands, sifting through them as recognition flooded in. It was a bank statement with Gary Managan's name at the top, along with a client ID and bank account number. Transactions were highlighted all down the front and back pages dating back several years. A total of $5,000 was taken out in small increments over the course of several days, all of it in the week leading up to Amanda's death. After that, the withdrawals stopped. She looked farther back in yearly intervals as she finally noticed the pattern. She moved to grab the police reports and lined up the dates. All were within the same week of the women being reported as missing or dead. The total amount in the account was incomprehensible. She turned to him and his face was a strange mixture of despair, anger and clarity.

"This was the link we couldn't find. This was the proof we didn't have. He was paying off judges. No wonder there was no record! It was done in cash, that sly fucking bastard!" he yelled.

"Maeve, we need to call Briggs. Right now. Look at this," he urged, pointing to the page as she leaned in. "Lara found the missing link. She fucking did it! She solved this case for us and was likely killed because of it."

"This doesn't mean anything decisively though, Ben. We still may get our asses handed to us if this is a coincidence," she reasoned, opening a bottle of water.

"A coincidence?! You can't be serious, Maeve...look at this money!"

"I know I know, but it's going to be hard to prove anything unless we talk to the judges themselves. Otherwise, it's just a man making cash withdrawals. We have no proof where that money went. We have an educated guess, but nothing definitive. Nothing that will hold up in court."

He started pacing as she fiddled with her long braid.

"It's a lead at least. It's something. We can work with this! There's someone else who can help us prove this theory. Without question. Something admissible," he stated, eager and driven.

"Who?"

"The warden himself."

She lifted her eyebrows. "And how are you ever going to get him to confess?"

"No idea, but it's worth a shot. This is solid proof right here in my hands. He's going to have a hard time denying it, Maeve."

"Fine. I'm calling the chief."

"That's more like it," he smirked, "we need this guy in cuffs."

Briggs had been silent on the line before he solemnly agreed to go down and bring his friend into the station. Even he couldn't deny the evidence. He'd ended the call by asking Maeve to report in with him right away when she got back to town. Ben was still sifting through pages, looking up at her when she ended the call, dread plastered on his handsome face.

"What is it?" she asked tentatively as she moved closer to him. He didn't speak as he slid the paper over to her. It was one of the pages that was covered in chicken scratch.

Warden Gary Managan, age 59, height 6'4", bald, single, moved to GP in...2009? Ish?
No history of women going missing or dying at Umbele until his arrival...not definitive...
Amanda Brinks, not suicide? What happened? F/U w/Mason Killing women? Why? MOTIVE? Where? HOW?
History of women being in solitary. Talk to 419, 417, maybe east side?
Who else would talk?
Background check into Gary...nothing before 2009. Where did he come from? Ask him? Other COs involved? Next steps? MAY 1, 2019 @ 17:00

The weekend was spent in complete chaos. The DNA testing of the car had yet to be completed, and the CCTV footage of its journey was inconclusive. They found grainy, short chunks of video of Lara's car being driven by a woman with red hair and sunglasses. The video showed the car moving through South Lake Tahoe at an alarmingly slow speed before it pulled off into a gas station, filled up, and disappeared from the video feed just past South Lake Tahoe, heading east.

The date stamp showed 23:58pm, May 2, 2019. The day after Lara was last seen. There was no indication as to how the car ended up in the bush, and the woman in the blurry videos seemed calm and emotionless. Nothing to indicate she was in any kind of hurry. They'd searched along the connecting roadways closest to the area the car was found, but no woman who matched her description could be clocked anywhere. No credit or debit card transactions on her accounts after May 1st. She must have paid in cash every step of the way.

Still, the woman was familiar. It was impossible to tell definitively if it was Lara, but it was plausible.

The prison tapes showed the warden leave just after eight on the evening of May 1st and return the next morning just after eight. At first, they were suspicious of how late he stayed into the evening, but when scrolling through the following nights, it was typical for him. Nothing out of the ordinary. If he was involved, he would've had to track Lara down hours after she'd already left, kidnap her and then return the following morning. It wasn't impossible, but it was a stretch.

The situation with the warden was even worse. He'd said absolutely nothing as he'd leaned back in his chair and a smug smile plastered over his face, toying aimlessly with his silk tie. Ben, Chief Briggs, and a Detective Sergeant from Medford had all tried to break him with no success. It'd been useless and they'd been forced to let him walk free after twenty-four hours.

A few short days later, they received a call from the forensics team in South Lake Tahoe. They confirmed that the only thing found in Lara's car was traces of her DNA through fingerprints and hair follicles, and a positive confirmation of a strand of synthetic hair. The detectives were sure it was proof that the woman driving the car had been wearing a wig and that it confirmed that it was not Lara. It didn't however confirm who it could've been instead. Although they had a new discovery, pattern, and evidence, it wasn't enough. It made Maeve sick to her stomach to watch the warden walk out the front doors.

. . .

Monday began the same way spring had, in a torrential downpour doubled with hostile winds and hurried, unyielding rain. Other than a short Facetime with her brother and his family, the weekend had been filled with work.

When she still hadn't heard from Ben by ten, she called. The sound of rain hitting the windows surrounded her like beating drums.

"Hey, has Dr. G called you yet?" Ben asked, forgoing any niceties.

"Um, what? No, Ben I'm calling because I haven't heard a peep from you or Briggs all morning."

"Oh. Yeah…sorry. Dr. G didn't tell me if he was also going to call you or if I should do it, so I was literally just about to text you when you called."

"Okay…call me about what?" she asked apprehensively.

"The watch. Apparently, Briggs called Liam to come check Lara's watch to confirm it was hers at the lab. Even though I thought it was very obvious, and I pointed that out to Briggs, he still insisted we get it documented. Anyway, after days of trying to get Liam back in there, he finally went to look yesterday. He confirmed it was hers. Dr. G also wants us to come down to the lab. He said it was important."

She felt her blood pressure rise. She wandered to her back doors as she watched her tulips get pelted by the rain.

"Why was it so hard to get Liam there? They've had that watch for a while."

"Not sure. It's probably all been very traumatic for him, though. Can I just meet you at the lab? I'm on the other side of town and Dr. G wants us to come down there as soon as we can."

"Yes Ben, you don't need to chauffeur me everywhere, you know. I'll meet you there."

Elena, Mason's support nurse, greeted the detectives warmly on their way by. Maeve knocked on Mason's door and a faint response on the other side beckoned them in. Mason was leaning against the back counter in his lab coat holding a brown file folder. When they came in he gestured for them to sit and he removed his glasses, before sliding into his own chair and tossing the folder on the desk.

"Thank you for coming in. With the results of the testing done by the Medford forensics team confirming Gary is a match for one of the partials on the watch, there was something else I wanted to make you aware of."

Maeve's stomach surged and Ben moved forward. "I'm sorry, what?"

Mason looked between them with concern. "I thought you knew? We received those results yesterday…after he was taken in for questioning and fingerprinted there was a match in the system."

Ben exchanged a heated look with her.

"No, I wasn't made aware. What the fuck?"

Maeve stepped in. "Sorry Mason, this is just a shock for us. So Gary's DNA is on Lara's watch?"

Mason nodded, taking a breath. "That's not all. It was confirmed with 99.8% certainty that there is a familiar paternal DNA match to Lara."

Time slowed as silence filled the small office.

"I can't even…I can't… How is that even possible? How did he…Jesus fucking Christ," Ben responded, shoving his chair back before he started pacing back and forth.

Maeve was too dumbfounded to even speak.

"I apologize for dropping that on you, detectives," Mason offered, pausing for a moment and clearing his throat. "That's not, however, the reason I brought you down here," he looked between them apprehensively.

"The watch is gone. I went to go complete my final report and send it back to your evidence storage and it wasn't there. I've looked everywhere. Elena and I have taken this lab apart. Nowhere to be found."

Ben stopped, hands on his hips as he took a step toward Mason.

"You're telling me the one piece of solid evidence we have…is gone?" he asked, his chest heaving. Maeve stood and placed a hand on his arm, forcing eye contact.

"Ben, just take a moment. I'll call the precinct and talk to Briggs. You sit here with Mason and hear him out. It's not like he would just misplace it." She turned to Dr. G.

"I haven't known you long doc, but you seem like the meticulously organized type."

Mason moved slowly out of his seat before returning to his spot against the counter, not the least bit shaken by Ben's anger.

"You're absolutely right, detective. I would never let anything like that happen under my watch." He stopped, hiding his oncoming smirk. "Sorry, pun not intended. I have a precise system and process for everything under my care. It was there when I had taken it out to show Liam yesterday, and it was gone this morning. I always make sure my lab is locked up tight."

Maeve nodded before stepping out of the room to call the chief. She tried his cell and work line with no success before she tried Beatta at reception. Beatta answered on the first ring and Maeve told her what was going on. She agreed to mobilize a team to Umbele immediately and to keep calling Briggs on her behalf. Maeve thanked her and returned to Mason's office.

"I called the office, no Briggs. Beatta is going to take care of it. We deal with this first and then we'll deal with the warden once he's in custody. Mason, can we take a look at your security footage?"

"I checked it this morning, but you can see for yourself if you want. The feed went black for a one-hour period last night and that's the only thing unusual that I noticed. That must have been when it happened."

They all made their way to a small room filled with electrical cords and two small computer screens. Mason lined up the security footage. Luckily Ben had calmed down enough to start asking his own questions as the pair watched the feed. Just as Mason had said, right at 19:15 the previous evening, the footage went down until 20:21. After they'd searched the previous days for anything suspicious, they stopped the tape.

"Where were you at this time, Dr. G?" Ben asked, attempting to keep his tone light and neutral.

"It was a Sunday, detective. I wasn't working."

They detectives exchanged a look. "Sorry, I didn't mean to imply you should be here every minute of the day. Just curious," Ben replied, placing a hand on Mason's shoulder.

Maeve turned to the doctor. "Was Elena here?"

"No, unfortunately not. She does help with data entry on some evenings and weekends, but not yesterday."

"What else does Elena do?"

"She sometimes assists me with autopsies as needed, but mostly data entry and office management. She only works casually, just enough to cover the bills and to help Jeremiah, her son. She works full time at the hospital, casual hours here, and I'm pretty sure she has a couple of other odd jobs around town."

They thanked him and left the office. The rain was still coming down in heavy, fat droplets, but the sounds of traffic had picked up as the city came to life.

"So, the warden is Lara's father?" Ben huffed from the passenger seat of Maeve's car.

"I mean, forgive me if this is ignorant, but I thought he was dead?" she said, laughing through an exhale.

"He was supposed to be. I would challenge this result if I didn't trust forensics, but still. I mean, how could we not see it?"

"Well, we have no photographic evidence of what he looked like back then. We had nothing to go on, we'd have no reason to question his death."

"That's true, I guess. So, Lara found out he was doing something sketchy with the women at Umbele and then found out they were related? Or was it reversed, did she know who he was before she started going there? Would she have recognized him? I mean, her last memory of him would've been from when she was five. Would he have recognized her? Or did he already know about her from the start?"

She looked out the window of the car, playing with her hair as she rambled on. "He fakes his death in Chico, changes his identity, and comes here? To see Lara, Liam and Lydia? No, to sit undercover working and living in and around them but never actually making contact. What the fuck is going on with this?" she finished, turning back to look at him. His eyes tracked her fingers weaving through her hair. She immediately dropped them back into her lap.

Ben cleared his throat, draping an arm over the back of her seat.

"As much as I love hearing the inner workings of your mind, we need to take action on one thing first. We need to bring him in. This is pseudocide.

It's not murder, but it's enough time for us to get to the bottom of this and make sure he stays out of Umbele while we do. Let's get to the prison. I want to watch this," Ben grinned eagerly.

• • •

Chief Maxwell, Chief Briggs, and the detectives had met to go over the strategy for the warden's interrogation and how they'd transition into getting information about the missing women. Chief Maxwell had more fortitude than anyone Maeve had ever met and he'd been committed to giving all of his time and energy to helping them solve the case. He had carried Briggs on his back as Sam had carried Frodo, and Maeve knew it would also end the same; with Briggs getting all the credit. She hadn't noticed how disorganized and incompetent her boss had been until she'd worked with Chief Maxwell.

After a full day of questioning from Maxwell, the warden confessed to the pseudocide. The abundance of evidence against him was enough to bury anyone.

The only issue was; that wasn't the confession they needed.

If the warden had committed the violent crimes they suspected him of, he'd covered his tracks well. The next interview would have to be perfectly executed, or they could ruin their chances of getting anything out of him ever again.

When they'd detained him before, Ben had gone on about the women and their families, what they had missed out on and what their lives could have been like. It was clear to all three of them that that particular angle wouldn't hold weight to a man like Gary Managan, or formally, Gerald McAllister. He didn't care about the women; he cared about himself. They'd decided to shift their strategy.

Ben moved to open the door of the interrogation room and Maeve found herself outside of her own body as she reached for his arm, holding him there.

"May I?" she asked as forced confidence flowed through her. Briggs was visibly tense, a bead of sweat dripping from his bushy brow as he gave her an intense but supportive smile. Ben also nodded, taking a step back and gesturing her through the door. He gave her hand a reassuring squeeze on the way by. She felt her anxiety ease as she realized that he'd always be there. In her corner.

She stepped into the room and a feeling of complete clarity and awareness settled over her.

Gary was in the chair opposite the metal table, leaned back in his usual easy posture, fingers intertwined in his lap. He was wearing a dark blue jumpsuit, the dull shade drawing attention to his glistening bald head. She took notice of his blue eyes for the first time. They weren't light like Lara's had been, they were darker. So similar to his son's. The same pair she'd looked into as he'd hovered over her in bed. She cursed herself for not seeing it sooner. She felt her throat tighten as she took in the similarities to the man she had spent a lust-filled night with to the monster in front of her. It gave her a visceral wariness that flowed through her entire body.

She took a moment to compose herself and redirect her thoughts. She wouldn't let it derail her. She couldn't.

Gary's lawyer stood in the back of the tiny room in a shiny brown suit, his thinning white hair showing his age and experience.

"Shall I call you Gerald? Or do you still prefer Gary?" Maeve asked, handing him some control.

"Whatever pleases you, my dear."

The man before her was not the same man she'd met at Umbele. He had a Hannibal Lecter quality she hadn't seen in him before. A predator, toying with his food. Circling it until it was so crippled with fear it could no longer find the will to flee in a desperate attempt of self-preservation. She refused to be the prey he wanted her to be.

Naturally, the fluorescents inside the room flickered.

She took another breath and re-directed her focus to the men she knew to be rooting for her behind the mirrored wall. She wanted to make them proud. She wanted to make herself proud.

She focused on Rebecca, Marc, Jason, Liam and Lydia. She focused on Lara's translucent skin riddled with marks formed through pain and agony. She focused on Jack and Judy Brinks' despair. She focused on each and every woman at Umbele Penitentiary. She focused on Ben and what he'd worked for. How it haunted him. How it haunted the whole town. She would not let them down.

"Gary, I'm just going to get right into things if you don't mind? You aren't the type for small talk, and frankly, neither am I."

He gave a small nod, somewhat thrown off guard as he moved to adjust a tie that was no longer there, dropping his hands when they grazed over the buttons of the jumpsuit instead.

"I'm just going to start at the beginning. Right at the beginning. You met Grace Brawley at a strip joint I presume? She was a stripper?"

He clenched his jaw, remaining silent. He hadn't expected this.

She glanced back at his lawyer and found him relaxed, texting something on his phone. She realized then that Gary had no intention of saying anything, the same tactic he'd used previously with Ben. It explained the nonchalance the attorney emanated. He knew his client. Gary was the best kind; intelligent, guarded, cunning.

Sometimes people's greatest strengths were also their greatest weaknesses. Maeve would use it to her advantage.

She shifted in her seat, pretending to adjust her top but instead drawing attention to the area. It was shameless work, but she had to use what she had going for her. They needed every advantage, and it was part of the reason she'd asked to go in instead of her partner.

Sure enough, his eyes wavered down quickly before coming back up to meet her eyes. The lawyer's did the same.

"Okay, so you fucked her and knocked her up…by accident, I assume? I mean, no one would voluntarily knock up a stripper, right? Especially a man as well-made and handsome as yourself."

His unblinking eyes bore into her own, the dark blue irises swirling with the beginnings of rage.

"Stop me if I get any of this wrong, I am new to this after all. So you knocked her up. She wanted to get an abortion, but seeing as that's a cardinal sin by your standards, you couldn't allow that, could you? You thought you could save her from that life, maybe become a big happy family. But you couldn't exactly go around having everyone in Chico knowing that you knocked up a stripper. That you'd stooped that low. I mean, gross man."

Maeve felt her insides churning at her own words. She was not the person she was pretending to be. She didn't agree with a single thing coming out of her perverse mouth. Strippers and sex workers did what they had to do to get by. Everyone was just doing what they could to get by in a system that worked against them.

"I assume she did some drugs while pregnant and you had no control over that too, right? You lost control over her and what your future would be like, didn't you? Did that make you feel vulnerable? Did you hate that she took something from you?"

Gary didn't respond, but a shift in his position made it clear she was on the right track.

"So, Lydia was born and you loved her, cause that's what you're supposed to do. It wasn't her fault for being born, after all. You resented Grace for what she'd taken from you, didn't you? You couldn't come back from that. She was taking your money and your freedom and doing whatever the fuck she wanted. Did that make you feel emasculated? I mean, you're the man after all. Shouldn't you decide what's best for your family?" she paused, holding eye contact.

"So, then she dies of a drug overdose a year after Lydia is born. Wow, that's so convenient for you. You really lucked out with that, didn't you? No more feelings of inadequacy I guess. Then you met Cora, and she was the exact opposite of Grace, and you thought it would be better the second time around. She came from money, she had a stable home, a kind, lively sister that she was close to. She had gorgeous flaming red hair and wore sundresses. She gardened and absentmindedly hummed melodies, and she loved you like you'd never been loved before. She healed you. Cherished you. Loved you. She was larger than life and she swept you up into her radiating presence. And she was the first person to truly appreciate you. So, naturally, you panic and put a ring on it because you feel threatened that she's going to leave once she realizes who you really are. She's too perfect to stay with your sorry ass, so might as well lock that shit in, right?

"Then you get her pregnant right away with Liam. I mean, no surprise, right? You have strong swimmers. You were fertile and masculine, and that woman needed to have your children. Maybe make up for the mistake you made with Lydia. Liam came along and he was a quiet kid. He played by himself, he was introspective and was the complete opposite of your beautiful Cora. She, of course, loved him endlessly, but he was a momma's boy. He didn't connect with you at all, and he preferred books and crafts instead of things boys should like right? Like sports and climbing trees.

"Then boom! Lara came along. She was all fiery and light and happy and bouncy. She was the opposite of her brother and even more beautiful. She looked exactly like her mother and embodied everything she was. She adored you and you adored her. She worshiped the ground her perfect daddy walked on. And finally, your family was complete. The years went on and something was still missing for you though, wasn't it? Did Cora get pregnant again? Was there a miscarriage? Did your sperm start to fail? Did you have technical issues in the bedroom, and you couldn't please her? Or was she just like a limp fish at that point? Boring and used and lost all of her appeal?"

Gary stood, slamming his fist on the table as his chair screeched across the floor.

"Don't you ever speak about her like that! Do you hear me?! You fucking cunt! Keep her name out of your filthy mouth! You know nothing about her!"

CHAPTER TWENTY-THREE

Maeve sat calmly, looking up at him.

An officer moved into the room, shoving him back in his seat. His lawyer placed a hand on his shoulder, speaking to him in whispered tones. After a few minutes in silence, Maeve dove in again. She was on a roll and didn't want to waste any time. Or any of Gary's anger.

"Okay, so we still love Cora. Good to know. So, one day she's found in the bathtub, wrists slit and bleeding all over the floor. Liam found her and called for you. You grabbed Lara into your arms to protect and coddle your little girl while Liam sits on the bathroom floor rocking back and forth, shaking. No coddling for him, right? He's the boy, so he should be fine.

"You'd lost both women in the span of a few years. I'd say that was convenient, but seeing the way you just lashed out at me, I actually believe you loved her. So, that means either you were jealous she loved her children more than you, or you were jealous the children loved her more than you. Either way, you felt threatened...surprise surprise," she taunted, pausing to take a purposeful sip from her water, letting silence fill the room for a moment.

"If you couldn't have all of her then no one could, right? That way, Lara would choose you. I mean she was the spitting image of Cora, so she'd replace her mother, right? She'd fill that hole in your life."

Gary's shoulders rose and fell quickly, his wrath held just below the surface.

"What was your childhood like? Did you have bullies for brothers or an abusive father that always made you feel you weren't enough? That you weren't man enough and you'd never amount to anything? Is that why you had something to prove? Was your mother also a slut? Did you have sisters that were unhinged?" she pushed, increasing in speed.

Gary leaned forward on the table, no longer looking at her but instead into the mirrored wall behind her. She was getting closer.

"Now, this is where I get a little foggy on things…you were working at the golf club in Chico as night shift security. Somehow, there's a fire, and you fake your own death. Now, I hope you can understand that you don't need to be a detective to deduce that you probably set that fire in order to skip town. But I'm unclear as to why? Were the police coming after you? I mean, you lost two women in the span of five years under suspicious circumstances. Was that it? Was it for life insurance? How did you get access to those funds?"

The truth was, they'd done their homework. They'd called the precinct in Chico and asked the officers there to pull the records. Gary, or Gerald McAllister, was being investigated for Cora's death as it related to the life insurance he took out on her a year prior. The claim stated if one was to take their own life less than a year after the insurance is taken out then the policy would be moot. Accidental death was covered immediately, but suicide was different. For that exact reason.

The detectives had looked deeper to find there was no paper trail substantiating the assumption that Cora was mentally ill. She hadn't been on any medications and hadn't seen her family doctor in ages, let alone a psychiatrist. There were no previous suicide attempts at any of the hospitals in the years prior, and when Maeve had contacted Charlotte Young after the funeral, she'd confirmed it.

"I looked up some old records as far back as I could find them, and I see you got a large payout when Cora died. You had life insurance on her and she had family money, didn't she? You received just under a million dollars. I also have here some records that Lara found when she was investigating you last year, and it looks like that money was withdrawn in large sums intermittently over the past fifteen years. The dates of your withdrawals seem to line up with some unsolved cases in the area.

So, you fake die and head off to god knows where, ending up in Grants Pass some twenty-five years later. In the meantime, the kids were sent to stay with Charlotte and were raised by her into their adult years. Nice, man. What a very fatherly thing to do, leaving your kids to be raised by someone else. You coward. Did your father do that to you? Just leave you to fend for yourself? Is that where you learned how to be a cowardly man?"

His interlaced fingers were flexing and tightening, causing them to turn white. His face remained surprisingly neutral.

"Somewhere along the way you must have ended up in Chico, watching the kids. How else would you have known that they moved to Grants Pass as adults. That's a little creepy, watching your kids grow up while you let them believe you were dead. How did that make you feel? Was Charlotte strict? Did she let them go out late as teenagers and cause havoc? Did you worry Lydia and Lara may also get knocked up without a strong father figure in their life? Did she forget to teach them about God?"

She paused, taking another drink from her cup and cracking her neck. Her eyes drifted around the room and she noticed that the lawyer had moved into the metal chair near the back wall. It was strange to see him seated there. Typically, counsel sat right next to their clients in a show of support. She assumed the direction must have come from her controlling detainee in his last-ditch attempt at flexing what little power and control he had left.

"Or did you just want to see Lara? Did you watch her grow into a beautiful, smart, strong woman like Cora? Was the true torture being an outsider in her life? The fact that you couldn't be the supportive father figure for her. Did it get to you? Did it make you angry when you watched her, lost and alone? You wanted her to need you like she needed Liam, right?

Did you want her to hug you like she hugged Liam? Lean on you instead of him when she cried. Liam had become that man for her, hadn't he? You watched as Liam took on that role you were supposed to fill. Your weak, godless son.

"So, I'm guessing eventually it got to be too much for you to try and stay away from her, and you tried to wade in a little deeper. You got a job at Umbele...close but not too close. You still came into GP and went for breakfast and acted like a local, but you kept your distance, just in case. I mean, they hadn't seen you in twenty-five years or so, I doubt they'd even recognize you. And you were betting on that, right?"

Gary started shifting, ever so slightly. She reciprocated his body language, leaning over the table as she rested on her elbows, tricking her body into confidence. She took a breath and drove it home.

"I noticed Shelley's Diner is right across the street from Bert & Callahan Law. I also noticed it's just a couple blocks adjacent to Kother Holistic Health. Convenient that your favorite place to eat breakfast is close enough to watch the day-to-day operations at Lara and Liam's places of work. The only children you cared about, right? I have no doubt you haven't checked up on Lydia over the years. She was the accident, the mistake. The child that shouldn't have been. She looked nothing like Cora and acted like Liam. Cold, docile, introverted.

"Anyway...I digress. So, you watch your kids, day in and day out and it kills you. It eats away at you that you can't touch them. Talk to them. Be there for them. You have no control or power over their lives as they make mistake after mistake without regard for the consequences.

I can see it in you.

"You think you're guarding your non-verbals, but you're not. Not to a trained professional at least. So, now, I'm kind of guessing here, but I think things changed when you saw Marc Hallman. You noticed Marc and Lara spending time together and it made you feel all types of ways, didn't it? Over the years you'd never seen anyone lay a hand on Lara, except her own brother. Then you saw this black man touching her. Loving her. Holding her. So, you stayed away for fear of what you might have done, right? 'Cause you have these urges...impulses...feelings you can't control when it comes to women. When they act like whores and have zero regard for the consequences. When they sin, over and over again. And it was all amplified by the fact that it was your little girl. The girl who was the spitting image of her mother. And she's staying out late…drinking…fucking…"

Gary stood up, his chair tipping back and slamming metal to metal, the sound echoing in the small room. His lawyer, Oliver, rose from his chair as he desperately tried to prevent an outburst from his client.

"My client needs a break, detective!"

She'd expected it. Any good lawyer would have jumped in. She nodded in agreement, gathering her papers. The last thing she needed was to make a mess of the interrogation and get accused of harassment. Briggs had warned her of such. One wrong move and the whole thing could be inadmissible.

She stepped out of the room and found herself being pulled forcefully into a body that felt like safety. Warm, smoky hues surrounded her. When she finally moved to pull back, he looked back and forth between her eyes as he lifted an eyebrow in silent question.

"I'm fine Ben, really. Thank you."

She stepped back, looking at Briggs hovering behind her partner, awkwardly fidgeting with the audio equipment. She'd forgotten that Briggs was in the room, and the interaction with her partner, although platonic in nature, was infinitely more than that. The chief had sensed it. He looked at them both with concern in his eyes.

Ben stepped back, pulling her attention back to him.

"This is going to work. I know it. You're so fucking smart to figure out the angle on how he feels about women. I knew it was something, but pinpointing the power, control, ego…narcissism. Brilliant."

She smiled warmly at him before turning to Briggs in an attempt to steer her partner back in the direction of professionalism.

"Ben's right darlin', you're doing very well in there. It's quite something to hear you talking like that, but I know what you're trying to do. Keep it up kid. We've got your back."

After a quick fifteen-minute break, Gary was seated back in his chair, his mask of impartiality firmly back in place. She was going to have to chip away at his resolve again. Luckily, she knew just how to do it.

She sat down, taking her hair out of its clip, the length falling over her shoulders.

"Where were we? Ah! Yes, that's right. Lara paraded herself around town with Marc. But first, I had a thought. There's something I want to go back to," she admitted, opening her file folder before crossing her arms and leaning forward.

"So somewhere along the way your impulses turned violent, right? You used to rip heads off dolls or hit your sisters when they acted out or you needed attention and control? Did you abuse Grace and Cora? Or just Grace? Was it just when they acted out?"

Charlotte had told them that Gerald had been abusive in the later years of Cora's life. Cora had visited her sister with bruises and old injuries she'd refused to explain. Unfortunately, it hadn't been a surprise to the detectives.

"Sometimes you'd get in such a frenzy that you'd blackout, right? Like your rage overpowered every other emotion. You'd bottle it up as best you could, but sometimes you just needed an outlet? Is that what happened at Umbele? Is that why you took a job in a women's penitentiary? Unlimited access to sinful women. Convicts no less. Lower than low. Women who deserved to be punished for their actions. Our justice system is too fluffy nowadays, isn't it? Simply being locked up wasn't enough for you, was it?

"These women would act out as they had their whole lives, without any regard for the consequences. An entire building of caged, feral animals. You used that to your advantage, didn't you? It was an entire building of women you could hold control and power over. You'd have them locked up in solitary. So, you could teach them a lesson? However, you couldn't just leave them there as punishment of course, no, there was more, wasn't there? That's how you satisfy that urge within you. That gut feeling that tells you they should be punished. Sometimes it went a bit too far, didn't it? Sometimes you got so wrapped up in that euphoric feeling, standing over them as they bled out on the floor, all crushed and broken, and you had to finish off that high. You needed all of it..." she paused, leaning back, apathetic and unbothered as she scanned her nail beds, the action juxtaposing her internal distress.

"So, you killed them. You strangled them. You held them down and finished the job. That was the only thing that helped you sleep at night, wasn't it? When you finally got to give into that urge...that craving...that power. You slept like a baby. It kept you going. You thought that because of the instant release you felt that it had to be a good thing. That it must have been a sign from your god that you were carrying out His will. What good is a judge and jury in comparison to divine justice, right? You weren't caught because He wouldn't let you get caught. He wanted you to rid the planet of those vile women. You were working by His hand. The path of righteousness..."

The warden's hands intertwined again, his knuckles tight as his emotion leaked out silently, filling the room like a dark shadow, poised and ready to strike.

"You know, I find it ironic when people use religion in an attempt to justify misdeeds. Some of the most morally, ethically sound people I know are atheists. Because they do the right thing because it's just that, simply the right thing. Not because they need to live up to a higher standard that their God or Gods have laid out for them. If you do all these good deeds, as your Catholicism teaches you, just to get into the Kingdom of Heaven, then, by nature, it's selfish, isn't it? To do good things so that you can have a possibility of living in the penthouse suite in the afterlife. Seems morally flawed to me. Or the other side...to avoid evil, sinful acts to avoid the fiery pits of hell. Why can't it just be that you want to be a decent human being? Why does there have to be a carrot hanging above your head?

"I mean, I'm biased, I get that. I understand that there are positives to religion, but I also know that some of the worst atrocities recorded in our history books have been done in its name. That being said, unlike a lot of my colleagues, I see the world through a gray lens. Even in this job, when I should be principled beyond a shadow of a doubt. How do I persecute the boy who stole a loaf of bread so he could feed his little sister, who lay starving and orphaned beneath a bridge simply because the system failed them? I don't see things in black and white. I believe in bending the rules for the right reason. But I don't see your justification. I can understand a lot of things, but not this."

She took a calming breath. "Anyway…eventually, your luck ran out. You chose the wrong woman. A woman whose family actually did care if she lived or died. And as luck would have it, they hired Lara to look into it. Talk about divine intervention.

"Lara, being the smart and capable lawyer she was, figured it all out and confronted you in your office. You were so thrown off guard by the fact that first, she'd figured it out, but second, that your own flesh and blood was sitting in front of you after all those years. Did you tell her who you were?" she probed, not leaving any time for him to respond.

"What happened after that? You lost control when she didn't greet you with a giant bear hug for her daddy like you thought? Instead, she was going to ruin everything. Everything you had worked so hard for years to cover up. And she likely hated you.

"Your own beautiful daughter hated you. This wasn't the dimpled, freckled bubbly little girl you raised. She was overconfident and threatening and thought she could get the better of you, didn't she? She forgot her place. She forgot that you were the one who would always be in charge, no matter what she made of herself," she paused, leaning back and crossing her arms.

"You lost it, didn't you? When she disrespected you like that? When she threatened you?"

Ben entered the room. He leaned down to tell her the last bit of information she needed to get the confession before positioning himself against the wall behind her.

"Sorry Gary, Ben just informed me that we have some credible information that Lara never left your office that day. We just had two separate witnesses come forward who gave us statements and some conclusive evidence. Once they heard you were in custody and knew they'd be safe, of course. We have one witness who confirmed the visitor log was altered as well as information around what was happening in the basement at your prison. We also have another who can confirm what happened to Lara's vehicle."

Gary's jaw clenched, his blue eyes shifting darker.

"Honestly, I'm just surprised that you would forget to tie up some loose ends like that. That's so careless. Lara got the better of you, figured it out so easily, and you didn't even cover your tracks. I mean, your own groundskeepers, under your employ, dug up one of your bodies for god's sake.

"Ironically, each of the women you hurt ended up out maneuvering you. Each of their deaths tells a story, doesn't it? It lays out a perfect roadmap to your killing spree. The women at the prison all became missing persons or died before they could be released properly, showing a pattern not only to us, but also to Lara. She figured you out before any one of us could with the limited resources she had. I mean, come on, tossing bodies carelessly in your place of work when you have thousands of acres of dense forest at your disposal. Bit lazy, isn't it? You didn't even fake your death well. It was just that no one cared enough about you to really look into it further or they'd have noticed the DNA didn't match. Your kids didn't give a shit, and you had no one. No friends, no family.

"No one gave a flying fuck that you died, right? Your kids probably hated you by that point anyway after watching their mother being mistreated year after year. I'm not entirely convinced you didn't put your hands on them too, to be honest. A violent man such as yourself teaching them right from wrong in the only way you knew how. Using god's name as you did. But they grew up and were no longer afraid of you. Everyone continued living their happy lives without you and you were forgotten…useless…worthless…and sloppy. We also discovered that you used to be a funeral director in California, didn't you? Was that how you disposed of the bodies before you moved here? Is that where you learned embalming techniques like the ones used on your daughter? It was a bit creepy to dress her up in that dress though, I'll tell you that much. What else did you do to her you sick fuck?"

Gary remained silent, and thankfully so did his lawyer. She pushed one last time.

"The women you killed laid out a perfect map to your life of violence and you were too damn full of yourself to notice that you made any mistakes at all."

"I didn't make any mistakes you filthy whore! I covered my tracks perfectly each and every time. There was no DNA to tie me to any of it and the world is a much better place now they no longer taint the world with their filth. I was meticulous in my work, but my daughter was corrupted, she was ignorant. She tried to outmaneuver me, and she failed. I still come out on top because I successfully rid the world of each and every one of those pieces of trash.

They all deserved it. God put me on this path. I am His hands. I carry out His will.

"I did everything right and I will be rewarded for my efforts. Dakota and Spencer can say whatever they want, they know what's coming to them. They all do. These women lied, stole, cheated, killed and even and bragged about it. Tell me I'm wrong for ridding the world of their rot. I did it efficiently and cleanly. I should be thanked…admired. You'll see. I took care of my Lara, she was my girl after all. She may not have lived up to her potential in life but will in death. She repented and she will be pure again."

Maeve smiled, piling up her papers as Gary sat in his own perceived victory. She did her best to pretend she wasn't interested as he recounted all the details of how meticulous he'd been, all the women he'd killed. Her charade of nonchalance motivated him to keep bragging. It was like a twisted confessional. A cap had come loose and the prideful ego maniac in him couldn't resist telling her why she was wrong and what great lengths he went through on his path of destruction.

His lawyer, dejected and nervous, was desperately trying to take control of the situation, but Gary had silenced him with a look. He talked about Jordyn, Anne, Amanda, and all the other women from Umbele. He'd orchestrated everything down to the fight between Amanda and Dakota. He'd chosen women who spoke back to him or acted out. He told her that he'd bring them into solitary and torture and abuse them for months until he felt it was enough punishment. Until they repented.

"Amanda Brinks deserved what she got, taking a kid's life like that. She only had to serve two years before she was up for parole. This poor excuse for a justice system lets killers just walk free. After I taught her a lesson, I strangled her and hung her in her cell."

"How did you do it?" Ben asked, moving forward. Gary smiled, touching his chest.

"Your ties," Ben whispered.

"What about Grace and Cora? I'm sure they didn't die from natural causes, did they?" Maeve asked, crossing her arms.

"I injected that slut with enough heroin to stop her heart before dropping her on the street where she belonged. As for Cora, she didn't have to die, but it was her fault. She brought it on herself. She was pulling away from me and she had no right. That's not how families work. She was turning my kids against me, and she had to be stopped or she would've taken them and run. I drugged her first before I put her in the bathtub and sliced her wrists. It was peaceful. She felt no pain," he said, his voice soft.

After he'd gone quiet for too long, Maeve pushed him again about Lara. He looked up at her and smiled, the effect contorting his features into something otherworldly, something sinister. He held the silence in an effort to make her squirm. After several long minutes she told him she didn't care, muttering they had enough evidence anyway before turning away. Oliver, the lawyer, tried to step in to keep him quiet but was waved off again. Now that the cap was loose, there was no shoving it all back in.

Gary's voice was quiet, raspy. "She asked to meet me that Friday afternoon. She was smart, didn't want to meet with me after hours. I should get credit for that. She got that from me. The other two were fucking airheads. I told my COs to steer clear of the admin building for a few hours because I needed them elsewhere. I told Spencer she could leave early, and she did, eagerly. She was a good girl.

Anyway, after Spencer left, it was just us. My daughter confronted me, and I couldn't have the news getting out until I was ready, so I grabbed the back of her pretty little head and slammed it against my desk. Once she was out cold, I took her to the basement."

The lights in the interrogation room flickered again as Maeve responded.

"The guards would've seen you if you had to go back out to the east and west wing junction to the stairs that lead into the basement," she said.

He smiled again, crossing his arms.

"Well, detective, not sure if you noticed, but the solitary cells are directly below the admin building. It happens to have an alternate entrance. I expected you and your partner to find that when you searched the place, but I guess I was giving you guys too much credit," he said, smiling.

"I kept her for eight months. I'd visit daily to try and set her right, because, you must understand, I didn't want to kill my own daughter. I wanted to give her the benefit of the doubt. To see if she could be purified. However, as you can guess, it didn't work. Even after we tried extensive persuasive actions, she was still as stubborn as ever, and too far gone. The devil himself had opened her up and climbed in. So, I took matters into my own hands" he finished, a look of smug satisfaction on his face.

"You strangled her with your tie?" she asked, nausea rolling through her. "I have a system, you see. It's how I remember my accomplishments. My gray pinstripe was for Mandy, my crimson red one for my sweet Lara, my navy-blue silk one for Jordyn," he revealed, leaning forward and closing the distance between them. Maeve held her position as his breath brushed across her face with his close proximity.

"And you wore them even after you'd used them?" she asked.

He scoffed. "Well yes of course. That was the whole point."

She nodded, moving to lean closer to him. "At what point did you rape your own daughter?"

Gary flinched, turning away.

"What, nothing to say? Just going to sweep that under the rug? I don't think that's very honorable of you. What does your bible say about that?"

He spoke quietly, just above a whisper. "I didn't rape her."

Maeve scoffed. "Well, the autopsy says otherwise. I believe in science, not vague denials."

He remained quiet, clenching his fists.

She moved on. "The floral dress was hers?"

"Yes. It was a dress I had purchased for her when she turned sixteen. I wrapped it up nicely and dropped it on her front porch at Lottie's place. I left an anonymous letter saying it was for her and watched from the trees as she squealed in excitement when she found it. It had warmed my heart so much to see that I made her that happy. She was perfect at that age. So well-mannered and pure. I just wanted her to be preserved like that after she was gone. That's why I got Mandy out of that casket she didn't deserve. I needed it for my Lara. I needed to know she was right there anytime I wanted to visit." he explained, dragging his tongue across his bottom lip.

She paused for a few minutes, bringing back a slip up she had tucked away for safekeeping.

"Gary, earlier when you confessed you used we. You said we tried extensive persuasive actions. Is there someone else who's been helping you?"

CHAPTER TWENTY-FOUR

Gary lifted his cool eyes to hers, a storm brewing within them. "No, I didn't. You must have misheard me."

"I didn't mishear anything and neither did these cameras," she replied, pointing to the red lights surrounding the space.

He fell into silence, refusing the bait.

"The notes I received…the threat that was left at my house and the warning on my car, was that you?"

He frowned but stayed quiet.

Maeve didn't know if she trusted the flash of confusion on his face, but she was done. She wasn't going to get anything else out of him.

Gary was moved to a cell at the station.

Ben had collapsed in her office, sitting on the ground as he buried his head in his arms and came undone. He'd spent the past year seeking justice for Lara and it was finally over.

"Can I ask you something?" Ben asked, looking up after a moment. She nodded, dropping down across from him.

"Do you really believe all that? What you said in there about god?" he asked quietly.

She took a breath. "Yeah, I do. It's hard to explain, but when you work as a nurse, when you work in healthcare and you've seen some of the worst atrocities play out in front of your eyes, extreme tragedies...you can't believe in a god. It'd cripple you. It would eat away at your sanity to know someone or something had the power to end the injustices and the suffering and chose to ignore it. To watch kids, babies, die from cancer, to watch the best kinds of humans suffer, to watch the balance of life and death play out in front of your eyes and believe someone is pulling the strings. It would fuck with you."

He was quiet for a while, contemplative. "Fair enough Maeve, fair enough."

It was the most respectful, level-headed response she'd ever received after explaining her beliefs. His civility took her by surprise.

"What about you?"

"Ah well, to be honest, I'm not really sure what I believe. I was raised Christian, being from the south and all, but after fighting overseas...let's just say I started leaning toward your side of the spectrum. I've seen a lot of shit. A lot of really fucked up things, Maeve," he murmured quietly, pausing.

"Americans fight for freedom, right? In god's name. Well, if that's the case, it comes at too high a price. It's okay to commit violent acts against each other in the name of patriotism or peace, right? Pretty fucked up logic if you ask me. It didn't feel okay. It didn't feel justified. In fact, it caused me enough moral distress to last a lifetime. In the end, we're all just human beings, regardless of where we live and what we believe," he said.

She nodded, unable to find words substantial enough to soothe his pain.

After a few quiet minutes he looked over at her again. "So. There could be a second bad guy."

She exhaled a laugh and tipped her head back against the wall. "Yeah, I guess so. And we have some loose ends. The notes and the sexual assault, both of which he denied. I don't know if I believe him, but he looked genuinely disgusted that I would say that. I mean, I get why he would deny the rape, but the notes...I know he didn't outright deny it but seems like a small thing to hold back on." She paused, playing with her ring. Ben was watching her, absentmindedly playing with his dog tags. "I also don't like how willing he was to divulge all of this to us. I know we pushed him to a confession and sometimes when people get that release the floodgates open, but it just seemed..."

"Like he didn't care?"

She looked at him, nodding. "Yeah. Like the idea of spending the rest of his life in prison wasn't all that much of an issue. He gave so many details we didn't even ask for. I know he's a narcissist and they love to brag, but I don't know. I got the impression he thinks he can get out of this somehow, like he has the upper hand. Which makes no sense. Or, I'm overthinking it and it's just his ego driving the car."

Ben was quiet for a moment. "No, I think your first hunch is right, Maeve." He looked up at her, their eyes locking. "Maybe he is going to get away with it. Maybe this is the plan. Maeve, if there's another person involved, we may have just waltzed right into a trap."

Over the next few days countless calls were made, officers and forensics teams were sent back out to Umbele, a press conference was held, de-briefs were executed, and there was coffee. So much coffee.

Ben had called almost every jurisdiction in California and Oregon asking about missing persons cases and any potential connection to Gerald McAllister. Briggs had finally caved and informed state police and the FBI. Grants Pass was about to become infamous.

Throughout the chaos, Gary sat in his cell, smiling coyly and watching in pride as they all moved about like worker ants. Once the detectives had pushed Dakota Patrieko and threatened to pull her early release, she told them she was the one who had pretended to leave Umbele and drive Lara's car to Lake Tahoe. She'd explained that the warden had given her the red wig to wear and told her where to leave Lara's car. It explained why Lara's hair was up in the video when she went into the prison and down when she left. It also explained the sense of recognition Maeve had had when she'd watched the footage for the first time. It wasn't until she noticed Dakota's fingers drumming on the steering wheel that it had confirmed the story. It was her tick. Maeve had seen her do it at the prison.

She'd called Liam and Lydia, brought them in and told them everything. Liam was reserved and stoic while Lydia broke down, leaning into her brother for support as they listened to the truth about their father. Liam had told the detectives that their father had been abusive and that he'd taken the brunt of it. Lydia had also been mistreated, but not quite to the same extent.

Their father had never touched Lara. Liam had informed Maeve that it was the reason Lara had become a lawyer in the first place, so she could protect those who couldn't protect themselves. All of it explained Liam's protectiveness. He'd grown up protecting his mother and his sisters as best as any kid was able at that age.

Both Liam and Lydia had both refused to see their father. Refused to give him the satisfaction. Maeve had then called Rebecca, Marc, and the rest of Lara's friends to tell them what had happened before it was leaked to the press. The case was slowly resolving, and people were finally going to be able to heal and move forward, but there were still unanswered questions. Questions that plagued the detectives.

As the days went by, Maeve was unable to let go. They'd finally solved the case that had flooded their minds like a parasitic fungus, growing, infiltrating and evolving until it had become their identity. However, even as things were wrapping up, there were still too many gaps.

First, there was the watch. Gary denied having it, and after a thorough search was completed of his home and office, it wasn't found. He'd also refused to speak about bribing judges, and since it was done in cash, his word would've been their only evidence. No official link to him altering the sentences for the women he targeted at Umbele. They knew he'd been paying someone off, but they didn't know who and to what extent the other person was involved. Then there were the notes, the sexual assault and the timing of it all.

Maeve had arrived only weeks before Amanda's body was uncovered. It was the first substantial lead that had led to the warden's arrest. Ben had been working with Briggs for an entire year with nothing to show for it. Was it a coincidence, or was everything happening for a reason?

Was there a chance it was connected to her arrival in Grants Pass?

Her paranoia was increasing by the day, and the general feeling of unease wouldn't let up. They'd attempted to get more information from the warden, but he refused to speak about anything other than the women themselves. It became increasingly apparent he was covering for someone, but they couldn't prove it, and Briggs kept pushing them to drop it. He was also under pressure to close the case.

Debrief sessions were facilitated by the FBI. All the personnel from the 59th precinct and Medford PD attended, including Chief Maxwell. On occasion, Briggs spoke about Maxwell, their time working together as rookies and his notorious closing percentage. He was one of the best detectives in the state and he'd been instrumental in days following the warden's arrest, stepping in where Briggs had floundered.

The taskforce that was stood up contained agents and officers from the state police, the sheriff's office, the FBI and the municipality. They'd gone over all the files associated with the case and sorted out what had been answered and what was still missing. There was a clear divide between those who thought Gary was lying about an accomplice, and those who thought there was actually someone else out there. Briggs fell in with the former line of thinking, confident the case was wrapped up in a nice little bow and excited to finally close the case and take back his jurisdiction. Maxwell pushed back against him, escalating his concerns up through the municipality, and the jurisdictional and bureaucratic complexities diverted attention away from the case itself. He'd cited Briggs's actions to be neglectful due to the delays in both the prison warrant and the untimely inclusion of the state police. The detectives had attempted to stand up for him, but had been shooed out before they could get more than a few words in. Briggs was on his own.

The delays were out of their control, but the detectives were restless. Just to add further complications, the feeling of someone watching Maeve had been unrelenting and debilitating. She wasn't sure if it was her paranoia feeding into her anxiety, or the other way around, but the hypersensitivity had only increased since they'd caught the killer.

Umbele had turned into a field of nightmares as they excavated all the bodies buried and scraped out the first six feet of earth as far as the eye could see in all directions. The land looked like a coal mining site. The beautiful, lush vegetation on the outer surface ripped out and the dark, heavy dirt beneath exposed. The earth was brutally undressed before their very eyes.

Maeve had walked the perimeter, watching her colleagues. She'd witnessed the stark contrast between the curated masterpiece of nature and the insensitive actions of its inhabitants. It was not just in the way countless nameless bodies were exposed, but also in the ruin that followed. The place was a disaster.

Gerald McAllister was a career killer. A serial.

The warden had buried fifteen bodies in the field behind the prison, and they still hadn't finished looking. Each of the women had shown varying levels of decay, some a decade old and others only a few months. The women's cheeks had sunken in and were riddled in gray and purple markings. The few pieces of hair left falling in stringy chunks down their bare skulls, the smell of their decay a mix of something like phlegm and compost.

Mason had been given reinforcements from the neighboring jurisdictions to form their own forensic analysis taskforce to help tag and examine the women that were uncovered. He'd been working just as hard as the rest of the force, arriving early in the mornings and leaving long after it was dark. He took it just as personally as Ben had, blaming himself for not noticing anything suspicious on Amanda's body the year prior.

Gary knew what he was doing when he let the women heal as much as they could before he killed them. He was smart enough to know it would look suspicious. Umbele, however, wasn't the beginning for him. They'd found embalming supplies in his basement and thirty-seven ties in his home, each with its own peg. Like a shrine. It didn't take a special agent to know the synchronicity behind it.

They'd looked into his time working as a funeral director in California, but it had been a dead end in terms of evidence. No better way to get rid of bodies than to cremate them. They wouldn't find any concrete evidence from those years before he came to Oregon. It also explained his ability to embalm Lara. He knew what he was doing.

Chief Briggs dropped heavily into a plastic chair and raised his voice over the sounds of chatter in the room. The three of them were in the break room, wrapping up for the day.

"Look guys, there's something else I need to tell you. Going back through these files I was looking for the alibis for the night Lara went missing. They all checked out except for one. I know Marc Hallman stated on record that he sent texts of his conversation with Lara that evening to you Ben, but we don't have anything on file at the precinct. I know he was with you the whole night, so it's not exactly damning, but there's a possibility she went missing before you met up with him. I don't have a copy of their text conversation. Do you have it somewhere?"

Ben frowned, crossing his arms. "Fuck, I may have forgotten, I can check my phone again, but Marc was with me the whole night. That would be a very small window of opportunity."

Maeve sitting on the ground, hair tossed up in a messy bun with a coffee in hand as she watched her partner get defensive. The long nights were beginning to get to them all. She hadn't showered in a few days and from what she could see and smell, neither had her colleagues.

"If we go with that line of thinking then we'd need to do the same for Liam. All Liam has is statements from drunk friends saying the same thing. Those are less credible than a detective vouching for your whereabouts. Plus, and hear me out here, we already have the guy who fucking did it! You're the one who believes he acted alone," Ben finished, raising his hands in the air, charged and animated. Anxiety rolled through her, the feeling like a balloon of air stuck just below her throat.

Briggs remained silent for a few minutes, clearly thrown off by Ben's disrespectful and insubordinate response. "You're right, Ben. I'm sorry. I'm just desperate here."

Ben relented, nodding in understanding before dropping a hand onto Briggs shoulder in solidarity. He looked at Maeve and swung his head toward the exit.

"Let's call it a day. We've all spent way too much time together while sleep deprived and hungry and it's getting to us. You too, Joe. You look like hell."

Briggs huffed a laugh but agreed. Twenty minutes later the three of them walked out of the station and into the pouring rain. It was the first time in days they'd left the precinct before midnight.

• • •

The patio at River's Edge restaurant had a cozy, intimate atmosphere. It was the perfect setting for a girls night. They'd snagged a table with a view overlooking the water, well positioned under the vine-wrapped pergola. It was a long overdue night off.

Maeve had chosen a figure hugging light blue silk dress with thin straps and a scoop neckline. She'd taken the time to curl her long dark hair and put in gold hoop earrings, finishing off the look with a pair of low strappy white heels. Letting out a gentle fuck it, she'd left the house feeling insecure about her outfit, but grateful about getting to dress up after weeks of minimal makeup and endless exhaustion. She'd gone back and forth about meeting up with her new friends, but in the end, Ben had convinced her to take a night away. She was grateful, she needed it.

The night went better than expected as the girls all drank way too many martinis. Nikko, Luna and Amelia helped take her mind off the case for a little while, but she was still uncomfortable. Even though it had been a nice break, the conversation light and easy, something still felt off. It had been the first day in many weeks that she hadn't spent with Ben, and it made her feel unsettled. Like she was forgetting something.

The women had shared their recent hikes and future travel plans for the summer and laughed at how much food they'd all eaten. They'd chatted about their partners and their exciting, and some, not-so-exciting, sex lives. After a few hours, as Maeve felt her head go fuzzy and her vision start to wobble, she decided to head out. Just as she finished paying her portion of the bill, goosebumps rose up along her arms and the pitches of the music shifted into an eerie low hum in her ears.

Maeve let her gaze track across the room and immediately locked eyes with Liam McAllister. The small town run-ins were never ending. He looked unapologetically handsome in a gray button-down dress shirt with the sleeves rolled up, his vascular arms on full display. His hair was styled back neatly, and he was making unrelenting, look into your soul eye contact with her. Once she met his gaze, a cocky grin emerged. He leaned back in his chair, one hand around a half-full pint and the other resting casually over the arm of his chair. A predatory quality poured out of him as he slowly ran his index finger through the condensation on his glass. Maeve felt her toes curl.

Three other people sat at his table, one woman who was leaning toward him and another couple Maeve didn't care enough to analyze. It was obviously a double date and the blonde sitting next to Liam was gorgeous, but his eyes did not waver from hers. She swallowed past the lump in her throat and stood on unsteady heels. She collected herself slowly before saying goodbye to the girls and strolling confidently back through the restaurant and toward the parking lot. She felt Liam's gaze until she stepped from the patio into the interior of the restaurant and her cheeks had turned crimson under the scrutiny her ass was no doubt receiving.

She was crossing the parking lot, her heels scraping against the pavement when he called her name, his voice closer than she was expecting. She turned as Liam moved within a few feet of her, undressing her with his eyes and making her feel even more unsteady.

His voice was deep, gravelly. "Hey, you."

"Hey," she replied, dropping her gaze off to the side to give herself a moment to breathe.

"You didn't want to say hello?" he asked, stepping in closer. The smell of his cologne surrounded her. Her vision doubled.

"Well, it looked like you were busy, and I didn't want to interrupt," she countered, finally lifting her eyes.

"I wasn't busy. I was bored, actually. You look devastating," he breathed, tracking his gaze hungrily over her hips before dragging them back up to her flushed face.

She gave him a friendly smile. "Thank you."

"Listen, now that this stuff with my sister is all over, can I take you out? Like for real this time?" he asked, stepping in even closer. Mere inches separated them. She turned, squinting as headlights appeared from the side, moving slowly toward them.

"Unfortunately, everything isn't over, Liam. We need to do our due diligence and there are things we still need some closure on. Ben told you that..." she trailed off, pointing to the car idling in front of them. "That's my Uber. I should go."

Liam stepped in front of her.

"What else is there, Maeve? You found my fucking father, right there in the open, kidnapping and killing women...my sister goes to see him and also finds herself in the same predicament. Seems pretty open and shut to me. Especially considering he admitted to it and all," he finished, the vein on the side of his head pulsing.

"It's not that simple. We need more details. Your father was out there killing for decades, Liam. We're bound to find a few more skeletons in his closet," she said, wagging her head at her choice of words and muttering an apology. The alcohol was inhibiting her usual restraint.

A group of patrons from the restaurant slowly wandered out of the front doors, their boisterous laughter filled the uncomfortable silence that had settled between them.

Liam shoved his hands in his pockets, taking a step back. "Are you seeing someone else then? Is it Striton?"

She didn't have the patience or the composure to explain herself to him. "Look, Liam, we can't do this here. Grants Pass is a small place and there's someone always listening. I'm the detective working on Lara's case and you're her brother. We can't be seen arguing and yelling out facts of this case for the whole world to hear, and you can't get all possessive and jealous because we had one drunken night together," she paused. "I'm going to go. If you still want to talk about Lara, you can call the precinct. Other than that, I need you to give me space Liam," she said, stepping around him to move toward her ride.

He turned to look at the group of people lingering near the entrance before taking a breath and dragging a hand through his copper hair, ruining the perfect style he'd molded into place.

"Fine, Maeve. I can respect that. Let me take you home at least. I've only had one beer and I'm not letting a woman who looks like that get a ride home from some random dude. Cancel the Uber."

Her blood pressure levelled up at his controlling tone. She was in an out-of-body experience as she found herself nodding in response and pulling out her phone. Liam, obviously content with her choice, walked over to the driver side of the silver Prius. She could see from their body language that an argument took place. She knew that she'd still have to pay for the ride, that was how Uber operated, but Liam wasn't backing down. She watched him slip the driver a bill before the car pulled out and took off. Liam walked back over to her, extending his elbow silently.

Despite her raging independence trying to push through, she gave in and grabbed onto it. She told herself it was because her feet hurt. Liam took her to the passenger side of his Forester, opening the door and helping her slide in. She kind of hated being treated like a princess but also kind of loved it all the same.

The drive was quiet but the air was charged. Somehow Liam drove even faster than Ben. He kept pace nearly 30 miles over the speed limit and weaved in and out of what little traffic Grants Pass had to offer at 11:53 at night. His elbow rested on the middle console and as her crossed legs drifted to his side of the car, the tension only increased. The long slit up the side of her dress didn't help. Liam's eyes had landed back on her exposed thigh more than once. She was still frustrated and annoyed at him, but it only seemed to increase her libido. Well, that and the cocktails. The sex had been great, but it wasn't worth all the drama that came with him. That, and it wasn't him she'd found herself thinking about recently.

Liam finally pulled up in front of her house and slid the car into park, turning to her.

"Look, I'm sorry I came on a little strong tonight. I was just having a terrible time there with those fake people and I saw you and I just couldn't let you leave without talking to you again. I know you have more work to do on Lara's case, but can you just give me full transparency for once and tell me that it's just tying up loose ends, right? You have the right guy?" he pushed, blue eyes intense and unraveling.

She did her best to evade his last question.

"There are just a few things here and there we need some answers on, but they'll come in time. But you should know that I don't think this is going to work out between us. It was fun, but I don't want to go down the casual dating road anymore," she said, picking at her cuticles.

"Good 'cause I wasn't thinking casual," he replied quickly, his darkening eyes digging into her own. Looking back at him, she found what had previously given her butterflies now made her feel uneasy. She turned her head to look out the window, absentmindedly playing with her hair for a moment before turning back.

"I just don't see us working out that way."

His eyebrows lifted for a moment before he nodded, taking the hint. "Thanks for the ride," she added, moving to open the door.

It was locked.

"Liam, can you please let me out?" she looked over at him, her heart rate increasing.

He didn't answer her, his gaze looking straight ahead with hand draped over the wheel. He clenched his jaw. Too much time passed. Maeve swallowed, wrapping her hand around her key.

Liam turned to look at her before hitting the unlock button with force, never lifting eye contact.

She quickly got out, her stomach in knots and her head spinning. She instinctively looked across the street to the patrol car. Wyatt was on shift, standing outside the car, his hands resting on his belt as he moved toward her, a question in his eyes. She nodded a response to him, confirming her well-being.

Somehow, she felt more unsettled by his presence than comforted. How come he hadn't checked on her sooner? She'd been in Liam's car too long and he looked like he had been watching the whole scene, unmoving.

She walked to the front door, letting herself in and locking it quickly behind her. She ever so slightly pulled the curtain back that covered the front window and peaked out. Liam's car was still idling in her driveway, but she couldn't see in because of the headlights. Wyatt remained outside the squad car, arms crossed as he watched her house.

She was sure she was overreacting, but she was also sure that Liam was too. She'd finally got a glimpse of how he could react when he became controlling and possessive, and she was glad she got out when she did. She shuddered as she realized the similarities between the man currently sitting behind bars and his son.

CHAPTER TWENTY-FIVE

Ben waltzed into Maeve's office carrying two venti Starbucks cups.

"Hey kid, d'ya miss me?" he asked, handing her one and offering a lazy grin. He was wearing denim jeans and a plain white cotton shirt. His badge was in its usual place around his neck and his hair had been freshly buzzed. She looked up at him and rolled her eyes, a small smile slipping through. He took a sip of his coffee and slid into his spot across from her.

"How was your day off?"

"Ugh, awful. I was so bored. I cleaned my house top to bottom, went for drinks with the girls, and did a mountain of paperwork. What about you?" she asked.

"Much of the same. Except I didn't get to have drinks with any girls," he replied, looking pathetic.

The sun pierced through her tiny office window and landed on the greedy cactus she'd put on the ledge. The weather had started off with a bang and it was already seventy degrees outside. Summer was just around the corner.

"We really need to figure out this connection," Ben started. "I think you're right. I think the warden manipulated these specific women for a reason, and he did it with help. He had someone on the inside who could help him cover this up. I don't think he had the time or energy to take these women, visit them in the basement, kill them and bury them all while running the prison. My gut is saying he wasn't working alone. And now for some reason he's a brick wall and won't speak. What the hell happened?"

"This is why I've been so restless all weekend, Ben. And if that's the case, it means we just took a day off while another homicidal rapist wanders the streets," She paused, scowling. "Maybe he didn't sexually abuse the women. Maybe his accomplice did," she stood up.

"That's how it worked...one of them got off on raping them for their own sexual gratification and the other got off on the violence and torture. Gary admitted to that part already, but he never admitted to anything else. Lara was raped. Repeatedly. And I bet the others were too. In Amanda's report it doesn't say she was sexually abused, but I also don't think Mason would have checked for that. Especially if it was just a suicide. For someone who claims he always wanted to keep his perfect little baby pure, rape doesn't fit his profile. Even if he is a sociopath. But, if I'm right about this, why would he let anyone else do that to his daughter?"

"You're onto something, Maeve. That's really something," Ben started, pausing. "The warden is either afraid of his partner, or that he still needs him. And he doesn't strike me as the kind of guy who's afraid of anyone. Now, seeing as we think our second suspect may have a link to the justice system, my guess is he thinks he can still get out of this. All he has to do is keep his mouth shut." He took a sip of his coffee.

"What I'd like to come back to is the fact that he blabbed on and on about what he did to these women only a few days ago and now all of a sudden he's impenetrable? What changed? I get that maybe he's protecting his guy, but I'm also a little concerned that he may have had a visit while he was here in his cell," he stood with her, stepping in to close the distance between them. "It may be a long shot, but there's a small chance his accomplice had access to this precinct. We need to get the video feed from the past few days and see who paid our friend here a visit."

Maeve's eyes were wide as she nodded her head.

"If this guy can alter prison sentences, I'll bet getting access to our precinct is a cakewalk. Going off the Bureau's profile, Gary's the planner.

The mastermind. The man behind the curtain...Oz, if you will. That aligns with him being a leader and doesn't exclude the possibility of a follower. Or followers. Look at Charles Manson for god's sake. Maybe his partner offered him a way to cover his tracks, and in return, he had his own time with the women. They had an agreement. Gary just needed reminding of that," she said, looking at her partner. "You're a fucking genius, Ben."

He gave her a shit-eating grin.

"Oh, I know, babe. Took you long enough to figure it out though."

Beatta smiled up at the detectives as they walked across the main reception area. The precinct was barren apart from her and a few officers that had been lingering near the break room. Ben shook his head at them as they walked by, but the officers were too oblivious to even notice the slight.

When Maeve had first started at the precinct, she'd thought Ben was just a cocky asshole who looked down on others that weren't up to his standards. After some time working at the 59th, she'd come to see that his hostility and resentment was justified. Briggs seemed to choose a very particular group of people to work for him, and Ben and Maeve were the exception.

The other major concern was that her and Beatta were the only women at the precinct. Ben had mentioned that there had been a few others over the years, but that they'd all left after a few months. Apparently, all of them had randomly quit on the spot or just weren't a good fit. To Briggs' credit, he'd given her extra attention and support since she'd started, but she'd assumed it was primarily because he was trying to keep a woman around longer than a few months. If only for appearances' sake. Either way, one thing had been clear from the start; the 59th precinct needed a change in leadership.

"Beatta, we need a favor. Can you call Stuart and ask him to load the feed from the holding cells from the time we arrested Gary Managan to present date?"

Beatta nodded. "Sure thing honey, I'll get him to meet you over there."

"Has Briggs called you back?" Maeve asked, as they crossed the room. Ben checked his phone, frowning before putting it back in his pocket and shaking his head. They both turned as Wyatt ducked his head around the door frame.

"Hey Striton, sorry to interrupt, but I can't find the chief, so I assumed you're covering for him?" At Ben's returning nod, he stepped in.

"This fax came through a few minutes ago and Beatta asked me to pass it along. She said you may need it for your case."

Ben read the paper, scowling. Long moments passed.

"Ben, use your words. Tell me what you're reading," Maeve demanded impatiently, moving to hover over him.

"It's just another missing persons report. Remember when we asked Beatta to track them for the past few months and to let us know if any new ones came up in the area?"

She murmured an acknowledgement.

"Well, this one is from Saturday. Beatta finessed the data extraction based on our target demographic and this looks like it fits. Marla Wayun, she's nineteen, five foot eight, brown hair, but she's not an ex-con. Her parents only filed this yesterday," he finished, lifting the sheet for emphasis. "Okay, well if we went through all the missing persons reports as they came up, we wouldn't have time to even go to the bathroom. What makes you think this is related?"

"I only asked Beatta to bring me the ones that could fit the pattern for our case and who lived in the area..." he said, trailing off. "I don't like this. This doesn't feel right. I bet Gary knew about this. I bet he knows about this!"

She moved in closer to him. "Okay, Ben. If you think this is connected, then I believe you. I won't lie, it's a stretch, but I've got your back. What do you want to do?" she asked, looking up into his turbulent eyes.

"I have no god damn idea."

• • •

Lara's vision cleared, head pounding as she took in her surroundings. She struggled to figure out where she was and what was happening, but the last few hours seemed to be mysteriously absent from her memory. Finally, after a few moments filled with agitation and uncertainty, the pulsing on the back of her skull let up and her awareness came with it. A cold surge of dread poured through her body as she felt cold metal around her wrists and ankles. Each arm and leg was shackled to the ground, all four points in each corner of the room. The metal hooks were formed into the concrete, the chains heavy.

She did a slow, reluctant scan of her environment. The room was entirely concrete, no windows in sight. A palpable dampness and earthy smell solidified the fact it was likely a basement of sorts. She turned herself around as best she could and spotted a door. It was made of solid concrete like the rest of the room, but there was a tiny slit in the bottom and a small square barred window at the top.

Horror overtook her as recognition made its way in. She was in a prison cell.

She took a breath in preparation to scream but she failed to drag in anything through her mouth, and the acute awareness of the duct tape seeped in. Still, she inhaled as deep as she could and let out as much noise as possible, screaming until her throat was raw, tears were streaming down her face and the small amount of air she could suck in through her nose was barely enough. Her head pounded like someone had taken a sledgehammer to it.

She wasn't all that confident they hadn't.

She moved to rip her arms from their chains, but the feeling of her rotator cuff tearing had her giving up on that tactic soon after. A mix of snot, tears, and saliva was dripping down into the ends of her red hair, messy and thick as it fell over her shoulders.

As her mind started to run through possible escape opportunities, the heavy door opened with a creak, and he walked in. Smiling, he locked it behind him before walking to face her, crouching down in front of her slowly, cocking his head to the side. His movements reminded her of the Cheshire cat. Goosebumps appeared over her exposed skin. He reached out and she jerked her head back so quick she sent a new wave of pain up the back of her neck. Closing her eyes, she took deep inhales through her nose. She felt a clammy hand grab under her chin forcefully and she opened her eyes, looking into a pair that were similar to her own.

"My beautiful girl. My beautiful, beautiful girl," he paused, dragging a hand down the side of her face. "You are so like your mother. You have her looks," he purred, scanning her face. "It's really too bad the inside is tainted, because the outside is still as perfect as your mother and I made it. I guess that's what happens when you grow up *without faith or a proper male role model in your life. I can see that it ruined you. This is your fault sweetie...you did this."*

He let go of her chin and pushed her face away, as if it hurt him to see her like that. Lara felt her resolve crumble as she started to cry, hyperaware of what was to come. No one knew she was there.

No one would come for her.

She hadn't told anyone that she was going to Umbele and what she'd figured out.

Her chest started to shake. Liam had been right. He'd warned her that she needed to start telling people where she was going, especially in her line of work. She'd been naive to think that having a cell phone would be a failsafe.

Her father stood, his knees cracking as he made his way to his full, six-foot-four stature. He took off his suit jacket and loosened his tie before rolling up his sleeves. She felt bile come up the back of her throat and she hastily forced it back down. She started screaming from behind the tape.

"Lara, no one can hear you down here. Please stop. I'm not going to hurt you, yet. We've planned for this for a long time. We aren't going to get rid of you that quickly my dear. I just need to prepare you, is all. See, we have a deal, him and I. But you should know that I would never have agreed to his terms if you were still pure. Don't worry, I'm not going to let him have his way with you. You still are my little girl after all, deal or no deal. You should know that. But like I said, you're tainted now. God doesn't want you this way, and neither do I. Now, be a good girl and play nice for daddy."

Lara felt despair encompass her as he knelt down to grab the bag he'd brought in with him. He pulled out an old dress and she recognized it instantly as the one she'd received on her sixteenth birthday. She'd been so excited when she had found it on Aunt Lotti's front porch along with a single white rose. She'd assumed it had been from Sam, the sweet shy boy who'd taken her to the movies the weekend prior.

She realized now how wrong she'd been.

"Do you remember this, baby? This was your favorite. You looked so perfect in this," he paused, smiling as he tilted his head. "You were perfect. The only good thing I made in this lifetime. Why'd you have to go and ruin yourself," he inhaled, lowering his voice to a whisper. "I kept it for you. Well, I kept it for me. I knew I'd see you in it again one day." He shook it out, smiling as he ran a hand down to press the wrinkles out of it.

Her father then spent the next ten minutes undressing her so slowly she felt every nerve ending fire in protest as she tried to kick and squirm out of the way. He was a huge man, he always had been. He'd been intimidating when she was five, but this was even worse. She'd always been scared of him, even when she wasn't sure why. The way he'd always looked at her so possessively. The same way Liam had started looking at her after he'd died. Or after they thought he'd died.

He had taken his time washing every inch of her with a cheap sponge and equally cheap floral scented body wash. A smell she'd never forget. He'd then brushed her hair lovingly before braiding it down her back. After he'd gotten her in the dress he stood back, sweating from the exertion of fighting with her. He looked pleased with himself as he stared at her for longer than he should have. The dress was inherently too small, as she'd been fifty pounds lighter and a great deal shorter when she'd last worn it. He hadn't been able to zip it up in the back, instead leaving it gaping and muttering that she'd really let herself go. Her entire body was trembling as she finally allowed herself to take in the immensity of the situation. He walked slowly toward the door, opening it and hovering for a moment.

"I'm sorry for this. I really am. But it's part of the deal, you understand," he muttered, before moving toward her with his blue tie and wrapping it around her eyes, securing it tightly.

She jumped as the sound of the heavy door slamming closed echoed off the concrete walls. She knew she should've felt relief as he left, but instead all she felt was extreme dread. A menacing force made its way into the room with her, crawling up the bottoms of her feet and into her throat as it tightened its grasp around the last bit of strength she had left.

He'd made a deal.

There was someone else.

Better the devil you know.

She started to whimper as the door opened again, slower this time. More purposeful. She heard someone enter, his breathing louder than her father's had been. His deep inhales and exhales filled the room. The man didn't speak but she heard his steps circle her spot on the ground slowly. Goosebumps appeared on her arms and legs as she started to sob. Then he spoke, his voice deep and rough as it rattled through her.

"Don't worry darlin', I'll treat you right. I'll cherish you like he can't."

She felt him stand behind her, grabbing the cuffs and removing her watch. He played with it for a moment before dropping it in his pocket. Bile came up again and she choked on it. She felt her body collapse onto the cold hard ground as he loosened the chains that held her in place. She tried with everything she had left to pull free, but realized very quickly the chains had only been extended long enough to allow her body to lay slack against the ground. She was still locked up. She heard his strained breathing again and the sound of the metal from his belt falling to the floor. The sound forced her into a catatonic state of being where she was no longer present in her own body, instead floating above, as the man she could not see did things she could only feel.

In the following months the man in the dark touched her gently. It was a stark contrast to what her father would do, often pulling his tie tight and pushing down across her neck until the hope of death taunted her before he'd let go and let her gulp down air she didn't want. It was always the same routine. Her father's aggression was welcomed in comparison to the man who would wash her, shave her, hold her, feed her, and have his way with her.

But by far, the worst part of it all was that it wasn't violent. It was purposeful, slow, and intimate. Which somehow made it much, much worse. They took turns, her father leaving her blindfold off as he taught her lessons, raising his hand and foot to her until she was barely breathing before the man in the dark took his turn.

She would take her father's beatings day in and day out to not be touched by the man in the dark. She wondered if her father knew what the man in the dark did to her. Surely, he wouldn't allow it. Surely he could protect her in some way.

She lived that way for such a long period of time she was eternally unaware of her surroundings. Her reality was far too grim to focus on the changing seasons or frequencies at which her captors paid her a visit. She never spoke, she ate only when the hunger pains moved her limbs involuntarily, and she never slept. At least, it felt that way, as her rest was filled with nightmares that she could no longer distinguish between dream and reality.

CHAPTER TWENTY-SIX

Ben, Maeve, and Stuart were hovering over the monitors on Stu's desk, arguing about the shotty audio playback. The only people who'd gone near the holding area where Gary Managan was held were all people who had reason to. Ben, Maeve, Briggs, Oliver, his vapid lawyer, and Liam. Every one of them had a perfectly justifiable reason for being there, but only one of them seemed suspicious.

Maeve locked eyes with Ben, panic and uncertainty quickly rising within her as she watched Liam hover on the other side of the locked bars, the view showing only the back of his head. His arms were crossed over his chest and it was impossible to read his non-verbals from the grainy video feed and the muffled audio. Gary had remained seated on the concrete bench with his head tilted back against the wall, fingers loosely intertwined on his legs as his lips moved silently on the screen. Even after re-watching it repeatedly, there was nothing incriminating on either side. Maeve had been unable to keep herself from pacing back and forth in the tiny room. Ben reached out and laid a firm hand on her forearm.

"Breathe. We don't know anything yet."

She nodded silently, taking a slow breath as her eyes moved back to the paused footage.

Ben thanked Stu before grabbing his phone and leading the way out of the tech room. Maeve followed close, her ability to focus and problem solve frozen solid, like her insides. She listened in as her partner called for patrol cars to get to Liam's house, advising them that they'd be en-route within minutes. He turned around to ensure she was behind him. He offered her a pitying look.

"Don't. Just don't...please. I can't process anything other than the fact that I am a detective and this is a lead. That's it."

He searched her eyes intently before giving her a discreet nod. "Normally I'd say we should go back and talk to our friend Gary there about his little visit with his son, but I'd put money on the fact that he won't say a damn thing and we don't have time to waste. I'll get Beatta to keep trying Briggs. I don't think he'll mind being pulled back in after we brief him on what's going on."

They arrived at Liam's place some twenty minutes later. Maeve trailed behind her partner as he made his way over to a stocky officer sporting white Oakley's.

"Afternoon sir, we didn't form a perimeter, but I've got a couple guys watching the back door. We didn't want to go in without your approval."

Ben nodded, unclipping his gun from his hip and palming it. "You did the right thing. I take it he's home?"

The young officer nodded but there was fear in his eyes. Maeve watched as Ben barked orders at the group and did his checks. His extensive military training was clear, and it had everyone focused and submissive. He was surprisingly good at being commander-in-chief as he remained calm and professional. The officers showed him more respect than they ever had with Briggs. Briggs had an easy disposition, and people often took advantage of that.

The officers would remain outside as backup just in case things went south, but the need for vests and forced entry was unnecessary. There was no proof of anything solid against Liam and they had no warrant. A few minutes later Ben gestured for her to join him behind his car, away from prying eyes. "Listen, I want you to stay here."

She huffed out a laugh, crossing her arms over her chest. "You've gotta be fucking joking, Ben."

He leveled her with a dark look and stepped in closer, pinning her between himself and his car as his arm came to rest on the roof, closing her in. Her stomach clenched.

"Does it look like I'm joking?"

"Ben, I have just as much of a right to be there as you do. I'm not going to mess this up. I know how to block things out. I know how to be professional and do my job. I'm asking you to trust me on this. I want this just as much as you do, and if Liam happens to be involved in this somehow, I'm happy to watch you take him down. In fact, I'd really, really enjoy watching that," she finished, in a teasing tone.

He stepped in closer and she dropped her eyes quickly, noticing his dog tags hanging on the outside of his shirt.

"It's not about you being incompetent, I would never suggest that, Maeve. You should know me well enough to know that by now. It's about your safety. That...that I don't fuck with."

His authoritative tone combined with his current proximity was making her feel flushed and light-headed. Or maybe it was the idea that she may have cozied up and slept with a serial rapist that they were potentially about to arrest. It could be either one, really.

"I'll be fine. I trust that he wouldn't make a stupid move with all of us surrounding the place. Plus, I think you probably know a billion ways to kill a man with your bare hands, so I feel good about that, to be honest," she replied, ending on a sarcastic note and biting her lower lip.

His eyes darkened as they dropped to her mouth, hovering there before he took his arm off the car and stepped back. Maeve felt the reluctance in it.

He turned his hat backwards and peeled off his sunglasses before giving her a sharp nod of acceptance.

They approached slowly, scanning the area intently before knocking on Liam's door. Maeve's heart was pounding out of her chest, and she could feel the sweat pooling in her bra.

Liam opened the door. His hair was disheveled, and he squinted in confusion. "Hey guys. What's up?" he started, before leaning around to notice the uniformed men on the street. "What's going on? Did something happen?" he asked, voice increasing with concern.

"Hey Liam, do you mind if we come in?" Ben asked casually, dropping his pistol back into his holster inconspicuously. Liam's eyes darted to Maeve's, scanning her face before nodding and stepping back.

His house was small but well maintained. It smelled like its owner, hints of mint and fresh linen filling the room. Her eyes landed on a bundle of wilting peonies in a vase near the kitchen sink.

"Liam, I'm just going to cut right to it. We have reason to believe that your father didn't work alone. I can't get into the specifics, but we're following the notion that he had help. Since we've had him in custody at the precinct, we've been watching who has come to visit him."

Liam nodded, dropping his hands in his pockets. Ben jolted, palming his gun again as Maeve quickly followed suit.

"Whoa whoa...sorry," Liam said, lifting his hands back out again, showing his empty palms. "Why are you guys so jumpy? Jesus, what did you think I was going to do?"

They both relaxed but each kept a hand on their respective holsters. "Liam, I need you to take a seat and not make any sudden movements, okay?" Ben ordered, stepping in front of Maeve. Liam's throat bobbed as he dropped into one of the stools that ran along his kitchen island. He had enough sense to look concerned.

"Okay, so you saw me visit my father, and now you think I helped him murder a bunch of women...including my sister?"

Ben took another step forward.

"We saw you visit him, and we just want to know why, that's it. We're just here to talk."

Liam made to stand but Ben gave him a look that had him dropping back into his seat in submission.

"Yeah, I went to see him. I know I told you guys I didn't want to, but I don't know, I just felt like I needed some closure. I hadn't seen the guy since I was a kid, and I just needed some answers. I asked Lydia to come with me, but she didn't want to. I just asked him about mom and Lara, but he didn't say much. He just went on about how much of a failure I was and how disappointed he was in me. Same old dad," he said quietly, offering a close-lipped disbelieving smile.

"Did he say anything else? Anything that would lead us to the identity of an accomplice?" Ben pushed, towering over him. Liam frowned, looking at Maeve before returning his gaze back to Ben.

"Nah, nothing else. I would've told you. Despite what you may think, I am not a fucking serial killer just because my father was. I'd like to think I shouldn't get accused of something because of who he is."

He turned to look at Maeve. "...and I think you should know me better than that. The fact that you think I could do something like that is disgusting. Take me to the station, put me on a polygraph. I'll do it. Then let's go through all of his victims and see how the hell I could have been involved. You think I've been doing this since I was a teenager? Are you kidding? You think I did this to my..." he turned away, voice cracking, "...to my sister? You think I spent this past year pretending to mourn her, to search for her...when in reality I was a part of the whole thing?!" he yelled, his face flushed with anger.

The detectives exchanged a look.

• • •

"I mean, it would've been handy if it had been him, but it still wouldn't explain the warden's connection to the system. Plus, I think people may have noticed the red-haired, tall, pasty, and preppy man-whore waltzing into Umbele," Ben muttered, looking out the window of the car as they made their way back.

"Also, the fact that Lara was a victim. I honestly believe him. I don't think he could've done that to his own sister," she reasoned.

"People can surprise you, Maeve. Trust me," he paused, taking a breath. "But I think you're right. I think it's a stretch. A stretch that doesn't answer all our questions and doesn't seem feasible, let alone something that can be validated. That, or he's a really good liar who knows how to cover his tracks and has us all fooled. But we've got nothing on him other than the fact he visited his dear old fucked up dad."

She relaxed into her seat as her partner dialed the station. "Beatta, have you been able to get a hold of Briggs?"

Maeve heard one side of the conversation, a short silence in between each of Ben's questions.

"What the hell? He usually answers my calls even when he's away. It's been hours and he hasn't even texted. I'm starting to worry. Swing by where? His house? He's home? Like on a stay-cation? Shit! Okay thanks Bee!" Ben blurted. He looked at her and she nodded her understanding.

They pulled up slowly next to Rebecca Raley's house, rolling farther along as Ben found a spot to park.

"Um, Ben, why are we at Rebecca's house?" she asked, scowling as she scanned the area.

He looked out of his window. "We're not, we're just passing it. This is Briggs's house right here," he explained, pointing to a smaller home.

"What? They live next door to each other?" she replied.

"Small town Maeve, small town."

The chief's house was all black stone with a large brown door and matching steps. His truck wasn't in the driveway but there was an attached garage. He was most likely trying to fly under the radar, especially in a small place like Grants Pass where everyone no doubt knew where the local police chief lived. Except for her, apparently.

She glanced uneasily over to Rebecca's house as Ben knocked on his front door. After no reply, he tried three more times before he started ringing the bell.

"Jesus Ben, you're coming on a little strong. He's probably just napping," she reasoned, shaking her head.

"Maeve, if we don't tell him about all this he'll have our balls. My balls...your...well you know what I mean. Contrary to my overconfident nature, I have not dealt with something this size before and I'm in over my head. I have no idea where to go with this and I'm panicked. He's the one who's supposed to be leading the taskforce. There's someone else out there and he is close by. I mean, he could have this Marla girl and then who's next...you?" he exhaled, shaking his head back and forth. "Not a fucking chance, over my dead body. I haven't forgotten those notes Maeve. If you have any idea what to do then please tell me, 'cause otherwise, I'm about to break down this motherfucker's door," he said, muttering quieter to himself. "...taking time off at a time like this..."

Finally, after two more rings of the bell, the door swung open. Briggs stood holding a beer, out of breath and sporting a wife beater and sweatpants. He obviously hadn't shaved in days. He looked chaotic.

"Fuck, Ben, I get it. I was cooking something in the oven and had no pants on, you gotta give me a minute. Didn't you hear me shouting to wait? I have neighbors. I have to be somewhat presentable at all times, you know. What the hell are you even doing here on my day off?" he boomed, anger pouring off of him. Amongst other liquids.

His tired gaze moved over to her. "Maeve! darlin'! Didn't see ya there. Sorry for my choice words. Shouldn't have done that in front of a woman," he said bashfully, tossing her a wink before focusing back on Ben. "What is it then? What's on fire?"

"Can we come in?" Ben pushed, taking an uninvited step toward the door.

"No," Briggs responded sincerely.

"Sir, I don't think you want us describing the details of this on your front porch," Ben reasoned. Briggs looked at him a long moment before finally stepping back and gesturing them inside.

Maeve felt an intense wave of wrongness as they stepped in, but she assumed it was due to the informality that came with going into your boss's house while they wore their at home pants. Ben looked at her as if reading her thoughts, lifting an eyebrow in an are you okay gesture. She nodded but he didn't take his eyes from her, his concern apparent. They followed Briggs toward the back of his home and into the living room.

The place was a complete disaster, bordering on hoarder level. Mismatched dirty furniture was haphazardly placed around the room, and a large television that took up an entire wall in the living room. No photos or art were present on the beige colored walls, and no personality whatsoever present in the home. There was, however, an insurmountable amount of garbage everywhere. Most of it was fast food wrappers and empty coke bottles, but it was substantial. The interior of his home was a direct contrast to the modern, renovated sleek exterior. It was like two completely different personalities lived there. What he wanted people to see on the outside and who he truly was on the inside.

She passed by the kitchen and noticed a door on the far side that was closed with a padlock. Curious, she started to turn quietly to get her partner's attention but was interrupted as Briggs stood in front of her.

"Sorry for the mess. Wasn't expecting company," he said, looking at Maeve as his breath was hot on her face. She swallowed, murmuring a response as she moved around him, trying to get Ben's attention. Luckily, Briggs took the hint as he pulled up his black sweatpants and padded into the kitchen.

Ben, finally sensing her anxiety, moved toward her. She was grateful for his grounding presence and substantially better body odor. It calmed her instantly. She was about to discreetly point toward the basement door when Briggs yelled from the kitchen.

"I'd offer you both something to drink but I don't particularly feel like a work visit on my day off so let's just get to the point, shall we?" he muttered, motioning them to follow him into the living room where he turned on the stereo. He sat in a burgundy armchair near the TV, and they moved to sit on the long gray sofa adjacent to it.

Maeve noticed blackout curtains all around the home and took in the mass amount of black electronic consoles and speakers jammed in under the oversized TV. Black electrical wires were everywhere, and about a hundred black DVD cases shoved in the console below. He must have been trying to achieve a movie theater-type setting in his own tiny living room.

She was trying and failing not to focus on the damp, musty smell that had filled her nose the moment she'd walked in. She felt slightly nauseated as Ben spoke, leaning forward and putting his forearms over his thighs. She leaned into his smoky cinnamon scent.

"Sorry for bombarding you like this Joe, but we wouldn't have come if it wasn't important. There's been some new developments, and we need your help."

Ben then took time explaining everything they'd discovered, and Briggs remained quiet as he leaned back in his chair, listening and nodding along. When her partner finally finished, a charged silence filled the room.

"Does anyone from the station know you're here? Have you put someone else in charge or did you leave them to fend for themselves? You're the most senior officer there Ben, tell me you told someone when you'd be back."

Ben looked concerned as he swallowed, his Adam's apple bobbing as he looked at Maeve for help.

"Uh no sir, we didn't tell anyone other than Bee. We only expected to be gone for half an hour or so, they have my number. I didn't think it would be a big deal. We'll go back as soon as we're done here."

"I'm going to get us all a drink after all," Briggs responded, getting up with great effort before he moved to the kitchen, breathing heavily as he waddled his large stomach past Maeve.

She turned to look at Ben. "This is so weird. I don't like this. Have you been here before?" she whispered, shifting closer.

He shook his head. "No. I've been outside a bunch of times but never been in. He never invites anyone over. All our work events or parties have been at the station. Now I see why. This is fucking nasty, " Ben replied, his lip curling in disgust.

She nodded as Briggs came back in, holding a tray with a large pitcher of sweet tea. He shoved some trash off the coffee table and poured Maeve a glass first. She took it reluctantly but held it in on her thigh. Ben downed his entire glass in half a second and moved to fill it up a second time. She felt the chief's eyes on her as he filled his own glass. She knew there were social expectations, but she hated sweet tea and her appetite had left her long ago. She reluctantly took a sip. It tasted bitter but bearable.

"So, what's our next step?" Maeve asked, wanting to move things along as quickly as possible. Briggs leaned back, scratching his stomach and pulling the lever on the side of the armchair to pop out the footrest.

"Well, Maeve, you've done some great work. You both have, that's for sure. There is one thing you didn't notice, though. The arresting officer listed on the files."

Ben and Maeve exchanged confused glances.

"If you'd bothered to look further into those reports, you'd have seen that I was the arresting officer on each of the files. I'm the connection you both missed. While frantically looking for some judge that could've gotten all these women out or put them in the system to begin with, you overlooked the most important piece of evidence," he purred, a taunting smile playing at his lips.

Ben turned to look at Maeve, and she saw intense fear in his eyes before they slowly started drooping. A surge of adrenaline poured through her as time slowed and everything became clear. She looked over at Briggs and attempted to move for her gun. He was disturbingly still, feet up, his fingers trailing over his large stomach as he looked at her.

She watched Ben the moment he fell completely unconscious, body collapsing into the sofa. Her body felt like jelly as she struggled to unclip her holster with one hand and her phone with the other. She fumbled and her panic set in.

The tea.

Her mind quickly became foggy and her vision followed. She rallied what energy she had left and pulled out her gun as her phone slipped from her other hand in the same instant. Finally, Briggs moved like she'd never seen him move before as he launched himself out of the armchair and across the room. She felt his large fingers grab her hair and dread surged through her as he yanked her down toward the coffee table before everything went black.

CHAPTER TWENTY-SEVEN

Maeve blinked back the fog from her vision as her head pounded, and blood pumped through her temples. She tried to bring hand up to check the damage and quickly realized they were both restrained behind her back. Which also happened to ache like someone had taken a crowbar to them.

A gag pulled tight against her cheeks inside her mouth and the taste of it smelled of her boss, the realization making her stomach reel. She looked down at her ankles and saw the black zip tie that held them together, not overly tight but still uncomfortable. She must be in Briggs's basement. She was likely dragged down the stairs on her back. Hence the crippling pain working its way up her spine.

The basement was the same size as the main floor, but it was entirely unfinished. The walls were covered in some sort of black foam that looked like it had been done by a ten-year-old, and the ground was all concrete. She was sitting on an old mattress on the floor near the back corner and she gagged as she looked at all the colored stains peppering it.

A low whining sound that had been going on since she woke sounded like it was coming from across the room in the area sectioned off by a large white room divider. Maeve leaned down on the side of her head on the mattress to get a lower angle to see what was on the other side but could only make out black metal grid lines underneath.

Panic consumed her as she struggled to accept that she was alone. She had no idea what had happened to Ben. She was more worried for him than she was for herself. At least she was still alive. She couldn't, with confidence, say the same for her partner.

She decided to try making noise, yelling as loud as possible through the fabric gag, but it was quiet.

Too quiet.

Not nearly enough for a neighbor to hear.

A neighbor...like Rebecca Raley.

Something shifted into her mind. A thought. A flutter of a discovery, light as a feather, floating through her brain. She tried to reach out and grab hold of it through the fog the drug had left in her system.

The watch. Lara's watch had been found on Rebecca's front lawn.

Originally Maeve had thought it was a well-rehearsed lie and that she'd had it all along, fabricating a convenient story. But now, now it made sense. She lived right next door to Briggs.

He must have had the watch.

He must have dropped it on his way past their adjoining lawns at some point, and once they'd had it tested in the lab, he'd be one of the very few people to have had access to Mason's clinic. He went in and took it back.

His trophy.

It was time to move. She was just about to start worming her way off the mattress when the door at the top of the staircase swung open. She stopped as she saw swollen, dirt-stained feet come down the old wooden steps. His steps were slow and deliberate, as if he was trying to increase the tension in the moment.

He finally landed at the bottom, his head hitting the string from the lightbulb that emitted a dull glow around the room. Her boss was shirtless. His large, hairy abdomen drooping over the band of his stained black sweatpants. He looked at her and smiled, and she could see something close to pride shining in his eyes.

"Hey darlin'..." he started, moving toward her slowly. "I've been waitin' a long time to see you like this. Just let me take a moment to really drink in this sight. You...here...ready and waiting for me," he breathed, running a large hand over his stomach as his labored breathing filled the room.

"I had a different plan for you at first, but this'll work too. I only wish you hadn't brought Ben into this. He was ignorant for so long and I wanted to keep it that way. It would be too obvious if you both up and quit as they say, but you both left me no choice."

She sat back up, wincing in pain before taking a breath through her nose and looking up at the man she'd once trusted. The man who somehow had shifted away from any sort of resemblance to Chief Joe Briggs and instead resembled a beast. He'd been cunning and meticulous.

He'd outsmarted everyone and he knew it.

He knelt down in front of her, disconcertingly close. She skirted back as best she could, but he grabbed onto one of her legs with one hand and tucked a strand of her hair behind her ear with the other. She had less than a few seconds to form a plan. She wasn't a victim. She wouldn't be a victim. This is why women choose the bear.

She was stronger than this bastard. All men had one thing in common, they underestimated women.

She leaned into his hand, tilting her head and rubbing her cheek along his palm as she closed her eyes. The gesture threw him off guard as his eyes widened and his breathing increased.

"You like that, baby?" he asked roughly, moving his hand across her cheek intimately.

She nodded, looking deep into his eyes to hold his attention before dragging them slowly down his body and back up again. A taunting, feminine move. As predicted, she saw his eyes light up, his mouth parting as he reached down to adjust his sweatpants. He tilted his head to the side, slowly moving his thumb in the side of her mouth under the gag. She made no move to bite it, instead running her tongue along its length as he let out an audible groan, moving to sit next to her on the mattress.

"Let me tell you, I didn't expect this," he said, voice raspy and deep. "I expected a fight from you. I'm a bit disappointed, actually. I like when they fight back. It makes it a little more rewarding when they finally give in to their situation and let me take care of them. But when they stop fighting, that's my favorite part. That being said, I was so looking forward to taking on someone with your...abilities. I guess this makes it easier for both of us. I'll take it either way darlin'." Smirking, he removed his thumb from her mouth and eyed her closely.

"You know, you've been teasing me since the moment you walked through the door. All those tight pants, how you were always right next to me every time we were working together on something. Especially that time at the funeral when you wore that tight little dress and teased me with your bare leg right up against my thigh, fuck that thing rode up so high Maeve. I wanted you to see my desire for you. I mean, the idea that you were looking at it, thinking about it, wanting it, well that had me straining through my zipper, Maeve. It took everything in me not to wrap my hands around these smooth legs and drag you on top of it" he exhaled, shuddering.

Maeve blocked him out as best she could, but it took every ounce of strength she had not to let him see her break. The high-pitched whining noise that was coming from the other side of the room started up again, louder than before. Maeve moved her eyes in its direction as profound, intrinsic fear pushed its way in.

Briggs grabbed her chin, pressing his fingers in enough to bruise as he forced her gaze back to him.

"Don't worry about that. There's bad piping down here," he said before he moved to stand, towering above her as his stomach blocked her view completely. Then, ever so slowly, he removed his sweatpants.

Maeve felt her legs start to tremble as she noticed he'd forgone underwear. She turned her head as he crouched in front of her, his excitement on full display as he once again forced her to look at him. A mere second passed by and she used it to dive back into herself. To block out emotion and refocus her mind before making an obvious display of looking at his unremarkable manhood, letting her eyes stay there longer than they should have. He reached into the pockets of his sweatpants that lay in a heap on the ground and pulled out a utility knife.

"You know, I see the way you look at Ben. Every fucking woman in this town looks at him that way. I wasn't going to let another beautiful woman like yourself slip through my fingers. Not after I worked so hard to get you here. You have no idea how eager I was when I saw your application. I've been waiting for you for what feels like a lifetime. You're so smart…clean…high quality compared to the other whores. That's why this is going to be so good, because you made me wait," he breathed, voice low and grading.

"Ben is dealt with, so you're all mine now. I can tell by the way you're looking at me right now that you also want to be mine. I can see the effect I have on you," he purred, running a hand down her arm as he watched her with his dull, shit-colored eyes.

"Don't worry, I'll take it slow for both of us," he said, reaching down as he grabbed the zip tie on her ankles before dragging her harshly toward him. Toward the end of the mattress.

She was unable to stop her body's innate response as she started trembling, but luckily, he was too focused on cutting her loose he didn't see her resolve crumbling. She couldn't let that happen. It was all she had left.

She wouldn't let him win.

He reached down and cut the zip tie, separating her legs as far as they could go. Holding down one of her legs, he tested letting go of the other and she laid there like a dead fish, unmoving. He seemed content with her reaction and reached up to rip her underwear off in one fell swoop. Only once he was kneeling in front of her on the edge of the mattress, looking down at her exposed flesh, he let go of her other ankle and moved his way to hover over her, closing the distance between them considerably.

"Now, usually I like to blindfold my girls, can't risk them identifying me in a small place like GP, you know, but with you, I don't think it's going to be a problem. You won't be leaving here alive, and I want to look into those dark eyes," he whispered in her ear.

Her arms were being crushed behind her back as they were still handcuffed together, but she engaged her core and brought her legs up as quickly as she could, kicking him right in the goods with everything she had.

Her act had worked, and he'd made the mistake of letting his guard down. Men and their egos. Without the privacy the prison provided and without his controlling, organized partner, he'd had to improvise, setting up a half-assed attempt in his basement and grabbing her and Ben on impulse. There was no way he could have known they were coming over to his house, so he'd been unprepared and impulsive. Both things Maeve had used to her advantage.

Briggs fell back, letting out a squeal that vibrated against the walls as he cupped himself. He rolled around as Maeve ran up the wooden stairs, turning herself around to try and get her cuffed hands to turn the knob. Her luck quickly ran out as she realized it wouldn't budge.

She went down a couple steps and threw her body against the door several times.

A hand weaved into her hair and wrenched her backwards.

Her scalp felt like it might be ripped off and she went tumbling back down the wooden steps to land on the concrete floor below. She felt like it had been hit by a train as she rolled around, trying to right herself as quickly as possible, her heart pounding in her ears.

Briggs stood over her, stark naked, with a mixture of rage and excitement on his face. He crouched down, as she tried to scramble away.

"You don't honestly think I'd be stupid enough to leave your escape route unlocked, do you? I may have had to make some adjustments, but I'm not a complete idiot. I've been doing this for decades darlin', give me some credit. He grabbed the back of her head, palming it like a basketball before slamming it into the lowest step. Her vision dipped to black for a few moments before the tingling sensation returned and flashing lights started up behind her eyelids.

The pain was paralyzing.

Tears burned behind her eyelids as she tried to keep it together, her teeth chattering. She blinked as much as she could but there was a hot, thick liquid filling her vision.

"Now, I usually don't like being too violent with my girls. That's Gary's thing. You know, he gets to act like the god he thinks he is, and I get to show the girls a good time. You see, I get these urges, I have since I was a boy. My daddy noticed when I started touching myself...rearranging myself around my friend's moms, my babysitter, my teachers. He told me about masturbation, and that worked for a while...until it didn't. The thing they don't tell you is that even with all these primal urges, some girls don't like it as much as men do. Sex I mean. You all have lower libidos. It's science, you know? But I didn't care. I needed it, whether they were willing to give it or not," he paused, sitting on the ground and pulling her head back onto his lap as blood running from her skull poured onto his skin. The smell of his body odor surrounded her and she gagged into the material tied into her mouth. He ran a hand over her hair in a gentle, petting motion.

"The first time I felt a girl was in sixth grade. Her name was Haley and said she liked me. She let me kiss her and I kissed her real hard back. I started touching her, but she didn't like that, so she slapped me across the face, and you know what? I liked it, Maeve. I mean, I really liked it. My pants got all tight and I forced my mouth on hers again. I didn't get very far before we got caught by some other kids and I got dragged to the principal's office. Back then it was easy enough to get out of, being the son of a well-known police chief and all," he said, ending in a breathy laugh.

"Anyway, the point is, I've always been this way. And the good thing with being the head of the department is that these women have nowhere to go. Before Gary came along I did it all myself. After I took what I needed from them, I'd tell them I was the police chief. That typically rendered them hopeless enough to leave it alone. The law couldn't help them, because I was the law. Who would believe them over me? They were nothing. You see? Foolproof."

Maeve was laying on her side, cheek pressed against his large thigh as she tried to let the blood flow away from her rather than down her face. He grabbed her ankle in his chubby hand as he held up a red brick that Maeve had failed to notice. He smiled down at her before slamming it as hard as he could against her foot. She felt the bones shatter in slow motion, one by one as she screamed in agony. Briggs dropped the brick off to the side as her tears flowed freely, mixing with blood and snot. She trembled, trying to focus on anything other than her insurmountable pain.

"Sorry about that, but I can't let you get the upper hand again, you see. I made that mistake once. I won't do it again. It hurts me as much as it hurts you, I swear," he said, sighing as he shifted her back into his lap even further. "After Gary and I struck our deal, it was easier. We had a system of course. We became fast friends, you know, him working at the prison and me at the station. We had a lot of interactions. I caught him first, down in solitary at Umbele with one of the girls, beating the living hell out of her. I made it clear we wouldn't have a problem if he let me have some fun too. The rest is history. A match made in heaven, him and I. I cherished the girls for what they offered me, and he punished them. As long as we both got what we wanted, we made it work," he paused, adjusting.

"That was until Lara of course. I knew it was a bad idea keeping her, but Gary insisted on it. He held me off for a long time, not allowing me near his little girl. I threatened him one day and he finally turned his cheek. He didn't know what I was doing to her. I think there was a line, even for him. So, I'd hit her to cover my tracks. I think he assumed I was just having some fun. She was so rewarding, she was so…feminine…" he said, closing his eyes. Maeve had been using his extended monologue to gather her strength, waiting for her opportunity to move. Adrenaline finally kicked back in as she shoved off him quickly, standing on her good foot as she managed to bring up her knee and drive it into his face. He rolled onto his back, howling as the blood poured from his undoubtedly broken nose. Maeve braced herself for the pain she was about to endure before she brought herself down, knee first, with full force onto his face. She got up and did it again and again relentlessly until she felt his skull crack.

His gargles soon became satiated with blood as he tried to clear his lungs from the bone fragments that were surely entering his circulation. After a few long minutes, he finally stopped flailing as his arms fell limply on either side of him.

Even though his face resembled shepherd's pie, she didn't take any chances as she grabbed the key chain from his sweatpants. She heard the loud whirring sound from the other side of the room escalate in intensity. Unable to form rational thought, she trusted her intuition instead and dragged her body across the basement. Her hands were still cuffed behind her and her head pounded. Her vision was still hazy and blood leaking down the side of her face. She did her best not to focus on the debilitating pain radiating from her crippled ankle. Peaking around the divider, her stomach lurched into her throat as she took in the battered body of a woman inside a cage. The metal rungs she'd noticed were those of black metal bars only big enough for a large dog. The woman was bound and bloody, her black hair sticking to her face as tears flowed freely onto the duct tape covering her mouth. The smell was overwhelming as Maeve took in how long she must have been kept in there without a place to relieve herself or even extend her limbs. The whirring sound came again, and Maeve sobbed along with the woman she now knew to be Marla Wayun. The woman who had just been reported missing. Ben had been right.

Ben.

After allowing herself another short moment to lay on the cold concrete in solidarity with Marla, she knew she was powerless to save her in her condition. They needed help. She made charged eye contact with Marla, trying her best to communicate that she was going to get help. Luckily, Marla understood, nodding briefly before collapsing back in a heap.

Maeve hobbled back up the steps one at a time, leaning on the banister as she went. Her body was trembling with a brutal mixture of panic and pain. She needed to find Ben.

She played the difficult game of trying to unlock the padlock while backwards and bleeding for several long minutes before finally feeling the key she'd stolen from Briggs slide home. A sob escaped her throat as sweet relief filled her and she turned it. Her heart raced as she glanced back down the steps to look for her captor before she jumped on one foot up the final step and out through the basement door. She knew it was impossible he was still alive, but her anxiety had taken control. Rational thought was long gone.

She made her way out of the basement and closed the door behind her, leaning back against it as she took deep breaths through her nose and past the damp gag in her mouth. Maeve was forced to drop to her knees as her good foot gave out, no longer able to support her hobbling. She dragged herself through the bungalow trying to find a phone. Her cries amplified every time her maimed foot touched something. The concussion she undoubtedly suffered from bridged and she gagged as nausea rolled through her, sharp and intense. The last thing she needed was to choke on her own vomit. Her gag would cause her to asphyxiate on it. Maeve rested for a moment, waiting for the nausea to pass before pressing on.

She kept glancing at the door to the basement. She was sure Briggs was going to burst through and grab her at any moment, even though she'd seen his brain matter leak all over the floor. After agonizingly long minutes of trying and failing to find a phone, she thought about going outside and getting help but quickly changed her mind. She had precious minutes. Her partner could be fighting for his life. She couldn't risk wasting any more time.

She searched the house as her adrenaline started to taper off and the pain became crippling. She was crying, her breaths becoming shallow as despair and hopelessness consumed her and she collapsed near the side door into the garage. She struggled to stay conscious. Hysteria swooped in when she noticed the door to the garage slightly ajar. Following a hunch she forced herself back up on one foot, she opened the door fully, a new surge of desperate energy flowing through her. Maeve saw the tailgate to Briggs' blue truck open. Hope fueled her as she hobbled down two steps and over.

Under the soft plastic that covered the flatbed, she saw him. Her partner was wrapped in a blue camping tarp, his arms and legs bound together with twist ties, a dirty shovel next to him. A stretch of duct tape covered his mouth, and he was unmoving.

He was too still.

She nearly collapsed not knowing if he was alive, but knowing she still had to get them help, she swallowed her intense emotions and overwhelming agony in order to finish her final task. She knew she was too weak to get him out herself, so she left him and hobbled back over to the side door. She pulled herself up the two steps and used her already damaged head to hit the large button that opened the garage door.

The garage door opened too slowly, a gust of wind and rain followed.

It wasn't enough.

She could bleed out by the time someone walked by and happened to search the garage. In one last desperate move, she crawled back toward the truck and opened the door. Pulling herself up on shaky arms she was about to pull every wire she could find under the wheel, but luck was finally on her side. Briggs had left the key fob on the console, likely in preparation for a quick escape. She turned backward, and with her cuffed hands she grabbed the fob, pressing every button until she found the right one. The truck lit up and started screaming the noise she used to resent but now would be eternally grateful for. Overcome with emotion she collapsed onto the concrete and fell into oblivion.

CHAPTER TWENTY-EIGHT

Maeve woke to the rhythmic sound of a machine beeping next to her left ear. She opened her eyes and did a scan around the room before sitting upright quickly, panic surging through her. The blood drained from her head down into the rest of her body much too quickly, causing a light-headedness that nearly knocked her back on the bed. She grabbed for the bed rail beside her.

"Whoa, whoa, whoa, calm down Maeve, you're okay," Ben reassured her, holding her forearm as he gently ran a hand over it in comfort. "It's okay. He's not here, he's gone, I promise, he's gone and you're safe. I've got you," Ben leaned in, moving the hair from her face as she searched his eyes.

She nodded, taking a deep breath and closing her eyes. It was over, it was all over. She laid her head back down and turned to look at him. His hazel eyes searched hers before she took in his unshaven, fatigued face. Profound concern rested there. The beeping was coming from the IV pump next to her bed and she noticed it was inserted into the lateral aspect of her wrist, pushing in normal saline.

The relief she felt upon realizing she was in the hospital was instantaneous. Another surge of emotions overpowered her sliver of control and tears began to flow freely. She kept her eyes closed and took in deep, grounding breaths. Ben was quiet but he kept his hand on her arm the entire time, tracing his thumb back and forth. She scanned her body and although she felt stiffness, pressure, and throbbing, there was no sharp pain. They must have given her something really, really strong.

She pulled back the beige blanket covering her legs to assess the damage. Her foot was in a large hard white cast that went from below her knee down to her toes. She shifted her gown, pulling it to the side to see her stomach and winced at the black and blue bruising that covered the areas around her left ribs and right kidney. Likely internal bleeding. Finally, she touched her face to find it swollen on one side, flinching as she palpated around her right eye as her fingers ran over the bandaging.

"Stitches," Ben explained, "eight of them there and another fifteen at the back of your head."

She reached behind and palpated the area that'd been shaven down and patched together at the back of her skull. She hit with a flashback of Briggs slamming the back of her head against the wooden step. She closed her eyes again, blinking back the scene and shifting to re-focus on her current surroundings.

"Maeve, are you okay? Other than the obvious ailments, " he sputtered, gesturing to her entire body. His buzzed hair was longer than usual, and he was wearing a set of blue scrubs that the hospital staff must've given him.

She gave him a weak smile as she grabbed his hand, giving it a small squeeze. "No, not really" she whispered, voice cracking.

She'd just started to cry again when the door busted open, and a short energetic nurse made his way in. When asked, he told her she had fractured nearly all the bones in her foot and ankle, three ribs, a lacerated spleen, a bruised kidney, and a subdural hematoma. She had undergone two surgeries since she'd been there, one for the stabilization of her foot and the other for her brain bleed. She would need several more surgeries for her foot, but there was a good chance she would regain full use of it with intensive physical therapy.

After the medical team finished their assessments and ensured she could go home soon, they left and closed the door. She was finally alone with her partner. His brow was furrowed with concern.

"Ben, have you been here the entire time?" she asked tentatively.

"It was nearly a week, Maeve. As if I'd just leave you alone here," he paused. "Why? Do I smell? Fuck! I bet I smell so bad." He lifted his arm to assess the damage.

She laughed and he eventually joined in, the sound filling the room. He leaned back, some tension rolling off his shoulders as he looked at her in admiration.

"Yes. I've been here. I'm not leaving you alone, ever, ever again. Plus, you have no family here. Well, yet I mean."

"Yet?! Ben tell me you didn't call them," she asked frantically, eyes darting to the window that overlooked the parking lot.

"Look, you were hurt pretty bad and you were in surgery and the doctor said you'd need a support system before you were discharged. I was just following orders," he responded, apology in his eyes.

She opened her mouth to argue but her protest was lost with the sincerity of his tone.

"I get it. Thank you for calling them," she said, feeling a warmth flow through her veins. "You look great in those, by the way. I'm kind of into the whole doctor vibe you got going on."

The effect of the Fentanyl was taking control of her mouth.

Pure unfiltered happiness flickered across his face for a brief moment before it dropped into a frown a moment later.

"Maeve, how dare you. What if I wanted to look like a nurse. Not all men in scrubs are doctors."

She let out a deep belly laugh, her stomach cramping in response as shooting pain from the area made her stop just as quickly. He chuckled along with her, raising an eyebrow before lifting his arms and flexing, his biceps bulging out of the material. A faint knock sounded at the door.

Spencer Caldwell stood awkwardly, holding some yellow daisies.

"Sorry to...interrupt. I can come back if it's a bad time," she said quietly, gaze darting between the detectives. Maeve smiled.

"No, not at all Spencer, please come in."

Ben stood. "I'll uh, go get us some coffee," he muttered, eyes darting to Maeve, seeking permission.

"I'll be fine Ben, go."

After he left, Spencer walked in and put the flowers on the bedside table before fidgeting with her hair.

"Sit down Spencer, please. What's going on?" Maeve asked, pulling up her blanket. After Spencer was seated she cleared her throat, finally bringing her gaze up to meet Maeve's.

"I just wanted to apologize," she said while spinning her thumb ring methodically.

Maeve frowned. "Okay. For what?"

"I was the one who left you the notes."

Maeve's reaction was instinctive. She pulled back quickly.

"I know I know, I'm so sorry. It wasn't a threat. I didn't mean it as a death threat of course, I was just trying to warn you. I knew if you kept looking he would catch on and you'd be the next girl to go missing. I knew something was going on there, all the warden's long hours, the girls in solitary, and the fact that Lara was last seen there before she went missing. I know I validated her signature when she signed in, but I now know he likely forced her to write in the sign out. Anyway, I tried again with the note on your car. I tried to warn you not to trust Chief Briggs. He was always hanging around and gave me the creeps. He used to say the grossest things to me, and he used to threaten me. He told me I couldn't tell anyone because no one would believe my word against his. I just wanted to warn you. I'm sorry if I scared you, that wasn't my intent," she said, tearing up.

Maeve searched her eyes.

"I just didn't know what to do. I didn't know what they were doing or how bad it really was, but I knew if I said something, or I left they would find me. They were always…manipulating me. The warden made me feel…I don't know…like I needed him or something. I was like always trying to impress him and make him proud of my work but the whole time I was also scared of him," she said, her voice dropping to a whisper.

Maeve put a hand over hers.

"You don't have to explain Spencer, you're allowed to be afraid. You aren't responsible for what happened there, and you were just trying to do what was best without putting yourself in danger. That's actually incredibly smart. I appreciate you putting yourself at risk to warn me, that takes a lot of courage."

Spencer sniffed, wiping her face. "I saw the chief come by often enough, I knew they were friends. He sometimes came when the warden was gone too. I didn't question it, I mean, who was I not to trust a police chief."

"You did the right thing. I honestly think you may have been in danger if you'd said anything. They are predators. They did this, not you. You did everything you could have. Just know that you are safe now and you can call me anytime you need, I'll be there. You're a good kid Spencer, don't let anyone take that from you."

. . .

Ben helped her home, and her mother, father, and sister had arrived a few hours later to help get her situated. Over the next week, Helen had kept herself busy with getting groceries, filling up Maeve's car and cleaning the house, while her father had just fussed and hovered around her in concern. Even though she knew it would be a short time before everyone started tripping over each other and getting on each other's nerves, she was thankful to have them around. She hadn't realized how much she'd missed the familiarity and comfort that they brought with them, and it went a long way toward her feeling safe again.

Matteo had tried to get time off, but he was unable to leave work and didn't want to leave his family alone. He promised he would make a trip with his wife and kids in the next few months when things calmed down for him, even against Maeve's protests. Her parents and Maya had offered to stay with her longer, but she was already feeling smothered after the end of the week. When Ben offered himself as an alternative option, she agreed without hesitation. He had come to know her needs so effortlessly, it was an easy choice. He knew how to be there without being an imposition. She reassured her family they could stay in a hotel and just come back during the day and finally, after some arguing back and forth, they agreed.

Ben had been there the whole week, laughing with her father and helping her mother with various projects. On the first day he'd done an extensive perimeter check and gotten her settled on the couch with her medications, tea and the paranormal activity box set he'd purchased for her and her "weird fascination with horror movies." He'd also jotted down all the instructions from her care team as she'd been discharged, reading them back to her throughout the day to ensure she was listening. He was annoyingly overbearing, but unlike the smothering feeling she got from being around her family, with him, it was perfect.

It had been a beautiful day; they had all spent it outside on Maeve's patio. Her father had made a fire and Ben had made everyone spiked hot chocolates as they ate and drank the day away. Her parents and sister had left promptly after dinner, Helen whispering that Maeve needed some alone time with Ben on her way out. Maeve had rolled her eyes, but butterflies had started up in her stomach.

Ben flopped down next to her, stealing the popcorn bowl. "Let's watch paranormal activities. Any real man can handle these stupid ghost movies anyway."

She hid her smile at his attempt to remember the movie title and snuggled close to him. As much as she wanted to tease him, something had changed in their relationship, and it didn't feel right. After they finished the second movie, she turned off the TV and turned to face him.

"We've avoided this long enough, Ben. We need to talk about what happened. I need to know. I need to know everything," she pleaded, adjusting her cast that was propped up on the coffee table.

He took a deep breath and nodded, searching her eyes before setting down his beer.

"What do you want to know? Where do you want me to start?" he asked gently, scanning her face.

"At the beginning. All of it. I need to know the details. I need closure from this nightmare. It's the only way I'll be able to move forward."

He nodded, grabbing her leg gently and bringing it over his lap, resting his arms over her knees casually.

"Gary or Gerald, whatever you want to call him, and Briggs met at Umbele. For years Joe would bring in women on made up charges and he'd make sure they ended up at Umbele. Then Gary pulled the strings enough to get away with detaining the women in their own personal torture chambers down in solitary. Sometimes they'd stay there for days, months.

Then once Gary got a little too carried away or got bored, he would toss their bodies in the forest behind the prison. Or, if he was feeling extra spicy, he'd let them go, hunt them down, and kill them," he said, taking another sip of his beer.

"Briggs was along for the ride but obviously wanted different things. They'd make their plans at Shelley's in the mornings, and when the area became hot with crime they'd back off and bide their time or branch out farther into Oregon. I received reports from the OBI of all the missing women and unresolved homicides that fit the bill, and after we got Briggs, I called my guy back there again to add rape into the search parameters. The files have already started to come through and the taskforce has been going through it all to try and see how many are connected to our fearless leader. Who, by the way, is dead, thanks to your extensive capabilities," he said, giving her a lazy grin before planting an obnoxiously wet kiss on her cheek. She huffed, pulling away dramatically and wiping her cheek in an effort to hide the flush covering her face.

"So, you did have the texts from Marc confirming Lara blew him off? God that had me spiraling thinking you were involved again" she said, looking back at him.

He sat back. "Yes of course! I just forgot to send them to the station.

Wait...again?! What do you mean again? You thought it could be me?"

She shrugged. "You can't trust anyone in this business Ben, you know that. I'm sorry I ever felt that way."

He relaxed, scanning her face. "You're right. I can't fault you for that, but I hope your faith in me is restored. Above everything else, your trust is what I value most. Also, don't change the subject, the fact that you saved many lives that night is not lost on anyone. They got Marla Wayun out alive because of you. She's okay physically, but she'll need a lot of support to deal with that trauma. You're a fucking badass Maeve, and don't you ever forget it. I was your damsel in distress, and I am damn proud of it" he said, putting his hand over his heart.

She allowed herself a moment to take his compliment as her eyes glazed over. When the emotion threatened to take her under again, she gestured to him to go on.

"So, anyway, after the team did a sweep of Briggs' house, we found trophies. Lots of them. He took their jewelry and kept them in a gross little box. Lara's watch was in there. After he found out Mason had it at the lab, he must have gone in and taken it back. Obviously, no one bats an eyelash when our chief goes to the medical examiner's office. And of course he lives right next door to Rebecca, who found it on the lawn that they share," he paused, shaking his head.

"Honestly, I was slightly concerned for a while there that Spencer was involved somehow. Obviously not the main culprit but it was a coincidence that she was taking care of both of their lawns at the time Rebecca found the watch," Maeve said, drowning in his hazel eyes.

"Yeah, that's fair, I think. I honestly suspected a lot of people at differing times. You can't overlook coincidences in this line of work. I can't believe she was the one to leave you the notes though. Good for her."

He paused, shifting closer. "Anyway, Briggs was also one of the people to visit the warden when he was in our jail cell. He was the one who threatened Gary to keep quiet. Obviously, we didn't think twice about our chief talking to someone we had in custody. No red flags there. Also makes sense why the warden was so confident in there. He thought Briggs would get him out of any situation."

"The call log," she croaked, zoning out.

"What?" he looked at her carefully.

"The call log. Remember when Jack Brinks told us he called to make a statement and Briggs said he'd look into it? We never heard about that again. It all makes sense. Jack Brinks was telling the truth. He had made a statement to Briggs and Briggs got rid of it."

Ben turned away, nodding. "Fuck."

"It all makes sense, the hold up on getting the warrant on the prison, him trying to throw Marc under the bus with the text message proof in a last-ditch attempt...all of it," Maeve finished. There was a long pause. Maeve saw hesitation and uncertainty in his face.

"Then there's the tapes," Ben said, fidgeting with her blanket covering them. He didn't look at her.

She stared at him, waiting for him to go on.

His voice was low. "There's tapes of everything he did. He filmed all of it. All those DVD cases under the TV."

Maeve held a hand over her mouth, before speaking through her fingers. "There must have been at least a hundred in there Ben..." she whispered. "One hundred and thirteen."

She closed her eyes as silent tears fell down her cheeks. Ben clenched his jaw so hard she could hear his teeth grinding together. They sat that way for a moment, respecting the impact of what they'd uncovered before he spoke again, his hand squeezing her thigh.

"The blinds, the eighty-inch TV, the media equipment, the soundproofing, he'd rewatch them. The tapes go back about fifteen years, and Gary isn't in any of them. He was preying on women in the area since he became an officer here. Jordyn Cunningham was working at the motel where he'd bring prostitutes, and eventually he figured she may talk one day, so that's where he grabbed her. She fought back and he had her arrested. No one believed her word against his and he smacked every charge he could against her until she ended up at Umbele. She was the victim who brought that sick partnership into fruition. He did have an agreement with Gary, but he went above and beyond that. Not all the women he assaulted ended up killed, sometimes they were just silenced. Briggs had connections. His family has been in the system for generations and he must have used that to his advantage, either through blackmail or through simple favors. He was as dirty as it got. The Bureau and Internal Affairs are having a field day. Apparently, a lot of women have come forward about Briggs since the story was leaked to the media. The irony that Grants Pass is the safest it's ever been with their police chief dead is not lost on anyone."

Ben's hand rubbed her leg gently before he stood up and proceeded to search her house again. Maeve didn't stop him. She knew he was looking for cameras or wires, something they hadn't considered the first time around. It took him a while before he could relax again, and she coaxed him back onto the couch with her.

"That fucker. Makes me fucking sick knowing what he did to you, preying on you all this time and coming so close to..." he tapered off.

Maeve let herself daydream for a moment about what it would've looked like if she'd had Ben, her former marine turned angry detective, have his way with Joe Briggs. It brought a smile to her face. He turned back around to find her smiling and softened slightly, leaning forward and bringing her closer.

"I'm sorry, but I'm not leaving you here alone until I do another search tomorrow. With lights and tools and lab geeks. I'm also going to the hardware store and you're going to get a security system and several padlocks. Also, a doorbell camera. Maybe a German Shepherd."

She smiled as he spoke, shifting to drop her head against his shoulder. "Keep going, Ben."

"Right, well, as for the warden, he was motivated. He dug six feet under, dragged Amanda out of her final resting place and put his perfect Lara in there. Also, convenient that he has a perfect view of all his trophies lying six feet under from the window in his office," he deadpanned, shaking his head. "The excavation isn't even done yet over there, they still keep finding..." he cleared his throat, "they keep finding more bodies, but none of them were embalmed like Lara was. The level of decay is significant, but maybe we can get some closure for some of these families. Naturally, he tried to pin it all on Briggs after he found out about his death, and after we told him what he did to Lara, but there's too much evidence against him. He's going away for the rest of his pathetic life. Briggs can't bail him out anymore. It's been all over the news too, something this big couldn't be contained. Liam, Lydia, and all their friends know all the gory details." He paused, taking another long drink of his beer and avoiding eye contact.

"Liam is pissed, but I don't blame him. People put their faith in their police force to protect and serve, and we're going to need some intense damage control and relationship building to mitigate this. Luckily, the stateys have basically taken over the precinct with the help of the Bureau. But to be honest, I don't mind one bit. I could use a fucking vacation," he said, dragging a hand over his head.

"OH, also, you're looking at the new Interim Chief of the 59th precinct. My first new order of business is burning Briggs's office furniture and then hiring more women," he said proudly before cringing as he heard his own words. "...not in a weird way...I just mean..."

She laughed, saving him. "I get what you mean, Ben. We could use more diversity at the station, and congratulations. I think you'll be an amazing chief. I can't wait to bust your balls."

His face lit up. "You're staying?"

She smiled, weaving her fingers through his. "I'm staying."

The moment was charged. He moved slowly, looking into her dark eyes as he slid a large hand around the back of her neck. Assessing her willingness for a moment he hesitated. When she leaned closer in permission he smiled ever so slightly before he brought her lips to his own. It was shallow but intimate, lasting only a few short moments before he pulled back and started searching her eyes for reassurance.

She raised her eyebrow at him, grabbing his shirt and bringing him back with force as she deepened it to another level. He made a guttural sound of satisfaction before they fell into perfect synchronicity, mouths moving over each other like they'd been doing it for years. It was familiar, passionate, and all consuming. He tightened the hand around the back of her neck and moved against her lips with expertise as butterflies filled her stomach.

She wasn't ready to take it any further after everything that had happened, but when she pulled away, she saw only pure joy on his face. He understood. She curled against him, and he tucked her under his arm before turning on the third movie.

ACKNOWLEDGEMENTS

Since the first moment I decided I wanted to write a book seven years ago, this process has been a labor of love. I first need to acknowledge the myriad of authors who came before me that inspired me to believe I could follow in their footsteps. The journey from reader to author was a grueling one, and if it wasn't for my love of reading, I would have never been successful. To go from "what a great story" to "I think I could do that" is the inception of a dream, and once I dream something, I refuse to not give it the time and effort it deserves. That I deserve.

Secondly, I would like to thank all my friends and family who supported me along the way. Without you, this would not have been possible. The endless requests for feedback and brainstorming, the constant support, and the way you all believed in me, was the ultimate recipe for success. I know you all probably got sick of hearing about this book and having to read it more times than I can count, but I deeply appreciate each and every one of you.

I would also like to address the mess that this novel was in before my editor, Cindi Jackson, got ahold of it. Writing a police procedural is a beast. Each and every clue needs to align, the details need to fit, and all loose ends must be tied up. That's no easy feat. As a nurse by background, I had no concept of the steps involved in an investigation, and Cindi was the brilliant mind to fill in the gaps and fix the mess. Without her, this would still be a chaotic collection of words on a page. A good editor will find all the things you missed when you were so deep into writing you forget where you were going.

Last, but definitely not least, my deepest thanks to each and every one of you that picked up this book and gave me the respect of giving it a chance. You are a part of my dream. You are proof that people want what I have to offer. You are proof that my creative calling matters. That my contribution to the world, no matter how small, matters. You are proof that people need art in their lives, and you owe it to yourself to pursue any dream that pops into your head. Who knows, one day it might impact the world. Thank you for showing me that my contribution to the world is important and valued. Thank you for supporting literary works. To be able to escape reality for a little while without looking at a screen, that is truly a gift. That is what life is about. Storytelling is magic, and it's a dwindling art. Let's keep it alive.

One last thing, to the book that kept me going, the book that reminded me of my why after all the late nights and ripped up pieces of paper. The book that took every piece of my soul and put it on paper, my manifesto. Thank you "Big Magic." Thank you, Elizabeth Gilbert, for creating and sharing.

"Fierce trust demands that you put forth the work anyhow, because fierce trust knows that the outcome does not matter. The outcome cannot matter…'you are worthy, dear one, regardless of the outcome. You will keep doing your work, regardless of the outcome. You will keep sharing your work, regardless of the outcome. You were born to create, regardless of the outcome. You will never lose trust in the creative process, even when you don't understand the outcome.'" – Elizabeth Gilbert, *Big Magic*

This book was intense, violent, dark and triggering. I went back and forth many times editing things out based on what was "acceptable" and more "digestible" before I spoke with other writers. They told me to write what I wanted to write without apology, you could never please everyone. If people didn't like it, they didn't like it. It's a fiction novel, it's a story I made up. My writing and my work will never be everyone's cup of tea, but that's not why I do it. I do it because I love it, and that's enough. Their advice was exactly what I needed and it was the reason I left it exactly as I wrote it. Raw and vivid and dark.

ABOUT THE AUTHOR

Megan Jamieson is a Canadian author and multipotentialite based in a small town outside of Edmonton, Alberta. Megan first started in healthcare working as a registered nurse before publishing her debut novel, The Ties That Bind Us. Megan has been a part of the Writers Guild of Alberta since 2023, and when she's not working or writing, she can usually be found travelling. She lives life to the fullest, a dreamer in its truest sense, and is always on the hunt to find her next adventure or experience.

NOTE FROM MEGAN JAMIESON

Word-of-mouth is crucial for any author to succeed. If you enjoyed *The Ties That Bind Us*, please leave a review online—anywhere you are able. Even if it's just a sentence or two. It would make all the difference and would be very much appreciated.

Thanks!
Megan Jamieson

We hope you enjoyed reading this title from:

BLACK ROSE writing

www.blackrosewriting.com

Subscribe to our mailing list – *The Rosevine* – and receive **FREE** books, daily deals, and stay current with news about
upcoming releases and our hottest authors.
Scan the QR code below to sign up.

Already a subscriber? Please accept a sincere thank you for being a fan of Black Rose Writing authors.

View other Black Rose Writing titles at
www.blackrosewriting.com/books and use promo code
PRINT to receive a **20% discount** when purchasing.